WHAT *the* EARL NEEDS NOW

MICHELLE WILLINGHAM

THE EARLS NEXT DOOR

Published by Michelle Willingham
www.michellewillingham.com

ISBN-13: 978-0-9906345-6-0

Cover by Carrie Divine/Seductive Designs
Photo by Novelstock
Period Images
Mariusz Patrzyk/Depositphotos
Eric Isselée/Depositphotos
LilKar/Shutterstock
Alexandr Labetskiy/Depositphotos

Interior formatting by Author E.M.S.

Published in the United States of America.

OTHER BOOKS BY MICHELLE WILLINGHAM

The Earls Next Door Series
(Victorian England)
Good Earls Don't Lie
What the Earl Needs Now

Warriors of the Night Series
(Medieval)
Forbidden Night with the Warrior
Forbidden Night with the Highlander

A Most Peculiar Season Series
(Regency)
A Viking for the Viscountess
A Viking Maiden for the Marquess

Secrets in Silk Series
(Regency Scotland)
Undone by the Duke
Unraveled by the Rebel
Undressed by the Earl
Unlaced by the Outlaw

Forbidden Viking Series
(Viking Age Ireland)
To Sin with a Viking
To Tempt a Viking

Warriors of Ireland Series
(Medieval Ireland)
Warrior of Ice
Warrior of Fire

MacEgan Brothers Series
(Medieval Ireland)
Her Warrior Slave
"The Viking's Forbidden Love-Slave" (novella)
Her Warrior King
Her Irish Warrior
The Warrior's Touch
Taming Her Irish Warrior
"The Warrior's Forbidden Virgin" (novella)
"Voyage of an Irish Warrior" (novella)
Surrender to an Irish Warrior
"Pleasured by the Viking" (novella)
"Lionheart's Bride" (novella)
Warriors in Winter

The MacKinloch Clan Series
(Medieval Scotland)
Claimed by the Highland Warrior
Seduced by Her Highland Warrior
"Craving the Highlander's Touch" (novella)
Tempted by the Highland Warrior
"Rescued by the Highland Warrior" (novella)

The Accidental Series
(Victorian England/Fictional Province of Lohenberg)
"An Accidental Seduction" (novella)
The Accidental Countess
The Accidental Princess
The Accidental Prince

Other Titles
"Innocent in the Harem"
(A novella of the sixteenth-century Ottoman Empire)
"A Wish to Build a Dream On"
(time travel novella to medieval Ireland)
"A Dance with the Devil"
(in the *Bedeviled* anthology)
"The Sweetest Christmas"
(in the *Kissed at Christmas* anthology)

Chapter One

London, England

Summer 1846

Lily Thornton reached for the doorknob and turned it. Inside, the room was dark, save for the fire at the hearth and a single candle burning on the mantel. The drapes were closed, shutting out the world.

"May I come in?" she asked softly.

There was no answer. She opened the door a little wider, uncertain of whether she should enter. Matthew Larkspur, the Earl of Arnsbury, had returned from India only days ago after her brother had accompanied him home. James had warned her not to visit him, for Lord Arnsbury had been captured and tortured by the enemy. *He is not the man you once knew,* he'd warned.

But he is my husband, she reassured herself. Even if no one else knew it but them, she had every right to see him. She took a single step into the darkness, wondering how badly he had been hurt.

Lord Arnsbury was seated in a large wingback chair a short distance from the fire. In the shadows, she could not see his face—only the outline of a man with his head lowered. In his posture, she sensed pain, mingled with frustration. Tension stretched out in the room, and she wondered if she should call out to his mother or a footman to join her as a chaperone. Both were lingering nearby in the hallway.

"Matthew, it's Lily," she murmured.

She prayed that when he heard her voice, it would break the spell of melancholy and bring him back. The silence grew heavier, and for a moment, she doubted herself.

"I've missed you so much," she said. "Are you all right?" *See me. Know that I love you and always have.*

At last, he raised his head, and it felt as if she were facing a wounded tiger. "Go away."

His voice was slurred, and she heard the traces of pain within it. Upon an end table beside the chair, she saw a glass. Had he been drinking? Or perhaps he had taken laudanum to help him sleep.

She ignored his command and pulled a chair across from him, sitting so close, he could touch her. Her heart was beating hard, and her emotions were tightly strung up inside her. With a glance toward the door, she saw that Lady Arnsbury was standing just beyond the door, allowing them a measure of privacy while still chaperoning her.

Lily spoke in the softest whisper, not wanting anyone to overhear her. "I am so glad you've returned," she said. "I've waited so long."

But again, he said nothing. It was as if he were a stranger, a man haunted by visions she could not see. His hands clenched the arms of his chair, and he demanded, "I want to be alone."

His assertion wounded her deeply. "I am your *wife*," she whispered. "How can you ask me to go? After all that we've meant to one another."

"I *have* no wife," he gritted out.

His head dropped forward, and for a breathless moment, she felt numb inside. The silver chain around her neck seemed to weigh against her throat. She withdrew it from her bodice and showed him the gold signet ring. It was *his* ring, the one his grandfather had given him when he was a boy.

"What do you mean, you have no wife?" Tears gathered in her eyes, and a wrenching fear gripped her. Her heart was pounding so hard, she felt physically ill.

Matthew leaned forward and stared at her. His brown eyes were dilated, chips of flint in a face made of stone. Gone was the rakish earl she had known, and in his place was a man filled with suffering. She searched his expression for some sign of affection, some glimmer of hope for them. But there was not even a hint of recognition, and it hardly seemed as if he'd understood a word she'd said.

"Leave me," he demanded.

The logical response would be to obey him, to wait another day until he was feeling better. It was clear that he was lost in his torment, and he needed time.

She didn't know what had happened to Matthew, but she would not turn away from him in his time of need. They would face this together and overcome it.

Lily reached out to touch his cheek. She stroked the dark bristle of his beard, not caring that he appeared so rough and unkempt. He had been to Hades and back again. Even his hair was longer than usual, and she suspected he hadn't cut it. Across his left cheek was a slash, a healing wound that seemed to have been cut with a curved sword.

"I promised I would never leave you," she said, stroking the outline of his face. "And you promised to take care of me. Don't you remember?"

At that, he caught her wrist and stood. He was so tall, she had to tip her head back to meet his gaze. His clothing hung against his frame, and the sharpness in his features suggested that he'd known hunger during his time in India.

"How could I promise such a thing?" A faint note of irony creased his expression. "Especially when I have never seen you before in my life."

The floor seemed to drop out from beneath her, and blood rushed through her cheeks. "I don't understand." Her throat tightened at the words. How was it possible for him to forget her? Her brother had said nothing about memory loss.

He started to sit down again, but he swayed like a man intoxicated before he stumbled into the chair, caught in a drugged haze. Something was not right, and she hoped that somehow she could alleviate his pain.

Lord Arnsbury glared down at her and pointed toward the door. "I don't know your face, and I don't know who you are. But I want you gone from here. Now."

She was paralyzed at his words, frozen in place. Then he took her by the wrist and forced her to rise, pushing her toward the door. "I said go!"

He released her only when she was beyond the doorframe, and then he slammed the door in her face.

Lily touched the wood, her fingers shaking. *Oh dear God.* Tears flowed freely over her face, for she'd never imagined this response from the man she loved.

Now what? she thought. This wasn't at all the homecoming she'd anticipated. She'd mistakenly thought that she could help him recover from his wounds, remaining at his side as a loving wife.

But he didn't even remember her face.

His body ached, and his mind was so weary, his eyesight blurred. How long had it been since he'd slept? Matthew couldn't remember. His days and nights blended together until he could not tell reality from dreams.

He dimly recalled the rocking motion of a ship and nights when he was racked with pain and fever. James Thornton, the Earl of Penford, had brought him back from India, but sometimes Matthew wished his best friend had left him to die.

He was a shell of a man, tormented by visions of the past.

He ran his hands over his beard, feeling invisible hands choking him. The candlelight speared his eyes, and he closed them, wanting to escape the horrors of his imagination.

But Lily's scent lingered.

He had lied, for he *did* remember her. At least partly. His memories remained fragmented after the nightmarish journey from India. He knew she was James's younger sister, a kindhearted woman who loved animals. Just as she had loved him, years ago.

Even her scent reminded him of lilies. Pure and white, surrounding him with the softness of an angel. In the candlelight, he'd glimpsed brown hair gleaming with gold and red. Her eyes were hazel, brown with hints of green. And they had looked upon him with love and yearning.

Matthew lowered his face in his hands, breathing slowly, until all traces of Lily were gone. His head was pounding, and the very room was spinning.

His mind felt clouded over by laudanum until he could hardly distinguish dreams from memories. It felt as if he had stepped back into another man's life. And though he'd recognized Charlotte Larkspur, the woman who had embraced him and called him her son, she felt like a stranger. The servants called him the Earl of Arnsbury, and there was evidence of wealth within this house.

But he would turn his back on all of it if it meant an escape from the nightmares.

Pain had been a part of each day for the past year. His captors had burned the soles of his feet, scarring the flesh until now he hardly felt anything at all when he walked. Sometimes, when the weather changed, his leg ached from where his captors had broken it. And then there was the healing cut upon his cheek, a mild sting he hardly noticed.

Though his physical wounds had mostly healed, his mind

had not. If he dared to close his eyes, he relived the agony of their torture, hour by hour.

It seemed incongruous, trying to return to his former life as an earl, attending soirees and taking his seat in the House of Lords. He felt utterly alone, and he didn't want to drag anyone else down into the torture he'd endured—least of all a beautiful young woman who had done nothing wrong except fall in love with him.

It was as if his mind and spirit had shut down, locked away with no emotions remaining. But amid the chaos, his thoughts drifted back to Lady Lily. The light touch of her fingers upon his face had jolted him back to the present. Like a siren, she beckoned him to follow her out of the darkness.

And he wondered if he dared to take the first step.

Lily returned home to her family's townhouse and found her brother, James, in the drawing room, staring out the window at the London streets. His face and hands were tanned from the hot India sun, and he, too, had shadows in his eyes.

"You look tired, James." She came up behind him and embraced him. He turned and gave her a crushing hug.

"I am. I've hardly slept in two years." He mussed her hair with affection and stepped back. Despite his good humor, the journey to India had changed her brother, too—she could see it in his eyes.

"Would you like something to eat?"

He nodded. "I haven't eaten real food in weeks. And afterward, I intend to sleep for a fortnight."

Her brother didn't sit down but returned to the window, staring outside. She waited a few moments for him to speak, and when he didn't, she voiced her true concern. "What happened to Lord Arnsbury while you were in India?"

James ignored the question. "I suppose you went to see

him, didn't you? Even though I warned you against it."

"You knew I would. But you never said anything about his memory loss."

Her brother let out a sigh and turned back to her. "God only knows what he remembers, Lily. We had to sedate him during the voyage. I don't know what the sailors gave him. Probably opium mixed with alcohol. I doubt he would remember much of anything after that." He studied her with sympathy. "I know you cared for him, Lily. But he's very different from the man you knew before."

There was a long pause, and Lily waited for him to elaborate. When he didn't, she prompted him once more. "What happened?"

He rested his palm against the glass window, hiding his face from her. "Suffice it to say, Matthew is lucky he survived. He was captured and tortured for information about the British troops."

She frowned at that. "But neither of you was in the army. Why would they take you prisoner?"

James shook his head. "We were in the wrong place at the wrong time. They believed that because we were English, we must know something about the war."

Her gut twisted as she imagined what Matthew had endured. "Will he be all right?"

"No one knows the answer to that question. Least of all me." James's shoulders lowered, and he turned back to her. "Some wounds don't heal, Lily. And right now, it would be best if you stayed away from him. Let him convalesce with his family."

She had no intention of doing so. It would take time, yes, but she'd spoken vows, promising to love him in sickness and in health. There had to be a way to break through his nightmares, to help him recover.

"You're not going to listen to a word I say, are you?" James sighed.

7

"If, by that, you mean will I stay away from him? No. I will not leave him." She moved forward to stand beside him. "Any more than I would leave you."

There was bleakness in his eyes, and he swallowed hard. "I'm alive, and we made it back to England. That's all that matters."

She took his hand in hers. "And what about you, James? What became of you in India?"

He remained silent. "I am not going to talk about it. I would rather hear about what I've missed these past two years."

She hesitated, uncertain of how to begin. "After Father died, we tried to send word. I don't suppose you received any of our letters."

James shook his head. "None. But then, we were traveling across India."

After a pause, she admitted, "I was afraid you might never return. We didn't know what became of you, and I feared the worst."

He let out a slow breath. "So did I, for a time. But I am here now, and I will do what I can to atone for my earlier absence." James put his arm around her and said, "I know I've been gone for a while, Lily. But I will do what I can to set things to rights." He gave her shoulder a squeeze. "I would not hold out hope for Arnsbury, though. He endured far worse than me."

"I love him," she murmured. "And I have nothing but hope."

James lowered his gaze and shook his head. "I fear he can do nothing but break your heart, Lily. He's lost in a world of his own nightmares."

She faced her brother. "Then I will bring him back to this world. No matter how long it takes."

Over the past few days, Matthew's memories had begun to return. He had ceased taking any medicines, for the sleeping draughts were causing hallucinations. But the deprivation made his hands tremble, and his head ached.

Still, he preferred clarity to the haze of forgetfulness. He sat in a wingback chair while his mother stood at the far side of the room.

"Matthew, please," she pleaded gently. "If you would just eat something, it might help." She pointed toward the breakfast tray on the end table beside him.

But his stomach twisted at the thought of food. He couldn't bring himself to eat, though he vaguely recalled his friend James forcing him to choke down stale bread on the voyage to England.

His tongue was dry, and he reached for the glass of water. The taste of it quenched his thirst, but his hands trembled against the cup. "I am not hungry," he said. "Leave me."

Charlotte ignored him and crossed the room. When she reached the window, she opened the drapes. The sunlight filled up the room, and he squinted at the brightness. "There, now. That's better."

She was wrong. The sunlight burned his eyes, reminding him of the hot India sun against the Thar Desert. The yellow sand had seared his skin, while the dust had choked his lungs. He drank more water in memory of the arid wasteland.

"Close the drapes, please."

"You've been in darkness for two days now. I know you're not feeling well, but the doctor says—"

"He knows nothing. And I won't take his medicines." The man had only given him laudanum, which dulled his senses.

"I'll bring another doctor to help you. Perhaps Dr. Fraser."

The name did sound familiar, and Matthew tried to place the man.

"He and his wife are visiting London," Charlotte continued. "I could ask them to stop in, if you like. I know Juliette would be delighted to see you."

He recalled now that the Scottish doctor was married to his godmother and cousin, Juliette. When Matthew tried to envision Juliette's face, he recalled that she had brown hair touched with gold and a few silver strands. She had green eyes, he was certain. And she had always been kind to him.

But then, the idea of facing more guests made him weary. "No, thank you."

"Matthew, you cannot do this to yourself." Charlotte stiffened, her hands clenched together. "You are home again and safe. Please, just try to get well. I cannot bear to see you suffer."

Suffering was all that he'd known for the past year, and the idea of returning to a normal existence was impossible. For so long, he had been unable to control his life. But here, for the first time, *he* was in command of when he slept and when he ate. Yet the very thought of any food turned his stomach.

A knock sounded at the door, and his mother called out for the maid to enter. The servant whispered softly to Charlotte, who thought a moment and then nodded. "Yes, bring her upstairs."

"I will not see any visitors," Matthew argued. But from the look in his mother's eyes, he suspected she would not listen. She appeared like a war general, intent on getting her way.

"I cannot imagine *why* Lady Lily would have any desire to see you in such a state," Charlotte remarked. "However, she is even more stubborn than I am. And perhaps a beautiful young woman may break through that thick head of yours." She smiled at him.

"I've no wish to see her." But as he spoke the words, something stirred within him at the mention of her name. Even after she had gone, he couldn't stop thinking of her.

Lady Lily's beauty had captivated him, but despite whatever

past they had shared, he didn't want her to pin hopes and dreams upon him.

"You *will* see her, and furthermore, you will behave yourself. Brownson will accompany her, in case you forget your manners." His mother returned to the door and offered a hesitant smile. "Lady Lily will help you."

But there were some pieces of the past he didn't want to remember. Idly, he touched the slash upon his cheek where the raw edges had come together.

Charlotte opened the bedroom door, revealing Lily's presence. The young woman wore a blue day dress with long sleeves that made a vee at her waist. Her hair was bound up beneath a matching bonnet, and in her hazel eyes, he saw a woman prepared to do battle.

His mother spoke as if he weren't even there. "Matthew is in a foul mood, I fear. But Brownson is here, if you have need of him. Would you rather I stayed with you?"

Lily shook her head and removed her bonnet, handing it to the footman. "I will be fine."

Her expression held a challenge, as if she were daring Matthew to throw her out again. She nodded to his mother, and Charlotte pulled the door closed behind her, leaving them alone.

Lady Lily stood far away from him, and her expression held a blend of curiosity and sympathy. "Good morning," she greeted him, braving a smile. "Are you feeling any better?"

"Not really." He leaned back against the chair, as if he didn't care if she stayed or left. "But I'm not dead today, so there's that."

"True enough." Her expression softened, and she moved closer to him, leaning against the same wall. "Do you...remember anything at all?"

"A little," he hedged. "It's coming back in bits and pieces." He didn't bother to hide his stare, and she met his gaze with an appraising look of her own. A flare of heat descended through his veins, and he was startled at the sudden emotion.

She took a step closer. "What do you remember?"

His mind taunted him with the vision of her lying naked upon his coverlet while he stroked her bare skin. Could that be true? God above, had he seduced this young woman and left her? The memories spilled through his brain like water droplets through his fingers. If nothing else, he needed to uncover the truth of what had happened before he'd left.

But he couldn't exactly say, *I remember you naked.* He wasn't trying to shock her.

Instead, he fumbled for another sentence and offered, "We met at your sister's debut."

Her face brightened, and she nodded. "We did. Many years ago." Lily moved to stand by the window, and the sun illuminated her brown hair with hints of gold and red. Her skin was pale, but her lips were the color of a pink rose. "What else do you remember?"

His mind conjured up soft curves and the gentle flare of hips. He closed his eyes, trying to maintain some grasp of dignity. But it was as if his imagination mocked him, leaving him with inappropriate visions.

Lily approached the untouched breakfast tray and picked up a strawberry by the stem, idly twirling it as she drew nearer. "Anything at all?"

Should he tell her the truth? It would likely drive her away. But then, perhaps that would be for the best. She should get on with her life instead of trying to mend the shattered pieces of his.

So be it. Matthew crooked a finger for her to lean in. When their faces were nearly touching, he murmured, "I remember seeing you upon a bed, wearing nothing but a sheet. I pushed back the sheet and drew my hands over your body. I touched your bare skin and pulled your hips against mine."

He rather expected her to slap him. Or at the very least,

glare at him indignantly and leave the room in a fury. But she didn't protest at all. Instead, her hazel eyes turned thoughtful.

"It wasn't a dream, was it?" he said quietly. "We were lovers."

To his surprise, she nodded. Color rose in her cheeks, but she confessed, "Yes. We were. On our wedding night, such as it was."

He didn't know what to think, though he suspected there was some truth in what she'd said. But he couldn't quite grasp why he would have taken her innocence and then left her behind. It wasn't the sort of man he was.

"Our reunion was not at all what I anticipated." She pulled out the silver chain with the ring and eyed him. "But my brother, James, told me that you suffered torture in India. And I believe that we should begin again as friends until you remember more."

"I'd rather be left alone."

Lily gave a slight nod. "I suspect that it's very difficult to return to all of this after what you endured." She drew back, holding the strawberry in her fingers. "But I will try anyway." She braved a smile, but it didn't meet her eyes.

"My name is Lily Thornton. My brother is James, the Earl of Penford, and I have a sister named Rose who recently learned to walk again after her illness. My mother is still living, but her mind wanders often." She straightened. "Now you cannot say that you don't know me."

Matthew held his ground, not knowing what she wanted. But he tensed with every step she took. She moved slowly, her hazel eyes filled with worry. And something deep within him froze.

Lily halted an arm's length away. His eyes had adjusted to the light, and the morning sun illuminated her delicate features. A flash of memory intruded, of the sweet taste of her lips.

Her very presence ignited a desire so fierce, his hands dug into the wooden arms of the chair. In his imagination, he thought of dragging her down to his lap, devouring her mouth, and giving in to the mindless beast of his lust. And he couldn't understand why he had this response to her. Clearly, his body remembered hers.

But Matthew didn't move. Not even when she brought the strawberry to his mouth.

"Do you want this?" she asked softly. And for a breathless moment, he wondered if she was speaking of herself. He did want her desperately, but he would never trust himself to hold back. This woman was driving him toward madness.

He bit into the strawberry, tasting its sweetness. Hunger roared through him, and she held the discarded hull. "Do you want more?"

He did. But not only did he want food, he wanted to taste this woman's mouth. He sensed that the last woman he had ever touched was *her*. The years of celibacy caught up with him, drowning him with need.

He wanted to kiss her, to explore every inch of her skin and make her cry out in ecstasy. Instead, he stood from the chair. For a moment, he looked down at her, waiting to see whether she would flee or stay.

"I—I'll get your tray," she stammered, moving toward the table where his cold breakfast lay. She reached for it and paused a moment, as if she needed to gather her courage.

"Do you still want me to leave?" She remained standing apart from him, and he understood that his open interest had transformed her mood from determined into that of a nervous young woman. But she was the one who had chosen to come here.

"I don't need you to feed me." His voice was gruff, encouraging her to go. The longer she remained, the more her presence unnerved him.

But she ignored him and took off her glove. She set it upon the table before she reached out for a piece of toast and spread it with blackberry jelly. When she offered it to him, he saw that her hands were shaking. Matthew ate it to avoid speaking, though the bread tasted like sand in his mouth.

She closed her eyes, as if trying to decide what to say. "I waited for you, dreaming of the day when you would return. I never loved any man but you, Matthew."

He could not respond, though he knew his silence bothered her deeply. It was clear that Lady Lily possessed a romantic heart. She had thought herself his wife and had spent the night in his arms. But any vows they might have spoken could not have been legal, for there had been no time for a marriage license before he'd sailed for India. She had to have known that. Why, then, had she surrendered herself? And why would he have agreed to it?

He could hardly remember any of the details. It was as if his mind had shut out the past, and every time he tried to reach back, there were only fragments of memories.

Lily reached for a fork, but her hand accidentally bumped against a teacup. The porcelain faltered upon the tray, before it tipped and shattered on the wooden floor. The sound was like a bullet coursing through his brain.

He jerked at the noise, his heart racing. In his mind, he heard his torturer's voice, softly pleading, *"Tell me where the soldiers are, and the pain will stop. I promise you."*

A cold sweat broke over him, but he refused to yield. Strong arms held down his ankles while a searing agony tore through his feet. The broken glass sliced through his burned soles, and she began again with the questioning.

"Tell me where they are..."

"Matthew!" Lily was shouting at him, but her voice was not enough to push away the vision. He didn't know where he was or what was happening. "Let go of the cup. Please."

He glanced down and saw that he had picked up the shattered porcelain, squeezing the broken shards into his palms until blood welled up in his hands.

The footman, Brownson, was already at his side. "My lord,

let me help you bandage that." He withdrew a handkerchief and pressed it gently into Matthew's palm.

Lily stared at him with fear in her eyes. "What happened? What did you see?"

He could only shake his head, unable to form the words. "You should go, Lady Lily. I am not feeling well."

She reached out to touch his cheek, but he pulled back, not wanting her to come close. Her expression held sympathy, but she finally stood and let Brownson escort her out.

The door closed behind her, leaving him with bloodied hands, a shattered teacup, and her fallen glove.

Chapter Two

Two years earlier

"You will be pleased to know that I have found a husband for you," her father said. "Lord Davonshire has made an offer for your hand, and I have accepted on your behalf."

Lily was aghast at his statement. From the pleased look upon George's face, he believed she should be delighted by his arrangement. "You did what?"

"I spoke with Lord Chesham, and you will marry his son, John." Her father had become close friends with Davonshire's father, the Marquess of Chesham, over the past year. She could only imagine that the pair of them had cooked up this scheme as a means of joining their families in marriage.

But she would have none of it.

"No, Father, I will not marry him." She had met the gentleman only twice, and Davonshire was practically a stranger. Not only that, but she had been in love with Matthew Larkspur, the Earl of Arnsbury, since she was sixteen. Her father knew this.

She believed with her whole heart that one day she would marry Lord Arnsbury. He was older than she was, but that didn't matter. He had danced with her at every ball and had even kissed her twice. The memory of those kisses sobered her, for the heated pressure of his mouth upon hers had hinted of far deeper pleasures. She had felt the intensity flowing through her blood, tempting her toward surrender.

"Lily," her father interrupted. "Are you paying attention to a word I've said?"

She shook the idle thoughts away. "I'm sorry."

Her father straightened and narrowed his gaze at her. "Lord Davonshire is the heir to a marquessate. He's decent looking, the same age as you, and quite wealthy."

With that, George eased himself into a wingback chair, propping his leg upon a footstool. Though he tried to remain cheerful, she didn't miss the shadow of pain in his eyes. Her father had fallen ill over the past few months, and though he had seen countless doctors, he refused to admit that anything was wrong.

He leaned back and added, "The wedding will take place before Christmas." He rubbed at his leg and sighed.

Lily bit her lower lip, trying to hide her exasperation. Her father believed that marriage was meant for increasing the family's wealth. Were it up to him, he would simply choose the richest suitor and marry her off. He truly couldn't understand why she wanted to follow her heart instead of her head.

She tried another tactic, though it was slightly unfair. "Why not ask Rose? She's older and ought to marry first."

"Davonshire doesn't want to marry a woman older than himself. And he specifically asked for you." Her father's chest puffed out. "Lily, be reasonable. You won't get a better offer."

"I already have," she blurted out, though it wasn't true. But it was the only way she could think of to distract him. "Lord Arnsbury has asked to marry me." Desperation edged her lie, for she didn't know what else to say.

Her father made a face and sighed. "Why would you settle for an earl when you could have a marquess?"

"Because I love him. And he loves me."

Or at least, she wanted him to. Lily knew that Lord Arnsbury cared about her a great deal, and perhaps he would love her after they were married. It was quite possible.

"I cannot marry Lord Davonshire," she insisted. "Tell him I am flattered by his offer, but no."

Her father rubbed at his leg again, wincing when he touched a tender spot. His expression grew serious and hardened. "I will not turn down this offer, Lily. Though I realize you are infatuated by Arnsbury, he's too old for you. And you hardly know him."

"I've known him for two years, and he's James's best friend. I don't know Lord Davonshire at all." It was time to stand up for herself and put her foot down. "I am sorry, Father, but I will not stand back and let you manipulate my life."

The iron cast to her father's face revealed that he intended to go through with this match and would not be swayed. "I am your father, and I am responsible for your future, Lily. I *will* ensure that you have someone to take care of you. And Rose, too, once I can find a suitable husband for her."

"There is time, Father," she stalled. "Just let it be." She was only eighteen years old, hardly a spinster on the shelf. "We will speak of this later."

He muttered something beneath his breath about the lack of time. She stared at him with a sudden realization. "What did the doctors say about your leg, Father?"

He grimaced. "They said I've been eating foods that are too rich. Nothing to worry your pretty head about." He braved a smile, but she wasn't so certain. She was about to ask again, when James entered the drawing room. Something about his demeanor made Lily uneasy, though she could not say why.

He glanced at their father and said, "I came to tell you that I am leaving in a few days."

George straightened in his chair and shook his head. "You cannot leave, James. There is too much to be done here."

"I intend to sail to India," her brother replied. "I expect to be gone for the next year, at the very least. Perhaps longer."

The air seemed to leave her lungs, and Lily gaped at him. "But why?" India was half a world away.

Her father struggled to rise from the chair, his face purple with anger. "Absolutely not."

And in answer, she saw the trace of rebellion in her brother's face. He met George's fury with indifference. "We have business dealings with the East India Company. I believe now would be a good time to expand our interests."

"You have responsibilities here," George insisted. "You are my heir, and you cannot go traipsing off on a fool's errand in India. I forbid it."

James gave a faint smile. "Of course you do." But he didn't appear at all concerned. "But I intend to go, nonetheless. And you cannot stop me."

Her father's face turned thunderous. "If you try, I will cut off your funds."

"I have my own wealth, Father. And I am quite certain that you can continue ruling Penford in my absence, just as you've done for the past twenty-five years."

He had planned this for some time, Lily realized. After he'd returned from school, her brother had been forced to obey their father's commands, learning to become the next earl. But she knew he had despised every moment of it.

"James, please," Lily reasoned. "India is so far away. I don't want to imagine you alone for an entire year. It may not be safe."

He reached out and ruffled her hair. "Oh, I'm not going alone. Arnsbury is accompanying me. It will be an adventure, and we will seek our fortunes before the chains of marriage are clapped upon us."

The very floor seemed to sway beneath her feet. "Lord Arnsbury is going with you?" It felt as if she were caught in a tunnel, and a roaring noise filled her ears.

She saw the look in her father's eyes and the smug satisfaction. If Matthew went to India, there was nothing to stop George from forcing this marriage. Even James would be gone and could not support her cause.

"Yes, Matthew is going to keep me out of trouble." James winked at her. "He can try anyway."

Lily took a chair and sat down before her knees buckled beneath her. She needed to see Lord Arnsbury to learn for herself if this was true. Her mind spun with all the consequences of James's journey. Her brother was arguing with their father, though she paid little attention to their words. This was a battle for control, and James had no intention of remaining their father's puppet. He would forge his own path, regardless of the consequences.

And it seemed she would have to do the same.

In the course of two days, Matthew Larkspur felt as if his life had been uprooted. His best friend had decided to leave for India, and he'd received a desperate message from Lily Thornton begging to see him.

James was seeking adventure, but from his friend's reckless nature, Matthew suspected that he would wander straight into danger. And he couldn't stand by and let it happen. James was the younger brother he'd never had, and he had a premonition that if he let the young man go, he would never return. Call it a ridiculous superstition, but he saw no choice but to accompany him.

And then there was Lily.

He didn't want to leave her behind, either. Despite their age difference, he could not deny the fierce attraction that drew him to her. Her brown hair framed an innocent face with hazel eyes and a smile that knocked all reason from his brain.

But God above, her kiss brought him to his knees. He had

stolen only two, but from the moment he'd taken her into his arms, he had desired her.

His footman had alerted him that she had come to call, and though he knew she would be angry with him for leaving, he needed to protect her brother. But he would not leave for India without saying goodbye.

He entered the drawing room, and the moment he set foot inside, she flew into his arms. She gripped him tightly, and Matthew drew back to look at her face. "You act as if I'm never coming back, Lady Lily."

Her hazel eyes held worry, and she admitted, "I need your help. My father is planning something terrible."

He tucked her gloved hand in the crook of his arm and led her to sit down. "What is it?"

"He is arranging a marriage between myself and Lord Davonshire." Her expression grew stricken. "I cannot marry him, Matthew. I hardly know him. And if you leave…"

"He will force you into it," he finished. She nodded and gripped her hands together as if trying to gather her courage.

He sat beside her, uncertain of what was right. Lord Penford was looking after Lily's welfare, trying to ensure that she would have everything she ever wanted—and Matthew could understand his reasoning.

But Lily held no power of her own, and he didn't doubt her father could demand the marriage. With her brother gone, she could do nothing to stop it. And neither could he.

"What do you want to do?" he asked quietly.

She pressed her lips together and thought a moment. "If we married in secret—even if you're gone—he could not force me to wed."

Matthew gave no answer at first, for he knew that she was seeing him with stars in her eyes. And while he wanted to believe that he could be the right husband for her, he was hesitant to trap her into a marriage when she was so young.

Her eyes widened at his silence, and she blurted out, "Do you…not want me?"

He reached out to caress her cheek and told her the truth. "I want you far more than I should, Lily." If James knew the thoughts coursing through his brain, he would be loading a pistol.

But his reassurance eased her panic, and she wound her arms around his neck. "You're the only man I've ever loved, Matthew. I cannot imagine wedding anyone else. Or worse, what comes after." Her cheeks flamed at the subtle mention of the marriage bed. "Please help me."

A flare of unexpected jealousy caught him, for he could never allow another man to touch Lily. When she lifted her face to his, he claimed her lips. Sweet and innocent, she offered everything of herself, and he could not deny that he desired her. Lily had a way of entwining herself within his mind until there was nothing else. He cared about this beautiful young woman, and he did not want her to be hurt or threatened while he was gone.

Matthew removed the gold ring from his little finger and passed it to her. It had belonged to his grandfather, and when he offered it, Lily's face brightened with joy.

"I will be so proud to wear this," she said, slipping it onto her finger. "Perhaps upon a chain around my throat until you return."

He kissed her again. "I will come back to you, Lily. I promise you that." An engagement might be enough to dissuade Lord Penford from demanding that his daughter marry another man.

She traced the edge of the ring and said, "I will arrange for a minister to hear our vows tomorrow night. But it cannot be here in London. Perhaps we could meet at an inn."

Her impetuous offer made him realize how serious she was. He caught her hands and was truthful. "Lily, we cannot marry this soon. You do not have your father's permission, and we don't have a license. It would not be legal." He didn't want her raising hopes that would only be dashed.

"I know it," she whispered. "But if my father believes we have consummated the union, he would not dare arrange a marriage between myself and Lord Davonshire. The scandal would be terrible." She closed her eyes for a moment, and her mood shifted. "Matthew, if you are gone for a year, let me imagine that it's real. Let me believe that I am your wife and that you love me." She rested her hands upon his heart. "It will be enough." Her hazel eyes filled up with trust, making him feel as if he did not deserve her.

"I will return to you," he promised. And if the illicit vows would protect her until he returned, keeping her from an unwanted marriage, so be it.

And when she kissed him again, he hoped he was making the right decision.

Chapter Three

Present day

"Lily, dearest, I must speak with you." Her grandmother, Mildred, Lady Wolcroft, leaned heavily against her cane as she walked into the small sitting room where Lily was seated with her sister, Rose, and their mother, Lady Penford. "I wanted to—"

Her grandmother's words broke off at the sight of her daughter. Lady Penford was seated by the fire, happily knitting, while she wore a ball gown and all her jewelry.

The older matron's face transformed into confusion. "Iris, what on earth are you wearing?"

Lily winced, shaking her head slightly. "It's not a good day, Grandmother," she told Lady Wolcroft. "Leave her be." Their mother's moods had been up and down over the past few days. She had been suffering from confusion ever since their father died two years ago. Sometimes she withdrew and hardly spoke, while at other times, she behaved like a child. There was no reason to upset Iris when she was safely at home where no one would judge her by her clothing.

Her grandmother ignored her. "This isn't a ball, Iris. You

really ought to go and change back into a day dress. You look ridiculous."

"But Rose is getting married!" Iris beamed at her eldest daughter. "And to an earl, no less. I am simply delighted for them both, and I thought it only appropriate to wear my best gown and jewels to the wedding."

During the past few months, Rose had recovered from a sudden illness that had stolen her ability to walk. Her sister had fallen in love with an Irishman who had helped her recover, though she still needed the support of a cane. And even now, Lily saw the flush of excitement on her sister's face at the mention of marriage.

"The wedding will be next month, Mother," Rose said, exchanging a glance with Lily. "There is time enough to wear our best gowns."

Iris reached out and squeezed Rose's hand. "Next month, yes. I will be ready."

"Have you thought about getting married here?" Lily asked, sending her sister a silent look. Although Rose was marrying an Irish earl, the wedding didn't have to take place in Ireland. "Wouldn't it be easier to have the ceremony before you go?"

Her sister sent a weak smile. "Iain doesn't want to. He wants our tenants to share in the celebration. And it gives him a reason to offer them supplies to last them through the winter. After the feast, the leftover food will be divided among the people."

Lily wasn't looking forward to the journey across the Irish Sea. She would have preferred to celebrate the marriage here, where their mother could be protected. Iris's spells of madness were growing more frequent, and Lily wasn't certain how many good days remained.

"Ireland is a godforsaken land riddled with famine," her grandmother pronounced. "I, for one, believe Rose and Iain should be married here." She raised her chin and then fixed her attention on Lily. "But I did not come here to discuss a wedding that is still weeks away."

Lily picked up her mending and began to sew up one of the holes in her stocking. She suspected she was the subject of her grandmother's censure but hoped she was wrong.

Lady Wolcroft chose a chair nearby and regarded her. "I came to discuss your scandalous behavior. It must cease, Lily, dearest."

Since her grandmother never used endearments, Lily understood that this was quite serious. "And what scandalous behavior is that?"

"You've been visiting Lord Arnsbury."

Lily saw no reason to deny it. "So I have. I've waited nearly two years for his return. Why wouldn't I?"

"Because your behavior is entirely too forward. It does not bode well for finding you a good match. Lord Arnsbury looks like an unshaved barbarian, and you would do well to avoid him."

"I will not leave him," she insisted. "Matthew has suffered, yes, but he—"

"Matthew?" her grandmother interrupted. "And what gives you the right to call Lord Arnsbury by his Christian name, do tell?"

Oh dear. Lily bit her tongue for speaking. She knew that Mildred did not approve of her interest in Lord Arnsbury, especially after she had spurned Lord Davonshire. Lady Wolcroft could not imagine any reason a woman would turn down a future marquess. But perhaps if she revealed the truth to her family, they might understand.

An abridged truth, to be sure, but one that would make them see why she would not give up on Lord Arnsbury.

She reached for the silver chain around her neck and unfastened it, revealing his gold signet ring. Then she slid it onto her finger. It was heavy and didn't fit, but that was irrelevant. "Because I married him."

An illegal marriage, yes, but Lily had spoken promises nonetheless. And she rather hoped that revealing the scandal might lead to the true, legal marriage she wanted.

Silence flooded the room, and her grandmother gaped. "You did what?"

"Oh, Lily," her sister breathed. Her tone mirrored Lady Wolcroft's, as if to ask, *How could you do such a thing?*

"Another wedding!" Lady Penford clapped her hands with delight. "Lily, don't you see? I was right to wear this gown." She preened and held out her wrist that was adorned by a pearl and diamond bracelet.

Lily ignored her mother and held out the ring to Lady Wolcroft. "Matthew gave me this ring before he left for India. We spoke our vows, and I promised him that I would keep the ring until he could give me a true wedding."

Lady Wolcroft's gaze narrowed. "And just who witnessed these vows? Some flighty minister whom you bribed?"

She flushed at her grandmother's anger, for it wasn't far off from the truth. "A minister did witness our vows, yes."

"And what of the license?" her grandmother demanded.

At that, she was forced to admit, "There was no time for a license."

Her grandmother closed her eyes and let out a heavy sigh. "Then it wasn't a true marriage, thank goodness. We can still uphold your father's arrangement with Lord Davonshire, now that enough time for mourning has passed."

"I spoke my vows before God," Lily argued. "It was a real marriage in that sense. And we intended to remarry when he returned from India." Matthew had warned her from the first that it would not be legal, but she hadn't cared. At the time, she'd needed a means of stopping her father's arrangement with the marquess.

But then George had died, and there had been no more talk of marriage. Her mother's grief had crippled her mind, and Lily had been free to wait upon Matthew's return.

Her grandmother stared hard at her. "You didn't allow him to ruin you, did you?"

Her cheeks flushed scarlet, and Lily didn't know quite what to say. "Well—I—do you suppose I would do such a thing, Grandmother?"

But Lady Wolcroft was not blind. "Oh dear Heavens, you *did.* That scoundrel. He will not get away with this." Her grandmother shook her head. "You do not know how fortunate you were not to get with child. Lily, how could you be so naïve? How could you allow it?"

"I loved him," she said simply. "And nothing happened. There was no child from our time together."

"Nothing? You simply ruined yourself for a man who may not want you anymore." Lady Wolcroft sent her a pitying look. "And everyone says he went mad after he was a prisoner in India. He has not set foot out of his house."

"I do not regret my choices. I loved Matthew, and I wanted to be with him." Lily replaced the ring upon the silver chain and hung it around her neck. "I still do."

But her grandmother's words weighed upon her. It was true that Matthew had demanded that she leave him. And there was no doubting his lack of awareness when she'd broken the teacup.

She had tried to stop him from touching the shards, but he'd clenched them in his palms, squeezing tightly until blood welled up. His eyes had been vacant, as if he were unaware of what he was doing.

Just like her mother.

A cold chill washed over her, and she felt her throat gather up with tears. They all knew that nothing could mend Iris's broken mind. But they loved her and would take care of her for as long as they could. Lily didn't want to imagine that the same had happened to Matthew.

Lady Penford had grown subdued and had removed her necklaces. She went to stand by the hearth, whispering softly to herself. Rose eased herself up from the chair and limped toward their mother, leaning on her cane.

"Lady Arnsbury is not aware of your secret wedding, is she?" her grandmother asked. Lily shook her head, and some of the tension left Lady Wolcroft's shoulders. "We have only one choice, as I see it. Since it was never a legal marriage, you are free to choose another suitor. I do believe this would be best, given Lord Arnsbury's…madness."

"He was wounded and tortured," Lily reminded her. It wasn't as if Matthew had lost his wits.

"Even so, he is not good husband material." Mildred squared her shoulders as if the matter were settled. "We will ensure that there are no legal implications and move forward from there."

"But I want to remain with him," Lily insisted. "He will recover, and I am certain we can wed properly." She wanted so badly to believe that he would recover.

Her grandmother rolled her eyes. "And here I thought you were the sensible one, Lily. I have one granddaughter who intends to marry a man and live as an exile in Ireland and a daughter who believes in imaginary wolves and adorns herself like the Queen of Sheba."

"I won't give up on Matthew," Lily said firmly. *At least, not until he gives up on me.* But today she had glimpsed a trace of the man she'd loved. When he'd spoken of their wedding night, it was as if the years had been lifted away for a moment, bringing them back together. She'd hoped he might kiss her.

Instead, the broken teacup had transformed him into someone else. She didn't know if he could be healed any more than her mother.

But she had to try.

Matthew was sitting in his mother's drawing room when James Thornton, the Earl of Penford, strode across the room. The man's fists were clenched, and fury blazed in his eyes. "I ought to kill you."

Given his friend's fury, Matthew stood and inquired, "Dare I ask why?"

"I should have left you to rot at the hands of your torturers after what you did to my sister." James lunged toward him, and his fist caught the edge of Matthew's jaw.

Pain blasted through him, but it was welcome. After days of hardly sleeping, he wished that someone *would* knock him unconscious.

"You ruined her." James threw another punch, and Matthew didn't bother to defend himself. His head snapped to the side with the force of the excruciating blow, and he tasted blood.

"Goddamn you." His friend stepped back, his fists still clenched. "Why would you take advantage of her? She was only eighteen." James loosened his fingers and shook his head. "I thought you were better than that." His voice lowered, and he sighed. "That's not the kind of man you are. Or, at least, that's what I believed."

Beneath the weight of his friend's stare, Matthew admitted, "I don't know what kind of man I am anymore, James." He stared back at his friend, the heaviness of exhaustion weighing upon him. He couldn't undo the mistakes he'd made.

"You let her believe you were going to marry her," James said, his tone holding cold fury. "And then you ruined her before leaving her behind. If there had been a child..."

"There wasn't." He held James's gaze. "And if you came here to tell me to leave her alone, save your breath. We both know I cannot marry her now."

"You bastard." James swung again, and pain lashed through him at the blow to his ribs, causing him to stagger backward. "That's why she came to see you, wasn't it? Because she loved you. And now, you think to abandon her?"

Matthew caught his friend's fist before the next blow could fall. "Yes. I am going to leave her alone to find another man who is far better than me. Isn't that what you want?"

"What I want is to break every bone in your body." James let out a foul curse. "How could you do this?"

"I never meant to hurt her." He knew he'd wronged Lily, despite the missing pieces of memory. He never should have touched her. For not only had he ruined her life, but he'd also destroyed the trust of his best friend. He couldn't change the past...but he could let Lily go. She could find a better man, one who would give her the life she deserved.

Matthew sank down into a chair, swiping at the blood on his nose. He lowered his head. "Tell her I'll add funds to her dowry as compensation for what I did."

James seized him by his shirt and jerked him to stand. "The last thing I want is for you to treat my sister like a common trollop. You ought to find a single shred of honor and marry her. Grant her that respect at least."

He didn't know how James could even consider it. He wasn't fit to be a husband to any woman just now. "No woman deserves to be bound to a man like me. Better that you should call me out and put a bullet through my brain."

"No," his friend answered. "I won't reward you with death. You ought to spend the rest of your miserable life groveling to my sister. You should atone for your sins, not find an eternal escape from them." He stepped back. "I'll expect you to call upon her with an offer."

Matthew's mouth twisted. "So you intend to punish her with a lifetime of unhappiness?" He couldn't imagine what James hoped to accomplish by wedding the pair of them. Lily believed there was something left of the man he had been, when they were hardly more than strangers now. She should try to find happiness with someone else.

"You should have thought of that before you claimed her virtue." James flexed his hands. "I saved your wretched life and brought you back from India because you were my friend. But you were never that, were you? Not if you betrayed my sister."

I was. I've always been your friend. They had been close, despite their ten year age difference. Their mothers had been good friends, paying calls on one another frequently. Sometimes when Matthew had visited with his mother, James had toddled after him, eagerly trying to engage him in playing with tin soldiers. He'd been the little brother Matthew had always wanted, and even now, he would protect James without a second thought.

He could say nothing to allay his friend's anger, for words wouldn't heal the invisible wounds he'd caused. His body ached, not only from James's blows, but from the darkness that shadowed his mood. "You should have left me there to die."

James paused at the doorway. "Yes. I should have."

Three days later

Lily had nearly reached the front door when her sister Rose stopped her. "What are you doing?"

She adjusted the basket over her arm. "Nothing."

"I don't believe you." Her sister took slow, halting steps. "You're trying to sneak out, aren't you? You're going to see *him* again." But instead of being angry, Rose gave a conspiratorial smile. "What's in the basket?"

"Just some food."

She'd asked Cook to prepare a basket filled with Matthew's favorite foods—in particular, strawberry tarts. They had shared some on their wedding night. A flush came over her face, remembering the way he had tasted the sliced strawberries and then kissed her until her knees went weak.

"I'm going with you," Rose said. "That way, James won't suspect anything. If he asks, we're going to pay a call on Evangeline." She caught sight of her lady's maid and ordered, "Hattie, please fetch my bonnet and shawl. I am going with my sister to pay calls."

"Shall I come with you?" the maid offered.

"No, thank you. I will take a footman with us." After Hattie departed, Rose leaned in closer. "How were you planning to travel?"

Lily kept her voice low, not knowing if she could trust any of the servants. "In our carriage, if I can manage it. But James is being overprotective. He's forbidden me to see Matthew."

Her sister's face turned serious. "And what do *you* want, Lily? You waited for this man for two years. Is he worth it?"

The weight of uncertainty bore down upon her. "I don't know. I want to believe that he will remember what we shared and love me again. But...nothing is the same as it was."

"And if he doesn't?"

Lily didn't want to consider that. For so long, she had shaped her life around Matthew. Without him, it was as if someone had torn away the foundation of herself. An emptiness stretched out before her, one she didn't want to face. "I don't know."

Rose walked with her to the front door. "My advice is to begin again, as friends. Treat him as you would a stranger, and perhaps, in time, his memories will return."

It was reasonable enough, but Lily admitted, "How? He doesn't even want to see me." She winced when she thought of him ordering her to leave.

"A man who has endured great suffering needs a reason to smile again, don't you think?" Her sister nodded toward the basket. "Your idea of bringing him food is a good one. But you should find a way to distract him from the past." Rose turned her attention toward their cat, Moses. He had sired four new kittens with their other cat, Geranium, a few months ago.

Two of the babies were following their father, and the sight of them made Lily smile. Moses nudged against her legs, seeking affection, and she leaned down to rub his ears. "No one loves you, do they, Moses? You are so neglected."

But she was beginning to see what Rose was suggesting. Matthew needed something to bring him back to the world, and was there anyone who didn't love kittens? She picked up a gray and white kitten and held him close. "Do you really think I should give him one of the kittens?"

Her sister considered it. "Possibly. Unless kittens make him sneeze."

Lily cuddled the feline, who rewarded her by sinking claws into her glove. She winced and extricated the animal, gently placing him in the basket with her food. "Well, I suppose we'll try it. At worst, I'll just bring the kitten back again." She followed her sister toward the front door, only to be interrupted by their brother.

James cleared his throat and stood at the doorway like an angry sentry. "And just where do you think you are going?" He folded his arms across his chest and raised an eyebrow.

Rose sent their brother a bright smile. "We are going to pay a call upon Evangeline. Lily decided to bring her a kitten."

His gaze narrowed. "Is that so? Perhaps I should accompany you."

No, don't, she pleaded inwardly. But her sister gave James a critical eye. "I wouldn't, James. Evangeline doesn't want to see you."

His expression held a hint of embarrassment. "And how would you know that?"

"Because when she found out you had returned, she said she would rather be devoured by eels than see you again. At least, I'm fairly certain that's what she said."

Lily bit back a smile. Sometimes her sister had quicker wits than anyone gave her credit for. There had been a time when their friend, Evangeline, had worshipped James from afar, but it had ended badly.

Her brother had the graces to look guilty, but he offered, "I imagine she's forgiven me after two years."

"It's doubtful," Lily added. "Women do hold grudges, you know." But James stepped aside and allowed them to leave. His expression revealed that he wasn't quite certain whether to believe them.

Rose climbed into the carriage with the help of their footman, and Lily followed, setting her basket down at their feet. With the door still open, her sister asked James, "Is there anything you'd like us to say to Evangeline on your behalf? Perhaps we should offer your apologies on being such a cowardly donkey's posterior?"

James let out a sigh and shook his head. "Whatever happened to sisters taking their brother's side? Are we not family?"

"Not in this instance," Rose said. "You abandoned Evangeline when she was in love with you and left for India without a goodbye. She despises the ground you walk on."

Thankfully, he appeared uneasy at the prospect of paying a call. "I suppose you are right. Give her my good wishes."

"She wouldn't accept them, even if I did." But Rose inclined her head with a warm smile. "But I will tell her you are sorry."

With that, the footman closed the door, and their brother waved them on. Lily studied her sister. "You are an accomplished liar, Rose. I'm not sure that's such a good thing."

Her sister reached for the kitten and tucked the feline into her lap. "It worked this time. But next time, we may not be so fortunate. Even if you do regain Lord Arnsbury's friendship, you should know that our brother believes Matthew ought to marry you for what he did."

Lily sobered at that. "I know." With a rueful smile, she added, "I had always intended to marry Matthew after he returned. But I believed he would want to wed me...not because he was forced into it."

"I can try to reason with James. But this should be your decision. And if you don't want to wed him, after all is said and done, you can come live in Ireland with Iain and me."

Her sister's suggestion was reassuring, though Lily had no desire to leave the country. It was only an offer of freedom, a chance to escape her troubles.

"Not yet," she said. "Not until I've done what I can to help Matthew recover."

It might not be enough, she understood. She didn't want to even imagine what he had suffered when he'd been a captive. But she would not turn away from him when he needed her.

The carriage pulled to a stop in front of the Arnsbury townhouse, and nerves gathered in her stomach. "Thank you for coming with me, Rose."

"You're welcome. I will stay here and have the coachman take me to pay a call upon Evangeline. I can keep my word to James, and you'll have time to be with the earl." She handed over the kitten, her gaze thoughtful. "I'll return for you in a couple of hours. Good luck, Lily. You'll need it."

Lily gathered the basket in one arm and tucked the kitten inside to keep the animal safe. And when she left the carriage, she prayed that she wasn't making a terrible mistake.

⌗

Lily waited for a quarter of an hour in the drawing room before Lady Arnsbury arrived to greet her. "Thank goodness you've come." The matron offered her hands and squeezed

Lily's. Her face held nothing but worry, and behind her, Lily saw Dr. Fraser and his wife.

Although the Scottish doctor had been born into a simple life, he had inherited his uncle's title of Viscount Falsham. Lady Falsham's brown hair had lines of silver in it, but she still held a classic, delicate beauty. "Matthew has worsened since you left," she said quietly.

A numb feeling settled in Lily's stomach. She should have come yesterday, despite her doubts. "What can I do to help?"

The doctor chose a seat nearby, steepling his hands together. "I've treated men like Lord Arnsbury before, Lady Lily. But the healing process is no' so verra easy." He exchanged a look with his wife, who had gone pale. "He's like a man come back from the battlefield. His mind has closed off all that he doesna wish to remember."

Even me, Lily thought. She reached down to the basket, suddenly feeling foolish. A man who had suffered from torture didn't need a basket of strawberry tarts or a kitten. Those were gifts for a child, not a grown man. Her cheeks reddened, and she wished she hadn't brought them.

"Perhaps I shouldn't have come," she ventured. "Especially if he is suffering so badly. I might cause him to remember something he wishes to forget."

"But your presence does seem to bring him back to reality," Lady Arnsbury pointed out. "I think he needs to see you, even if he does not understand the reasons." Her face faltered, and a flush rose over her cheeks. "I know he was...not himself the other day. But I will accompany you now."

It was an understatement, given the shattered teacup and Matthew's response to it. But Lily said nothing at all. She was here to help him and would do all that was necessary.

"I will also join you both," Lady Falsham offered.

Lily thought about leaving the basket behind, but was rather worried that the kitten would wander away. The lid was latched, but the animal might begin meowing. She picked it up, feeling the sway of the kitten's movement inside.

"Will you remain downstairs for a moment?" Lily asked the two women. "I will call out if I have need of you." She wanted a moment alone with Matthew to determine his mood.

The ladies agreed, and Lily went up the stairs, praying she could help the man she loved.

With her heart in her throat, she knocked at his door.

Chapter Four

Matthew sat in the wingback chair, his eyesight blurring, his shoulders aching. He was caught in a haze of sleeplessness, and he didn't remember when he'd eaten last. Nor did he care. The black pit of his existence surrounded him, the darkness pushing away everything, save an endless sea of weariness.

His bedroom door swung open, and he jerked at the noise. There she stood, a vision in white. Lily's golden brown hair was combed back to a knot at her nape, and she carried a basket in one arm. Her cheeks were flushed, as if she had hurried on her way to see him. And in spite of his melancholy, he was glad to see her. She disrupted the darkness, pushing back the shadows.

"May I come in?"

"You're already inside," he pointed out. "A few steps more won't matter."

She smiled at that, and something stirred within him. Her hazel eyes warmed to him, and she cracked the door behind her. "How are you today?"

"Alive. And quite disgruntled at the world and everyone in it." He didn't bother hiding the truth from her, and Lily didn't seem to mind. In a way, it felt good to be brutally honest with someone.

"Are you angry with me?"

He stared at her for a long moment. "No, not angry. But I do know that I'm behaving like an ill-tempered dragon."

"You have a strong reason for being ill-tempered." She sat down and put the basket upon a side table. "But I did promise to love you in sickness and in health." Her mood was different this time, as if she was no longer afraid of him. Still, she kept her distance. For a moment, she studied his bedroom. "It *is* rather dark in here. Do you prefer it that way, or shall I open the drapes?"

"I don't care what you do." He lacked the desire or the energy to move just now. But his curiosity was piqued by the basket. He thought he heard a rustling noise. "What did you bring me?"

"Strawberry tarts," she said. She pulled aside the drapes, and the sunlight pierced his eyes. Matthew shielded his face, and in the meantime, he heard the rustling noise again. What on earth was it?

He tensed, his hands tightening upon the armrests. His gaze shifted to the breakfast tray he'd ignored earlier and the silver cloche upon it. Had a mouse managed to get inside the basket? He started to ease his hand toward the cloche, wondering if he could trap the mouse beneath the tray cover.

"You seem a little better today," she offered. "At least, you haven't demanded that I leave you."

"Yet," he emphasized.

"I feel certain you might, perhaps within the next minute." She raised an eyebrow at him. "But I will take the risk."

Those hazel eyes studied him, as if she were trying to understand him better. "I've been thinking a great deal since I left you last. And you're right...we cannot simply pick up where we left off. You've changed, and you are not the same man anymore."

"Neither of us is the same," he agreed. "And our reasons for the...unconventional marriage are no longer valid. I cannot undo what happened in the past, but I can give you back your future."

Her expression dimmed, but she gave a nod. "I thought you might say that. But what you need is someone to help you out of the darkness. You need a friend." She extended her hand to him, but he didn't take it. "Let me help you, Matthew."

A tightness filled up the emptiness within him. He was so weary of living. She might want to be his friend, but he had nothing left to give.

"I won't ask that of you." He kept his voice frosted, needing her to go away. Didn't she understand that the man she had once loved was gone? He wasn't that man anymore, and he refused to try. He eyed the door and added, "Now would be a good time for you to leave."

But instead of rising from the chair, she reached for the basket.

"Wait," he warned her. "Something is moving within that basket. And I highly doubt my strawberry tarts are...alive."

"Oh, that." Her demeanor turned guilty. "I brought you something else, along with the tarts. It may not have been a very good idea. But I'll show you nonetheless."

She went over to the basket and unlatched it. A moment later, he spied a gray and white kitten emerging, covered in strawberries and crumbs. When Lily saw her ruined tarts, her expression grew pained. "Oh dear."

Matthew got up and went to inspect the animal. The kitten was just large enough to fit in his hand, and he picked it up. The feline stared at him with wide eyes. Its fur was matted with sticky strawberries, and he brushed off the crumbs.

"I suppose you won't be having a strawberry tart." She winced. "I thought I had wrapped the tarts safely in napkins, but the kitten managed to get into them."

Matthew eyed Lily. "And what are you expecting me to do with him?"

A hint of a smile slid over her lips. "Well, I didn't intend for you to eat him, that's for certain." She reached out for the kitten. "I suppose I should wash him off. He'll be quite cross with me."

"Isn't he too young to be separated from his mother?"

"He's a few months old, so he'll be fine," Lily said. "At least, I think he's a boy."

Matthew couldn't help but ask, "Why did you bring me a kitten?"

Lily shrugged and thought a moment. "Because you're unhappy. You've endured so much, and I thought you needed something to lift your spirits." She lifted her gaze to his. "He might help you to live in the present instead of dwelling in the past. And besides, I can't think of anyone who doesn't like kittens."

Lily brought the kitten over to a basin. She poured water inside it and gently washed the strawberry filling from the kitten's fur. The animal squirmed while she cleaned him, letting out a high-pitched squawk. When she was finished, the kitten appeared indignant.

"There now." She picked up one of Matthew's fallen shirts and wrapped it around the animal. "You'll dry off. It's not so bad."

"That *is* my shirt you've used as a towel," he felt compelled to point out.

She dried off the kitten until it resembled a knotted ball of damp fuzz. Then she held him out. "Here, take him."

Matthew hesitated but finally accepted the animal. It began squeaking, eyeing him as if he were at fault for the bath. And despite his earlier mood, he softened. "He seems quite angry with us."

"He'll get over it." Lily picked up the basket and examined the contents. "Oh, look—there's still one of the tarts wrapped up in a napkin. I don't think he touched this one." She pulled out a white linen cloth and unwrapped it, revealing a small pastry with a red filling. "Do you want it?"

The kitten sank its claws into his arm as it climbed up his shirt. Matthew gently lifted it onto his chair, and it crouched into a hunter's stance before it pounced at a pillow. It struck him that this was as close to an ordinary day that he'd had in some time. The kitten's antics were a distraction he'd never anticipated, and it wasn't unwelcome.

Lady Lily took a step closer, holding out the tart. A few strands of brown hair framed her face, and he didn't miss the shining hope in her hazel eyes.

God above, he shouldn't have let her in. This had been a big mistake, and he had to make it clear that he could not be her friend. Not with his life in such a tangled mess.

"Lady Lily, I don't think—"

She lifted her hand and cut him off. "I know you're going to send me away. But before you do, taste this." In her hand, she held out the strawberry tart.

She clearly wasn't going to give him a choice. And why on earth it was so important to her, he didn't know. But he accepted the pastry and took a bite. The sweet taste of strawberries flooded his mouth, and Matthew blinked as it evoked an unexpected memory.

The last time he'd eaten a strawberry tart, Lily had been with him. He had shared it with her, kissing her hard until the taste mingled with her tongue. He had been desperate to touch her, and the memory of her hands upon his skin struck hard.

The deep sweetness of the berries conjured the taste of her lips, the memory of her head falling back as she arched beneath him. Her hands had clung to his hair as he kissed a path down the softness of her neck, down to her rounded breasts. He had taken a nipple into his mouth, the erect tip rising as she cried out in pleasure.

Matthew set down the strawberry tart, shaken by the

vision. He could not deny the arousal of his body as memories flooded through him. He had pleasured her until her body had convulsed against him in ecstasy. He gritted his teeth to force back the unexpected memory.

"Do you like it?" she asked.

He couldn't answer, still caught up by the daydream. Lily had done this deliberately, wanting him to remember the past. She'd brought him strawberry tarts and a kitten, hoping that he would care for her again.

He forced himself to harden his emotions toward this woman. She didn't understand how broken his mind was, and he didn't want to drag her down into his own private hell. After months of torture and pain, he didn't know how long it would take to recover.

Lily believed that time and friendship would bring him back…but he couldn't believe that. If he lost himself to a vision again, he might hurt her without meaning to. He was barely holding on to sanity, and he couldn't take that risk.

And though it was cruel, he needed to cut the bonds between them and free her from the past. This was his battle to face alone.

"Lily, whatever memories we had are in the past. The truth is, I took advantage of your innocence, and we were never legally married. I don't want or need your help, and you must accept the fact that we cannot be man and wife. It's best for both of us."

❧ ⁂ ☙

It felt as if Matthew had struck her in the heart. Though Lily had braced herself for this, it hurt far worse than she'd imagined. She set aside the tart on his breakfast tray, turning her face away to hide the unshed tears.

She should have known that the past could not be fixed so easily. She'd been such a fool to visit, raising her hopes, only to have them dashed into pieces. The urge to leave came over her so strong she could not deny it.

But a knock at the door interrupted. She had nearly forgotten about Lady Falsham and Matthew's mother, Lady Arnsbury. The last thing she wanted was to see them right now.

"Your mother and godmother are just outside the door," she informed him, tucking the napkin back inside the basket.

"I suppose you'll have to let them in." He sat down in the wingback chair, and the kitten crawled into his lap.

With reluctance, Lily went to the door and opened it. Lady Arnsbury and Lady Falsham stood there, but she noticed the absence of Dr. Fraser. Perhaps he'd decided to stay behind in the drawing room.

"Come in." She braved a smile she didn't feel at all.

The two women eyed one another before crossing the threshold. Lady Arnsbury studied Lily as if to ensure that she had not been harmed. Matthew's godmother, Lady Falsham, moved across the room to him, stopping short when she saw the kitten. "Why, Matthew, what's this?"

"Lady Lily thought I needed a companion." He picked up the damp kitten in one hand and gave it over to her. "We had to wash him, since he was covered in strawberry tart."

The viscountess was startled when the kitten climbed up her arm, sinking its claws into her gown. "Well, he is a darling thing, isn't he? What will you name him?"

"I've no idea." Matthew leaned back against the chair and turned to Lily. "Have you any suggestions?"

She hadn't given it any thought. Right now, her thoughts were scattered as she tried to determine what to do now. "No."

His brown eyes locked upon hers. "Perhaps I should call him Beast. For that is precisely what he is."

Lily tightened her lips, knowing he spoke of himself. She had wanted to try again, to help him recover from his ordeal.

But he kept pushing her away. He didn't want her help, and he didn't want her. The very thought broke her heart.

She sank into a chair, hardly knowing what to do now. Should she continue to visit with him, if only for the sake of helping him recover from his wounds? Or would it cut too deeply to be near a man who no longer loved her?

Lily barely heard the conversation between Lady Arnsbury and Lady Falsham. The air was suffocating, and she stared back at Matthew, wondering what to do now. But his emotions were shielded like armor.

Lily reached for her basket. "I wish you well with your Beast. Good day." She needed time to be away right now, so she could bury her face in a pillow and sob her heart out. Never in her life had she imagined he would shut her out, refusing to let her help him.

She started to leave the room but heard his footsteps behind her. She had no desire to speak with him, not when he didn't want her in his life anymore. She couldn't bear to look upon his face and remember what was lost between them. But he was well aware of her misery.

"Lady Lily." Matthew caught her wrist in the hallway and stopped her from leaving. "It's better this way. Go back to the life you knew before me."

She turned to face him and this time didn't bother to hide the tears slipping free from her eyes. "I only wanted to help you, Matthew."

"You can't. It's not your battle to face."

Her battered emotions were bruised, and she had no words that would change his mind. Before she left, she removed the chain from her neck that held the gold ring. She slid it free and held it out. "This belongs to you. I should have returned it sooner."

He sobered and slid it onto the smallest finger of his left hand. "I hope you find happiness, Lady Lily. It was never my intention to hurt you."

His handsome face was haggard, worn down from all the sleepless nights. She reached up and traced the outline of his face, and in his eyes, she saw regret. Whether it was guilt over ruining her, she didn't know. But she couldn't heal a man who didn't want her help any more than he would let her love him.

She needed to gather up the fragments of her life and decide what to do now.

And with that, she turned away, leaving behind the shadow of the girl she'd once been.

Lily sat in the empty dining room of her family's townhouse with a decanter of brandy and a glass. She had never before tasted spirits, but tonight she intended to become well and truly foxed. It was nearly ten o'clock at night, and she'd ordered the servants to leave her alone.

She poured the brandy into the glass and took a small sip. It tasted like liquid fire, burning through her stomach, and she couldn't stop herself from coughing. But the second sip went down easier.

She toasted an invisible Matthew. "To a marriage that never should have happened," she whispered. The brandy had a smooth taste that warmed her from the inside.

Moses jumped onto the dining table and nosed her with his head. "Go away, kitty." But he flopped across the wood, staring at her.

Perhaps it was foolish, but she decided the cat was as good a confessor as any. She rubbed his ears, and he began purring.

"I was a silly, selfish girl," she informed him. "It was all my fault. I fell in love, and I used the poor man to avoid a marriage I didn't want." She poured herself another glass of brandy, and the cat batted at her fingers.

Her mood darkened, and she bit back tears. "I should never have forced him into it. And now I don't know what to do.

Should I leave him, the way he wants me to? Or should I stay?" The cat rubbed himself up against her hand, and she whispered, "He's been so badly hurt. I don't want to abandon him...but he doesn't want me there."

The door to the dining room opened, and Lily glared at the blurry intruder. "I do not wish to be disturbed." But then her eyes adjusted, and she realized it was Rose.

"Oh. It's you." She toasted her sister and took another sip of liquid courage. "Cheers."

"Lily, what are you doing?" Rose leaned upon a cane, taking careful steps until she could sit beside her at the table. "It's very late."

So it was. And she found that she hardly cared. "I'm not sleepy at all. You can retire for the night if you wish. I will remain here."

Rose reached for her hand. "Was it so terrible paying a call upon Lord Arnsbury?"

"He doesn't want to see me again." With an unsteady hand, Lily poured herself another glass of brandy. "Do you want to drink with me, Rose?"

"No, thank you." Her sister's expression grew pained. "I'm so sorry, Lily."

"So am I. And now, I intend to get so intoxicated I won't even remember Matthew's name." She lifted her glass in another mock toast and drained it. The velvety brandy slid down her throat in a light burn.

My goodness, that was nice.

But Rose took the glass from her and set it aside. The room swayed, and Lily was surprised to find that the table was moving, too. How fascinating.

"What happened? What did he say?"

"It's over," she told her sister. "My marriage that never happened." She tried to reach for the brandy decanter, but Rose took her hand instead.

"What do you mean? Did Matthew hurt you in any way?"

"Only my heart. It's empty now, you see?" She blinked at the brandy, noticing that there were three different decanters. This time, she reached for the middle one, and her hand closed over the crystal.

"What are you going to do?" her sister asked. Rose had a way of listening and making her feel as if she would support her, no matter what choices she made. And with her question, she had cut to the heart of the matter.

"What *can* I do? I suppose I'll remain on the shelf and never marry anyone." She reached out for her glass, and this time, Rose allowed her to take it. The brandy no longer burned her stomach but instead filled her with a pleasant buzzing sensation.

"Lily, I'm so very sorry. I wish there was some way I could help."

As her hand clenched the empty glass, she turned back to her sister. "Then you know how I feel about Matthew. I know he's hurt. I know they broke his body and his mind, but he wants me to walk away from him. How can I do that?" She traced the edge of her glass. "I can't leave him behind when he's suffering so badly. And it hurts so much that he wants me to go." Tears flowed over now, and she admitted, "I don't know what to do. He'd rather shut me out and keep me at a distance."

"A wounded man will do or say anything to avoid appearing weak, Lily."

Her sister's words sliced through her sadness, and she wondered if those were his reasons. "Perhaps. But I just...wanted to start over. I wanted to be his friend, to show him that I still cared."

She didn't even know the sort of woman she was without Matthew. Her life felt as if it had little purpose. And no amount of brandy would show her what she was meant to do with her life.

Moses got up and arched his back, nuzzling against her

before he hopped off the table. She stared at the amber glass, feeling broken and lost.

"Do you want me to help you to bed?" her sister asked.

"No. I want to sit here a little longer."

Rose stood from the table and balanced herself against her cane, embracing her. Lily hugged her back, and a rise of dizziness washed over her. "You are strong enough to overcome this. I have faith in you."

She only wished she could have that kind of faith in herself.

Chapter Five

Five days later

It was outright war between Lily and her grandmother. She crossed her arms and regarded Lady Wolcroft. "I am not going, and that is final."

"You need to let go of that blackguard and find another husband to replace him. Where else would you find one except at Lady Arnsbury's ball?"

"I do not wish to marry right now." It was the very last thing she wanted. "I would rather remain home and contemplate the useless nature of my life." And perhaps what she could do to change it.

"You are *not* useless, Lily. But you are obstinate. Be reasonable about this. If your older sister is foolish enough to marry an impoverished Irish earl, at least *you* ought to marry a man of means."

"Perhaps I should wear a price tag about my neck," she grumbled. "Or better, you could auction me off to the highest bidder."

"Unless you improve your temperament, no man would buy you." With an exasperated huff, her grandmother continued,

"Lily, I don't see why you are being so difficult about this. What is so wrong with marrying a wealthy man, bearing him children, and spending his money?"

She couldn't give an answer, for it was clear that Lady Wolcroft was in earnest. Her grandmother appeared perplexed at the idea that a woman could be anything other than a wife.

Lily squared her shoulders. "I want a life in which I can be more than just a brood mare with a penchant for shopping. And there are no men attending the ball who would allow that."

The most eligible London bachelors were men of tradition who wanted decorative wives. She found the idea impossible to swallow. Not to mention, her heart was still wounded from the loss of Matthew. If he had given her any sign at all that he cared, she would have waited. But now she had no choice but to forge a life without him, in spite of the hurt.

"I will not have a bluestocking or a spinster for a granddaughter," Mildred continued. "And your life is not at all useless. It will serve a great purpose when you bring an heir into the world."

She didn't agree at all. She had spent the past two years pining for the man she'd married in secret, believing they would reunite in a proper, legal union...only to find out he had come home a different man, one who no longer wanted her. No, being a wife had not served her at all. It had only shown her that she had allowed herself to become a shell of a woman, living and dreaming for the return of someone else.

It was no life at all, and she'd had her fill of it.

"You will attend the ball and speak with Lord Davonshire or someone else," her grandmother pronounced. "That is final."

Lily crossed her arms and faced down the elderly woman. "Is it?" She spun and crossed the room, feeling the need to escape the house. It was stifling inside, and she ordered a footman to bring her bonnet and shawl. Perhaps a drive around town might ease her spirits.

While she waited, she spied her mother walking down the

stairs. Iris was murmuring to herself, and she was dressed in a blue morning gown. The moment she reached the landing, her gaze centered on Lily.

"Oh, there you are, Lily. I thought we could go out and pay calls together. I should enjoy your company." While her mother's words made perfect sense, there was a slight vacant expression upon her face that suggested she was recovering from one of her madness spells. It might be dangerous to take her out.

"Are you feeling well?" she asked Iris directly.

The matron nodded. "A little anxious, but I think some brisk air might do me some good." Her face softened, and she added, "I promise I will not leave the carriage before we arrive." Her embarrassment was evident, and she said, "I know I have not been myself as of late."

It occurred to Lily that they had been keeping Lady Penford prisoner in the house, too afraid to let her go anywhere. True, Iris suffered from moments of delirium where she saw and heard things that were not real. But to lock her away was no life at all.

She moved forward and linked her arm with her mother's. "Everything will be fine. And we will take two footmen with us to make sure we are safe."

The grateful brightness on her mother's face was like a morning sunrise. "Thank you, Lily," she whispered.

It took half an hour, but eventually, they drove through the streets in the open carriage while Lily held her parasol. The sight of her mother's happiness eased the strain she had been feeling.

"Grandmother insists that I attend Lady Arnsbury's ball and find someone else to marry," she confided. "But it's not so easy."

Her mother tucked her hand in hers. "No, it is never easy to let go of someone you love. But he may come back to you once you have set him free."

The thought was heartbreaking. And right now, she didn't think she had it within her to begin again.

"I don't want to go to the ball at all," Lily confessed. "The idea is unbearable. I cannot imagine the idea of looking for another man to love."

"Perhaps you shouldn't be looking for someone else," her mother said quietly. "It might be that you should be looking for yourself instead." She reached out and squeezed Lily's palm. "Why not go with the intent of having fun? Do as you please. Laugh and dance and make merry."

The warmth of her mother's hand in hers was a welcome comfort. She hadn't thought about attending the ball with a reckless sense of fun. When had a ball ever been anything except a disastrous attempt at matchmaking?

"I hadn't thought of that," she admitted. "Grandmother would never condone my having fun."

Iris smiled. "You ought to try it. And instead of grieving for what you have lost, look and see what you may find instead."

In that moment, her mother's advice brought a welcome balm of healing to her wounded heart. It was true that she had never envisioned a ball as a moment of fun. And what if she did? She might discover that it was enjoyable, particularly if she had no intention of finding a husband.

"All right," she agreed. "I will go. But only for fun."

"Good." Iris sighed, and for the next few minutes, they drove through the streets toward no destination in particular. It was a fine day, and Lily enjoyed the warmth of sunlight on her face. When they passed the street where Matthew lived, she felt a twinge of sadness before she forced it away. Iris asked, "Did you want to stop and pay a call upon Lady Arnsbury before this evening?"

It was the very last place she wanted to be. "No. I am certain she is very busy with the plans for the ball."

Her mother nodded absently. "All right, then."

"Thank you for the outing, Mother," she told Iris. "You've made me feel so much better about the ball tonight."

"I will send Hattie to dress your hair and help you," her mother said. "James will accompany you, and Rose might attend if she feels well enough to dance." Lily knew how much Rose wanted to prove that she was no longer an invalid.

"All right," she agreed. But as they returned to the house, she imagined herself wearing a brightly colored gown that would make her feel beautiful again. She would try to smile and enjoy herself.

Her mother's suggestion was a sound one indeed. Lily would not at all look for a new husband to marry—she would try to find the joy in each moment.

His mother adored parties and always had. From his bedchamber, Matthew could hear the lilting sounds of music coming from their small ballroom. The evening was warm, and Lady Arnsbury had opened up the doors to allow guests to spend time within the garden. It was a small space, walled off from the rest of the London streets, but he'd always found a sense of quiet among the greenery. It was nothing more than a stone patio with gravel pathways that encircled a large fountain. In the summer, roses bloomed along the brick wall, and his mother delighted in sitting upon a bench beneath a small lilac tree.

He stood with his windows open, gazing down at the darkness below. A few lamps had been set out in the garden, and he watched the guests milling about. Truthfully, he was searching for one guest in particular—Lily Thornton. Not to bother her but simply to know if she was here. A footman had confirmed that she had indeed come to the ball. But despite endless minutes of watching over the garden, he had not seen her.

Matthew had no intention of going downstairs. He wasn't dressed for an evening ball, and the thought of being surrounded by crowds of people was unthinkable. No, he would not dare to attend.

Yet, he'd felt remorse after the way he'd behaved toward Lily. She had wanted to help him, to offer her love and sympathy. He simply couldn't bring himself to drag her into his darkness. It was better to give her the freedom to walk a different path.

Matthew closed the windows of his room, stepping over the Beast who was curled up in one of his shoes. The kitten had been a most unexpected gift, but the animal had offered a quiet companionship. It was difficult to brood properly when a fuzzy creature was cuddling and purring beside you.

He realized that he *wanted* to see Lily tonight, even if he never spoke a word to her. If he ventured downstairs, he could remain in the shadows of the staircase, watching over the guests in his mother's ballroom. No one need know he was there.

Matthew reached for his evening coat and buttoned it, before he glanced at himself in a looking glass. His face appeared like the stuff of nightmares, almost wild and frightful. The angry red scar made him look like a pirate, not to mention that he hadn't shaved in days, and his eyes were bloodshot from lack of sleep. It would send any young woman screaming from the sight of him.

A monster in the shadows, indeed. Still, there was nothing to be done for it. He ignored the mirror and strode out of the room, closing the door behind him. From below, he heard the lilting stringed instruments and the melody of a waltz.

Matthew took the stairs slowly, not wanting anyone to see him. When the hallway was empty, he hastened down the remaining steps, slipping back behind the left side of the staircase. From here, he could glimpse the open ballroom and the men and women dancing.

Dozens of guests filled the space, and he searched again for Lily. She could be standing against a wall with her sister or grandmother. But no, she was not among the wallflowers.

He thought he heard her voice, and then he spied a young woman dressed in vivid purple with a pearl necklace that dipped to the curve of her breast. Lily's brown hair was swept into an updo with two curls on either side of her face. And she was smiling.

Matthew took a step forward, staring at her. She was laughing at something her companion had said, fanning herself lightly. It looked as if she was enjoying herself, and something tightened within him.

It was better for both of them if she found happiness with someone else. He knew that. And yet, he took another step closer, his hand gripping the wooden bannister.

She laughed again, and then her gaze shifted to the hallway where he was standing. Without knowing why, he took a few steps forward, letting her see him. He crossed his arms, nodding to her in silent greeting.

Her smile faded, and then she turned back to her companion, behaving as if she hadn't seen him...though he knew she had. The question was whether she would return to the ball, as if nothing had happened.

Matthew waited a moment before he slipped into a smaller hallway that led to the outside garden. He opened the door and breathed in the warm night air. Gravel crunched beneath his feet as he walked along the perimeter of the house. The lighted windows offered stolen glimpses at the guests, but he ignored them. He had seen what he'd wanted to see.

His mind and conscience battled with one another. He wanted to talk with Lily and perhaps apologize for his behavior the other day, though he ought to leave her alone. For a moment, he stood beside a tall arbor vitae, trying to decide whether to return to his room or approach her.

Fate made the decision for him when he saw her walk

outside into the garden with her sister standing nearby. Matthew emerged from the shadows but remained far enough away that he was not intruding upon their conversation.

Lily surprised him, however, when she strode across the gravel pathway and stopped directly in front of him. "Are you all right, Lord Arnsbury?"

Her use of his title instead of his first name was not lost on him. Clearly, she was trying to maintain distance between them.

"I am, thank you. I thought I would take a short walk."

The deep purple of the gown brought out the green in her hazel eyes, and her thin shawl did little to hide the curve of her shoulder. Unbidden came the memory of pressing his mouth to that shoulder, kissing a path lower. A sudden rise of heat came over him, and he gritted his teeth against the unexpected desire, forcing it back.

She hesitated, asking softly, "Is this the first time you've been outside since you returned?"

"It is." Part of him wanted to return upstairs, but it *was* tedious there with only a kitten for company.

Lily was staring at him as if she wanted to say something more but couldn't find the right words. He offered a light shrug. "I suppose I should go back to my room. I'm likely frightening away my mother's guests."

"This *is* your house, as you said before. They can go away if they're frightened of you," Lily answered. He was surprised to hear her defend him. Then she stole a glance back at her sister, as if trying to make a decision. "My mother told me I ought to enjoy this ball, to do whatever I wished."

"Within reason." He was rewarded by a faint smile that vanished from her face a moment later.

"Yes. And I think I would like to walk through the garden now."

He wasn't certain whether she was dismissing him, but she waved for her sister Rose to come closer. "Do you want to join us?"

He thought about it for a moment. He had remained inside his room for over a week, and the atmosphere was stifling. This was something he needed to do to push back against the darkness and take a step forward.

Part of him believed he shouldn't accept her help, not after he'd rebuffed her earlier. And yet, he saw nothing demanding in her expression—only the offer of friendship. This was a walk in the garden, nothing more. And so, he offered his arm.

Lily placed her hand upon it, and when her sister drew near, leaning on her cane, he gave his other arm to Rose. Her brown hair was dotted with blossoms, and she wore a bright blue gown. The young woman smiled brightly at him. "Hello, Lord Arnsbury. It's good to see you out and about once again."

"It has been a long time, Lady Rose." He bowed his head in greeting, and she smiled when they began walking. Lily's sister had to lean against him, since she could not walk quickly, but he didn't mind. It was a good distraction from the strange feeling of being out of doors once again. The air was warm by London standards, but it lacked the brutality of the desert sun. Each step was easier than the last.

In the moonlit darkness, he led the women along the gravel pathway. Lily barely said a word, though it had been her idea. Rose, in contrast, admired the flowers blooming.

"Have you enjoyed your evening?" he asked Lily, attempting conversation.

With a hint of a smile, she answered, "I tried something different. Instead of being a quiet, shy young woman, I answered questions with complete honesty. I'm not certain the gentlemen liked it very much."

"Then they were not right for you," he said. He ignored the tightness in his gut that rose up at the mention of other men.

"I agree," Rose added. "Honesty is the best way to begin any relationship."

Lily broke out in a laugh. "When you began your

60

relationship with Iain, you nearly stabbed him with a rake. I'm not certain that was honesty."

"Of course it was. I was completely forthright that if he tried to hurt me, he would be skewered." Rose smiled brightly, and a flare of amusement caught Matthew in the gut.

The emotion seemed foreign somehow, but he said, "A man always likes to know where he stands."

He led them toward the stone fountain comprised of a cupid statue with water streaming from its arrow tip. Lily took off her glove and reached out to the water, letting it spill over her fingers. Then she sent him a mischievous sidelong glance, flicking water over him.

Droplets spilled over his scar, and Matthew stared at her in disbelief. "That wasn't wise," he warned.

He removed his own glove and reached under the running water, preparing to strike back. Lily couldn't stop her smile, and she taunted, "You wouldn't dare."

"Lily, don't provoke him," Rose warned, stepping away from them. She leaned on her cane until she reached the safety of the shrubbery.

Matthew lowered his hand from the water, and Lily beamed at her sister. "See? I told you he wouldn't."

He rewarded her answer by squirting her in the face with the water he'd concealed in his palm. Lily shrieked with laughter and reached into the fountain, splashing more water at him. Matthew dodged it and grinned at her. "That wasn't very ladylike, Lily."

"But it was great fun." Her hair was slightly wet, and the burst of laughter brought the sparkle to her eyes. "I should apologize."

"Well?" he coaxed.

"But I don't want to."

He noticed that Rose had retreated further away to give them a measure of privacy. He saw it as an opportunity and drew closer. Her face held mischief, and he rested one hand on the edge of the fountain.

"You may want to run, Lily."

"Why?" Her sidelong glance showed she didn't believe he would follow through with his threat.

"Because you're tempting me."

A sudden blush flooded her cheeks, but she didn't move. Instead, she slid her hand into the water. "Perhaps you are the one who should be careful."

He removed his own glove and took her hand beneath the water. It was freezing cold, and it numbed his hand. But he held her palm, preventing her from doing anything foolish.

"Let go, Matthew."

"Why?" His thumb caressed her hand beneath the water, and he found himself captivated by her lovely face and the softness of her skin.

She stood on tiptoe until her face was a breath away from his. "Because." Her lips were sensual, her eyes filled with yearning. It evoked the memory of her kiss, and a sudden heat swelled within him.

Without warning, a sudden shock of frigid water hit his neck, and he yelped, releasing her hand. Lily laughed, lowering her hand. "Because I said so."

He wiped off the water and glared at her, though he didn't truly mean it. Despite the trick, he was enjoying her playful mood. "You should be careful next time, Lily."

She smiled and placed her hand in his arm. "Perhaps." He led her away from the fountain, and she added. "I *am* glad you seem to be feeling better now. And I do hope you've begun to eat again." Her hand pressed lightly against his arm. The gentle pressure offered a quiet support, and he was grateful for it.

He led her through the garden back to Rose, who was waiting for them. "I am glad to see that my sister did not drench you in the fountain."

"She did try. But I managed to defend myself." He raised an eyebrow at Lily, who winked at him.

Rose limped slightly as she took a step toward them. Matthew offered his arm for support, and she took it. "Would you care to go back inside, Lady Rose?" Though he didn't particularly want to make an appearance among the guests, neither did he want her to stumble.

"I should like to sit for a moment," Rose answered. "If you will help me to hobble over to the bench, that will do."

He assisted her over to the bench while Lily trailed behind them. Once Rose was seated, she sighed with relief. "Lily, will you stay with me for a moment?"

"Of course." She moved to sit beside her sister, and Matthew understood that this was his hint to leave them alone.

"Thank you for the walk," Lily said to him.

He bowed to the women. "Lady Lily. And Lady Rose." With that, he returned to the doorway leading inside.

Just as he was about to enter, he glanced behind him at the women. Lily was speaking with her sister in a hushed tone, but then she glanced back at him. For a moment, she met his gaze with a frank stare of her own.

The very sight of her made him aware of exactly what he'd given up. And how very difficult it was to let her go.

Chapter Six

"Would you care to dance, Lady Lily?"

She turned and saw a dark-haired gentleman, impeccably dressed in black. His hair was cropped short, and his brown eyes held undeniable interest. He appeared familiar somehow, but she did not recall his name.

"I am Adrian Monroe," he said. "We were introduced earlier this evening, but I suppose you may not remember me."

She lifted her shoulders in an apologetic shrug. "Forgive me, but I have met many people tonight."

"As have we all," he agreed. "If you are not spoken for, perhaps we might take a turn?"

She pretended to glance at her card, though she was aware that all her remaining dances were free. "All right, Mr. Monroe."

He smiled at her and offered his arm to guide her toward the other dancers. They joined the circle, and he took her hand, leading her in the steps. "I saw you speaking with my cousin a few moments ago," he said. "Matthew Larkspur, the Earl of Arnsbury, I mean."

She felt her cheeks flush. "Yes, I have known Lord

Arnsbury for several years. I did not realize you were cousins."

"Distant cousins," he clarified. "On my father's side." Mr. Monroe spun her lightly, his gloved palm holding hers. "I understand he was unwell after his return from India."

Because he was tortured, Lily thought. But in answer, she said, "He is still convalescing. I am certain he will make a full recovery."

Mr. Monroe nodded to that. "Perhaps. I suppose he'll be seeking a wife soon enough. He'll need an heir after all."

"It's really none of my affair," she answered. "I'm certain Lord Arnsbury will do whatever he wishes."

Mr. Monroe's demeanor softened. "Forgive me. I was merely wondering if you were already spoken for with my cousin. I know you were very close to him not so long ago."

We were married, she wanted to say. Although it hadn't been legal.

"We are friends now, but that is all." The words felt like a lie, even as she spoke them.

But Mr. Monroe appeared pleased. "You do not know how happy I am to hear this." He gave her hand a gentle squeeze. Yes, he was a handsome man, but she did not feel any attraction toward him. As soon as the dance ended, she excused herself, saying that she needed to find her sister.

But Mr. Monroe seemed determined to follow her. "I could not, in good conscience, allow a beautiful lady to go alone without someone to watch over her."

"Thank you, but I will be fine. I am only walking outside those doors to my sister."

"I insist," he said, tucking her hand into his arm. His sudden forward behavior bothered her, though she suspected he meant only to protect her.

Lily pulled her hand free and faced him evenly. "You are making me uncomfortable, Mr. Monroe. I have already said no."

At least he had the good graces to appear apologetic. "That was never my intention, Lady Lily."

She excused herself and returned to the garden where her sister was sitting. This time, Mr. Monroe allowed her to leave with no interference, but she saw his gaze fixed upon her while she walked outside. She found Rose where she'd left her, and her sister smiled. "Did you enjoy yourself, Lily?"

"No, not really. Mr. Monroe was rather overprotective." She sank down on the stone bench and sighed. "I still don't think I want to be here for the Season right now. The idea of dancing and flirting seems so wrong." She had wanted to believe she could indulge in mindless merriment, but it was not so easy.

"Your heart was broken," Rose agreed. "It's too soon."

That, and it was worsened by the fact that she had seen Matthew again. He *was* looking a little better, and it was good to see him walking outside. For a few moments tonight, it had felt like old times again during their mock water fight. And it only renewed the yearning within her.

"I should return to Yorkshire," she said. "Perhaps some time away from London will help." But it was truly time away from Matthew that she needed. She knew he had meant nothing by the water play, but being near him had brought back all her buried feelings to the surface.

"Perhaps you will come with me to Ireland instead," Rose offered. "Iain has already gone back home to prepare for our wedding, and I've promised to join him soon. If you would like to stay with us, you are more than welcome."

The offer was a kind one, but Lily was not so certain she wanted to remain in Ireland for very long. The potato famine had caused hundreds of thousands of people to starve, and she knew that it was a dangerous place with so many fighting for food.

"How bad do you think it will be at Ashton?"

"It will be difficult," Rose said softly. "But I think it will be a challenge worth embracing. We will feed the hungry and rebuild the estate to its former splendor."

It was then that she understood what her sister was truly offering—a chance to be useful. She could immerse herself in helping others, and that might take her mind off her broken heart.

"Do you know, I believe I would be glad to escape London for a time," Lily agreed. "I need a means of occupying my time."

And maybe then, her heart would learn to let go of Matthew.

Days passed, but Matthew knew better than to believe that his mind was healing. The lack of sleep had driven him to such madness that at last he'd asked his valet to buy another sleeping draught, one that was much stronger.

The dark-brown bottle was labeled as Dr. Calaban's Sleeping Tonic. When he uncorked it, the scent reminded him of whiskey. Matthew poured a small dram into a glass, hardly caring what was in it. He drained the glass and tasted the sharp burn of alcohol. He would drink anything if it cast him into a deep sleep.

It was early in the evening, but his hands were trembling from exhaustion. During the past three nights, he'd awakened nearly every hour, his mind filled up with images of torture and pain. He needed to be unconscious, completely devoid of dreams. If a sleeping tonic would bring him some form of relief, he would welcome it.

A soft knock came at his door, and when he answered, his footman said, "I am sorry for the interruption, Lord Arnsbury, but you have a caller. Lady Lily is here."

Matthew was surprised to hear it, and he wondered why she had come. He rose from his chair, reaching for his frock coat. "I will come downstairs in a moment." The room appeared to sway, but he pushed back the effects of the tonic, steadying himself.

The footman inclined his head. "She awaits you in the library."

Matthew walked down the narrow stairs, holding on to the banister for support. With each step, he felt dizziness sweeping over him. It was clear that he would not be able to spend a great deal of time visiting with Lady Lily, or else he'd end up unconscious on the carpet. A bitter taste filled his mouth, and he felt as if his body were buoyant.

He entered the library and found Lily standing beside the bookcase. She turned and said, "I…wanted to see if you were feeling better. It was nice to see you more like yourself the other night."

"Each day gets easier," he answered. Even so, he sensed there was another reason for the call. She appeared hesitant to say more, but in her eyes, he saw the concern.

"I wasn't certain whether I should come," she admitted. "But then, I thought you would want to know that I am leaving for Ireland to attend my sister's wedding. I will be gone for quite a while."

"I am glad you came to say goodbye," he said. And he was. She could have left the country without a word, for she owed him nothing. He was glad of her company, but he hardly knew how long he could remain standing after the effects of the medicine. "Would you like tea?"

Lily shook her head. "I cannot stay for very long."

Matthew closed the door behind him, knowing how improper this was. For a moment, he remained next to the door while his vision blurred, and he felt lightheaded. The tonic was indeed working, and he would need to say his farewell quickly.

He crossed the room to stand by her. "I am glad you are here, Lily. And I did enjoy our walk in the garden the other night." For a moment, he regarded her, fully aware of her beauty and the faint perfume of her soap. If he were a different man, he wouldn't have pushed her away. He might have renewed his pursuit.

"In spite of all that's happened, I do want to remain friends." She ventured a smile at him, though he could not return it just now.

The effects of the tonic had grown stronger, and there was now a ringing in his ears. It felt as if he were viewing Lily's face from underwater, and the room tipped sideways. He reached for a chair, catching his balance.

"I realize I've not been myself since I returned." He sensed that once she left for Ireland, nothing would be the same. He traced the outline of his signet ring upon his finger, remembering how it had hung on a chain around her throat.

Lily gripped his hands a moment, as if she were trying to hold on to the past. "I suppose I was naïve to imagine that we could continue on as we were before. Two years is a long time."

The medicine seemed to intensify his emotions and heighten his senses. He could smell the fragrance of her hair, and the smallest details sharpened. Her hazel eyes were the deep green of summer grass, rimmed with a circle of light brown. Her mouth was the color of a rose, and memories flashed through him of the last time he had shared her bed.

"Is something wrong?" Lily asked. "You look....odd somehow."

He *felt* odd. He sat down upon the chaise longue and blinked, trying to clear his vision. "I took a tonic a little while ago. To help me sleep."

Lily glanced at the doorway and came closer. "Your eyes don't look right, Matthew. I think you should lie down before you fall over."

It seemed as if his mind were caught in a tunnel, and his voice slurred when he spoke. "I agree." But then his mouth continued speaking, "You could lie down with me."

She bit back an amused smile. "I don't think that would be proper. But this medicine does seem to put you in better spirits, doesn't it?"

It felt as if his mind and mouth were disconnected, and he heard himself say, "Do you know how beautiful you are, Lady Lily?"

This time her smile faded. "Please don't say that, Matthew. I need to go now."

"Don't go," he murmured, reaching up to cup her cheek. She froze, and those hazel eyes turned stricken.

"Matthew, you're not yourself." But she didn't pull away.

His pulse quickened, and he could feel the blood racing through his veins. He couldn't say what possessed him at this moment, but he needed to kiss her, to taste that soft mouth. He threaded his hands through her hair, drawing her lower.

"W-what are you doing?"

"I want to remember kissing you," he answered. And the moment his mouth touched hers, it was as if the rest of the world fell away. The deep hunger rose within him in a fierce crescendo, one he could never quench. Though he knew it was wrong to press her like this, on a deeper level, he wanted so much more.

Lily kept him at a distance, but he sensed the moment when she relaxed against him and kissed him back. This woman fit with him like no other. Her hands moved down his face to his shoulders. His shirt had come loose, and she slid her palms beneath it, pressing her hands against his bare back.

The sudden flash of memory seared him the moment she touched his scars. His mind blurred with the hazy effects of the tonic, and Lily's face disappeared, replaced by the woman who had tortured him.

No longer did he see hazel eyes staring at him with passion. Instead, he saw a woman's brown eyes and her mocking smile that revealed he was her prisoner. When he glanced down at the chair, he saw a wooden stool.

His arms were bound behind him with ropes that cut into his wrists. The hot desert sun burned upon his bare skin, and he wore nothing except his smallclothes.

Behind her stood a hooded man in robes. In the man's hand, he saw a glowing red poker.

"Where are the British troops?" she demanded.

"I am not part of the army. I don't know where they are." He tensed as the hooded man drew closer, holding the hot poker near his face.

"You lie. My men saw you with the soldiers." The woman nodded toward the assassin. "Start with his back," she said. "He will tell us everything."

Matthew struggled to free himself, but a searing pain blazed upon his shoulders. He could smell burning skin, and a hoarse cry escaped him. The poker was lifted away, but fire radiated through his scorched flesh.

"The pain will not stop until you tell us what we want to know." Her voice was calm, and seconds later, the man laid the poker across another part of his back. Matthew flinched at the agonizing heat, trying to numb himself to the pain.

The torturer continued her questions, and he began lying even more, telling her where the British were camped, even though he had no knowledge of this. He struggled against the ropes, arching his back as the torment continued.

Abruptly, one of his bonds broke, and he lunged toward the woman, knocking her to the ground. A sudden strength filled him, and he reached for her neck, intending to snap it.

The woman screamed, fighting back against him. He gloried in the sound of vengeance, though she was twisting in his grasp. Now she would feel what had been done to him. He seized her shoulders, twisting her arm so she could not fight back.

For the first time, he was in command of her. She would never torture him again, and he would end the nightmares when he killed her.

"Matthew, please," she begged. Her voice was not the same. He hesitated a moment, hearing the woman's sobs. The tone of her voice was English, not that of a foreigner. And when his mind cleared away the unwanted vision, it felt as if he'd slipped outside of himself.

Lily was lying on the floor, and he was holding her down while she struggled to escape him. His vision shifted, and in horror, he saw that she was crying. He released her immediately, and she clutched her arm in pain. The skin was reddened and would undoubtedly bruise.

Dear God, what had he done?

Her tearful hazel eyes met his with fear. "Get away from me, Matthew! Don't touch me."

Shock and self-loathing washed over him. He had lost himself in memories of the past, and because of it, he had hurt this woman.

He'd mistakenly believed that he would never be able to harm Lily Thornton. Instead, he had fallen into a madness that proved otherwise.

Matthew sank back upon the chair, and dizziness disrupted his balance. "I'm so sorry, Lily," he managed. But the words would not undo the damage he'd wrought.

She stumbled to her feet, protecting her arm. Tears flowed down her cheeks, and she regarded him as if he were a monster.

And so he was. He couldn't be trusted to be alone with this woman, not after this. "I'll summon Dr. Fraser to look at your arm." It was all he could offer. He despised himself for what had happened.

"Don't," she said, backing toward the library door. Her hazel eyes held only fear, and when she reached the threshold, she added, "I am leaving. And…I think it is best if we do not see each other again. Not for a long time."

Matthew kept his distance from Lily, but inwardly, it felt as if his body had been immersed in ice. He was responsible for this, and she had every right to hate him.

When the door closed behind her, he sank to the floor with his knees drawn up. Although he was aware that the tonic had caused him to lose sight of reality, the fault lay with him. He had known it would be hard to live an ordinary life once again, but he'd never imagined he would turn violent.

He reached down and unlaced his shoes, drawing them off, then his socks, until his feet were bare. With trembling fingers, he touched the sole of his left foot. The scars were red, the deep grooves carved into his heel. There was no sensation at all in his foot when he touched the skin.

Matthew stared at the rows of books, neatly aligned with their spines perfectly level. For weeks now, he had wanted a normal existence, one where he could eat, sleep, and exist as any other man.

But if he couldn't even tell the difference between dreams and reality, how could he ever go back to the life he'd known before?

❧

Her maid, Hattie, fussed over Lily in the carriage as soon as she saw her. "What's happened, my lady? Your arm, it's—"

"Take me to see Dr. Fraser," she ordered the driver. Her arm had swollen up dreadfully, and she was in so much pain, she gasped when she climbed inside the carriage.

"It was an accident," she told Hattie. "I slipped and fell."

But the moment the carriage began rolling across the city streets, every jostle intensified the agony. Matthew's eyes had been pinpricks, and he hadn't heard a word she'd spoken. He had been so lost in his nightmares, he'd believed she was somehow his torturer.

The pain sharpened her sense of reason, for Lily now understood what he'd been trying to tell her. The years in India had changed him into a broken man who was incapable of being her husband.

Tears rimmed her eyes, but they were as much from her wounded heart as her arm. She let them fall silently, weeping for the lost man she had loved. Until today, she had believed that his tormented mind could be healed, but now, he frightened her.

The carriage arrived at Lord Falsham's townhouse. Dr. Fraser and his wife, Juliette, had always been kind to her, and she trusted him to help mend her arm.

Her footman opened the door for her and helped her out of the carriage while she cradled her arm. The pain was a constant throbbing, and she was barely conscious of being escorted up the stairs. She prayed that Dr. Fraser was at home to help her.

Thankfully, it took only moments for his servants to lead her to a private room where she met his wife. Lady Falsham gave orders for the servants to bring her tea, and she assured Lily, "We will give you medicine to take away the pain while Paul looks at your arm. How did this happen?"

She hesitated, not knowing whether to speak the truth. But then, Juliette had seen her godson upon his return from India. His mental condition was no secret to her, and Lily confessed, "Matthew became lost in a nightmare. He thought I was one of his torturers, and he pushed me to the ground and fell on top of me. My elbow twisted beneath me."

The woman inhaled sharply and closed her eyes. "I am so very sorry, Lily. We knew he was still having...difficult spells, but I never in my wildest dreams thought he could ever hurt you."

Juliette's compassion made it impossible to keep her composure. Lily's emotions crumpled, and she wept—not from the pain, but from the realization that she could not break through the barrier between them. Matthew had continually pushed her away, rejecting her friendship and desire to help him. And now she understood why. Though she'd never believed his hallucinations would cause him to hurt her, she had no choice but to accept it now.

When Dr. Fraser arrived with his bag, Juliette explained to her husband what had happened to Lily. His face held sympathy when he regarded her. "I am sorry this happened, lass, but I canna say that I'm verra surprised. Lord Arnsbury has endured more torment than most men, and it's his mind that suffers now. I'd wager he knew nothing of what he was doing."

Lily tried to gather herself while Dr. Fraser pulled up a chair and examined her arm. "H-he didn't know. He said he'd taken a sleeping tonic."

"Not one I gave him, I should think." Dr. Fraser put gentle pressure against her arm, and Lily couldn't help but yelp when he touched the swollen place. "Sorry, lass. It's no' broken, but he might have dislocated it when he fell on you."

He nodded to Juliette. "Darling, give her a bit of laudanum in her tea. She'll not be wanting to feel very much when I mend this."

Juliette reached for a small bottle and added a few drops to the tea. "Paul is a very good physician, and he'll fix your elbow for you. I've seen far worse. You can look away if it hurts too much."

She wasn't certain if she wanted to, but Lady Falsham insisted that she drink the tea to help relax her muscles. The laudanum did make her head feel muzzy, and after a little while, Lily was less concerned about the pain. She found it was rather interesting to watch as he adjusted the position of her arm. A little twist here, a bend there, and the pain was suddenly easier to endure.

"Keep it in a splint for a day or two to be sure it doesn't slip out of place again," the doctor advised. "The swelling will go down soon enough." The splints held her arm in the proper place, and he wrapped it tightly in bandages to secure it.

"How long did it take you to learn all of this?" she asked Dr. Fraser.

"Years of study, lass. I went to medical school in

Edinburgh, and I've been practicing medicine all my life. Even though I inherited my uncle's title afterward, I still prefer to be known as Dr. Fraser, rather than Lord Falsham."

Lily was intrigued by how much he'd had to learn in school, and yet, she imagined how fulfilling it must be to heal others. She had never known any woman to study medicine, and undoubtedly it would not be allowed. The musings helped to distract her from her injured arm.

"Do you have any books I might borrow?" she asked. "I would like to know more about healing. That is, perhaps cures for household ailments or injuries."

He exchanged a glance with his wife. "If you want to read about it, I've no objection." Then his expression turned serious. "But the cure for Lord Arnsbury is no' one you'll find in books. You canna splint his broken mind or wrap it in bandages."

"This is not for Matthew. This is for me, so that I can find something to occupy my time. I've spent far too much of my life pining away."

Juliette sent a silent message toward her husband and then interjected, "Why don't you come and pay a call again when you're feeling better? Perhaps Paul could show you some poultices and medicines that might interest you." She smiled and then ran her fingers along a row of books resting on a shelf on the side wall of the room. "Or this might also occupy your time." She handed Lily a green leather book titled *The Pharmacopoeia of the Royal College of Physicians of London.* "It may not be very interesting."

But Lily found herself intrigued by the challenge. "Thank you, Lord and Lady Falsham."

More than anything, she needed a distraction from Matthew. Though she knew he had not intended to hurt her, it broke her heart to think of how much he'd suffered. Deep inside, she was grieving for the husband she had loved and lost.

If losing herself in books would ease the gaping emptiness, she would read the dictionary itself. But perhaps the medical book might offer an escape, a chance to learn about something else that could help others.

She held the book in her lap while Lord Falsham fashioned a sling for her arm. "It will take a few weeks for this to heal properly," he told her. "Come back to me after you've returned from Ireland, and I'll see how it's healing."

She thanked him again for his help, and he gave her a packet of powdered medicine to take with a cup of tea at night to help her sleep.

"Lady Lily," he said, as she stood to leave. "I will look in on Lord Arnsbury and find out what's happened to him. Some medicines have a verra powerful effect upon the mind."

She nodded, holding on to the book. But as she departed the house, she promised herself that she would no longer hold on to the past—instead, she would look toward a different future.

Chapter Seven

The darkness closed over him, drowning Matthew in a sea of hopelessness. God above, how could he have hurt Lily? She had done nothing wrong, and she had only come to say goodbye. Because of his drugged state, he had thrown her to the ground like an animal and hurt her arm. He despised himself for what he had done.

Matthew stood at the window of his room, staring out into the London streets. The dim flare of the gas lamps illuminated the night, and below him were men and women returning from the workhouses, along with other strangers.

He remembered the face of his torturer. Nisha Amat was her name. With black hair and deep brown eyes, she had smiled at him on the first day he'd been taken prisoner. She was beautiful in the way that a poisonous snake held one mesmerized. Her voice was soft and soothing, even as she had ordered her men to break his bones or burn his flesh.

But it was his mind that bore the greatest scars. The memories of guilt and horror washed over him, and he sat down in a chair, wondering why God had let him live. He was nothing and no one.

And now he had hurt Lily.

If he could go back and undo the mistakes he had made, if he could stop himself from drinking the sleeping potion, he would do it.

The insidious voices rose up within him, tempting him. He could take a blade and slash his wrists until he bled to death. Or he could throw himself from a balcony, smashing his skull against the pavement. His hands shook as the effects of the sleeping draught made him hallucinate all the different ways to die.

He wanted to forget the years of the past and present. When he tried to imagine a better future, he could not grasp any release from this prison.

A sudden blur of motion dove at him, and Matthew nearly lashed out at his attacker...only to realize it was his kitten, Beast.

"Damn you," he muttered. His heart was pounding wildly, and a thin layer of sweat coated his skin. The kitten crawled up the leg of his trousers, sinking its claws into the fabric. The animal had no idea how close it had come to being thrown across the room. Matthew picked it up and set it down in his lap, but the kitten only stretched and attempted to swat at his cravat.

Were he an ordinary man, he'd have found the animal's antics amusing. Instead, a bone-deep weariness settled over him. He didn't know a way out of this nightmare. He couldn't be trusted with anyone or anything.

Matthew held the kitten with one hand and rose from his chair. He went to pour himself a glass of brandy, but his hands shook upon the decanter, sloshing the alcohol onto the tray. He took a slow, deep breath, and then drank the entire glass. The brandy burned his throat, but it did nothing to calm him.

The kitten gave a weak meow and sank its claws into his shirt. He kept a close hold on the feline, as if it were the single thread keeping his wits together. A part of him longed to surrender to the dark place within him, the one that tempted him to take his own life.

His guilt at harming Lily weighed upon him like a mountain of stones. There were no words to apologize for what he had done. Whether she knew it was a moment of madness didn't matter. He had hurt the woman who had tried to heal his broken spirit.

With trembling fingers, he sat down and stared at the hearth, not knowing what to do. His mind was not whole, and he dared not trust himself anymore. His fingers curled into the warmth of the sleeping kitten. The animal offered a quiet, unconditional love that he didn't deserve.

On the edge of the desk rested the bottle his footman had purchased. If he drank the remainder of the draught, he might fall into a sleep from which he would never awaken. The temptation increased, though he knew it was a coward's path.

But never would he forget Lily's terror or the horrifying visions that plagued him. He dared not see her again for fear of doing irreparable harm.

His fingers closed around the bottle.

"Paul, we must hurry," Lady Falsham insisted. After they had set Lily's arm, her instincts warned that Matthew was in grave danger. To the outside world, the earl was only her cousin and godson. But she had been close to him his entire life, and she could not stand by and let him suffer. Her husband knew the true reason why. "Please. If he was aware of what he did, I fear the worst."

Paul rapped on the carriage ceiling and ordered the driver to go faster. "He was no' himself, Juliette. I'm sure of it."

"I agree. But after what happened to Lily, he may be a danger to himself. Aunt Charlotte needs to keep a close watch over him." She gripped her hands together, and her husband moved to sit beside her.

"I won't be letting anything happen," he assured her, taking her hand in his. She squeezed his palm, her heart racing. Although she trusted her husband, Juliette could not let go of her instincts that all was not well. Her heart bled at the thought of what Matthew had endured in India and the pain he must be facing now.

When they arrived at the house, Paul helped her from the carriage and a footman greeted them at the door. The man's face appeared concerned at the sight of Paul. "Is aught amiss, Dr. Fraser? Did Lady Arnsbury send for you?"

"I came of my own accord to see the earl. He's no' feeling verra well, so I was told." Paul stepped into the house without awaiting permission. "Show me to his room."

The footman obeyed and closed the door behind them, before leading them to the main staircase. "Lady Falsham, would you care to take tea while your husband tends to Lord Arnsbury?"

"No, thank you. You may let my aunt know we have come, but I intend to see Matthew myself." She was impatient and started climbing the stairs.

When she reached the first landing, her aunt emerged from her room wearing a dressing gown. Her face transformed with fear, and she demanded, "What has happened? Is it Matthew?"

Juliette hesitated and told her husband, "Go and find Matthew while I speak with Aunt Charlotte."

Paul followed the footman up the stairs, and she went to stand beside her aunt. "I know you were not at home when Lady Lily came to see Matthew earlier. She came to bid him farewell, and in the middle of their conversation, he had a spell of madness come upon him. Lily believes it was some medicine that he drank." She met her aunt's stricken face with a steady gaze. "He dislocated her arm, believing she was trying to torture him."

Charlotte blanched and covered her mouth. A moment later, she murmured, "Dear God, how could this have happened?"

"I'm afraid for him, and I fear what he will do now." The very thought of Matthew's pain echoed her own. Juliette had no qualms about raising heaven and earth to help.

"You're right," her aunt agreed. "We must go to him."

"I am prepared to pray all night, if necessary," Juliette said. "In my heart, I fear the worst."

When the pair of them reached his room, Charlotte didn't bother knocking but opened it instead. Matthew was lying prone near the hearth, while Paul was trying to force a liquid down him.

Oh God. Her heart nearly stopped at the sight of him.

"Is he alive?" Juliette asked. Terror slid through her veins at the thought of him dying. She could not imagine anything worse.

"He drank brandy with whatever was in that bottle," Paul snapped. "If we canna purge him, he willna live to see the dawn."

Juliette began to pray as she fetched a basin for her husband. "Was it laudanum?"

"Opium and alcohol," Paul said. "Hardly better than poison. It would stop the heart of most men." He turned Matthew over. "Bring the basin. This willna be pleasant, but it's all we can do."

The fear within her turned to an iron resolve. She would not let him die. If she had to force him to retch for hours, they would do whatever was necessary to save his life. And she thanked God that her husband had the medical knowledge to do so.

"Tell me what we must do."

The bleakness on Paul's face was numbing. "You must pray. Both of you."

Juliette kept up her vigil for the rest of the night, until it seemed that Matthew had nothing left in his stomach. It was ghastly, seeing him so broken. Even the kitten Lily had given him was meowing weakly.

But after a few hours, Paul nodded. "I think that's everything. We'll get him to bed. And he is no' to have laudanum, alcohol, or anything else for a long while. His body must heal itself."

And his mind, Juliette thought. She didn't want to believe that he had done this to himself on purpose, but he needed help to get through these next few weeks.

Her husband lifted Matthew back to the bed, and Charlotte sat beside him. "I knew he wasn't sleeping." Her voice held heartbreak and devastation. "But I never realized he had lost himself so deeply."

"He was far worse than we realized." Juliette took the opposite side so that Matthew was surrounded by those who cared about him. Her husband rested his hand upon her shoulder, but she was weeping openly. There was no point in trying to hold back her emotions when they filled her with such fear. They could have lost him this night.

"He may live," Paul said. "But he'll be needing a reason to pull himself out of the hell he's living in."

Juliette lifted up the kitten, nestling the animal closer to Matthew. The animal snuggled against his side, taking comfort from the warmth.

"We will all help him," she swore. "But I think the person he needs the most is Lily. She still loves him, and I believe he needs her."

"Do you think she can bring him out of this melancholy?" Charlotte ventured.

Juliette touched Matthew's hand and stroked it. "I don't know. But she is the best hope for him now."

Chapter Eight

Lily had not expected the journey to Ireland to be so disheartening. The voyage across the Irish Sea wasn't so terrible, but she had been shocked by so many faces of starving men, women, and children. Her sister had warned her about the conditions after the potato famine, but she had vastly underestimated the devastating effects.

James had arranged for a coach to bring them across Ireland into County Mayo, where the Ashton estate lay. The railway did not yet extend westward, so they had little choice but to travel along the roads. It would take at least a week to reach Ashton, after they had already traveled across England during the past fortnight.

Lily's arm was healing, but she tried not to think of Matthew. In her heart, she had known he was not himself—but his actions had terrified her.

This morning, since the skies were sunny, her brother, James, had decided to ride with the driver. It gave Lily the chance to be alone with her mother inside the coach. Iris sat across from her and smiled warmly. "You miss him, don't you?"

It was as if her mother had read her mind. Lily tried to feign ignorance. "Of whom do you speak?"

"Why, Matthew, of course. I can tell that you're thinking of him."

Although Lily wanted to believe that Iris was imagining things, it was quite clear that this was one of her better days. "Why do you say that?"

Her mother smiled. "Because I know you, Lily dear. And you mustn't blame him for what happened." Her gaze drifted down to her healing arm.

"Matthew was not to blame," she lied. "I fell, and that's how I hurt my arm."

Iris's expression didn't change. "A person's mind is a powerful thing. And when you become lost in your thoughts, the ordinary world doesn't exist. Dreams become real, and what is real becomes a dream." She reached out to squeeze her daughter's hand. "I know what it is to be imprisoned by the visions of your mind. It's more frightening than anyone could know."

The clarity of Iris's words made Lily's heart ache. "Are you...aware of the moments when you've lost what is real?"

Her mother released her hand and stared out the window. "Sometimes I have no memory of what I've said or done. Other times, I dream of what happened, and it embarrasses me. I only know if it was real after I've spoken to someone who was there."

Iris's eyes gleamed with tears. "You cannot imagine the guilt or humiliation you feel. But I do believe that Matthew needs you. And if he was...somehow responsible for hurting you, you must know that he did not mean it." Her voice lowered in volume. "The voices catch hold of you and whisper. And it's hard not to listen when you believe what they say."

Her words sent a chill over Lily's spine. On the night Matthew had hurt her, she'd been so terrified, she didn't want to see him ever again. But her mother was right—he had not been himself.

"He drank medicine that night," Lily heard herself confess. "And I could tell from his expression that it affected him. His eyes were not right, and he appeared to be caught in a haze."

Her mother nodded. "He lost himself, didn't he?"

"He believed I was one of his torturers. He was trying to push me away, to free himself from the madness." She let out a sigh. "Do not tell James," she warned. "He would kill Matthew for this."

"I will not." Her mother gave a wry smile. "James believes I'm half-potted, and I'm not certain he's wrong."

"You have good days and bad days," Lily admitted. "And I do not blame you for it. We manage as best we can."

"I do miss your father," Iris admitted. "It's an empty hole inside of me. Without him, I feel like only a piece of myself."

Her mother's word resonated, mirroring the way Lily had felt when Matthew was away in India. And now that he had returned, she still didn't know how to fill the emptiness.

"I miss him, too," she admitted.

"And Matthew?" her mother prompted. "Do you miss him?"

Lily leaned back against the seat, lowering her shoulders. She didn't want to think of Matthew anymore. Her heart was too broken, her spirits too confused. "I don't know."

She had tried to put it all behind her, but she could not stop her mind from wondering about him. It had not ended well between them.

As the coach passed through the town, the stench of rotting potatoes in the fields was unmistakable. She raised a handkerchief to her nose and realized that everything could be far worse than it was.

She had come to Ireland to celebrate the wedding of her sister to the man she loved. It was meant to be a time of joy, not sorrow. And for now, she would look to the future and put the past behind her.

Two weeks later

"Rose, you look beautiful," Lily proclaimed. She hadn't expected to feel this emotional at the sight of her sister wearing a wedding gown, but her eyes welled up at seeing Rose so happy. This was the sort of wedding she had wanted for herself and Matthew before the illusion had shattered.

Her arm had been healing, and now it felt only tender. She'd claimed it was an accident from falling down the stairs. Everyone believed her, except for a small few who knew the truth.

Lily bent down and smoothed an invisible wrinkle from the ivory gown, hiding her tears. Her mother wore a bright purple gown, and a dreamy smile covered her face. It seemed that today she was lost in visions that made her happy. Perhaps she was remembering her own wedding day. As long as her mother did not become agitated with moments of madness, Lily believed all would be well.

Rose wore a long veil made of Irish lace loaned to her by Iain's mother, Moira, Lady Ashton. The matron had been quiet and pensive ever since they had arrived. At first, Lady Ashton had been opposed to the marriage between her son and Rose. But ever since she had returned to Ashton, there had been a change in the woman. It might be because Rose had promised to help her daughters find husbands in London.

But more likely, Lily suspected that Moira had begun to regret her actions, accepting her future daughter-in-law. Even now, the woman stood back from them as if she didn't feel that she had a place here. Something was troubling Moira, and she eyed Rose with uncertainty.

While her sister was occupied, Lily stepped closer to Lady Ashton. "Are you all right?" she murmured beneath her breath.

"Yes," the woman answered. "It's only that I never thought to see that veil worn again. I didn't wear it during my second wedding." Her expression held sadness.

"Was it lost?" Lily asked.

Moira shook her head. "I didn't want to wear it, for it only reminded me of my first marriage. I suppose I knew the second marriage wouldn't last long, for Garrick was older than me. I only married him to provide for the boys. He gave me two daughters, but he died soon after Colleen was born. They never knew him." She let out a sigh and braved a smile again. "I am glad that Rose will wear the veil now. It may bring them happiness."

Lily glanced outside the bedroom window and saw that the bridegroom was already walking outside the manor house, while hundreds of guests gathered. Rose and Iain had decided to hold the ceremony outside, so all the tenants could witness their union.

Rose joined her at the window and tension knotted her face at the sight of so many people. "Where did they all come from? And how will we feed them all?"

James moved to her side. "Leave that to me." He told her about the supplies they had brought with them. Then he related a story about an investment Iris had made with Evangeline's father. "Cain Sinclair stepped in while I was away," James continued. "He wanted to ensure that our family was provided for, and now we need not worry about money. I am grateful for his intervention."

"So am I." Rose smiled, revealing her relief. Her mother reached out to touch her hair, and the soft smile on her face held clarity.

"It's almost time for the wedding," Lily interrupted. "Are you ready?"

But Lady Ashton's expression held wariness, as if she was uncertain of whether to go. Instead, she asked Rose, "May I speak with you a moment?"

Lily suspected that Moira was taking an opportunity to bridge the distance between herself and Rose. It boded well for their future, and Lily smiled to herself.

She guided their mother outside the door, taking Iris's arm, while James walked ahead of them.

"One day it will be you taking vows," her mother murmured.

"I think I am destined to be a spinster." Lily tucked her mother's hand into her arm, helping her down the stairs. "I shall give in to my urges to become a bluestocking and be wedded to books." She had spent the past few weeks reading *The Pharmacopoeia of the Royal College of Physicians of London.* Thus far, she had learned how to make extracts and compound powders, and the distraction had been exactly what she needed.

"Oh no, my dear." Iris clucked her tongue. "You cannot possibly remain unmarried. It isn't natural." She was muttering something about sharing a man's bed, and Lily cut her off.

"Let's not speak of it, Mother." The last thing she wanted was her mother's advice on lovemaking. Her cheeks grew warm at the thought. "We will go and enjoy Rose's wedding day."

But Iris stopped at the bottom of the stairs. "No, Lily, there was something I was meant to give to you. What was it now?"

She had no idea what her mother meant, but it would not be the first time Iris had been unable to remember. "Do not worry about it. We'll go and join the wedding guests. James will be there." Her brother had a way of calming their mother, perhaps because Iris felt protected.

But her mother shook her head. "He gave it to me. It's

very, *very* important." Her eyes filled with anxiety, and she began searching her gown for a pocket that wasn't there.

"It's nothing, Mother. I promise you."

"No!" Iris stood her ground, her expression turning fiery. "I *have* to remember this. I will not let myself forget. I promised him."

"Promised who?"

Iris began clenching and unclenching her hands, growing more agitated. A tear rolled down her wrinkled cheek. "Why can't I remember anything, Lily? What is wrong with me?"

"Could you have put it in your reticule?" she asked gently.

Iris opened it, but there was nothing inside. She gritted her teeth, and Lily feared that if her mother didn't find it, she would cause a scene.

"What if I return to your room and search? Would that help?"

Her mother shook her head. "I didn't leave it there. It was far too valuable." She wiped away her tears, and it was then that Lily caught sight of a silver chain beneath her mother's high-necked gown. Her pulse began to quicken, and she reached out to touch it. "Was it this?"

Iris pulled the chain out from her gown and brightened. "Why, yes. That's it, exactly. He told me to show you this ring. He said it had once belonged to you. And that he was terribly sorry and wanted to speak with you."

The moment she saw Matthew's signet ring, Lily's skin flushed with a blend of nervous energy. How had her mother received the ring? Had he traveled across England and Ireland to bring it to her? She could not imagine him making such a journey—especially not after all that had happened.

"Is he here?" Lily ventured.

Iris shrugged. "I cannot remember." She took off the chain and put it around Lily's neck. The gold ring was heavy, but the familiar weight brought back all the emotions she'd tried to forget. She tucked it beneath her bodice, not understanding the meaning of Matthew's gift.

Lily walked with Iris outside into the morning sunlight. She searched among the wedding guests for a glimpse of Matthew. It was possible that he wasn't here, that he had simply given her mother the ring before they'd left for Ireland. But somehow, she didn't believe that.

She guided Iris to stand beside her brother, and Lily stood on the opposite side of them. The people of Ireland were dressed in clothing hardly better than rags, and their faces were gaunt with hunger. Even so, she saw young boys fidgeting with excitement while their mothers gripped their wrists in warning to behave. The delicious aroma of the wedding feast was a distraction for all of them, and more than once, the people glanced toward the long tables set up for the celebration after the wedding.

James looked far better than he had when he'd returned from India. His brown hair was still lighter from the burning sun, and his face had lost some of its tan. He had filled out from eating better food, and it did seem that he was recovering from his own ordeal.

There was a glint in his eyes, as if he knew something she didn't. Lily leaned in, keeping her voice low. "Where is he?"

"Where is who?" Her brother stared straight ahead, but she could tell he was trying to keep something from her.

"You know who I mean. Where is Matthew?" She reached across her sling to touch his arm.

"I suppose he is among the guests. He *was* invited to the wedding, after all." Her brother turned and scrutinized her face.

Lily looked around at the sea of faces until at last she spied Matthew at the very back of the crowd. He wore a simple black coat and trousers, and he met her gaze evenly. Then he glanced at her arm, and a look of regret crossed his face.

She ought to be afraid of him after what happened. Logic ruled that she should. And yet, despite everything, she knew he hadn't been aware of his surroundings or of anything else.

That night, he had been caught up in his nightmares, unable to grasp reality.

It reminded her of Iris's words. *The voices catch hold of you and whisper. And it's hard not to listen when you believe what they say.*

She turned back to the wedding party and saw Iain Donovan, Lord Ashton, waiting upon her sister's arrival. The man was dressed in a frock coat of dark blue with a white waistcoat and a red rose in his lapel. His face held awed wonder when he saw her sister approaching.

Rose wore a long-sleeved white gown with a narrow waistline and a flared skirt that billowed out into a train. Her reddish-brown hair was caught up in an intricate knot, and she wore pearls around her throat. Moira's lace veil cascaded over Rose's shoulders, down the back of her gown.

But it was the look of love shared between Rose and Iain that made Lily's heart ache. The groom looked at his bride as if she were his reason for being alive. And the joy upon her sister's face held a happiness that went beyond words.

The large crowd gathered as close as they could to the bride and groom, listening as they spoke their vows. From behind her, she sensed a shifting movement of people, and then she became aware of Matthew's presence. Her brother glanced back at him and gave a nod of acknowledgment, but Lily said nothing. She was too confused by her own emotions.

From behind her, Matthew's hand bumped against her uninjured arm. Then she heard him whisper, "Forgive me, Lily."

She stiffened, not wanting to interrupt the ceremony. His hand brushed against hers again, but she pulled it away. She wasn't ready to face the emotions—not yet. But she would have to confront Matthew today and decide what was to be done.

After the wedding ceremony was over, her sister kissed Iain, and all around them came cheers of happiness. Bagpipers played a merry tune, and Iain lifted her up, turning her in a slow circle. Her sister laughed with happiness, her veil getting tangled up as her new husband embraced her.

It was the perfect distraction, and Lily hurried forward to help her sister. After Iain finished kissing his new wife, Lily said, "I'll take your veil for you, Rose."

Her sister beamed with happiness. "Yes, thank you."

Rose helped her remove the pins holding it to her hair. Then Lily gathered up the long veil under one arm. The newly married couple walked among the crowd toward the tables set out for feasting while Lily returned to the manor house with the veil folded up as best she could.

Within moments, Matthew was at her side. "May I help you with that?"

"It's not heavy. I can manage." She started to walk past him, but he stepped in her path.

"Lily, I've traveled hundreds of miles to see you. I came to apologize for what happened." His tone held utter sincerity, and she paused a moment.

Upon his cheek, the reddened scar had begun to fade. His brown hair was trimmed back, and he had shaved. She detected the faint scent of sandalwood, and his eyes held the familiar weariness that plagued him.

She could tell him no, refusing to see him. But what good would that do? Better to face the demons than try to bury them. "Walk with me inside, and we will talk."

At the house, he opened the door for her and allowed her to enter first. Inside, several maids hurried past them, carrying steaming trays of food. All of the servants were attending the wedding, and Lily smiled at the sight of an elegant three-tiered cake. The cook was careful to balance it, and two servants opened the door for her.

"I'll put this in my sister's room," she started to say, but Matthew took the veil from her and placed it on a side table.

"Just a moment, Lily." He glanced around the hall, and

most of the servants were either back in the kitchen or outside. "I wanted to ask if you are all right."

She lifted her arm to show him. "It's healing."

He was quiet for a moment, watching her. "I thought about what you said, that I should stay away from you. Believe me that I never, ever meant to harm you." He let out a slow breath. "I took a tonic I never should have drunk. Dr. Fraser said it was opium mixed with gin." He eyed her and added, "Words won't change what happened to you. But I did want you to know that I am sorry."

"I know you are." For a time, she heard only the ticking of the grandfather clock in the hall. He seemed unsure of what to say now, and finally, she added, "I wish I knew how to help you, Matthew."

He studied her for a while. "I would like to begin again as friends, Lily. Even if it is never more than that, when I am near you, I don't feel so distant from the world."

His brown eyes clouded over with regret and a quiet resolution. "You may never forgive me, and I understand that. But I don't want to lose your friendship."

She didn't know how to answer him. A part of her was angry that he had suffered so much during his time in India, that his normal life had been stolen from him, bringing him so low. It was difficult to trust him now, but she still cared deeply for Matthew.

"I need time," she said at last. "For two years, I believed I would be your wife. That we would marry properly when you returned, and it would be me standing beside you in a church, speaking our vows." She nodded back toward the wedding guests outside. "I feel as if that part of me is lost now. And I don't know who I am or what I want anymore."

She pulled out the chain holding his signet ring and removed it from her throat, returning it to him. "I will be your friend again, Matthew. But I cannot promise you anything more."

Chapter Nine

The dancing and feasting continued into the night, and Matthew had to admit, the Irish knew how to celebrate. More than once, men had tried to share whiskey with him, their cheeks reddened with drunken joy.

Iain's sisters, Colleen and Sybil, tried to encourage Matthew to join the dancing, but he could not bring himself to leave the shadows. He had come to Ireland to apologize to Lily, not to indulge in the celebration. But Charlotte and Juliette were attending the wedding, and he knew that she and his cousin were always watching him. He had nearly ended his life, albeit unintentionally, and he hardly trusted himself anymore.

After he had awakened with the doctor and his family surrounding him, he'd felt a sense of shame for what had happened. And so, he had begun each day as a single step. He bargained with himself, claiming that he would try to become a better man and atone for his failings.

He forced himself to get out of bed each day and eat food that tasted like dust. He'd attempted Dr. Fraser's suggestion of standing outside for minutes at a time. But even a few moments made his heartbeat quicken with fear.

A few paces away, he saw that Lily's face was flushed, and she was laughing at something one of the older Irishmen had said. The man had reached for her hand, but she shook her head. "Forgive me, sir, but we've only just met."

He wondered if the man had made an improper remark and stepped in. "Is everything all right, Lady Lily?"

"Yes, of course. Padraig here has asked me to wed him, but I could not be so bold." She was still laughing, and he returned her smile. The Irishman had to be eighty years old, if not older. His blue eyes twinkled with mischief, and he had no teeth left in his wrinkled smile.

"You're a fine *cailín*, to be sure," he cackled. "And in my day, all the women wanted to wed me."

Matthew raised an eyebrow at that. "How much whiskey have you drunk, sir?"

"Not enough," the old man remarked cheerfully. "When I'm no longer standing, that'll be enough."

"I'll leave you to it," Lily said, joining Matthew. Her hazel eyes were bright with merriment. "My goodness, I never imagined these people would love a wedding so much."

"Are you enjoying yourself?" he asked.

"I am." She smiled warmly at him, and he took in the sight of her beauty. Her brown hair was nearly red against the firelight, her skin flushed from the dancing. He could not stop staring at her, and Lily seemed to sense his interest. She averted her gaze. "Rose and Iain have already departed, but the guests will undoubtedly eat and drink until dawn." Her voice came out faster, as if she was trying to fill the space with conversation.

He didn't want her to feel awkward or afraid of him, but he offered his arm. "Would you care to walk with me for a while?"

Lily hesitated and glanced back at the others. Idly, she rubbed at her arm. "It's getting late. I should probably go back to the house."

"I'll escort you there."

He waited, and she gave a nod of agreement. After they walked a few steps, she inquired, "Why *did* you travel so far, Lord Arnsbury? It truly wasn't necessary. You could have simply sent a letter."

He slowed his pace, wondering quite how to explain it. She didn't know of his close brush with death that night. But he said, "I couldn't go on as I had before. Not when I had sunk so low. I needed to leave London and prove to myself that I could begin again. The journey gave me the time I needed."

She stopped walking and faced him. In the moonlight, her face held sympathy. "And now?"

He reached out to take her hand, and her fingers curled over his. "Each mile helped me to clear my head. Not only from all the medicines and draughts, but it gave me the chance to find out what was left of me after India."

Her expression sobered. "I know what you mean." After a pause, she added, "Forgive me for speaking so plainly, but after we parted ways the last time, I saw that my father was right. I was only eighteen when you left for India, infatuated with the idea of an elopement. You and I didn't truly know one another."

"I never meant to coerce you into an unwanted marriage, Lily."

"I know. It was my own fault. And perhaps it's better that it was never legal."

It was an easy solution, one that enabled them to have their freedom. And yet, he didn't like the idea of abandoning Lily. He remembered the night he had shared in her arms, and he had accepted the gift of her innocence. It felt wrong to walk away from her now, but he knew she deserved better.

Before she could take another step, one of the drunken men stumbled into her. The Irishman was a large bearded man, and he reached for Lily, leaning in. "Here, now. You're a pretty thing. Come on and give us a kiss."

Without thinking, Matthew shoved the man away from her. The raw urge to protect Lily overshadowed all else. *Leave her alone.*

The drunken man lunged at him, and Matthew dodged a blow to his stomach. In an instant, the world appeared to slow down, and his surroundings blurred. His hands curled into fists, and he struck the man hard, welcoming the crunch of bone and bruised skin.

"Matthew!" Lily cried out.

He was dimly aware of men cheering while someone cried out for him to stop. But truthfully, it felt good to defend her honor. He was fully in command of his senses, and within seconds, the drunkard was lying face down on the ground, unmoving.

He hadn't fought in months, but a surge of righteousness filled him. No one would harm Lily while she was under his protection.

Yet somehow, she appeared terrified at his actions, frozen with fear.

"Lily," he said quietly. "It's all right. He won't harm you."

But when she took a step back, he realized that she had not been afraid of her attacker—she'd been afraid of *him.*

"I should go," she said. And before he could reassure her that he'd been fully in command of his senses, she had disappeared into the house. He could have pursued her, but he didn't want her to feel threatened in any way.

No, she hadn't understood what had truly happened this night, but for him, it marked another step forward. He was not trapped within a world of harsh visions and torture—instead, he had begun to move on.

And it felt good to be whole once again.

London

Lily sat by the fireplace in her bedroom, books scattered on the floor all around her. She had been reading about how to concoct an infusion of chamomile. A knock sounded at the door, but before she could rise from the hearth to answer it, the door swung open. Her grandmother never bothered to wait on a reply before she entered.

"Lily, why are you on the floor? Ladies do not sit before the hearth unless they are scullery maids."

"Hello, Grandmother." She stood and kissed Lady Wolcroft on the cheek. "I did not expect you to come calling."

"I live here from time to time, if you have forgotten." The older matron chose a chair and sat down. "Now then. I have accepted an invitation for you to attend Lady Falsham's supper party. It will be an intimate gathering, and she has promised to invite several eligible gentlemen."

Lily sighed. "Grandmother, I am not going to be married." She had made up her mind not to wed again.

"Nonsense. Of course you will. We simply have to find the right man for you to manage. Someone handsome, of course. And wealthy. A marquess or a duke, perhaps. I still believe Lord Davonshire would make an excellent match."

"After Father died and Mother was struggling to make ends meet, he wasn't so eager to wed," she pointed out.

"Only because he was a young man who wasn't ready yet. But he may have changed his mind."

She couldn't quite bring herself to agree with her grandmother. The thought of being courted by any other man troubled her. Lily stood by the glowing coals of the hearth. "I need time to get over Matthew."

Mildred shrugged. "He's no longer suitable for you, and you know it."

"I suppose you heard about the fight that broke out at Rose's wedding." Undoubtedly that was one of many reasons why her grandmother did not approve.

But to her surprise, Mildred laughed. "It was indeed entertaining. I will grant Lord Arnsbury that—he did defend your honor from that drunken lout."

"I had never seen him fight like that before. I was afraid he would kill the man."

"Oh, fiddlesticks. He knew precisely what he was doing." Her grandmother straightened in her chair. "No one else bothered you after that, did they?"

"I wouldn't know. I left the celebration and went back to my room."

"Oh, yes. You didn't hear about all the Irish women swooning over Lord Arnsbury." Was her grandmother actually...defending Matthew? She had no reason for it, especially given her desire to match Lily with someone else.

"Half of the ladies were throwing themselves at him," Mildred finished. "Offering to kiss his bruises and all that nonsense."

A strange ripple of jealousy took hold. "And what did he do about it?"

"Why should you care? He's not your concern anymore. You're going to find a man who is dull and terribly wealthy. Who would want the excitement of a man brawling over you?"

Was it her imagination or was her grandmother's tone somewhat ironic? Lady Wolcroft smiled serenely. "Now then. You will attend the supper party and find someone else. Believe me when I say it is for the best."

"I intend to be a spinster, Grandmother. I will be perfectly content wedded to my books."

"Not if I have aught to do with it." Lady Wolcroft stood and regarded her. "You have a romantic heart, Lily. You were never meant to be unmarried, and well you know it."

She could give no answer to that. But she sensed that her grandmother had set forth a strategy to do battle.

Heaven help her.

After he returned to England, Matthew began immersing himself in the estate ledgers, seeking ways to occupy his time. There was a mountain of correspondence he'd neglected since his return from India, which gave him a purpose.

He noticed that they had received several letters from a woman named Sarah Carlisle. He had no notion of who she was, but there were at least six letters from her, all sent within the past year.

He slit open the first letter and was about to read it when his mother interrupted with a knock upon the open door. She strode into the room in a swirl of blue skirts. "Matthew, you really ought to venture out of this study," Charlotte bade him. "Your cousin Juliette is hosting a supper party this evening."

Matthew winced at the thought. "I hardly think it would be wise. I am not interested in anyone's company just now."

"You have a seat in Parliament," his mother pointed out. "And you must try to take your place in society. It is your responsibility as the earl."

Then she sent him a pointed look, adding, "It is also your duty to marry a young lady from a good family and sire an heir."

Matthew could not imagine how his mother could come up with such a suggestion. "I am hardly fit to marry any woman."

She moved closer and touched his arm. "But each day grows a little easier, does it not?"

He didn't know how to answer that. "I need time, Mother. Just leave me be."

Charlotte let out a quiet sigh. "Lily's grandmother wants her to find a new suitor and marry. I understand your cousin Adrian intends to court her."

The idea of Lily dancing with Adrian made him tense. Or any other man, for that matter. He struggled to force back the possessive thoughts he had no right to. "My cousin would not be an appropriate match for her."

"Then you had best attend the gathering and stop him, hadn't you?" With a smile, his mother departed the study.

She had known precisely how to aim her arrow, and it had struck true. He had given Lily time and space, but he found that he missed her company. Was it worse to remain here in this house or to see her with another man? He had no answers to that.

By way of a distraction, he picked up one of the letters from Sarah Carlisle and read it. Then he blinked and read it again. Five hundred pounds? This woman expected him to pay her such a vast amount? And what was she talking about, protecting his secrets?

This was blackmail, pure and simple. His mood darkened when he opened the second letter and then the third. All of them repeated her demand for five hundred pounds.

But there was one portion of her note that stopped him cold. *Your father and I had an arrangement. See that you keep it.*

Had his father been paying this woman an ungodly sum over the years? For what purpose? His mood grew grim when he wondered if they had indulged in an affair. A rush of resentment filled him at the thought. He had always idolized his father, believing there was no better man.

He tossed the letters onto the stack, promising himself he would think no more upon it. There was nothing this Sarah Carlisle could do, now that his father was dead.

And he had no intention of discussing any of this with his mother.

For nearly half an hour, Matthew stood on the outskirts of the room, wishing he hadn't come. Although his mother had demanded that he attend Cousin Juliette's gathering, he preferred to remain apart from the others.

Yet, when Lily arrived with her mother and grandmother, she studied him with a strange expression before she crossed the room.

Her brown hair was braided in a soft updo with a few flowers tucked in the strands. She wore a light-rose gown with two flounces trimmed with lace. But as she drew closer, he saw that her attention was caught by something on the floor behind him. He turned and saw Beast crouched upon the floor.

"What on earth?" Matthew couldn't imagine how the kitten had managed to stowaway and sneak into Lady Falsham's ballroom.

"Did you bring a guest?" Lily asked, reaching down to pick up the kitten.

Beast purred, and Matthew ruffled the animal's ears. Her expression held amusement, and he shrugged. "Honestly, I have no idea how he got here."

She studied him, her hazel eyes softening. "Perhaps he crawled into your coat pocket and slipped out when the footman took it from you."

"I think I would have noticed if there was something moving in my pocket." He plucked the animal from Lily's hands and set it upon his shoulder. The kitten began nudging his face, and she laughed.

It reminded Matthew of the first night he'd seen Lily, all grown up as a young lady. It had been years since then, but he was still fascinated by her, perhaps now even more so. And there had been a runaway cat, even then. He smiled at the memory.

"Well, however he got here, we'll have to make sure your Beast gets home safely." As if in answer to Lily's suggestion, the animal began crawling down his frock coat.

He noticed that she had relaxed her demeanor around him, and he answered her smile with his own.

"You're in trouble now," she warned.

When the kitten hopped down, he saw Beast trotting toward the guests. His cousin Juliette was approaching, and Lily offered, "I'll go and get him before he's trampled." She excused herself and hurried after the animal.

His cousin met his gaze with a warm smile, oblivious to the kitten. "It was so good of you to come this evening, Matthew. We haven't seen enough of you as of late." He tried to manage a smile, and she teased, "I am certain Charlotte had to drag you here, didn't she?"

"Indeed." He narrowed a glance at Lily, who was following the kitten as he moved toward the center of the ballroom. She looked ready to pick up her skirts and pursue the animal but was trying not to be too obvious. Instead, she walked slowly toward the kitten, as it disappeared behind the guests.

"Well, I intend to steal you away for a moment." Juliette linked her hand in his arm and brought him over toward the far side of the room. Matthew sent Lily a silent plea for help, and she nodded, her gaze turned downward to search the floor for the kitten.

He could only imagine the horrified screams, if Beast happened to attack the skirts of any young ladies. Though the animal was quite a handsome feline, the element of surprise would make any woman screech.

"Are you feeling better?" Lady Falsham asked, in all seriousness. Her green eyes held concern, and she added, "Your wounds seem to be healing."

"They are." He glanced back toward Lily, who was standing still in the middle of the ballroom. From her posture, it appeared that she'd trapped the kitten beneath her skirts.

"And what of Lady Lily?" his cousin prompted. "Have you renewed your friendship?"

"We have," he said, though he didn't know if Lily was still frightened of him. At the moment, he was grateful that she was trying to prevent the Beast from being trod upon. When he glanced back at her, he saw that her face was flushed. People were beginning to stare, for she was standing in the middle of the room for no apparent reason.

"That's good," Lady Falsham said. "Her grandmother hopes that she will marry. I know Lady Wolcroft has her heart set upon Lord Davonshire, but I think you might have a chance if you gave her a reason to hope."

An older gentleman had caught sight of Lily and was approaching now. Matthew saw no choice but to rescue her swiftly. "An excellent idea, Cousin. In fact, I believe Lady Lily promised me the next dance. If you will excuse me." He bowed, not giving her the chance to stop him.

The older man approaching Lily was portly, and he lifted his hand to her in a wave. It was Lord Tyson, a widower who had fourteen grandchildren at last count.

Matthew saw the amused looks on the faces of the bystanders, and he crossed to Lily's side quickly before Lord Tyson could reach her.

"The Beast is under my skirts," she said. "I can't move or he'll escape."

"What do you want to do?" Matthew couldn't exactly kneel down and peer under her gown to find the creature.

"Pretend as if we are in a conversation, and I'll crouch a little lower to keep him from escaping. With any luck, he'll stay imprisoned by my petticoats."

"Lady Lily!" Lord Tyson smiled broadly as he reached them. "You look simply beautiful this evening. I know you must be itching for a dance."

"Thank you, Lord Tyson, but I intend to sit out the next set."

His smile didn't diminish at all, but he withdrew an ear trumpet from his coat pocket. "What was that?"

She raised her voice slightly and answered, "I said I prefer not to dance."

His face furrowed, and he inquired again, "What did you say?"

This was getting out of hand. Matthew took Lily's arm, and said, "I am escorting the lady back to her mother, Lord Tyson."

"Whatever for?" He appeared genuinely puzzled.

"Please excuse me, Lord Tyson." Lily crouched down in a mock curtsy and kept her skirts trailing along the ballroom floor.

"I am in need of a wife, you know!" he called out. But she pretended not to hear him, shuffling across the floor.

Matthew led her away and inquired, "How long have you known this man?"

"I met him two days ago." She placed her hand in the crook of his arm, trying to hurry him along. "Let us go to the terrace, and then I'll lift my skirts for you."

He couldn't stop his smile at her remark. "That sounds scandalous, Lady Lily."

She blinked a moment and then laughed. "You know what I meant." As they continued walking toward the doors leading outside, she continued dragging her skirts. Then abruptly, she stopped walking. Her face paled, and she pursed her lips together.

"What is it?"

"He's crawling up my petticoats." Lily winced, and he knew there was no choice but to get her outside quickly. Unfortunately, there were other guests milling about the gravel pathway.

"I'll help you." He led her outside, and Lily hurried with him. There were lanterns hung around the small walled space, lighting the darkness.

"Oh, heavens, his claws are like needles." Her face wrinkled, but she reached toward her right hip and tried to grasp the fabric. "Help me, Matthew."

They moved toward the furthest corner, and he said, "Face the wall. I'll try to find him."

"You cannot go rummaging through my skirts in front of everyone," she hissed. "Ow, ow, ow. Let go, Beast."

He saw the bulge of silk and said, "Trap him there, against your hip. I'll kneel down and try to get him out. If you keep your skirts wide, I should be able to reach underneath and seize him."

"I don't think this is a good idea," she protested. "Someone will see you."

"Would you rather I stand in front of you while you search?"

She gave a slight shriek, clapping her hands over her mouth. Then she began shaking her skirts, hopping on one foot, then the other. A moment later, a ball of fur came bolting out from beneath her skirts. Matthew dove for the kitten and seized him. "Not so fast, Beast." He managed to grasp the animal, and then sat up on the gravel path.

Lily's shoulders were shaking, and she was laughing so hard, tears came to her eyes.

"I'm so sorry. I know I shouldn't laugh, but he's so mischievous. I still cannot believe he managed to follow you here."

The sound of her laughter was infectious, and he could not help but laugh as well. Never had he imagined he would be sitting on gravel at a social gathering, holding a runaway kitten. Lily's laughter warmed him, and he stood, holding fast to Beast. "Perhaps he missed seeing you."

Her face softened, and he was caught by the flush upon her cheeks. In the lantern light, her eyes were bright, and he was transfixed by the beauty of her face. "I might have missed him, too," she murmured. "It's good to hear you laugh again, Matthew."

He held out the kitten to her, and she stroked his ears. Her fingertips brushed against his, and the slight touch sent a flare of interest through him.

It was a new beginning, he decided. And one that held promise.

When Lily arrived back at the carriage, she adjusted her wrap against the chill. The autumn air had turned bitter, and her mother was chattering endlessly about the supper party and the dancing. She stepped inside with the help of her footman and slid onto the leather seat, half-listening to Iris's exclamations.

They drove through the streets, and her mother asked, "How is Lord Arnsbury? I saw him walking with you in the garden."

"He is improving with each day." And she admitted to herself that she *had* enjoyed seeing him again, in spite of the kitten's mischief. Matthew had remained at the ball, after giving Beast into the care of his footman with instructions to take him home.

Iris smiled warmly and added, "I do like that young man. You should marry him."

The words came out of nowhere, and Lily bit her lip. "I—I don't think so, Mother. I do not intend to marry anyone."

"Nonsense. You need to marry and have babies. I do miss my babies." Her mother sighed and leaned back. Her face clouded over, and Lily recognized that Iris was starting to slip into one of her spells. Since Rose's wedding, her mother had enjoyed several weeks of clarity, but Lily feared it was all an illusion.

"Rose will have a baby soon," Iris murmured. "I do believe so. Especially with that handsome Irishman she married." Her mother pressed her hand against the carriage door. "I miss

George so very much, you know. There are days when I wish I could join him."

"Mother, no." Lily didn't like the direction of this conversation. Out of desperation, she offered, "The babies will need their grandmother."

Iris appeared confused for a moment. Then she rapped at the carriage and called out to the coachman. "Nelson, stop for a moment."

Lily didn't like the look in her mother's eyes, but the coachman obeyed and pulled the carriage over to the side of the road. "What is it, Mother? Are you not feeling well?"

Before Iris could answer, she threw the door open and bolted out into the streets. Lily hadn't expected it, and she tried to follow, but her skirts tangled up. "Nelson, stop her!"

The coachman gave the reins over to their footman and hurried after Lady Penford. Lily gathered up the yards of fabric in her skirt and left the carriage to chase after them. It was dark outside, and she knew this wasn't a good idea to be out in the London streets with only a coachman and her mother.

But what choice did she have? Her mother could easily be trampled by horses or accosted by a stranger.

It wasn't easy to pursue Iris on foot, but she eventually caught up to her. Nelson had restrained Iris, who was kicking and shoving at him. "Let me go, or I'll have you dismissed from your post."

"Lady Penford, please. It's not safe here." Nelson kept a firm grip on her, but the older woman began to scream.

"Help!"

A few bystanders turned to look, but before anyone could approach, Lily saw a dark figure hurrying toward them. When he reached the light, she saw that it was Matthew. His carriage was nearby, and a sudden rush of relief passed over her.

"Lady Penford, what is it?" Matthew asked. He motioned for Nelson to let go of her. The coachman waited until he was closer and then obeyed.

"I want to be with George," Iris wept. "I'm so lonely. I just…need George to be with me."

Matthew exchanged a look with Lily.

Help me, she pleaded silently. Her mother's grasp on reality was slipping away. Lily worried that she might have to take Iris back to Penford, if she continued to have bad spells.

"May I escort you home?" he asked her gently. "You must be weary after this long night."

His sympathy seemed to break through Iris's frustration, and she looked back at him with tear-filled eyes. "I—I don't know. What's happening?"

"Mother, let us go and have a hot cup of tea," Lily urged. "It's very cold outside, and you need to get warm. Matthew will accompany us, won't you?"

He nodded and offered his arm. "I should be glad to take you home." He ordered his coachman to drive on without him.

Iris rested her gloved hand in the crook of his elbow, weeping silently as he helped her walk back to the carriage. Lily overheard him giving orders to Nelson to drive around the city for a while, giving Lady Penford time to calm herself.

When they were safely inside the vehicle, he took a seat beside her mother, talking all the while. His calm tone seemed to soothe Iris, and she leaned back in her seat, closing her eyes after a time. The rocking motion of the carriage helped, and Lily whispered, "Thank you, Matthew."

He gave a nod. "How long as she been like this?"

"Ever since my father died. It broke her heart, and I know she wanted to join him in death. Rose and I had to take her to the country, and even then, she has not been well. She may never be the same."

The worry over her mother was a burden she would always carry. But for now, it eased her to have someone else to share the responsibility.

"She is lucky to have you," he said quietly. In the darkness, his steady gaze warmed her. Lily felt the comfort of his presence and braved a smile.

"Will you stay a while, just to help me get her inside the house? You could have tea with us, even though it's late."

"I will stay as long as you have need of me." His quiet reassurance filled the space between them. He reached out to take her hand, and she squeezed it in thanks.

A moment later, the carriage lurched, and she went crashing forward into his arms. Matthew caught her, and Iris awakened.

"What's happened? Was there an accident?" Her mother's eyes had gone wild, and she twisted her hands together. "Why have we stopped?"

"Wait here." Matthew helped Lily back to her seat. "I'll find out." He opened the door and closed it behind him.

Lily rubbed at her shoulders, which were bruised from the collision. She didn't know what had caused them to stop, but it was her mother's fear she had to manage.

"I'm certain everything is all right," she said. "You aren't hurt, are you?"

"No." But Iris appeared agitated by the accident. She began twisting her hands together, staring out the window and muttering to herself about wolves. Lily reached out to take her hand. "Matthew will be back in a moment. I'm sure it's nothing."

But it was indeed taking a while. Lily started to open the door, and then she saw Matthew approaching. He was no longer wearing his coat, and he was carrying a bundle of something enormous, dark, and furry. Was that an animal bundled inside his coat? Lily saw the concerned look on his face and asked, "What is that, Matthew?"

A whimpering sound came from the coat. "It's a dog," he said. "It ran out in front of the horses and startled them. I don't know if he'll live, but I didn't want to leave him there."

In the darkness, Lily could hear the dog panting and whining from pain. "Bring him inside the carriage, and we'll take him home. I want to have a look at him." She had read the medical book Dr. Fraser had loaned her, but she wasn't certain if she knew enough to help the animal. Perhaps not.

And yet, she did want to help in some small way. The dog was enormous, with black and white patches of fur, though she didn't know what breed he was. His fur was matted and filthy, and his ribs were evident through his skin.

Matthew climbed inside the carriage, and the dog nearly filled up the entire space. Lily moved across to the opposite seat, and the animal was so large, his head rested in her lap. "He looks half-starved."

"It's likely he had to fend for himself in the streets." Matthew closed the door to the carriage and reached for her hand before she could pet the dog. "Be careful. A hurt dog might bite you, and we don't know anything about him."

"Oh dear," Iris muttered. "Oh dear, oh dear. It's a wolf you've brought." She edged backward against the seat, but Matthew blocked the door with his leg. Lily met his gaze, trusting that he would prevent her mother from fleeing.

"It's not a wolf, Iris. It's a dog who has been hurt. Lily wants to try to heal him."

"But he's so big," Iris whispered. "I don't know. He could be a wolf."

"He's not, I assure you. And I will not allow him to harm you," Matthew promised. Then he turned to Lily. "Do you think it's all right that I brought him here to you?"

"I would be more upset if you had left him to die." She looked up at him. "I don't know if we can heal him, but I want to try."

They rode through the streets, back to the Penford townhouse. Lily started thinking back to the books she had read and remembered that she should not give him any food or water—at least, not until she was certain there were no serious injuries. This dog needed their help, and she was going to do everything she could to save him.

When they arrived home, Matthew carried the dog inside. Lily guided her mother into the house and gave orders for hot tea. She also requested a blanket, water, bandages, and salve for the animal's wounds. "Oh, and bring me the laudanum, Hattie." She didn't know if it would help the dog, but it was all she had.

"Where do you want me to take the dog?"

"Into the study. We can lay him upon James's desk." She told Hattie to take her mother into the parlor and give her tea. "Mother, will you be all right?"

"Yes." Iris paled at the sight of the dog. "I would rather not be in the presence of a wolf just now."

"He's only a large dog who has been badly hurt," she repeated. "I am going to take care of him. But Hattie will bring you some tea and see that you're feeling better."

"Yes...I...that would be fine," her mother murmured. It did seem that she was still frightened of the dog. She took several steps away from them. "I'll just have my tea now while you look after him."

Lily didn't like the way the dog appeared so still and quiet. He was hanging in Matthew's arms like a dead weight. "Follow me. I want to see his injuries right away." It was too difficult to tell how wounded the animal was, but his flesh was scraped raw in several places.

Matthew walked down the hallway with her until they reached her brother's study. She was surprised to find James seated inside, surrounded by papers. "I need your desk, James."

Her brother stood, eyeing the bundle in Matthew's arms. "What have you there?"

"It's a dog," Lily answered. "I am going to tend his injuries, and I need a large clean surface for that. Clear off your desk, if you would. I don't want to get blood on your ledgers."

Her brother's expression was a blend of amusement and

fascination, but he obeyed. "Lily, what do you know about tending wounded dogs? He'll bite your hand off."

"No, he won't. Matthew will hold him for me." She wished she knew how to sedate the dog. The laudanum might work, but she wasn't certain of the dose.

"Oh, so you're going to have him bite Matthew's hand off, is that it? That's all right, then." Her brother cleared off his desk, and Matthew set him down on the surface. Now that they had more light, she saw that the dog was larger than she'd realized. It must have been an enormous strain to carry him this far, but Matthew appeared indifferent to the weight.

The dog's black and white fur was matted and coated in blood, and his head was large with a rounded snout. She had not seen a dog like him before, but it was his soulful eyes that caught her heart. He stared at her, trembling with pain, and she murmured, "I'm going to fix you, Dog. Just hold still, and I'll make it better. I promise."

"Keep your hands away from his mouth, Arnsbury," her brother warned.

"Indeed." Matthew used his coat to restrain the forelegs and head of the dog. The moment he held down the animal, it frantically tried to twist and buck against him.

"I need to sedate him," Lily said. "When Hattie comes, we'll do that first. And I think it would be wise to muzzle him gently. Perhaps with your cravat."

Matthew nodded in agreement and rested his hand upon the dog's head. "Easy, there."

"What sort of dog is he?" Lily asked. She had never seen a dog so large before.

"I believe he's a Landseer breed. They are usually quite calm and gentle."

The dog's whimpering grew louder into cries of pain. It bothered her deeply to see the animal in such agony, and Lily vowed to herself that she would heal him to the best of her ability.

Hattie arrived at last with the bandages, blankets, and a basin of water. She set them down upon the desk and then pulled out the laudanum and salve from her apron pocket. "Is this all you'll be needing, Lady Lily?"

"Yes, thank you." Her mind was spinning with what to do. First, she needed to take the edge off the dog's pain.

"I have tea and biscuits on a tray in the hall," Hattie added. "Shall I bring them in?"

"No, take them to my mother," she replied. She could not imagine having refreshments right now. To her brother and Matthew, she asked, "Should I try the laudanum on him first?"

"Whiskey might be better," her brother suggested.

"I am not about to get this poor dog intoxicated." She reached for the laudanum, deciding that it would be best to start with a few drops and observe him. Lily poured a tiny spoonful and gave it to him to lick, but the dog ignored it and lay back panting.

"Hattie, I've changed my mind," she called out to the maid. "Bring me a biscuit for the dog." She needed a means of getting him to take the laudanum, as bitter as it was.

"He might not eat anything," James warned. "He looks as if he's barely conscious."

She suspected as much, but they would try. When Hattie returned with a biscuit upon a plate, Lily poured a few drops of laudanum upon it. "Hold his mouth and teeth for me, Matthew." The dog appeared to be stunned by all that had happened, and her brother was right. The animal showed little interest in the food, despite his frail and starving state.

Instinct warned that the moment she began probing his wounds, he could lash out at Matthew. A muzzle was most definitely needed, but not until she got him to drink some of the sedative.

"Since he won't eat, we're going to have to pour it into him," she warned Matthew. "I want you to hold him steady, and I'll take care of it." Given the dog's size, she suspected he would need more than she'd imagined.

Matthew drew his forearm across the animal and used both hands to pry open the dog's mouth. Lily eased a spoon inside and poured the droplets upon his tongue. Once she was finished, Matthew released the dog. The animal licked at his chops as if he loathed the bitter taste. "I know that's awful, but it will make you feel better."

"Now you can muzzle him," she said to Matthew. He removed his cravat and gently wound it around the dog's mouth, tying it off behind his ears. They waited for a time until the dog's heavy panting seemed to ease, and he closed his eyes. She prayed she had not given him too much.

From the bent angle of his back leg, Lily could see that it was broken and would need to be set. The top layer of his skin was shredded from being dragged across the road while dried blood and dirt matted his fur.

She would need to clean the wounds to prevent him from getting a fever. "I'll need you to hold the basin," she said to Matthew. To James, she added, "Go and bring me three more pitchers of water and some towels. I will also need two short pieces of wood, about this length." She demonstrated with her hands, knowing the broken leg would need to be splinted.

Her brother obeyed and retreated into the hallway.

"You're doing well with the dog, Lily," Matthew said quietly. "I believe you will heal him."

She was grateful for his quiet faith. "I will do the best I can." But his confidence in her offered a support she hadn't known she needed. She had read about treating wounds, but never had she attempted it herself.

James arrived with the remainder of her supplies, along with a large basin. Lily gave it to Matthew and asked him to hold it beneath the dog's wounds. With the pitcher, she began pouring water over the scraped flesh, washing away the dirt and debris. The dog jolted when she touched his raw skin, but she spoke softly to him. One wound was a large gash, but it didn't appear deep. She was careful to avoid his broken leg as she ensured the other three limbs were intact.

Some of the water spilled upon Matthew, but he shrugged away her apologies. "It's no matter to me." She saw that several splinters of wood were embedded in the dog's flesh, and she pulled them free as best she could.

The dog nearly came off the table when she touched a tender spot, and she was glad that Matthew had muzzled him—else he might have lunged to bite her hand. "I'm so sorry," she murmured to the dog. "I'm trying to be gentle."

Lily could feel the dog's ribs through his skin, and what he needed was good food and a warm place to sleep. She continued caring for the dog, all the while speaking to him in a soft voice.

"You are such a good boy," she praised him. "So very brave." She put some of the thick salve upon his cuts and bandaged the larger gash, wrapping the linen bandages around his torso. The dog continued to whine, and when she touched his broken leg, he whimpered.

"I'm going to splint his leg," she told the men. "Matthew, I want you to hold him down while I try to set the bone." He kept a firm grip on the dog, and she palpated the leg gently, trying to feel where the bone had broken. The break didn't seem too bad, and she studied his other legs to determine how to set it. The animal yelped when she moved his leg, but the bone did appear to slide back into position.

Lily took the thin pieces of wood James had brought and placed them on either side of his leg, binding it with bandages. Then she inspected the splints to be sure they would not move out of place.

"There now. That's done." She inspected the dog for further injuries, but it seemed that she had tended everything. His fur was wet, and she tried to dry him off as best she could.

Her earlier nerves had dissipated, replaced by a strange

sense of triumph. This animal would heal because of her. Even now, she could see him resting easier, and the thought filled her with satisfaction.

"I'm going to make a place for him to sleep by the hearth," she told the men. "James, will you stoke the fire?"

Her brother did, while she went to fetch the blanket Hattie had brought earlier. After she spread it out on the floor, she reached toward the dog.

"Let me carry him, Lily," Matthew intervened. "He's far too heavy for you. Especially now, when he's had so much laudanum." He lifted the dog from James's desk, and she saw the tremendous effort he used to carry the dog. She could not help but notice his taut muscles straining against his shirt when he placed the dog upon a blanket near the hearth. A sudden flash of memory overcame her, of when she had felt Matthew's skin against hers on their wedding night. She had traced the lean planes of his body, learning each and every muscle. A warmth suffused her skin at the thought, and she tried to push it away, focusing her attention upon the dog.

Lily knelt down beside the animal. "There now," she murmured, stroking his ears. She tucked the blanket around him "Sleep until morning." To Matthew, she asked, "Should we unwrap the muzzle?"

"Not just yet," he said. "We do not know the dog, and pain is often worse the second day. If he awakens and is hurting, he may try to bite those trying to help him. When you feed him, we can take it off."

Lily suspected he was right. She reached out to pet the dog, stroking his damp fur. He laid his head down and closed his eyes as she soothed him.

"You have a gentle touch, Lily," Matthew said. "And I believe the dog will live."

She smiled, feeling at ease for the first time in a while. "It feels good to have a sense of purpose. Even if it is only a dog."

"I am certain he appreciates it, though he can only growl or bark." Matthew joined her on the floor, reaching out to stroke the dog's fur. The animal gave a low snore, and Lily started to draw her hand back. Matthew rested his palm atop hers, covering her hand. For a moment, she let him touch her, feeling the heat of his hand on hers.

Her brother cleared his throat, reminding them both of his presence. "Shouldn't you be going now, Arnsbury?"

Lily gave a sheepish smile, for she had forgotten all about James standing near the fire. "In a moment, he will. Matthew, thank you for your help tonight. And especially with Mother when she ran away."

Her brother's gaze narrowed, for she had neglected to tell him of Iris's attempt to escape. "What happened?"

Lily gave him a short version of the story and said, "I think she gets lonely, and it causes her bad spells to worsen. I was glad Matthew was there to stop her from fleeing."

Her brother appeared uneasy by it. "Thank you for your help, Arnsbury. Calvert will see you to the door."

But Matthew kept his hand atop hers, his expression turning amused. "I can stay longer, if you like."

"That won't be necessary." Her brother sent him a pointed look, and Lily understood the silent message.

"Unfortunately, I think James is right," she said. "It is rather late."

"Someone should stay with the dog," Matthew suggested. "It's a strange house, and he might awaken in pain."

"I was planning to keep the door to the study closed," Lily said. "I believe he will be fine." But she was quite conscious of Matthew's touch. Instead of petting the dog, his thumb was stroking her hand.

"Good night, Arnsbury," James said, opening the door. "I'm certain you can see yourself out." It was a not-so-subtle reminder of the time. But instead, Matthew grinned at her brother as if James were the one leaving. "Goodnight, Penford. Sleep well. I'll see you at breakfast."

James tipped his head to the side and regarded him. For a moment, there was a silent battle between them, but Lily could not tell why. Then her brother surprised her by saying, "Do you know I've a mind to let you stay with the dog. It would serve you right to sleep on the floor with a hairy creature who smells terrible."

"It's not that far from the truth," Matthew remarked. "I *do* spend my nights with a hairy creature, though I cannot say that I sleep very much."

Lily hid her smile, turning away at his mention of the kitten, Beast. "He can stay if he wants to, James. I see no harm in it."

"Have you lost your mind, Lily? People will talk. And why on earth would I allow him to stay?"

"Because I am worried about the dog. And because he offered to watch over him for the night." She made no mention of her own desire for Matthew to stay. "You can lock him in the study if you are worried about my virtue."

James's face darkened, and his gaze fixed upon Matthew before it turned back to her. "It's a little late for that, isn't it, Lily?"

A flush slid over her cheeks, for he already knew of her lost innocence. She had made that mistake years ago, and there was no undoing it.

"I intend to go and see about our mother," she said, ignoring his remark. To Matthew, she added, "Go or stay. It doesn't matter to me."

But as she left them behind, she rather hoped he would remain.

Chapter Ten

Matthew sat on the floor beside the sleeping dog. The coals burned low in the hearth, but it provided a pleasant warmth for both of them. It was a miracle that the animal had not been crushed by the carriage wheels, but somehow, he had survived.

A low whining sound came from the dog's throat, and he twitched in his sleep. Matthew eased himself to lie down beside the animal and rested his hand upon the black and white fur, stroking gently. The dog seemed to relax, taking comfort from his presence. The glow from the hearth seemed to cast a peaceful spell over them, and as foolish as it was, Matthew rather enjoyed resting beside the dog.

He knew what it was to be alone and suffering, yearning for someone to take away the pain. And somehow, the dog's presence seemed to fill up the emptiness that burdened him even now. For this moment, there was only the two of them and the warmth of the fire. He kept one arm over the animal, until its breathing grew deep and even. It was strange to feel the same weariness passing over him. He stared into the fire, and he relaxed against the furry presence.

Sleep had eluded him for so long, but he closed his eyes and let his mind drift back to more pleasant memories. Lily's beauty had struck him speechless, and he hadn't known what to say or do.

She had arrived with her sister, Rose, as well as her parents and her brother, James. Although it was her sister's debut, Matthew had been caught up in the soft dreaminess of Lily's face. She hung back from the others, drinking in the sight of the ballroom as if she had never imagined to be there. Although he'd seen her on occasion while visiting James, Matthew had never imagined Lady Lily would transform into such a breathtaking woman.

His mother had all but shoved him toward the Thornton girls, but he held himself back. Instead, he found a way to discreetly stare at Lily. Her brown hair was caught up in a soft updo with hothouse gardenias tucked amid the strands. In the light, there were tints of red and gold, and he was transfixed by her presence.

"She's beautiful, isn't she?" His cousin, Juliette Fraser, moved behind him and touched his shoulder. "I suppose you have not seen Lady Lily in several years, since she only just returned from school."

He didn't quite know what to say, but it was easier to nod.

"Would you like to speak with her?" Juliette asked.

"It's not necessary," he replied. "Her sister is making her debut, and I should not interfere with that."

His cousin's eyes were kind, almost maternal as she smiled at him. He had always been close to Juliette and had even spent a summer in Scotland with her family.

Her expression turned conspiratorial. "Leave everything to me, Matthew." She crossed the ballroom and went to speak with Lily's mother, Lady Penford.

He didn't know whether to stand his ground or seek an escape.

His cousin disappeared behind one of the doors and returned a moment later, leaving the door slightly ajar. She approached Lady Penford and spoke to the woman quietly before leading the countess toward him, with Lady Rose and Lady Lily following behind. Matthew straightened and saw his cousin wink at him. What had Juliette done now? He suspected it had something to do with her hasty disappearance.

"Lady Penford," she began, "I know you remember my godson and cousin, Matthew Larkspur, the Earl of Arnsbury?"

"Of course," the matron responded, winking at him. "Matthew and James have been friends for years." Then she nodded to her daughters. "You already know Rose and Lily, I'm certain."

"It has been a long time." Matthew kissed Lady Rose's hand, and when he took Lady Lily's hand, he held it a moment longer than he should have. She flushed but ventured a faint smile.

"Matthew, I—oh dear." Juliette's words broke off, and she sighed. "That cat. What am I to do with him?" He turned to see what she was speaking of and saw a brown- and black-striped cat walking across the refreshment table.

Lady Lily's face transformed into a delighted smile, and she said, "Don't worry, I'll get him for you."

She started toward the table, and her mother apologized, "Lily loves animals. I fear she may not give the cat back."

"Matthew, go and help her," his cousin bade him. "I wouldn't want Lady Lily to be scratched by Tom."

Understanding dawned upon him. So that was what she had done. The merriment in Juliette's eyes suggested that she had known full well that the cat would begin exploring the ballroom. He had to admit, his cousin was indeed clever.

He bowed to the women before he followed. Lady Lily was already reaching for the cat, but Tom stretched out on the table and batted at her gloved hands.

"He thinks it's a game," Matthew told her. "Tom isn't the most obedient of cats."

"And that is why I love them so," Lily answered. "They are deliciously selfish. I have an older cat of my own whom I adore."

Matthew recalled that their family had owned a cat, but he'd never paid much attention to the animal. "What is his name?" He reached out and scooped the cat off the table, but he didn't remove Tom from the room. He now had the perfect means of speaking to Lady Lily, and he intended to hold on to the feline.

The young woman bit her lip. "His, ah, his name is rather ridiculous, I fear. I've had him since I was a young girl, and I named him when I was five years old."

He waited for her to continue, but Lady Lily said nothing at first. Instead, she reached out to pet Tom's head, rubbing at his ears. The cat purred, and her gloved hand brushed against his chest as she continued to give the animal affection. At last, she confessed, "I called him Princess, for I wanted a girl cat."

"And you still deride his masculinity with the name?"

She was trying to hold back laughter when the cat caught her glove with his claws. "His full name was Princess Caledonia. My father had more inappropriate names for him, since Princess insisted on scratching the furniture—but I shall not reveal those."

Lily was trying to extricate her glove from the cat's claws, but every time she tried to free herself, the cat snagged another bit of fabric.

"The inappropriate names are far more interesting." Matthew tried to help her remove the claws, but instead, it resulted in him sliding her glove off her hand. The cat was delighted to have the glove and it squirmed in Matthew's arms, trying to bite the delicate material. "Will you help me remove Tom from the ballroom?"

"Of course." Lily walked alongside him. She made no comment about the door being ajar but pushed it open further and followed him into the hallway. "Where should we bring him?"

"Outside in the garden should do well enough. He can hunt until it's time to return." He nodded toward the doorway at the far end of the house. "Could you go and open that door for me?"

She hesitated a moment. "We should have gone the other way, I think. My mother will be angry with me for being alone with you."

He remained standing where he was. "It was not my intent to frighten you, Lady Lily."

"No, I realize that your hands are filled with the cat. It's unlikely that you intended to accost me or damage my reputation."

Matthew took a step closer to her and set the cat down. Without asking permission, he held out her glove and took her bare hand. Slowly, he slid it over her fingers, then kept her hand in his. The air between them seemed to grow warmer, and her hazel eyes flared with heat. He held her hand a moment, and the cat slid between them, rubbing his head against their legs.

And when Lily smiled at him, the ground beneath his feet seemed to crumble.

***

The next morning, Lily was startled to learn that Matthew *had*, in fact, stayed with the dog. She opened the study and found him sitting beside the animal, stroking his fur.

"I didn't expect you to stay," she admitted. "I suppose there will be talk, won't there?" For him to stay overnight at the house, even with her brother at home, was quite a scandal.

"Only if you tell them," he said. He rose and stretched by

the fire, and she was caught by the outline of his body against the linen shirt. His skin still held a deep tan from the India sun, and she longed to touch it. Lily didn't know what was the matter with her, but she could not deny her attraction to Matthew. It had not dissipated even a little over the years, despite all that had happened. She turned away to force back the unbidden feelings.

"How is the dog?" she inquired. "Was he in a great deal of pain?"

"I think he had enough laudanum to knock him senseless. I don't recall him whimpering very much, once we both went to sleep." Matthew went to stand before her, and she saw that the dog was breathing easier.

"I've asked Dr. Fraser to come and look in on him," she admitted. "I know it's only a dog, but I want to be sure I set his leg properly."

Last night, for the first time in her life, she had felt such pride in taking care of the dog. She hadn't thought about her inexperience or lack of knowledge, but had charged forward, wanting to help the animal.

"He looks better," Matthew answered. As if in response, the dog yawned and tried to get up from the hearth. He avoided putting much weight on the broken leg and slumped back on the blanket, his tail wagging.

"He'll need more laudanum," Lily said. "I'll put some in his breakfast. But only a little." She decided to start him with a meat broth, not knowing how much food he could handle, if any.

The dog attempted to stand once again, but swayed on his feet. He sniffed at the rug, in spite of the muzzle, as if searching for food. Lily rang for a servant. "He may be hungry, but I don't want him to eat too quickly."

The door swung open, and James joined them. "I see you disregarded my wishes, Arnsbury."

Lily couldn't quite read her brother's mood, but she

stepped toward him. "James, there was no harm done. He slept with the dog, and that was all."

A hint of amusement crossed her brother's face. "A fitting bedmate, I should think."

Matthew stared back at James. "I could say something, but we are in the presence of your sister, and it would not be appropriate. For now, I'll say only that you should cease the derisive remarks." Though his tone was stern, she saw the twinkle in his eyes that mirrored her brother's humor.

The footman arrived, and Lily ordered the meat broth for the dog, along with warm water, towels, and soap. To the men, she added, "You can both have breakfast in the dining room. I want to stay with the dog and clean his wounds again."

"I'll remain here," Matthew responded. "You couldn't lift that dog if you wanted to."

He was right about that. Even though the animal was thin and starved, he was still about seven or eight stone in weight. "Very well. You may stay."

"If he stays, then *I* intend to stay," James intervened. He ordered the footman to bring breakfast into the study. "We may as well dine here together."

The dog limped unsteadily closer to Matthew, still sniffing the floor. Lily was about to ask him to lift the dog back to the desk, when the animal cocked his leg and relieved himself on Matthew's ankle.

"What on earth?" He rolled his eyes in disgust. "After the night we spent together, you would do this?"

James howled with laughter. "Oh God, that's the best dog I've ever seen. Lily, you have my approval if you wish to keep him."

She glared at her brother. "Go and fetch Matthew a pair of trousers to replace these." To Matthew, she added, "I'm so sorry. We should have taken him out, and...I suppose he couldn't hold it."

After James left, the dog limped under the desk and lay down, as if ashamed of himself. Matthew sighed and leaned against the desk. "I liked that dog until now."

"He didn't mean anything," Lily insisted. "You must know it was only an accident."

Matthew raised an eyebrow at her and shook his head. "Accident or not, I suppose my clothes are ruined, and it hardly matters what happens now." He crossed the room and lifted the dog into his arms. The animal squirmed, and when Matthew set him down on the desk, the dog whined.

"Thank you," Lily said. "I want to check his wounds again to be certain I didn't miss anything. And he may likely need a bath."

"So could I," Matthew remarked, wincing as he eyed his trousers. But he helped her by holding the dog gently and stroking his head. Soulful brown eyes stared into his, and the dog jolted when Lily touched a sensitive place.

The footman returned with their breakfast while a second footman brought the meat broth, the towels, and a basin. Lily dipped the linen cloth into the warm water and wrung it out over the wound. The dog tried to scramble away, but Matthew held him in place.

"There, lad. You'll be all right." He leaned in close and whispered, "You're a good dog, even if you did piss on me."

She cleansed the raw skin again, wrapping fresh linen bandages around the animal. But the dog's flesh was bruised and swollen, and she didn't doubt that he was feeling the pain. It let out a mournful groan, and she gentled her touch. "You'll be well soon enough," she told the dog. "I suppose I ought to give you a name for now." She thought a moment and then decided, "I will call you Sebastian." The dog perked up slightly at the name, his tail thumping. She rubbed his ears, and he leaned back, trying to roll to his back.

"What will you do with him?"

She hadn't truly thought about that. "I cannot simply throw

him back into the streets. It wouldn't be right." And yet, she wasn't quite certain what to do with the dog. He was sniffing at her fingertips, struggling to get up. At first, she tried to hold him down, and then it occurred to her what he wanted. "Matthew, will you help me remove the muzzle? I want to give him some more laudanum in the meat broth."

He set the dog on the floor, reached for the linen cravat and gently untied it. The dog shook his head once it was gone, licking his lips. Lily mixed a few drops of laudanum into the broth and set the bowl down in front of Sebastian. The dog took a tentative lick and then began to drink. He stood, keeping weight off his broken leg, and slurped at the broth as if it would be taken away at any moment.

When he had finished, he licked his chops as if begging for more. "Later," she promised him, stroking back his ears. Her fingers brushed against Matthew's, and she froze at the unexpected contact. He took her hand in his and held it for a moment.

The touch unraveled her good sense, but she fought the urge to pull her hand back. Instead, she fumbled for conversation. Anything. "H-how did you sleep last night?"

The moment she asked, she realized what a bad question it was.

"Actually, I slept well last night," he admitted. "I think Sebastian helped." He rubbed at the animal's ears again, and the dog licked at his fingers.

She softened at the sight of the pair of them. "I am glad to hear it."

But then, Matthew drew closer. "It has been a long time since I slept for more than a few hours at a time." His tone was husky, reminding her of what it was to sleep in his arms after a night of lovemaking. A soft rush of desire heightened her sensitivity, making her long to be touched by this man. And for a brief moment, it was as if the man she'd loved was standing before her once again.

James interrupted her wayward thoughts when he returned with a pair of dark trousers. He approached, holding them out to Matthew, and ordered, "Go upstairs and find a room where you can change into these. I'll have yours cleaned and sent to your house later."

Matthew took the trousers and regarded Lily with a look of interest. Her pulse quickened at the sight of his brown eyes watching her. *You must not think about him undressing.*

She would try not to remember his muscular thighs or the way his body had felt upon hers, skin to skin. Her traitorous body went breathless at the memory.

Matthew gave her a knowing smile before he left her behind with the dog.

"You're looking flushed, Lily," her brother remarked. "Is everything all right?"

"Yes. It's just very warm in here." She picked up another linen cloth and began drying off the dog.

"You haven't touched your breakfast," James added. "You should eat."

Her brother was right, and she made a plate of food, bringing it to his desk. Then he pulled a chair beside her, and she picked at the eggs that had gone cold.

"Stay away from Arnsbury," her brother warned in a quiet voice. "I can see the look in your eyes. Do not forget how dangerous he has become."

"He's getting better," she argued.

"He's not the same man you knew once. Don't believe that Arnsbury is safe—he's not. Just like that dog over there could snarl at you and bite. And you don't know when his mind will break again."

She knew he was trying to protect her. "I'll be careful." To change the subject, she inquired, "Are you attending the Duchess of Worthingstone's ball this evening? Evangeline will be there, so I've heard."

A stony look crossed her brother's face, as if he knew

exactly what she was doing to turn the subject. "Stop trying to play matchmaker."

Lily stabbed a bit of sausage with her fork. "Oh, I wouldn't dream of it. Evangeline loathes you."

"Then why would you mention her name to me?"

"Because I would find it most interesting to watch the pair of you together," she said. "I wonder why it is that you are still at odds. I know after you left for India, she was furious, but it seems a long time to hold a grudge."

"We are not at all suited. Every time I walk close to her, she attempts to blend in with the wall. Or she hides behind a potted plant. She is shy and ought to marry a man as quiet as she is."

Lily wasn't so certain. Evangeline was indeed a wallflower, but beneath her shyness was a strong woman. "I thought you were friends at one point."

"I am not going to discuss this with you. Suffice it to say, it is best if we go our separate ways." A troubled look crossed her brother's face, but she didn't press him.

She pushed her plate away, and when the footman came to clear away their dishes, he added, "Dr. Fraser, er, that is, Lord Falsham has come to call."

"Excellent. Please send him in," Lily said.

The footman started to put away the food, but Lily stopped him. "No, leave it for now." Matthew had not yet eaten. She stood from the desk and waited for the doctor to come into James's study. Her nerves tightened, and she hoped she had tended the dog properly.

When Dr. Fraser entered, she smiled at him. "I am very glad you could come."

"It was no trouble at all." To James, he nodded, "Penford, it's good to see you again."

"And you," her brother answered. "Forgive my sister's summons. She was quite upset when this dog was injured last night. She felt it necessary to send for you."

Dr. Fraser shrugged it away. "He's one of God's creatures, is he no'? We'll have a look and see. I suppose this is the animal, aye?" He knelt by the hearth. Sebastian's tail thumped, but he didn't rise. "There's a good lad."

Lily moved toward the animal and knelt beside the doctor. "He is. I think his leg is broken, and he has many cuts. I tried to clean them with water, and I put some salve on them."

The doctor studied the dog's wounds. "You were right. His leg is broken. But Lady Lily, I must be telling you that 'tis rare that a dog can heal from a break such as this. Most veterinary surgeons would be killing it."

She was horrified at the very idea. "It's only a broken leg. Why should he die from that?"

Dr. Fraser stood up. "Many of the surgeons believe that 'tis no' worth tryin' to heal a pup, especially if he could have rabies. Some might take the leg off."

"He deserves to live as much as a sheep or a cow." Lily stroked Sebastian's fur, and the dog turned to lick her hand. "And I'll not allow you to amputate his leg."

Dr. Fraser smiled. "I didna say that I would be doing such a thing, Lady Lily. Only to warn you that other surgeons might act differently."

Her shoulders lowered with relief. "Thank goodness." She took a breath, stood, and asked, "Did I set his leg properly?"

He reached down to feel the leg again, and the dog whimpered. "Just a little pinch, lad. Naught t'be worried about." Dr. Fraser made a slight adjustment to the limb, and the dog let out a short yelp. "There now, that's better." He wrapped the bandage around the dog's leg tightly and secured the end. "You nearly had it right, lass."

But it bothered her to think that she had set the dog's leg in an improper position. Had she not summoned the doctor, the bone might have healed wrong and crippled the animal for the rest of his life. She wished she knew more about healing, even with only a book to help her learn.

Dr. Fraser stood and asked, "Will you attend the Worthingstone ball this evening? Juliette and I would be glad to see both of you there."

"Yes, I will come. And so will James," Lily asserted.

The doctor nodded. "Then I'll be seeing you there." He leaned down to rub the dog's ears before he left.

Matthew entered the room at that moment, wearing her brother's trousers. "Lord Falsham," he greeted the doctor. "I know Lily was glad to have you look in on the dog."

"Ah, lad, you can be calling me Dr. Fraser. I was that long before I inherited the title of viscount. It feels as if you're speaking to someone else," the man remarked. "I didn't realize you had come to call."

"I was here earlier when the dog decided to relieve himself on my leg. James was kind enough to loan me a pair of trousers."

The doctor barked out a laugh and shook his head. "Animals have their own ways, do they no'?" Then his gaze sharpened upon him. "You're looking better than the last time I saw you."

"A little," Matthew agreed. But Lily noticed that there was a slight trace of tension between the men.

"He's sleeping with dogs now," James said, clapping him on the back. "It agrees with him."

There were times when she wanted to strangle her brother. "Matthew offered to watch over Sebastian the first night. I was grateful for it." To end James's teasing, she offered, "Perhaps *you* would like to sleep with the dog this evening?"

"Not at all," James replied. "I prefer more pleasant company."

Dr. Fraser picked up his bag and said, "I should be going now. Juliette will be wanting to know where I am."

They bid him farewell, and after he had gone, Lily realized that Matthew hadn't eaten anything yet. "Would you care for breakfast?"

"If there's anything left." He took a seat near the desk.

Lily fixed a plate for him from the leftover food and sat beside him. Sebastian sniffed the air and hobbled his way over to rest at Matthew's feet. "I suppose he is hoping you'll drop food for him."

"Just so." He dug in with his fork and "accidentally" let some of the eggs fall to the carpet. The dog devoured them hungrily.

Lily smiled and turned back to her brother. "You will go with me to the duchess's ball tonight, won't you, James?"

Her brother sighed. "If I must. But I am not going to dance with Miss Sinclair." His tone held a warning, but she cheerfully ignored it and smiled at him.

"And what of you, Matthew? Are you planning to attend?"

She posed the question idly and was surprised when he answered, "She is my cousin, so I might. If you want me to."

She thought about it for a moment and realized she did want to see him there. During the last ball, she had enjoyed his company, despite the runaway kitten. "Yes, I would like you to come."

Matthew reached for her hand and held it a moment. "Then I will."

Lily wore a lilac-colored ball gown and had tucked violets into her hair. Right now, she stood beside her friend Evangeline, who wore a short-sleeved gown the color of dust, with a neckline that covered any hint of a bosom. The grayish-brown silk did nothing for the young woman's complexion, and her hair was twisted into a severe updo.

"You look lovely tonight, Lily," Evangeline said. "Especially in that color. Have you changed your mind about finding a husband?"

"Not at all. Thank you." She studied her friend, trying to decide if she dared to broach the subject of Evangeline's attire. "I do not mean to offend, but was this truly a gown of your choosing?"

Evangeline beamed. "It's perfectly dreadful, isn't it? I asked the modiste to find silk the color of mouse fur. Now I can safely remain a wallflower, and no man would dare ask me to dance."

"It is...certainly a different color than any I've seen before."

"My mother was horrified. She thinks I should make a greater effort to find a husband, but why would I want a man to govern my life with his own rules? I am perfectly happy with my books. And my father seems content to let me remain a spinster."

Evangeline's father, Cain Sinclair, had a darker reputation among the men. Born a Scottish commoner, it was well known that her father would not hesitate to shoot any man who dared threaten her virtue. He would likely dress his daughter in black crape and a veil, if he could.

James crossed the room and joined Lily, pretending he didn't notice Evangeline standing beside her. "Lily, would you care to dance?"

"Not just now, thank you. But I am certain Evangeline would be happy to take my place." She sent him a smile filled with mischief.

"I would sooner stand in a corner and peel wallpaper," Evangeline answered cheerfully. "But thank you for the offer."

James's posture grew rigid at the insult. "I see your manners have not improved, Evangeline." To Lily, he apologized, "Forgive me, but I am trying to avoid being matched up by the meddling mamas."

"Matchmaking meddling mamas," Evangeline repeated. "Now there's a phrase I'd wager you couldn't say three times without twisting up your tongue."

"I don't recall that you are part of this conversation," James snapped.

Now why on earth was her brother being so rude? Lily was startled to see the flare of anger between the pair of them. Evangeline's cheeks were fiery red, and she took a step toward James. "I don't know that I want to be part of a conversation with you." Without another word, she spun and strode away, disappearing into the crowd.

Lily was horrified by her brother's behavior. "Why on earth would you behave like such an awful man? I've never seen you this way before."

"We do not like each other," he said calmly.

But there was far more to it than that. Her friend was normally a quiet young woman who made pleasant conversation—not at all a fierce termagant who looked as if she were contemplating murder.

But before she could think upon it further, Adrian Monroe approached. He bowed to her and said to her brother, "Lord Penford, it is good to see you back from India. I know your sister was most overjoyed at your return."

"You are already acquainted with Lily, then?" James mused.

"We shared a dance a few months ago," he said. With a warm smile, he invited, "Would you care to join me, Lady Lily?"

There was something about the man's tone that struck her as insincere. Since it would be rude to decline, she told him, "I fear I have already promised this dance to my brother." She tucked her hand in James's arm. "Perhaps another time."

Her brother did not seem pleased as she led him to join the dancers. There was tension within him, and he remarked, "You were trying to avoid Mr. Monroe. Why?"

"He was too forward the last time I danced with him." Something about the man made her uneasy, and she preferred to keep her distance.

"Shall I speak to him about his behavior?" James took his place across from her and bowed while she curtseyed.

"No, let it be. He's harmless." She took his hand, and they

136

joined in the country dance. Her brother was quite a good dancer, though reluctant. She found herself relaxing and enjoying herself as he spun her in place.

But his expression remained serious. "Is Matthew courting you again?"

She shook her head. "We're friends, nothing more." But despite her dismissal of the idea, she had felt a shift between herself and Matthew. She enjoyed spending time with him and had appreciated his help tending her new dog, Sebastian.

The dance ended, and he asked, "Would you like lemonade or something to eat?"

She nodded. "I would, yes. Shall I come with you?"

"If you wish."

They began walking toward the refreshments when Lily caught a glimpse of Matthew in the shadows near the hall. It warmed her to know that he'd kept his word about attending the gathering. "Actually, I think I will go and talk with Lord Arnsbury for a moment."

She nodded toward the hallway, and James raised an eyebrow. "I hardly think that's proper with no chaperone."

"The door is open, and I know you will join us within a moment or two." She narrowed her gaze at him. "Don't you trust me?"

He shrugged. "I trust you. I am not so certain I trust *him*."

"It's only for a moment, James." Without waiting for his consent, Lily crossed the room and slipped into the alcove leading toward the hall. Matthew was standing in the shadow of the stairs, dressed in evening finery.

"I see you've found a place to skulk." She smiled at him. "And I hope there are no stowaway kittens this time."

"None at all. I am free to skulk at my leisure. Or watch the people from a distance."

Then he took her hand and guided her back so that she could see from his vantage point. "Do you see the woman in white over there?"

His voice was husky against her ear, evoking a silent thrill of sensation. She was nearly in his embrace, and if anyone caught them together, the gossips would whisper about them.

"Y-yes. What about her?"

"She is making her debut."

Lily was far more distracted by Matthew's breath against her cheek. At this moment, all she could think about was kissing him and touching the muscled edges of his body.

"Do you know her?" she managed.

"No. But I find it fascinating to observe the guests." His hands drifted to the small of her back, and a flare of yearning slid over her body. The very touch of his hands made her skin rise with anticipation.

She struggled to put together her thoughts. "Are you... planning to remain here, hidden from view?"

"I am. It's better this way."

"Why?" Was he still feeling unnerved by crowds of people? But his hand moved over her spine.

"Because then I can watch over you."

The words slid over her like a caress, and she warned herself not to fall beneath his spell. Her brother's warning echoed in her thoughts. *Don't believe that Arnsbury is safe—he's not. And you don't know when his mind will break again.*

She knew James was right...but she also remembered how much she had once loved Matthew. And she didn't know if that same lover was beneath the surface of the man who stood behind her.

"I should return to the ballroom," she said. But she couldn't quite bring herself to move. Here, in the shadows, she wanted to pretend that Matthew was her husband, that they were stealing a quiet moment together.

"You could stay," he murmured. "Just for a little while."

Lily wanted that, so badly. She remained motionless and answered, "Sometimes I daydream of the way it used to be, before you left for India."

"We were different then." His mouth rested against her hair, and goose bumps rose over her body.

She was acutely aware of his touch, and though she tried to distance herself, she yearned for him. "We were. Do you remember it now?" Her voice came out as a broken whisper.

"I remember everything." His hand trailed up her spine, and she felt the touch deep inside herself. "I remember your smile when I came to see you. And the way you threw yourself into my arms when we were alone."

A faint note of nostalgia brushed over her. "I was impulsive then. And you tried to make me see reason."

"Every time you kissed me, I lost all sense of reason. There was none, and I didn't care." His mouth lowered to her nape, and her body reacted instinctively to the touch of his mouth upon her skin.

She was torn between wanting to flee back into the ballroom...or turning to kiss him back. Instead, she remained frozen, his touch awakening her senses. "Matthew, what do you want from me?"

"A second chance." He kissed the back of her neck, and his lips were like warm silk against her flesh. "I lost two years of my life, and memories of torture haunt me at night. I want to replace them with something better."

Shivers erupted upon her skin, and she longed to turn and pull him closer. But not here. "We could be seen at any moment," she whispered. "Take me somewhere else."

He took her hands and guided her deeper into the shadows, to a darkened corner by the stairs. She went with him, her heartbeat quickening. It was almost as if the old Matthew had returned to her once again.

But this time, she was no longer a girl with foolish dreams. She understood that his mind could not heal as swiftly as his body.

He didn't speak at all, but his hands framed her face. Strong fingers traced the outline of her cheeks, and she felt herself softening beneath his touch. Her bare arms prickled with gooseflesh, and he raised her hand to his lips, kissing it.

"I am sorry," he murmured. "For all that I have done."

Lily touched his cheek and answered, "Forgiven." She wanted Matthew now, just as she always had. No one else made her feel this way, and she wanted to believe that the jagged edges of his past could heal back into a whole man.

His arms moved around her waist, drawing her close. For a time, he didn't move, and she understood that he was giving her the choice to refuse him. She could pull away now, and he would allow that.

Matthew cupped one cheek, tilting her mouth toward his. Then he kissed her gently, and the heat of his mouth conjured a craving she knew would never be satisfied. He claimed her lips as his own, plundering her mouth until she could scarcely breathe. Hot blood rushed through her veins, and she clung to him for balance.

Just for a moment, she told her brain. *I need this.*

And God help her, she kissed him back. Her tongue mingled with his, and she lowered the boundaries of her conscience. Matthew shielded her from the outside world, pressing her back against the wall as he kissed her. She knew that they could be discovered at any moment, and the danger felt reckless. Between her legs, she grew wet, wanting so much more than this stolen moment.

He had taken her innocence two years ago, and she feared she lacked any willpower when it came to the fierce desire between them.

Her breasts ached, and she could scarcely gather her thoughts when he pulled back at last. There was only the sound of their hushed breathing, and she knew that her mouth was swollen from the intensity of the kiss.

"You should return to your brother," he warned. "Before he comes looking for you."

She took a step backward. Then another, trying to gather

her composure. In the end, she turned and fled back to the ballroom, not wanting to face her tangled thoughts and dreams.

Her cheeks were burning, and she fanned herself, seeking a sanctuary among the older women. She didn't want to dance or endure the flirtations of men—not now. When she spied Lady Falsham, she crossed the ballroom and joined her.

"Lady Lily." The viscountess smiled and motioned for her to join them. "I am glad to see you this evening." Her face softened, and she added, "Have you seen Matthew, by chance?"

Lily nodded. "He preferred to remain away from everyone else."

Lady Falsham's face held concern. "I had hoped he was starting to get better." She kept her voice low, but there was no hiding her worry.

"I believe he is improving, but he does not wish to be among everyone else just yet." To change the subject, Lily added, "By the way, I wanted to thank you and your husband for the book you loaned me. I find medicine most fascinating." She told the viscountess about the dog. "And I do appreciate Dr. Fraser paying a call upon Sebastian."

Lady Falsham smiled warmly. "While my husband doesn't normally tend dogs, I believe he enjoys a challenge." Then she thought a moment. "If you are interested in veterinary medicine, you might visit the Royal Veterinary College. They may have pamphlets you could read."

The idea intrigued her. She had always loved animals, and although the Royal Veterinary College was known for treating horses, they might allow her to borrow books or study about the treatment of animals. She had not considered it before, but it might be a distraction from her family's goal of finding her a husband.

"I will ask," she told Lady Falsham.

Chapter Eleven

Matthew had come to call upon Lily, only to find her leaving her brother's house, a footman assisting her into the landau. He thought about calling out to her but decided to simply follow. Presumably she was going out shopping, and he could speak with her there. He ordered his driver to follow, but was surprised to see that the carriage did not bring Lily toward the linen-drapers in Mayfair. Instead, the vehicle took a northeastern path.

Soon enough, they stopped outside the Royal Veterinary College. Now what was Lily doing there? He suspected it was related to Sebastian but couldn't be certain. Instead, he kept a discreet distance and watched.

Lily entered the college with her maid shadowing her. They disappeared inside the entrance, and Matthew ordered his driver to bring the vehicle closer. Nearly half an hour passed before she strode out. From her posture, she appeared furious. He waited until her carriage drove away and then disembarked from his own vehicle, with his footman trailing behind.

When he reached the entrance to the college, the footman

opened the door on his behalf. Matthew walked inside, and he studied the registrar with mild interest. "I saw a lady leaving just now, who seemed in some distress. Was there a reason for it?"

The gentleman sighed. "She wanted to enquire about books and papers regarding the treatment of dogs. I told her that we do not offer such reading materials to ladies."

"Because you specialize in horses and cattle, I presume."

The registrar shook his head. "No, because it would be inappropriate for women. She ought to spend her time reading about poetry, not material such as this."

Matthew resisted the urge to argue, for he doubted he could convince the man of anything. "Because you believe she would not be intelligent enough to understand it?"

Far from it. Lily was indeed a bright young woman, and Matthew didn't doubt she could easily grasp the material.

But the registrar nodded in agreement. "Precisely. It would be quite a waste."

Matthew could only imagine what the man had said to Lily. But he had another idea in mind. "I wish to purchase a set of books for the first year of veterinary studies. And I require any books and materials you have regarding the care of hunting dogs, and all other animals."

"Do you wish to seek admission to the college?" the registrar inquired.

"A correspondence course," Matthew corrected. "I am Matthew Larkspur, Earl Arnsbury." He gave the registrar an imperious look. "I have an interest in reading about veterinary medicine, but my duties would never permit me to attend classes. Nor would I want to engage in such pursuits." He looked down at the man, making his point clear. "If my requirements are met, I will bestow additional funds upon the college to assist with further research studies."

The registrar's eyes gleamed as he caught Matthew's meaning. "Of course, my lord. We should be glad to provide you with all the materials you desire. Particularly for your hunting dogs, if that is your interest."

Matthew nodded. "Give the materials to my servant, and I will await them in my carriage."

"At once, my lord. And I bid you a good day." The registrar appeared delighted with the prospect.

And as Matthew departed the college, he looked forward to seeing Lily's reaction to his gift.

Later that day, Matthew found Lily at home sitting on the floor with Sebastian. The animal's head rested in her lap, his paw draped over one of her legs. The sight of them together made him smile, and the moment he entered James's study, the dog's tail began to wag. Lily's mother was standing by the window, her expression frozen as she stared. Likely, it was not a good day for Lady Penford.

"Hello, Matthew," Lily greeted him. Her eyes narrowed at the sight of all the parcels in his hands. "Were you out shopping today?"

"In a manner of speaking." He set the wrapped books down on the desk and went to sit beside her. Sebastian rolled to his back, exposing his stomach. Matthew rubbed the dog's belly, and his tail thumped with delight. "He seems in good spirits."

"I don't like the look of some of his cuts. They seem quite red and swollen." She rubbed the animal's ears, and the dog appeared delighted with the attention.

Matthew nodded in acknowledgment and then asked in a low voice, "How is your mother today?"

Lily only shook her head. "It's as if she isn't there. She doesn't know me at all."

He reached out to squeeze her hand out of sympathy. "I'm sorry."

Her face grew pained, but there was nothing either of them

could do. Sebastian rolled over and trotted toward Iris, sniffing at her skirts. The matron jolted backward and demanded, "What is that wolf doing here?"

Lily exchanged a glance with Matthew, and they both stood. "It's all right, Mother."

"I won't stay here and be eaten by a wolf," Iris insisted. She twisted her hands together and backed away. Lily pushed Sebastian back, but her mother hurried to the door and left, closing it behind her.

She was about to follow, but Matthew said, "Let her be. It might upset her more."

Lily paused but then nodded. "I suppose. I will check on her in a few minutes."

"Go on and open the parcels," he suggested. "See if they are what you wanted."

"I didn't need any gifts," Lily said, but she went to unwrap them. She touched the brown paper and guessed, "Are they books?"

When he did not answer, she tore the first one open. It was a copy of *From Farriery to Veterinary Medicine*. He waited to hear her response, but she had gone utterly silent. Her back was turned to him, and he could not gauge her reaction until he moved in front of her.

Lily was holding the book with both hands, and her expression held tears. "You followed me to the college, didn't you?"

"I came to pay a call and saw you leaving. I was curious," he admitted.

"They refused to even speak with me," she confessed. "That arrogant man told me I should go home and tend to my embroidery. Or perhaps I should put my time to better use in finding a husband."

Matthew could not quite read her reaction to the gift. Had he offended her somehow? "Was I wrong to ask for the books? Are they not what you wanted?"

She shook her head and clutched the volume to her chest. "They are everything I wanted." A brilliant smile spread across her face, and she set the book down. "Help me open the others."

It was like Christmas morning, watching her unwrap the books and pamphlets. When she found one on the care of hunting dogs, she threw her arms around him. "Matthew, this is perfect!"

Her reaction warmed him, and he drew his arms around her waist, holding her a moment, before she could turn back to the books. She pulled back slightly and rested her palms upon his heart, her face shining with happiness. "Thank you."

"There's more," he murmured, framing her face with his hands.

"What else?" There was a note of excitement in her voice.

Matthew was not going to waste this chance, and he bent in to rest his forehead against hers. Her hands moved to his shoulders, and he murmured, "A correspondence course. If you want to complete the written assignments under my name, that is. They would not allow you to take the lessons in person, but you could learn whatever you wanted to, in this manner."

Her eyes widened, and she drew her arms around his neck again, hugging him tightly. "I do want to try."

He remained close to her, drinking in the comfort of her touch. And when she raised her mouth to his, he kissed her back.

The moment she kissed him, Lily felt the heat pouring through her skin. She could not resist the urge, and Matthew's gift had touched her deeply. No other man would have done this for her.

His kiss was coaxing, reminding her of the way he had tempted her last night. She lost herself to the man she once loved, and when his tongue slid inside her mouth, her fingers dug into his shoulders. Though he did nothing more than kiss her, she could feel herself rising to his call, needing more from him.

He drew back, staring at her. His eyes were dark with desire, his mouth firm. "I missed this. I missed you, Lily."

She rose up on tiptoe, kissing him again. "I feel the same way."

Matthew lifted her up, bringing her to a wingback chair where he sat down and kept her upon his lap. Then he kissed her again, and she felt the ridge of his erection straining at his trousers. The memory drew her back to the night he had first made love to her. Lily remembered how it had felt with their bodies joined together, and a moan escaped her as he kissed her over and over.

"I will stop any time you want me to," he swore. His voice was husky with restrained need, and she knew he meant it.

"I don't want you stop," she whispered. "Not just yet."

For now, she wanted to touch this man, to remember what it had been like between them. She wanted to erase the years of loneliness and fear, returning to a time when she had loved him. Her own needs pushed away any doubts she might have had.

He kissed her roughly, and she felt the need to be closer. She changed her position so that she was kneeling astride him, her skirts cascading over the chair. It was scandalous, utterly improper, but she hardly cared. He gripped her hips and sat forward in the chair, bringing them even closer.

This is sinful and wrong, she told herself. *Someone could walk in on us.*

But she silenced the voice of reason and loosened his cravat and his shirt, sliding her hand against his bare chest. His skin was hot to the touch, and his heart was beating as wildly as her own.

"Lily," he breathed, drawing his palms beneath her skirts.

"What I wouldn't give to touch you right now." He spoke against her mouth softly, tasting her lips. "If you were naked in my bed, I would lean down to your breasts and take a nipple into my mouth. I would swirl my tongue over your flesh and watch you unravel."

The words evoked her imagination, and she felt her body growing aroused. Her breasts were tight beneath her chemise, and she felt her breathing hasten.

Matthew palmed her spine, arching against her. She felt every hard inch of him thrusting with only a thin layer of linen between them. In her mind, she could imagine him freeing himself from his trousers, finding the slit between her undergarments, and sliding in deep. She closed her eyes, afraid of the wild thoughts that conjured within her mind.

"I want to touch you intimately," he said, slipping his tongue inside her mouth. He entered and withdrew, and she ached for this man.

Lily pulled back from his kiss, trying to gather her sanity from this madness. But she remembered too well the ecstasy of his hands upon her. He drew his hand lower, down to her right ankle, and she bit her lip at the silent question.

He didn't move, and she understood he would not push her too far. But she wanted this man, and her body was eager for him.

She reached down to his hand and guided it higher, over her stockings to her pantalettes. He brought his other hand there and palmed her bottom, kneading it gently. She rocked against him, his shaft pressing her until she felt a shimmering sensation building. He had found the slit in the pantalettes, and now his fingers were against her intimate flesh. When Matthew's bare hand stroked her womanhood, she let out a half sob of wrenching need.

She shouldn't allow this—not after all that had happened. But he bent forward and took her earlobe in his mouth, just as he stroked the cleft of her.

"You're wet for me, Lily." His voice held years' worth of frustration, but he found the center of her pleasure and caressed it gently. "Do you want me to pleasure you?"

"Y-yes," she gasped. And though it was wanton, she was caught up beneath his spell. He delved two fingers inside her, stroking the hooded flesh with his thumb. She began to tremble, her nails digging into his shoulders. Without shame, she sat against him, burying his fingers inside her before rising up. It was an exquisite torture, and her mind fantasized that his shaft was buried within her body.

"That's it," he murmured in her ear. "Imagine you are riding me, Lily."

She moved her hips in counterpoint, and the rise of sensation overtook her, spiraling higher and higher. She was arching against him, her body trembling. He pressed against the pearl of her, and she felt the intensity gather into a ball of white-hot pleasure, spearing through her senses, until she sobbed against him.

"More," he demanded, stroking and touching her until the shuddering broke over her, and she erupted in a breathtaking release. She was so wet against his fingers, her body spasming as he thrust and withdrew his hand.

Lily came a second time when he captured her mouth, kissing her hard as he penetrated her with his fingers and pressed against her center. A gasp escaped her, but he silenced her cries with his mouth, letting her ride out the storm of the orgasm.

Lily had forgotten the reckless pleasure of being in his arms. Right now, she felt as if every muscle had gone fluid within her. If she tried to stand, her knees would buckle beneath her.

Drawing back, she looked into his brown eyes and saw only desire. He spoke no promises but only held her.

And she wondered exactly what she had started between them.

Two days later

"You have a caller, my lord."

Matthew glanced up from his ledgers, wondering if it was Lily who had come to visit. He yearned to have her back in his life at his side. They belonged together. Somehow, she had managed to forgive him for his sins, making him want to be a better man for her sake.

"Who is it?" he asked the footman.

"A lady who calls herself Miss Carlisle. She said she had sent you several letters, and there was no reply. Should I tell her you are not at home?"

He tensed at the mention of the blackmailer's name. It seemed that ignoring her actions had not silenced her. Worst of all, he'd found evidence in the ledgers that his father had indeed paid Miss Carlisle over the years—and he doubted if his mother knew anything about it. It was best to meet the problem face to face.

"Show her in," he told the servant.

Matthew stood from his chair, fully prepared to throw the woman out, once he reassured her that he would not pay anything for her silence. If his father had indulged in an affair, it was over. He refused to have anything to do with a mistress.

But the woman who entered his study was not at all the sort he'd expected. She was dressed in a black serge gown, and she appeared to be in her midfifties. The lines of her face held weariness and suffering, and he half expected her to drop to her knees in prayer. And there was a familiarity about her, as if he had seen this woman somewhere before.

"Thank you for agreeing to see me, my lord," Miss Carlisle began. "I understand that you may not have received my letters."

"I received them," he said curtly. "That does not mean I intend to pay you any blackmail money. Whatever secrets my father was trying to keep do not matter. He is dead, and we have gone on with our lives. As must you."

Her brown eyes held sadness. "I did know Lord Arnsbury well, long ago. I was young and foolish and fancied myself in love with him. I thought he would marry me after I was caught in a compromising position, but he refused." Shame darkened her cheeks. "He decided to wed Charlotte instead."

A sudden uneasiness caught in his gut, though he could not understand why. He had already guessed that this woman was one of his father's old paramours. But why would she return now believing he would pay her anything?

"Have you never wondered why your eyes are brown, like mine?" she murmured. "Neither Lord Arnsbury nor Lady Arnsbury has the same color as ours. We look like one another, do we not?"

A coldness flooded through him, and he said nothing. It was as if her words were a razor, slashing through him. Never, in all his life, had he allowed himself to consider that Charlotte was not his mother. It was unthinkable.

Miss Carlisle took a step forward. "It is well known that Lady Arnsbury was barren for at least ten years. She went away for nearly a year and returned with you, claiming you as her child. And then Lord Arnsbury raised you as his heir."

"Get out," he said. He had no wish to hear any more of these insinuations. "I will pay you nothing. But I *will* have you arrested on charges of blackmail, unless you cease these accusations."

"Your father ruined me," she said softly. "And he knew it. He was also willing to pay a yearly sum so that I could live in comfort."

"I am not willing to pay it." He took her by the elbow and guided her to the door. "You will leave now, before I have you removed."

"The Earl of Strathland was my brother," she said. "I have hidden myself from society over the years because of his misdeeds. But if you ask Lady Arnsbury about our family, she will tell you what truly happened."

He started to open the door, but she touched his hand with hers. "How much is your good name worth?" she asked. "All I ask is a small amount to live on. And in return, no one need ever know you are a bastard."

In response, he led her outside the study, closed the door, and shut her out. His hands were shaking from fury and denial. All his life, he had been the beloved only son of his parents. He had never wanted for anything, and his mother had treated him like a precious gift.

There could be no truth to Sarah Carlisle's words. She was only trying to solicit money from him, and he would not consider it.

Have you never wondered why your eyes are brown, like mine? God help him, there was indeed a similarity between them. That was why she had appeared so familiar. He saw bits and pieces of himself in her face.

She is not my mother, he swore to himself. He would not allow such thoughts to take root. But he could not dispute the fact that his father had indeed paid this woman a great deal of money over the years. Whether it was guilt over having ruined her...or the price for secrecy, he could not say.

And God help him, he didn't want to know the answers.

For the next few weeks, Matthew pushed the matter to the back of his mind, keeping his attention on courting Lily. Ever since he had nearly seduced her, she had shied away from him, ensuring that James was always there to chaperone. Although she never once turned him away when he came to call, it was clear that she was uneasy about being alone with him.

And so, he took a step back, giving her time to adjust to the idea that he wanted to be with her.

Some men might use flowers or jewelry to court a woman. Instead, Matthew brought Lily books and pamphlets on veterinary medicine. He considered it a challenge to find new gifts for her, and it pleased him to see her smile.

The dog's wounds had healed, and today Matthew saw Sebastian curled up at Lily's feet while she studied. She wore a dove-gray gown, and her brown hair was caught up in an updo with two curls hanging down to her throat. Her fingers were ink-stained, but she continued to write.

Her footman cleared his throat, announcing his presence. "Lord Arnsbury has come to pay a call, Lady Lily."

"Show him in, Calvert. And tell James that he has come." She glanced up from her work and smiled.

"I regret that your brother is not here just now," Calvert said. "Shall I send for your mother to chaperone?"

"Yes, please." Lily set her pen down and stood from her chair. The dog rolled over, and the moment he spied Matthew, his tail began to wag. Sebastian stood and stretched, then trotted over to sniff Matthew's shoes.

Lily gripped her hands together and nodded in greeting. "Hello, Matthew."

He moved forward and lifted her hand to his lips. "Good afternoon, Lily." With a glance toward the papers scattered around her, he asked, "How do you find the correspondence course?"

She smiled and answered honestly, "It is unfortunate that I have to lie about my name and pretend I'm a man. But they seem pleased with my progress. I'm learning about rabies in dogs at the moment." She reached down to ruffle Sebastian's ears, and he licked her fingers.

Matthew offered her a package wrapped in brown paper, and she smiled at him. "Another book?"

"If it were, I would need to bring you a bookcase as your next gift. But no, it's something different this time."

She unwrapped the parcel to reveal a box. He watched her expression while she opened it. Lily withdrew a silver bracelet with a dog charm hanging from the chain, and her face softened. "Oh, Matthew. It's as if you captured the image of Sebastian." She raised shining eyes to him, and her happiness filled him up with satisfaction. He helped her put on the bracelet, and her hand rested upon his. "It's wonderful."

When he held her fingers captive, she hesitated. "I fear I will stain your hands with my ink." Her face flushed, but he didn't let go.

Instead, he rubbed his thumb across her knuckles. "I'm hardly worried about ink, Lily." He cupped her cheek, tilting her face up as he kissed her lightly. "I am very glad we don't have a chaperone yet," he murmured against her mouth. "I've missed kissing you." He started to deepen the embrace, but she pulled back.

Lily's cheeks were flushed, and she rested her hands on his shoulders. "I—I don't know where my mother is," she stammered. "I wonder if she's feeling well today."

Matthew didn't know whether he'd frightened her or overwhelmed her. But he relaxed his hold, not wanting to pressure her. "Am I making you uncomfortable?" He guessed he had pushed her too far when he'd touched her the last time.

She rested her hands upon his chest, meeting his gaze. "I feel a bit like I've been tossed through a storm. I hardly know what to think."

He stroked back a fallen strand of her hair. "I am courting you, Lily. I want to start again and rebuild what we once had."

She hesitated and covered his hand with her own. "I do want you to be well and whole again, however long it takes."

He understood then that this was about trust. She didn't know if he would fall back into the darkness in which he had been imprisoned. "I was a different man when I was taking those medicines," he admitted. "I haven't touched any since then, and it has helped."

"It wasn't the medicine that wounded your spirit and your mind," she reminded him.

"No. But I have shut out that part of my life. It needs to stay in the past, and I won't think of it again." He believed that it was the best way to move on and let the nightmares remain where they belonged.

She was silent for a time, but her hand moved across his heart. "A part of me wants to agree and pretend that everything is back to the way it was before you left." She raised her eyes to his. "But neither of us is the same person. And I don't believe locking away bad memories will make them go away. I'd rather face them with you."

"I won't ever speak of what happened in India." It was easier to behave as if that time had never existed.

She studied him with a pensive expression. "It might help you. But I will not ask it of you. I'm only afraid of what will happen if you lose yourself again."

"It will not happen," he swore. "I have no reason to take laudanum or opium anymore." He leaned down and kissed her lightly. "All I want is to spend time with you, Lily. I feel more like myself when you are near."

Her hazel eyes softened, and she answered, "I am glad of it. And I hope that each day grows easier."

Matthew wanted to ask her to marry him but sensed that they were still rebuilding trust. He drew back slowly but kept her hands in his. Before he could say anything more, Lady Penford entered the drawing room. She smiled at the sight of them and said, "Lord Arnsbury, you are looking well."

The dog went up to Lily's mother and sniffed her skirts, his tail wagging. From her lack of fear, it appeared she was having a lucid day. Matthew nudged Sebastian aside and kissed Iris's hand. "It is good to see you, Lady Penford." She wore a light-blue day dress and a rope of pearls around her neck.

"Have you asked my daughter to marry you yet?" she inquired, smiling at him.

Matthew returned the smile and saw Lily's hesitant expression. "Not yet. I need to be certain she will agree before I ask her."

"Nonsense. You were nearly married once before." Iris turned to her daughter. "Don't you want to marry Matthew again? You told me you had always planned to marry him again, once he returned from India."

"I—I might. I don't know." She seemed to be grasping at reasons to delay her answer. "I should finish this correspondence course for now."

Matthew reached for Lily's hand. "I see no reason why you could not finish it after the wedding." He squeezed her hand lightly and leaned in to her ear. "Play along, Lily. Let her have a little joy." Her face relaxed when she realized he had no intention of pressuring her into marriage.

"I quite agree," Iris said. "Perhaps you could wed next month. That would give you enough time to have the banns read."

He winked at Lily and asked, "What do you think?"

She looked at her mother, and a slight smile spread over her face. "It might be better to have a Christmas wedding in a few months. It's rather cold and rainy just now."

"Oh, I *do* like that idea." Her mother beamed. "We could have a wonderful party with holly and a fir tree lit with candles."

Matthew released Lily's hand and bowed to her mother. "And dancing." He offered his hand, and Iris took it. He led her in a country dance to the end of the room, and as he spun her, the older woman laughed with delight. Sebastian barked, his tail furiously wagging as if he wanted to join them.

But it was the gentle understanding in Lily's eyes that caught his attention. She knew he was trying to bring a bit of light into Iris's life, a moment of happiness. And when he bowed to Iris at the end of their dance, she sank into a chair, still laughing.

"Oh my. I haven't danced in years, I don't think." She reached for a fan on a side table and opened it, fluttering it in front of her face. Sebastian trotted toward her and rested his face in her lap. Lady Penford rubbed his ears, still smiling. Then she reached into a fold of her skirt. "I'd nearly forgotten. Calvert asked me to give you this note. It's from Evangeline Sinclair." She held it out to her daughter.

Lily stepped back and tore open the note. She read aloud:

Dear Lily,

I fear my dog is dying, perhaps of boredom. Annabelle lies next to the hearth all day, doing absolutely nothing. Will you bring Sebastian and perhaps we could take them both on a walk?

Warmly,
Evangeline

At the very mention of the word walk, Sebastian perked up, his tail wagging. Though his broken leg now seemed to be healed, she had not attempted much in the way of exercising him. Lily bent down. "Would you like a walk, Sebastian?"

The dog's excitement grew, and he danced in a circle, as if he understood their conversation. Lily smiled at his antics. "Well, then. I suppose that's my answer." She rang for Calvert, and when the footman arrived, she gave orders for the carriage to be brought around. "Sebastian will be coming with me. I will need his collar and leash."

"Do you and Evangeline need someone to accompany you on the walk?" Matthew offered.

Lily shook her head. "I'm certain that Evangeline will

want to gossip freely, so not this time. We will take our footmen with us, though."

"I will bid you good day," he said, kissing her hand. But he held it a moment longer. "Your mother's idea of a Christmas wedding is a good one, Lily." He slid his signet ring from his finger and pressed it into her palm.

She blushed, her expression filled with joy and uncertainty. "I will think upon it, Matthew."

"Thank you for coming over to look at my dog," Evangeline said, leading Lily inside their townhouse. Sebastian appeared delighted to visit, and he sniffed at the carpet, his tail wagging furiously. "I've been wondering if Annabelle is ill. She's hardly moved from the fireplace in a week."

"I am glad to look at her for you," Lily said. Though her studies had only a little information about dogs, she was beginning to see the similarities among the animals.

From the moment she entered the sitting room, Sebastian's demeanor transformed. He pulled hard on the leash, struggling to reach Annabelle. The plump cocker spaniel eyed him with suspicion, and Sebastian crouched low with his tail in the air, desperate to play.

"I think we should take them both for a walk now, don't you?" Evangeline suggested. She reached for a leash and slid it over her dog's head. "Annabelle is quite fat, and I've no doubt it was caused by sitting and eating all day long."

Lily wasn't so certain, but before she could get a closer look at the dog, Evangeline's father, Cain Sinclair, blocked the doorway. "And just where d'ye think you're going, Evangeline?"

"Lily and I are taking Sebastian and Annabelle for a walk."

Sebastian sniffed at Annabelle's backside, his tail wagging. Then he trotted over to Evangeline's father and rolled to his back, exposing his belly.

A faint smile creased the man's mouth. "You're a braw lad, aren't you, dog? A fine animal indeed." Then he turned back to his daughter. "Your mother told me that Thomas Kingford, Viscount Burkham, intends to pay a call on you this afternoon. She's wanting you to stay."

Evangeline's face turned pained. "Lord Burkham was once betrothed to Rose, have you forgotten? He abandoned her when she was ill."

"Aye. But your mother said he isn't so bad."

"He's a fortune hunter, and I will not let him court me," Evangeline insisted. "Not to mention, Mrs. Everett has sunk her claws into him. She intends for him to wed her daughter. Good riddance, I say."

Mr. Sinclair did not seem at all disappointed in his daughter's reluctance. "If you wish to never marry, that's all right with me, lass." Evangeline only rolled her eyes and said nothing. Then Mr. Sinclair added, "What of you, Lily? Have you decided upon a husband as of yet?"

She decided to tease her friend. "I've had an offer from Lord Arnsbury," she confessed with a smile. "I am thinking about it."

Evangeline's mouth dropped open. "Do you mean to say that Matthew asked you to wed, and you didn't tell me? You let me go on about dogs when your life is about to change?" She appeared aghast at the idea.

"I haven't said yes, Evangeline." Because he'd only said it to soothe her mother, she wasn't certain it was a true offer—but then again, he *had* given her his signet ring again. She wore it beneath her gown on a chain around her throat.

"Oh, but you will." She looped her arm in Lily's and smiled at her father. "Please give Mother my excuses. Lily and I must be off now so I can learn everything and talk her into the marriage." She tugged upon the leash, but her dog planted herself firmly upon the floor and refused to budge. In exasperation, Evangeline picked her up.

"Take a footman with you," her father warned. "And be back within two hours, or I will come to collect you." Although his words were spoken calmly, Lily was well aware that Mr. Sinclair was an overprotective father.

"So we shall." Evangeline kissed him on the cheek. "Though we both know you will send three men to guard us. Goodbye, Father."

Lily gave a slight tug on the leash for Sebastian to join them, and the dog followed behind.

"Thank you so much for coming to call," Evangeline breathed. "I know Mother means well, but I have no desire to let Lord Burkham court me. The man is empty-headed and not at all suited to me." Her friend stepped inside the carriage, arranging Annabelle at her feet. "Now tell me everything about Lord Arnsbury. Leave nothing out."

While Lily filled her in, Sebastian leaned his head outside the carriage, his enormous tongue lolling out. His ears flapped in the wind, and she held on to him to ensure that he didn't go leaping out.

When they reached Rotten Row, the carriage slowed to a stop. Evangeline disembarked with the help of a footman, but when she set Annabelle down upon the pathway, the dog lay down on the ground and did nothing. Sebastian, in contrast, was anxious to be off, after being confined indoors for so long.

"Would you care to trade your dog for mine?" her friend suggested. "Mine has become terribly lazy."

In answer, Lily held out her leash. Evangeline traded with her, and Lily picked up the cocker spaniel for a closer look. She was indeed plump, but the reason for her excess flesh was exactly the reason she suspected. The dog was quite pregnant.

"Evangeline, I believe Annabelle—" Before she could finish her sentence, Sebastian perked up and began sniffing the ground. He pulled hard on the lead before he made his way toward a gentleman. Then he tore his way free of

Evangeline and jumped up with his paws on the man's shoulders.

"Oh, dear!" Evangeline seized her skirts and hurried to retrieve Sebastian. Lily kept Annabelle in her arms and joined her, praying her dog wouldn't hurt the stranger.

"Stop it, Sebastian!" she called out.

But then she saw that the dog was licking the hands of a tall blond gentleman. "My goodness," Evangeline breathed. She stopped running and touched her heart.

When Lily drew nearer, the man was laughing and petting Sebastian's head. He gave the dog something from his pocket and then turned to smile at the women. "Now there's a good boy."

The moment she recognized him, Lily's face fell. It was John Wilson, the Earl of Davonshire. It had been months since she'd spoken to him last, and then, only in passing. For a moment, she wondered what to say to him. Finally, she offered, "I'm terribly sorry, Lord Davonshire. The dog got away from us."

The gentleman's smile tightened, and he tipped his hat. "Lady Lily." The awkwardness seemed to fill the space between them. "I am glad to see you again."

But all Lily could think was the heartbreaking notion that Sebastian *knew* Lord Davonshire. He was petting her dog and behaving as if *he* were the true owner.

"It has been a long time," she managed. Then she handed Evangeline's dog back to her. Sebastian was still licking Lord Davonshire's fingers, utterly delighted with himself. And the earl appeared just as happy to see the dog. That didn't bode well at all.

"Have you met Sebastian before?" she asked. "You seem to know one another." The dog continued to circle the gentleman, his tail wagging furiously.

The man snapped his fingers, and her dog instantly lay down. "Louis, be still."

Louis? Was that his true name?

"I beg your pardon. What did you call him?" Lily ventured.

Lord Davonshire turned back to her. "Louis ran off weeks ago and was lost. We could not find him anywhere until now." He offered her a grateful smile. "I believe I am in your debt for taking such good care of him." He leaned down and gave the dog another treat from his pocket.

A harsh lump rose up within her throat, for Lily had never considered the possibility of losing Sebastian. She bit her lip to hold back tears, feeling bereft.

He glanced over toward the place where Evangeline had been standing. "Was I mistaken, or didn't you have a companion with you?"

It was then that Lily realized Evangeline had disappeared. She was no longer standing on the pathway—instead, she was hiding behind a shrub.

"Miss Sinclair is rather shy," Lily explained. She thought about calling Evangeline to come and meet Lord Davonshire, but then again, her friend might be humiliated by all of this. She returned her attention to Sebastian, kneeling beside him. When she ruffled his ears, he rolled to his back, exposing his stomach for her to rub.

"You know his favorite spot to be touched," Lord Davonshire remarked. "And I can see that you've taken good care of Louis. I am eternally thankful for it."

She tried to hold back her tears, but she had grown attached to the dog in the past two months. The lovable Sebastian had stolen a piece of her heart, and frankly, she didn't want to give him back, even if he did belong to Lord Davonshire.

"How long have you had him?" she ventured.

"Three years. Ever since he was weaned as a pup," he answered. "He was large, even then."

But something about his words rang false. She could not recall her father ever mentioning a dog when he went to the residence of the Marquess of Chesham. Then, too, Sebastian's leg had healed quickly—suggesting that he was younger in age. He behaved like a dog of one year instead of three.

Yet there was no denying that Sebastian was sniffing Davonshire's pockets and seemed excited around the man. It was indeed possible that he was the dog's true owner.

"I am sorry," Lily said, feeling foolish. "It's just that I rescued Sebastian from the streets when he was hit by a carriage. I've grown very fond of him."

"He is a favorite of mine. I have two other dogs, but none so fine as Louis." His blue eyes warmed as he spoke of them. "I am so glad to have him back again."

She leaned down to study the dog, trying to decide what to do. The earl gently pressed the dog down and gave him another treat.

"I will miss him desperately," Lily admitted. "I can't bear the thought of going home without him." Her heart was shattered at the thought of losing this animal who snuggled at her feet. He was the first creature she had ever saved, and she loved him. But she understood Sebastian was not hers.

With regret, she remained standing in place while Lord Davonshire bowed to her. "Lady Lily, I am most thankful for your good care of my Louis. If I may pay a call upon you from time to time, perhaps I might bring him to visit?"

"Yes, of course." But her voice broke with emotion. The earl removed Sebastian's leash and handed it back to her. She leaned down and hugged the dog, unable to stop her tears when he licked her face. She ruffled his furry ears and stood, feeling utterly bereft. "I would like to see him to know that he is well."

Lord Davonshire took her gloved hand and held it for a moment. "And I would like to know that *you* are well." With a slight smile, he added, "Our fathers were such good friends, after all."

From behind her, she heard Evangeline's intake of breath. Although her friend was fascinated by the earl, Lily didn't feel the same way at all. She had been so frustrated by her father's attempts at a betrothal, she had no interest whatsoever in Davonshire. Not like her feelings for Matthew.

"Until we meet again." Lord Davonshire released her fingers and turned back on the pathway with Sebastian trotting at his side. The dog obeyed his master without question. Although Lily she knew she had made the right choice for him, it hurt so badly to let him go.

Evangeline emerged from the shrubbery and returned to her side. "I'm so sorry, Lily."

She blinked back her tears. "So am I."

Chapter Twelve

Matthew entered his family's townhouse and gave his hat and gloves to a footman. The servant took them and added, "My lord, Lady Arnsbury is taking tea in the drawing room. She asked if you would join her when you returned home."

"So I shall." He crossed through the hallway until he reached the blue drawing room. The wallpaper was the color of a robin's egg with drapes that were white and blue. He saw his mother seated upon the settee, and her expression brightened when he arrived.

"Matthew, I am glad you were able to join me." Charlotte poured him a cup of tea and added sugar, offering it to him. "I've been wanting to speak with you."

His first thought was of Miss Carlisle. Had the woman carried out her threat of spreading stories? Matthew took the cup and joined his mother, sitting across from her. "What is it? Has something happened?"

She paused a moment and said, "I wanted to see how you've been...feeling during the past few months. We haven't truly talked in a while."

He understood what she meant now. Ever since the night when he'd fallen into despair, his mother had hovered over him, afraid he would do the worst. And the truth was, after he'd hurt Lily, his own life had seemed useless and wasted.

"Each day grows easier," he admitted. "Sometimes the nightmares come, but I have found that I am now able to sleep at night."

"And you are eating again." Charlotte smiled warmly at him, offering a plate of sandwiches. He took one to satisfy her, though he wasn't truly hungry. "You do not know how worried we were."

It had been a dark time, but he did believe Lily's forgiveness had helped. "It was not easy."

Charlotte poured herself a cup of tea. "And how are things with Lady Lily? Dare I hope that we can post the banns soon?"

"I have asked her to marry me," he admitted. "But she has not yet agreed."

At that, his mother set down her cup. "Why ever not?

Because she does not yet trust me, he thought. But he managed an excuse, saying, "She is studying veterinary medicine."

Charlotte stared at him as if he'd confessed that Lily was trying to grow wings. "Why on earth would she do that? Is she interested in horses?"

"Lily prefers smaller animals, such as dogs. She saved the life of a Landseer, and she also gave me that Beast of my own." He nodded toward the kitten who had wandered inside the drawing room and was poised to attack the furniture. Matthew leaned down to scoop the kitten into his lap.

"I hope you will continue to court Lady Lily," his mother said. "I like the girl and her family. She is good for you, Matthew."

"She is. And I intend to keep paying calls on her."

A strange look crossed his mother's face, one that held a hint of wickedness. "It may sound Machiavellian, but I would not hold it against you if you were to seduce the girl."

He said nothing, for he'd already done that two years ago. It had been passionate and impulsive, and he'd made promises of marriage that he'd fully intended to keep upon his return.

But both of them had changed over the years. And though he wanted her by his side, he understood her wariness.

"Lily is a good woman," he reminded his mother. "And I intend to win her heart on her own terms."

"With flowers and jewels?" Charlotte prompted.

"No. With books and pamphlets on veterinary medicine."

His mother let out a rueful sigh. "You, my dear son, have much to learn about how to court a woman." Charlotte rose from her chair and came to embrace him. "And do not delay too long, for I should like to have grandchildren before I die."

Though her tone was teasing, his mother was in her mid-sixties now, and he understood her desire for babies. As for himself, he wasn't entirely ready for children. At least, not yet.

"Time will tell," was all he could say.

"By the by, I am concerned about your cousin Adrian. I hear gossip that he has considerable gaming losses."

"If he does, that is on his shoulders, not mine." He had never particularly liked his cousin.

"It's just that...he is spending as if he will come into a large sum of money."

Matthew's mood turned grim, and he wondered if Sarah Carlisle had spoken to him or to anyone else about his birth. "Because he believes he might somehow inherit my title?"

Her face paled and she returned to her seat. "H-how can you imagine such a thing?"

Matthew set down his cup and leaned forward, resting his arms on his knees. It struck him that his mother appeared more worried than enraged. There was no anger—only fear. And so, he pried a little deeper.

"A woman named Miss Carlisle paid a call upon me a few

weeks ago," he began. "She spoke of a payment my father gave her on a yearly basis. A blackmail payment. Now why would Father allow this?"

He wanted to see his mother's outrage and denial. He wanted to hear from her own lips that there was nothing wrong. But Charlotte's hands were shaking, and she did not answer. He waited, then demanded, "Well?"

"I—I don't know." Her voice was tremulous, and she would not look at him. Something was wrong, something she would not say. And God help him, he needed to know if there was any truth to Sarah Carlisle's claims.

He pressed again, "Why do I have brown eyes, Mother? I don't look like you or my father."

He expected her to speak of a grandparent, but instead, her face blanched. "Close the door, Matthew."

A sudden coldness iced through him, but he obeyed. When he turned back to her, he saw that she was staring down at her hands. She looked all the world like a woman suffused with guilt.

No. He did not want to believe any of this. He wished he had not brought it up, but now, it was too late to go back. He needed the truth, even at the risk of his inheritance.

His mood darkened, and he demanded, "Is it true? Am I a bastard with no claim to the earldom?"

"Your father formally recognized you as his heir," she said quietly. "But please...do not ask any more questions. Let things be as they are. Your father and I treasured you, and you were raised to be the earl."

He felt as if the floor beneath him had buckled, his life torn apart by her words. "Is that woman my mother?" he gritted out. "Did she have an affair with my father, and is that why he paid her?"

"N-no," the countess insisted. "Matthew, I swear to you, she is not your mother. Your father was never unfaithful to me."

He didn't believe her. The terror in her eyes and her visible fear revealed far more than he wanted to know. And he would have the truth now, even if it meant confronting the woman who threatened his very future.

"How do I look?" Evangeline breathed. Instead of wearing the ball gown the color of mouse fur, she had chosen a soft rose silk. Around her throat, she wore a chain of diamonds, and two tiny pink roses were tucked into her black hair. "Will Lord Davonshire notice me, do you think?"

Already half of the gentlemen had noticed her, but Lily feared it was because of the diamonds around Evangeline's throat. Everyone knew of her wealth, and many unscrupulous men might try to take advantage of her.

"You look beautiful," Lily told her. And her friend had indeed transformed. Evangeline's cheeks were flushed with excitement, her eyes bright with the prospect of meeting the earl.

"Will he be here this evening, do you think? Lord Delicious, I mean."

"Lord Dog Thief," Lily corrected. Although she knew it was right to surrender Sebastian into his hands, she felt the loss of the dog keenly. She missed the enormous animal trying to snuggle against her while she read her books and the patch of drool upon her skirts.

"He did not truly steal Sebastian," Evangeline reminded her.

"Oh, I know it. But I do miss my dog. He was mine, even if only for a short time." Her heart was still wounded at the memory.

"Annabelle had her puppies last night," Evangeline said. "If you would like one, I can give you one of your own, once the puppies are old enough to be weaned. A new Sebastian, if you like. Although this one would be much smaller."

Her friend's offer was so generous, but Lily didn't know if she was ready for a new dog yet. "Perhaps."

Evangeline squeezed her hand in silent sympathy, and Lily forced away the sadness. "Do promise me this. If Lord Davonshire *does* attend this gathering, you cannot hide yourself behind the drapes."

"I might faint," her friend warned.

"Were I you, I would visit with other ladies and gentlemen before he arrives. Then, at least, you'll be ready for a conversation."

"I will never be ready," Evangeline murmured. "Not for a man like him." She let out a heartfelt sigh, fanning herself.

"I suppose you have given up on James, then?" It did seem that Evangeline wanted nothing more to do with her brother.

But her friend's demeanor shifted into sadness. "It's not really giving up when he had no interest in me in the first place."

There was nothing Lily could say to that except, "I'm sorry."

Evangeline braved a smile before it suddenly faded. "Oh goodness, Lord Magnificent is here." She fanned herself rapidly and clutched Lily's palm with her other hand. "What should I do?"

"Try smiling. He might come and speak to you."

But Evangeline's expression was pained. "I never should have hidden in the shrubbery that day. He might come talk to you, but never to me." She closed her eyes. "I should go into the hallway by the stairs and collect myself."

"You are not going anywhere." Lily tightened her grip on Evangeline's hand. "Calm yourself. Take a deep breath and count to ten."

The young woman made a valiant effort, but she seemed unable to resist her urge to disappear. Thankfully, after a few moments, she seemed to gather her composure. And that was likely because Lily had not released her hand.

But Lord Davonshire did not approach. Instead, Matthew's cousin, Adrian Monroe, walked toward them. He wore a black evening tailcoat with a snowy waistcoat. Mr. Monroe bowed to them and then turned to Evangeline. "Miss Sinclair, would you care to dance?"

His invitation was the last thing Evangeline expected. Her expression resembled a gaping fish, so Lily intervened and handed her friend over to Mr. Monroe. "Of course, she would." It was far better for her friend to dance and distract herself from Lord Davonshire. "Enjoy yourself, Evangeline."

Adrian tucked her gloved hand in his arms and winked at Lily. "And will you save a later dance for me, Lady Lily?"

"If you wish." It did seem that Monroe had recognized that she wanted only friendship, and she was grateful for that.

For a moment, she stood among the wallflowers, watching over the dancing. There had been a time when she had remained among them because she had not wanted any man to court her. Now, she wasn't so certain. When she glanced back to where she had last seen Lord Davonshire, she now saw Matthew.

His heated gaze fixed upon hers, and she felt the echo of an invisible caress upon her bare skin. The very sight of him unnerved her. He knew her intimately, and it was as if the rest of the crowd had disappeared, until only the two of them stood before one another.

Lily had made a conscious effort to distance herself over the past few weeks, declining all invitations. She needed him to trust her with the truth before she could give him her heart without reservations. And indeed, with each day she was apart from Matthew, she found herself missing him more and more. He had been kind enough to continue sending her the books on veterinary medicine, but the books only augmented her loneliness.

Right now, she wanted to cross the room and embrace him, feeling his strong arms around her.

You are so weak, she told herself. She wanted to believe that his mind had healed from the torment he had endured. And yet, his unwillingness to tell her anything about India suggested that he had buried the past instead of trying to face it.

He watched her for a time, a slight smile curving upon his mouth. She met his gaze, realizing how much she cared for this man.

Lily heard a slight sound behind her, a woman's cry of dismay. It distracted her enough that she turned to see what it was. She saw her mother standing in the hallway, just beyond the ballroom. What on earth was Iris doing here?

"I did not realize you were attending the soiree this evening, Mother."

But when she came closer, she saw that Iris was wearing a day dress and not an evening gown. Around her neck, she wore a chain of dried daisies, and her gaze was distant. "The wolves are circling, Lily. And I fear they have come for me."

Lily's heart froze, and she moved beside her mother immediately. "I am here, Mother. I am sorry you aren't feeling yourself. I'll summon the carriage and take you home."

"No, you mustn't leave," Iris said. "He will be here soon."

Lily didn't bother to unravel the mysteries of her mother's conversation, nor did she ask who "he" was. Instead, she reached out to take her hand. Iris was not wearing gloves, and her palm was ice cold. "Will you walk with me, Mother?"

"They're circling...all around," she breathed. "Don't you see them? They will devour us all."

Desperately, Lily looked around in case Matthew had come any closer. Or even her brother, but neither could be found. She needed someone to help her escort Iris outside before anything happened. Right now, the madness had overtaken her mother, suffocating out all reality. If Lily tried to force her to leave, Iris might protest and make a scene.

When she tried to tuck her mother's hand in her arm, Iris pulled back. "It's not safe here, Lily."

"What isn't safe?" came a deep baritone voice. Lily turned and saw Lord Davonshire standing nearby. He smiled warmly, but she was afraid of what her mother might do. "Is everything all right, Lady Penford?"

"It's nothing," Lily answered on her mother's behalf. She needed to send him back to the ballroom before her mother's condition worsened. "Lord Davonshire, I fear my mother is not feeling well. I am about to take her home."

But then her mother took another step back. "Who is that man, Lily? Why is he here?"

She tried to keep a serene expression on her face. "I know you remember John Wilson, the Earl of Davonshire, Mother."

But there was no response at all. Her mother was staring off into the distance, one hand upon the stair bannister. *Oh no.*

"Forgive me, Lord Davonshire, but I really must take my mother home. She is quite ill."

He inclined his head. "I understand. But before you go, you should know that Louis misses you."

The tightness in her gut twisted, and she wished he had never mentioned the dog. "I miss him, too," she confessed. While she spoke, she kept an eye on her mother, in case Iris attempted to run.

"He seems to be searching for you," Lord Davonshire said. "And he keeps trying to sit in my lap."

Lily managed a smile. Though she wanted to ask him more questions, her attention was focused upon Iris. "I am glad to hear that he is well."

Lord Davonshire turned to Iris and saw that the older woman was still staring off at the end of the hallway, utterly silent now. "I beg your pardon, but your mother seems—"

"Yes, I know." Though she was trying not to panic, Iris's behavior strongly resembled that of a woman caught within a trance. "I really should be going now."

"Then allow me to accompany you both home. It would be no trouble."

No doubt Evangeline would be terribly disappointed if she agreed to such a thing. "Thank you, but no. We will be fine." Then she added, "When we met the other day, my friend Evangeline Sinclair was too shy to meet you. She is here this evening, and I know it would mean the world to her if you asked her for a dance."

The earl's attention rested upon her for a moment. "And would it mean a great deal to you if I did?"

This conversation was not at all going the way it should. She didn't understand why he would be so attentive. Their engagement two years ago had been concocted by their fathers, and after George died, they had mutually ended it. Lily needed to make it clear that she was not at all interested. "Lord Davonshire, I think you should know that—"

A piercing scream tore from her mother's mouth. "No! Please! Help me!" Iris clenched her hands at her sides and broke into a run toward the ballroom.

Lily raced after her. The moment Iris entered the crowd of people, all conversation ceased. Her mother continued to scream, and Lily felt utterly helpless. The madness was upon her, and nothing she said or did would make any difference.

But then, Matthew emerged from the crowd. He crossed the room and caught hold of Iris, speaking in a low voice. Gently, he guided her away from everyone. Lily had never been more glad to see him. She hurried to catch up to them and overheard him murmuring apologies to their host.

In that moment, she realized that this was the sort of man he had always been. He didn't care about what others thought or about what they would say. He knew her mother needed help, and he gave it without hesitation. And despite her fears that his mind had not healed from his ordeal in India, she was grateful to him now.

When Lily reached them, she lifted her eyes to his and whispered, "Thank you."

"Do you want to stay?" he asked. "I can take her home for you."

She shook her head. "I wouldn't dream of it."

Behind her, she was well aware of the whispering. While many of the ladies knew that her mother had retreated from society, the family had managed to carefully hide her madness—but no longer. Lily wished she could undo the past few minutes, but the damage was done. They needed to bring her back to Penford into seclusion. And it hurt to think of it.

Matthew rested his arm around her mother's shoulders while Iris sobbed about the wolves. "They're here. All around me, ready to devour me alive. And I cannot stop them."

"We will protect you," he said, as they guided her outside. Lily asked a footman to bring around the carriage, and he did so.

She had mistakenly believed that her mother's condition was improving, for she'd had more moments of clarity. But now it was clear that Iris would never be the same.

Lily wanted to weep for the mother she'd lost, wishing she could bring back the woman who had taught her how to dance and how to make daisy chains.

They guided her inside the carriage, sitting on either side of Iris so she could not break free again. Her mother's gaze was fixed outside the window, and beneath her breath she was murmuring to herself.

"I need to take her back to Yorkshire, to Penford," Lily said. "We cannot stay in London."

"I will go with you," Matthew said.

She ventured a smile. "Now what sort of scandal would that cause? Though I appreciate your offer, we both know you cannot."

"I am not staying with you," he pointed out. "I will make other arrangements with my cousin Amelia. She does not live far from you, I believe."

His offer took her by surprise, and she studied him in the

darkness of the carriage. "Why would you do this, Matthew?"

"Because you need help. Your sister is married and in Ireland. Your brother has the estates to manage, and this has fallen upon your shoulders."

He meant it. He truly intended to come with her to Yorkshire, whether she wanted him to or not.

"James will accompany us, since Parliament is out of session," she reminded him. "It isn't necessary."

"Do you want me to come, Lily?" His voice was low and deep like a caress in the darkness.

Her wayward heart soared, for she could not deny the feelings that continued to rise up. She ought to tell him no, that her family would manage her mother and do what was best.

And yet, she could not stop the whisper. "Yes. I do want you to come with us."

His thumb slid against her palm, making gentle circles. It felt as if he were touching bare skin everywhere, though it was only beneath her glove. Had her mother not been with them, she believed he would have kissed her.

"Then I will be there with you."

"I understand you are leaving for Yorkshire."

Matthew turned at the sound of his cousin's voice. He was walking toward his London townhouse when he spied Adrian approaching. The man wore a russet striped waistcoat and a black coat with dark trousers. He carried a walking stick with a silver handle, while a sly smile spread over his face.

"I am traveling for a short time," he agreed. "A fortnight or so." In fact, he had ordered his servants to begin packing his belongings for the visit. God willing, he would return to announce an engagement between himself and Lily. But he knew his cousin was not here to exchange pleasantries. More likely, the man intended to ask for money, given his gaming debts. "What is it you want, Adrian?"

"A question that is best explained over a drink and perhaps a round of cards," his cousin suggested. "Let us go and talk at White's. We will toast your good journey."

Matthew wanted to refuse. He had no desire to spend time with Adrian, especially given the threat of Miss Carlisle's blackmail. His cousin might try to use that information to his advantage. But Matthew still didn't know the entire truth. He should have pressed his mother for the answers, but she had been so distraught, he had held back.

Worst of all, Charlotte had not denied the rumors. It felt as if his entire childhood had been a lie, and he didn't know how to react. Though Matthew doubted he would lose his inheritance, Adrian could cause a scandal that would destroy his mother. The man was a wastrel who would ruin the family. Matthew could not stand aside and let him do such a thing.

"Well?" his cousin prompted. "Shall we go?"

"Fine." He followed his cousin along the street, the tension stretching taut within him. The London air was thick with the scent of poverty and unrest. When he passed a group of street urchins, it struck him hard that he could have come from that. He could have been born from anyone, adopted into his parents' home.

His mother had sworn that Sarah Carlisle was not his mother. But their eyes were the same, as were their features. He had no interest in giving Miss Carlisle a single penny…and yet, she held the answers he needed.

Adrian opened the door to the gentleman's club and entered the smoky room. Several men greeted them, and Matthew raised his hand in greeting. His cousin chose a table far away from anyone else and ordered drinks for them.

Once they arrived, Matthew took a drink and sat back, studying his cousin. Why had he never noticed that they looked nothing alike? He resembled no one in his family, not with his dark hair or brown eyes.

Adrian raised his glass. "To your journey, Cousin."

Matthew did the same, noticing the gleam of interest in the man's eyes. "Why did you want to speak with me?"

His cousin drained the rum. "I've heard a number of stories recently that I find fascinating. In particular, about your mother, Charlotte. Did you know she was barren for over ten years? And then suddenly...you came along."

He knew precisely what his cousin was implying. But he could not allow Adrian to threaten the only family he had left. Whether or not he was a bastard didn't matter—what mattered was protecting Arnsbury and his mother.

And so, he parried Adrian's verbal strike with one of his own. "My father was overjoyed when I was born. He was glad to have a son."

"*Is* that who you truly are?" his cousin said silkily. "Or were you a convenient child adopted at the right time?"

Matthew leaned forward, making sure Adrian understood him. "My father, the Earl of Arnsbury, acknowledged me as his son to everyone. I became the earl upon his death, and he never had any doubts of who I was."

"Perhaps he should have asked more questions," Adrian said. He met Matthew's stare openly. "I understand a mutual acquaintance of ours, Miss Carlisle, was most disappointed that you refused to pay her annual pension. I, on the other hand, am prepared to reward her handsomely for her assistance."

It was time to end this conversation. Matthew stood from the table and looked down upon Adrian. "Lies and stories will not change what is. I am the Earl of Arnsbury, and nothing will alter that."

Adrian rose from his place and gave a mocking smile. "We shall see."

Chapter Thirteen

It was a hard truth for Lily to accept that her mother was not getting better. Although Iris had experienced periods of melancholy before, none had been as bad as this.

The leaves had fallen from the trees, and Lily admired the beauty of late autumn as she walked through the estate at Penford. Her mother had secluded herself from the outside world, although Lily had tried to coax her to take walks. Her sister had promised to visit from Ireland soon, and perhaps that would lift Iris's spirits.

In many ways, Lily rather wished she had Sebastian with her, for the dog had been a gentle presence in their lives. She still felt the ache of loss, though she knew he belonged with his owner. One day, she would get another dog of her own.

She shielded her eyes against the morning sunlight and saw a rider approaching. The sight of Matthew made her smile. True to his word, he had accompanied them to Yorkshire, and he was staying at the residence of his cousin Amelia Hartford, the Countess of Castledon.

Lily waved, and he dismounted, leading his horse by the reins. He wore a chestnut riding coat and a black silk hat. She found herself studying the horse, noting the animal's health. She had mailed in the remainder of her assignments for the correspondence course under Matthew's name, and the newest books involved the health and care of horses.

"You are looking beautiful today, Lady Lily," Matthew greeted her. "Would you like to come riding with me?"

"In a little while," she agreed. "But first, there is something I would like to show you."

Matthew gave his horse over to the coachman, Nelson, and followed her. "I have been asked to bring you to Castledon for tea today. Amelia's daughter Verity demanded it."

"Is something the matter?" Lily asked.

"One of her pets is quite ill, and she would like you to take a look at it." Though his tone was serious, Lily detected a note of amusement in Matthew's bearing. "Iris is welcome to join you, of course."

"We both know my mother is incapable of making such a journey now."

He nodded. "I suspected as much, but the invitation stands. Bring your maid, Hattie, if you want."

She led him toward the walled garden, wanting him to see it. "I suppose, but it is a long ride."

"Amelia would be quite grateful if you could examine Verity's...pet."

Again, the odd smile on his face. She was instantly suspicious of it. "What is it you're not telling me, Matthew?"

He shrugged. "You'll find out for yourself soon enough. And I look forward to seeing your methods of helping the animal."

"It's not an ordinary pet, is it?" She suspected that whatever ailment the animal possessed would be one she was incapable of curing.

"Not precisely."

Lily could have pressed the subject but decided not to. "All right. I will come for tea." She led him inside the garden, pushing open the doorway. The grass had turned brown, and the rosebushes had been pruned down to bare canes. Still, the chrysanthemums and primroses offered color amid the dying plants.

A pool of water rested near a willow tree. Lily pulled her shawl across her shoulders and leaned down to dip her fingers into the water. "I wanted you to see my parents' garden. It's even more beautiful in spring." She lifted her dripping fingertips from the water and smiled at him. "What do you think?"

Matthew barely looked at the garden, and instead, his attention was focused upon her. "It is beautiful, yes." He moved closer to her and framed her face with his hands. "Just as you are." He brushed a fallen lock of her hair back, leaning in to steal a kiss. "I want you to marry me, Lily."

Her heart should have rejoiced at his words. Yet the shadows of the past were still there, and she could not forget the haunted man he had been.

"If you had asked me months ago when you returned from India, I would have said yes without hesitation."

"But you can't forget that I hurt you." His mood turned grim, though he caressed her cheek. "And you won't forgive me for it."

"That's not it." She caught his hand and drew it down. "You became someone else that day. And it wasn't only the opium—you were lost somehow."

"I am stronger now," he told her. "It won't happen again."

"But you still will not tell me what happened to you in India. I know it was terrible. But I don't think you will get over these nightmares until you speak of it."

He nipped at her mouth. "I know a better way to get over the nightmares." His tongue slid against the seam of her lips, and the heat of his kiss brought a rise of sensation throughout her body. She held on to his shoulders, feeling her knees soften.

"How?" Her voice came out soft, filled with yearning she could not deny.

"By replacing them with better dreams." He kissed her more deeply then, inviting her to fall beneath his spell. The autumn air was crisp, but she hardly felt the chill with his warm, hard body pressed to hers.

She was drowning in this man, feeling all her boundaries melt away until she could not stop the heart-pounding desire.

"I thought we were going to your cousin's house for tea," she murmured, trying to catch hold of her thoughts.

"We can be late." He offered a wicked smile, moving his hands over her waist. She closed her eyes, feeling the rush of longing. But reality intruded, and she forced herself to step back.

"No. It will take an hour or so to ride there." She rested her hands against his coat, but he tipped her chin up and stole one last kiss.

Then he slid his hand against her throat, touching the silver chain she wore. He gently tugged at the chain until he pulled the heavy gold signet ring from beneath her gown. The metal was warm from her bare flesh, and he held it for a moment. "Because you're wearing this, I can only assume that you will think about my proposal."

He was right. In spite of his demons, she did still love this man. But her feelings had reshaped into a deeper understanding of who he was. Matthew wasn't the perfect man she'd believed him to be, but he knew her in a way no one else did. Her throat constricted with emotion, and she could only bring herself to nod.

"I will think upon it."

"How is your mother, Lily?" Amelia asked, pouring a cup of tea. Matthew's cousin, the Countess of Castledon, had a warm smile and mischief brewing in her eyes. Her blonde hair had streaks of gray, and the fine lines around her eyes spoke of a woman who had many reasons to smile.

"She had a setback in London." Lily saw no reason to hide it, for likely Lady Castledon already knew of this. "We brought her to Penford to recover. My brother is staying with her now."

"I am sorry to hear of it. I had sent an invitation asking James to attend the hunt, but he sent his apologies."

"He wanted to look after our mother," Lily explained. But it suddenly occurred to her that James had been declining many invitations, keeping to himself—just as Matthew had done.

She had not thought about what her brother had encountered in India. He might have more of the answers she was seeking. Lily sipped at her tea, letting her mind drift.

The countess offered them refreshments, and before long, a young girl stood at the doorway of the drawing room. She cleared her throat, and Lady Castledon brightened. "There you are, Verity. Come inside and meet our guests."

The girl looked to be about twelve or thirteen, caught in the awkward stage between girlhood and adolescence. Her hair was pulled back in a long dark braid, and her blue eyes were clear and thoughtful. She gave a slight curtsy, and when she was introduced to Lily, her expression turned pleading. "Mother says that you are studying veterinary medicine."

"I am," Lily agreed. "I am mostly interested in dogs and cats, but I've studied a bit about horses."

The girl's face turned grave. "I hope you can help Mathilda. She's been so sick. Papa tells me it's no use, but I want to believe that she'll get better. Will you look at her please?"

"I should be glad to." Lily gave her a reassuring smile, though she wasn't certain exactly what she was promising.

"Good. If she doesn't improve, I fear the worst may

happen. She may become luncheon." A tightness clenched her cheeks. "I cannot endure it."

Luncheon? She could only guess that Verity's pet was a pig or perhaps a lamb.

Amelia lowered her gaze, but her attempt to hide her mirth did not go unnoticed. Verity glared at her mother. "It's not a laughing matter! Mathilda is very dear to me and has been since she was little."

Lily stood from her chair. "Shall we go and look at her now? I can make no promises, but I will try." She considered which books might be of use. It was possible that the animal had consumed tainted food and had become sick.

She had brought a bag with her including a few instruments Matthew had purchased from the college. One of the newer devices was a Laennec stethoscope made of wood. She had found it quite useful in listening to Sebastian's heart and lungs.

Verity appeared quite relieved. "Yes, of course. I will take you outside."

"I will come with you," Matthew said. Amelia did the same, rising from her chair.

After a footman brought their cloaks, Lily followed the young girl out of the house toward the barn. Outside, frost coated the ground, and her breath formed clouds in the air. A young pony was tethered nearby, but Verity walked past it and pushed open the barn door. "I had to keep her somewhere safe so the dogs wouldn't try to eat her."

Lily continued toward the stall that Verity opened. Inside, upon a nest of hay, she saw a reddish-brown hen.

"Is this...Mathilda?"

The young girl nodded. "She's been sneezing and struggling to breathe for a few days now. My older brother, Edward, claims that she's only fit for soup." Tears welled up in her eyes. "He's hateful. I've had Mathilda ever since she hatched as a chick. I would never cook her and eat her."

Matthew was smirking. "What do you think, Lily? Can you cure this *fowl* disease?"

She wanted to groan, and he winked at her. Truth to tell, she knew very little about chickens—but she was not about to let this young girl cry over her pet. She knew how easy it was to form attachments, poultry or not. "I will try."

Lily knelt beside the chicken. "Can you hold her and bring her out where there is more light?"

Verity nodded. "Yes, I will." She lifted the hen into her arms, and the animal sneezed. The ailment was clearly lung related.

Verity brought the chicken out of the stall. Lily decided the best course of action was to give the animal clean water, good food, and to keep it isolated from the other animals.

When they reached the edge of the barn, Verity stopped and held up the chicken. "There. Do you want a closer look?"

Not exactly, Lily thought, but she didn't say so. Still, she examined the hen closely, trying to determine if anything was out of the ordinary.

The hen's feet were normal, and she saw nothing unusual about the feathers. There was a slight discharge from the chicken's nostrils and it sneezed yet again. *Rather like a cold*, Lily thought.

But she knew that diseases in animals could spread rapidly, and there were no known cures for these ailments.

"How long has she been like this?" she asked Verity.

"About a week. She isn't eating or drinking the way she should." Verity appeared troubled. "I don't know what to do."

"I'll need to do some reading. But in the meantime, be sure that she is kept away from other animals. Her drinking water should be completely pure, and she must be kept in a clean area." Lily thought a moment about the chicken sneezing and added, "We can make a solution of salt water and wash her nostrils with it. It may help."

"Thank you, Lady Lily." Verity bobbed a curtsy. "I will do as you say." She hurried back to the barn with the hen.

Once the young woman was gone, Matthew touched the small of Lily's back. "That meant a great deal to her."

"I don't know anything about chickens."

"Perhaps not. But you do know about kindness. And for her, it was enough."

One week later

"Lily! She's here!" Iris burst through the bedroom door, not even bothering to knock.

Lily was startled at her mother's intrusion and asked, "Who is here?"

"It's Rose and Iain." The happiness glowed upon her mother's face, and she seized Lily by the hand. "You must come and see them."

Lily followed her mother down the stairs and was delighted to see that her mother was right. Her sister and her husband had written a few weeks ago of their plans to visit Penford, and they had just arrived. Calvert escorted them into the drawing room where her grandmother was waiting.

"Isn't it wonderful?" Iris exclaimed. The joy on her face made it impossible not to smile. Lily hurried forward and embraced her sister. "It's so good to see you, Rose." Then she hugged her brother-in-law. "And you, Iain."

He returned the embrace. "It's good to see all of you again." The Irishman was tall with striking dark hair and deep-blue eyes. "And Lady Wolcroft, you're looking very fine indeed."

"Just so." Mildred nodded regally. "I am glad you have come to visit, though it must have been a long journey."

Though Iain smiled warmly, there was a trace of worry on his face toward his wife. Rose leaned upon her cane as he helped her into a chair.

"How long will you stay with us before you have to return to Ireland?" Lily asked, pulling up a chair beside her sister. It was then that she noticed Rose's pale complexion. Was it her imagination, or did her sister seem sickly? Iain rested his hands upon his wife's shoulders, idly stroking a lock of her hair.

"I am not certain," Rose said. "Perhaps a few weeks." She exchanged a look with her husband, but Iain was having none of it.

"Possibly until the spring," he contradicted. "I would prefer that Rose stays at Penford where she can rest and recover."

"I am not ill, Iain." She covered his hand with her own and then blushed. To all of them, she admitted, "You would think a woman had never had a baby before. Iain's just a wee bit overprotective."

Iris began to cry tears of joy, sobbing into her handkerchief and laughing as she went to hug her daughter. "Oh, Rose. I am so glad for both of you."

Lily waited until her mother pulled back and then reached for her sister's hand. "This is wonderful news. I wish you both all the happiness in the world."

"Thank you. I wanted to tell you sooner, but Iain insisted that we come and share the news on our visit." She narrowed her gaze at her husband. "I think he has the half-brained notion that I must be secluded for most of the year, tucked into bed where I must do naught but stare at the walls."

"It would be safer than staying at Ashton," he admitted. "Our tenants are surviving, but the rest of the country is still facing famine. I fear that they may try to steal the food we have. I won't risk Rose's safety."

"I will not be separated from you," she insisted. "It is my place to remain in Ireland, and we will stay there together."

But Lily could see that her sister's husband did not feel comfortable with the idea of Rose being in danger. "We will discuss it further when you feel better."

Calvert brought in a tea tray with refreshments, and Iain took a sandwich for his wife. Rose sipped at her tea but only picked at the bread crust.

"The first few months are not easy," her grandmother said. "I remember when I carried Iris. I was sick every day from dawn until I went to sleep at night. The doctor told me I would only be sick in the mornings. Bah! It was all day, every day for four months." Mildred smiled at Iain. "A man could never endure what we women face."

The Irishman's expression tightened, and he appeared uneasy about Lady Wolcroft's revelation.

"I cannot say I am enjoying it," Rose admitted, "but when the baby comes, I am certain everything will be fine." Iain did not seem to share her confidence, but he did take a chair on the opposite side of his wife.

"And what of you, Lily?" Rose asked. "Has Matthew's health improved at all?"

She nodded. "He is better, yes. Though, as you can imagine, he is reluctant to venture back into society."

Rose met her expression evenly, and Lily didn't know what to think of that. Her sister seemed to read beneath her thoughts somehow. She glanced at their mother and then back again, silently conveying the reason for their retreat to Penford. Rose smiled and nodded her understanding.

They were about to go in to supper when Calvert announced, "Lady Wolcroft, your guest Lady Castledon has arrived for tea."

"I didn't realize she would be joining us," Lily remarked.

Her grandmother shrugged. "I did not find it necessary to

ask permission. If I want Amelia to be my companion at tea, I shall invite her."

But Lily knew better than to imagine that the two women were innocent. She suspected they were plotting something. But what?

When Calvert returned with their guests, he gave Lily a letter. "Lady Lily, this arrived for you just now." She thanked him and placed it in her pocket, intending to read it later.

The countess entered the room with her husband, Lord Castledon, and she greeted everyone with enthusiasm. "I was simply delighted to receive the invitation to tea today." She sat beside Lady Wolcroft and said, "Mildred and I are having a disagreement. I say we should tell everyone and let them decide."

Her grandmother rolled her eyes. "Amelia believes she is always right, as usual."

"Indeed," Lady Castledon agreed with a bright smile. "But I am certainly open to hearing other opinions. David thinks I intend to interfere in affairs that are none of my concern, but I told him it was nonsense."

"Of course you will interfere. It's what you do best, Amelia." Her husband shook his head as if there was nothing to be done for it. And yet, he did not seem bothered by the notion.

Lady Castledon laughed and winked at her husband. "I am quite good at meddling. I won your heart, didn't I?"

"You had your sights set elsewhere at first." David gave a slight smile. "But yes, you did. Even if you did accuse me of having the personality of a handkerchief."

At that, Amelia stood, crossed over to her husband, and touched his cheek. "I met my match, indeed. As for Lily here, I think we could move things along for her. *That* is the subject of my disagreement with Mildred. She believes Lily should find another man, whilst I believe Matthew Larkspur is exactly what she needs."

"I beg your pardon?" Lily gaped at Lady Castledon, wondering exactly what the woman was plotting.

But Amelia only smiled and turned toward Lady Wolcroft as if Lily had not spoken. "Yorkshire can be quite romantic in the autumn. And I believe Cousin Matthew is very much in love with Lily here."

Lily flushed at her words, uncertain of whether she wanted to be the subject of Lady Castledon's matchmaking. She sent a silent plea for help to her grandmother.

Mildred only shrugged. "Lord Arnsbury already made a mess of things. He may not be worth it. *I* say she should reconsider Lord Davonshire. He is a future marquess after all."

"I disagree," Lady Castledon said. "Matthew suffered through an ordeal, and he needs the love of a good woman to see him through it."

The pair of women were discussing her as if she were not there. Lily turned to her sister. "Have I suddenly become invisible, Rose?"

"Oh, do let them go on. It amuses them to meddle. In the end, *you* are the one who will decide what's best." Rose shared a smile with Iain. "And I can highly recommend the state of matrimony. It is quite wonderful."

A pang caught at her heart when she saw the love between the two of them. Iain rested his hand upon the small of his wife's back. His concern for Rose warmed her, and Lily could not deny her own sense of envy that they were happily married with a child on the way. Rose was happier than Lily had ever seen her.

"Come to our estate in the morning, Lily," Lady Castledon urged. "David is going fox hunting with some of our neighbors, but Matthew does not wish to attend the hunt. He will be wanting company, and I thought you could stroll through the grounds."

"Ha. If Amelia had her way, she would have you strolling

through dark corridors with no chaperone," Lady Wolcroft sniffed.

"There is no need for a chaperone in the gardens," Lady Castledon said. "Anyone could see them from the windows. You, yourself, could watch over them from the comfort of your chair."

"Amelia, I think she could do better than Lord Arnsbury. Why not introduce her to some of your neighbors? Surely one of them might make a better husband. Have you invited them to the hunt?"

"I *am* still here," Lily reminded them, but neither seemed to notice. "And I *am* capable of making my own decisions."

"Pish tosh," her grandmother said. "Look where that got you the last time."

Lady Castledon narrowed her gaze, as if she knew what had happened. Clearing her throat, she said, "Lily, please do come to my house tomorrow. I am certain Cousin Matthew would be quite glad to see you. Rest assured, I do not intend to go out riding in pursuit of a poor, helpless fox." She reached out and patted Lily's hand. "Just come and enjoy our company."

"As long as you aren't fawning over Lord Arnsbury," Lady Wolcroft added. "You should choose another gentleman instead. Perhaps a duke, if you can find one."

"The only duke of my acquaintance is married to my sister," Amelia said. "And I don't think Victoria would appreciate anyone casting eyes at Jonathan."

Lily was quite finished with their discussion. "I am busy enough with my studies." She raised her chin and regarded them with a firm this-matter-is-closed look.

"Do you want to place a wager, Mildred?" Amelia said. "Fifty pounds if she weds Lord Arnsbury. I'll give you the same if she does not."

Lily gaped at the venture, appalled they would suggest such a thing.

"Prepare to lose, Amelia," Lady Wolcroft said. "For I intend to give every last penny of your wager to Lily."

"We shall see about that," Lady Castledon answered with a smile.

Chapter Fourteen

The next morning, Matthew rode out alone while the other gentlemen went on the hunt. He had no interest in fox hunting, and Lily had promised to meet with him later today. The autumn air was crisp with the scent of damp leaves and an underlying chill. He could see traces of his breath in the air as he rode toward Penford.

Matthew spied Lily approaching with her footman, and she smiled when she saw him, lifting a hand in greeting. Her hair was tucked up beneath her black hat, and she wore a deep-green riding habit. The color accentuated the red undertones in her brown hair. He slowed his horse until he reached her side, and pulled the stallion parallel to her mount. "Good morning."

"And to you." Lily's smile remained, and a faint blush rose upon her cheeks. "I see that you decided not to join the others in the hunt."

"Cousin Amelia thought I should spend time with you instead. I agreed with her." He took her hand and kissed it.

Lily motioned for her footman to ride ahead to Castledon,

giving them privacy as they rode at a slower pace over the next few miles. It took nearly an hour, and she relished being in the company of the man she loved.

"Will you check on Mathilda once we arrive?" he asked.

Lily appeared embarrassed. "I know nothing about chickens, Matthew. I do hope she isn't dead yet. I should hate to disappoint Verity." She winced and added, "But yes, I will see if she has improved at all."

The air of trouble lingered upon her face, and he asked, "Is everything all right, Lily? How is your mother?"

She tried to shake away her mood. "The same as ever. But there is something I wanted to talk to you about. I received a letter yesterday from your cousin Adrian."

Matthew stiffened at the mention of the blackguard. No doubt his cousin was attempting to spread more stories in an effort to gain control of Arnsbury. But he forced himself to ask, "What did he say?"

Lily slowed the pace of her horse as they drew nearer to Castledon. "He warned that you have been lying to me, and said that *he* is the rightful Earl of Arnsbury." She turned to him. "Matthew, what is he talking about? Why would he say something like this?"

Anger flared within him, but he kept a tight control over it. The last thing he wanted was to frighten Lily. Instead, he kept his voice calm.

"Adrian has been jealous of me all his life. There are some rumors that he's trying to feed to raise himself up—primarily for his own monetary gain. He can never be the earl, and he knows this."

Once they arrived, Matthew dismounted and summoned a groom. Then he helped Lily down from her horse. The groom took both animals away, and Matthew guided her toward the kitchen gardens to have a moment to speak in private. The herb gardens were withering away in the frozen air, but there were still a few patches of rosemary and mint. A gravel pathway led through the gate, and he stopped at the edge of the garden.

"My mother and father struggled for many years to have children," he told her. "Adrian wants everyone to believe I am not their legitimate heir."

He didn't reveal the possibility that it could be true, for he had few answers right now.

Lily took his gloved hand in hers and squeezed it gently. "I am sorry he is causing trouble for you."

"I won't allow him to spread rumors that will harm my mother." He suspected Adrian's letter was meant to sow the seeds of doubt in Lily so she would not consider marrying him. It seemed he had no choice but to return to London to put a stop to his cousin's schemes.

For now, he wanted to distract Lily from her worries. He lifted her wrist to kiss it and caught the scent of oranges. "You smell delicious," he said, pressing his mouth to the underside of her wrist.

"It was a breakfast indulgence," she admitted. "Oranges are Mother's favorites, and James managed to get some from Italy, though I'm not certain how."

He lowered her hand, softly stroking the pulse point of her wrist. But before he could answer, a resounding gunshot broke the stillness. Then another.

Lily jolted at the sound. Matthew dropped down, instinctively shielding her, though he was certain the shots were not close to them. She was trembling with fear, and the sight of her terror transformed him.

His heart pounded, and a rushing noise filled his ears, though there was silence surrounding them. It felt as if the rest of the world fell away, and he was plunged into an icy cold pool of memories.

The unwanted visions roared through him with the force of a locomotive. His vision blurred, and he was dimly aware of Lily's presence. A dull rumbling resounded, and the echo of the gunshot reverberated in his mind. Lily's face twisted into the face of his torturer.

Tell me where your soldiers are, and your pain will end.

I do not know.

Then the horrifying agony of white-hot pain made his back seize. He closed his eyes, trapped within the nightmare. Just as before, he felt as if he were drowning, caught up in a prison of the past. Even his skin was wet, though he could not tell if it was sweat or rain.

But this time, the scent of oranges broke through the nightmare.

He clung to the aroma, and a part of him became aware that he was not in India, but in England. The mossy ground beneath his fingertips was not desert sand, and he struggled to fight off the vision. The muddy scent of the earth, coupled with the falling rain, forced him to see the truth.

It isn't real.

Someone was speaking to him, and he fought hard to listen to the words.

"Matthew, you're safe," he heard Lily say. "I am here."

He lowered his face to her wrist, breathing in the scent of oranges again. The citrus tang pulled him back until his awareness returned. He breathed slowly, steadying his heartbeat. Her hands smoothed his damp hair, and he held her close, forcing his mind to be still.

"Are you all right?" he asked her.

"I should ask you the same." Her worried hazel eyes stared at him. "I was startled by the gunshots, though I should have expected them."

"The shots reminded me of India. It provoked another memory." He realized they were both sitting on the ground. It was raining steadily now, and Lily's hair was damp against her throat. He needed to take her inside, out of the bad weather.

"But this time, it was different. You did not stay lost in your visions." Her voice was gentle, and she took his hand in hers. "You came back to me."

It was the scent of oranges that had done it. Or perhaps it was Lily's presence that broke through the past. Regardless, it was a small victory to know that he had not fallen into the darkness this time.

He kissed her hand, not knowing what to say. Then she leaned down and kissed his mouth. It was reassurance and love mingled in the touch of her lips, and he deepened the kiss. He hardly cared that the entire household could see them from the windows or that they were being rained upon.

He cradled her face with his hands, savoring the taste of her mouth until at last, she pulled back. "Will you ever tell me what happened to you?"

He gripped her hand and nodded. Somehow, he felt that she was right. If he told her everything, it might help alleviate the bad memories and lay them to rest. "I will, yes."

He stood up from the ground, helping her do the same. "But first, I would like to get out of the rain and have a glass of brandy. Would you join me?"

Lily smiled in answer, taking his hand.

❧

Lady Castledon clucked her tongue at the pair of them when they returned inside. "I cannot believe this weather. Ruining everything, isn't it? Now then, let's get you both something hot to drink, and you will want to sit by the fire."

"Actually, I would like to change my riding habit first," Lily said. "But I know Lord Arnsbury wished for brandy."

"In a moment, dear, in a moment," the countess reassured them. "Come into the library. There's a warm blaze going, and I'll bring the brandy."

Lily rather felt like she was being tossed back into a storm, for Lady Castledon took her hand and led her down a narrow corridor, followed by Matthew. It was a longer walk than she'd imagined, and the library was nowhere near the main rooms of the house. Instead, it was tucked away in the west wing, in its own corner.

Inside, she found it to be much nicer than she'd imagined. As the countess had promised, there was a bright fire in the hearth, as well as a chaise longue with comfortable pillows. Lady Castledon poured them each a glass of brandy, though Lily would have preferred hot tea.

"Now, if you'll sit here and relax, I'll see to it that you have some food." Lady Castledon smiled warmly and walked back to the door.

"I'm really not that hungry," Lily protested.

"Nonsense. I will send a footman with food. Wait here." And with that, the countess left the room, closing the door behind her. She had an air of triumph, and Lily could not imagine why.

"Is it me, or do you feel like she's up to something?" Lily walked back toward the door, wondering what was happening. She opened it, not wanting to start gossip by being alone in the library with Matthew. It was quite possible that Lady Castledon was trying to win her bet by causing a scandal.

"If it's Cousin Amelia, you can be sure she's always up to something." Matthew sipped at his brandy and leaned against the fireplace mantel.

Lily tried not to stare, but she was transfixed by the handsome planes of his face. The rain had darkened his hair, and she felt the sudden urge to touch it.

"I should probably go," she murmured, as she reached for her own glass. Though she normally didn't indulge in spirits, she worried about Matthew's troubled interlude earlier. He still suffered from the visions, though it did seem that he could control them better.

She drank a small sip of the brandy, and it burned down

her throat, warming her from the inside. "I'll see if Lady Castledon has some dry clothes I can borrow."

There came a knock at the library door, and a footman entered, carrying two large baskets. "These are from Lady Castledon, with her very best wishes."

Lily's suspicions heightened, for it was too soon for a servant to return with food, given the distance to the kitchen. "Isn't the countess going to join us?"

"She must attend to her other guests. But she bade me give you this note." The footman gave Lily an envelope and departed, closing the door behind him. Lily thought she heard an odd click, but it must have been her imagination.

"I don't like this, Matthew. She's matchmaking again—I'm sure of it. She and my grandmother made a wager about us." Lily held up the note, which was sealed with wax. "She would not have had time to write this or to assemble the baskets."

"It certainly seems that way." He walked toward her. "Why don't you read her note, and we'll find out what Cousin Amelia is up to?"

Lily broke the seal and began reading.

Dearest Cousin Matthew and Lily,

Please do forgive me for interfering, but I could not stand by and allow two people so deeply in love to walk away from a life together. Lily, I know how Matthew cares for you, and Matthew, I know how long Lily waited for your return. Perhaps my methods might be rather scandalous, but I hope you might see this for what it truly is—a chance to be together.

Yours,
Amelia

"I'm almost afraid to open those baskets," Lily said. "And what does she mean, she doesn't want us to walk away from a life together?"

"I told her that you have not yet accepted my marriage proposal." Matthew moved to the door and turned the knob. With a grim expression, he turned back to her. "It's locked."

"Oh, good Lord." Lily lifted her gaze to the ceiling, feeling exasperated by the situation. "I cannot believe she would do this." She had expected Lady Castledon to meddle and try to match them up together. But this was going too far.

Matthew rolled his eyes. "And of course, she chose a room far away from the rest of the house. We would have to shout to the rafters for anyone to hear us. I imagine Amelia has given the servants orders to ignore us." He studied her. "What do you want to do?"

Her riding habit was sodden, and she stood up, shivering. "I don't know. I need to think first."

He noticed her discomfort and asked, "Are you cold from the rain?"

"A bit." Lily moved a chair over beside the fire. With a sigh, she said, "Well, I suppose we should see what's in the baskets. Perhaps it will give us an idea of how long she intends to leave us here."

A part of her feared that Amelia was intending to keep them locked away for the rest of the afternoon. Or even worse, all night. She tried to think of how many people knew she was here and realized it was only her immediate family and Amelia. No one else had seen her.

Matthew opened the first basket and withdrew a bottle of wine. "It looks as if my cousin has packed enough food for the rest of the day." Then he pulled out another bundle wrapped in cloth. "I believe we have bread and cheese here, some cold meats, and a cake." One by one, he withdrew parcels and set them upon a nearby table. "One thing is certain—we won't starve."

Lily opened the second basket and found several vials of what looked like oil. Then there were pieces of a sponge and...was that a length of black silk? "What on earth is this for?"

Matthew eyed the contents of the basket and grimaced. "No one could accuse Cousin Amelia of subtlety."

Lily had no idea what he was talking about. "I don't understand. Why would she put this silk in here? Is it meant for a napkin? And what is this bit of a sponge for?"

Matthew's shoulders were shaking, and he took the fabric from her. "She's only matchmaking, Lily. It's nothing to worry about. Don't pay it any heed."

But she was still curious about it. She returned to stand by the fire while Matthew unwrapped the rest of the food. A part of her knew they ought to call out for help or, at the very least, attempt an escape.

And yet, she was not entirely displeased by having a few hours alone with Matthew. It *would* give her the opportunity to hear what he had endured in India. She felt as if it might exorcise his demons, allowing him to share his burden. If a scandal ensued, so be it. Only a few knew she was here, and his cousin Amelia was part of the matchmaking.

Lily removed her bonnet and set it aside. Her hair was wet and hanging against her shoulders, so she removed several of the pins.

Matthew was still holding the black silk, and he approached her slowly until they both stood by the fire. "Do you want to leave, Lily? I could break the door down, if need be."

She felt a tremor slide over her, and her skin prickled with gooseflesh. "Not yet." Her voice came out in a whisper, and she let her hands fall to her sides. "Unless you want to."

"Not yet," he repeated. He leaned in and rested his forehead against hers. "I know you have not yet given me an answer to my proposal. But if we stay here, it will cause talk."

"I know it." She drew her hand to rest upon his cheek. "But I want you to tell me about India. I need to hear it before I can marry you."

"You may not want to marry me after you hear it," he admitted.

"It haunts you still. And perhaps it will ease your burden if you share it." She traced her fingertips over his rough cheeks, feeling the stubble of a growing beard. His brown eyes were fixed upon hers, and in them, she saw hunger and desire. The intensity of his gaze speared through her, and he drew his arms around her.

"Do you know why Cousin Amelia locked us inside this room?" he murmured. His warm hands slid down her spine, before he cupped her hips and drew them close. She could feel the hard ridge of his arousal, and her breasts peaked beneath her chemise and corset.

"I—I think so. She wanted to force us into marriage."

"Through seduction," he clarified. "That second basket is filled with everything necessary for lovemaking."

Her mouth formed an O, and she blinked a moment. "Well. That wasn't at all what I was expecting."

He stole a kiss, his mouth nipping at hers. A hundred questions filled her mind, but she silenced them. His kiss evoked such strong memories of the past, of the man he had once been. When his tongue slid against her lips, she welcomed it, feeling the echo of desire between her thighs.

"There are extra clothes in the other basket," he told her.

The thought was tempting, but she was still uncertain about what would happen between them. "Pour some more brandy," she told him. "And then start at the beginning. I want to know what happened when you were in India." She had a feeling she would need spirits to fortify her courage.

Matthew stepped back and returned to the table. He poured two glasses of brandy, handing one to her. "You should sit down, Lily."

She chose a chair beside the fire and gestured for him to join her. He did, pulling his chair so close to hers that their knees touched. Lily took a sip of the brandy by way of a distraction. The second glass went down easier, and it warmed her throat.

Matthew set his glass on the table but did not touch it. In the firelight, she could see the troubled lines of his face and the scar across one cheek.

"James was angry with your father," he said quietly. "George wanted him to take more responsibility, to bury himself in the affairs of the estates. Your brother was young and wanted to live his life before being shackled to the earldom."

"He didn't know our father was sick," Lily said. "Or he wasn't willing to acknowledge it."

"I think he suspected...but he wanted to deny it. Both because he didn't want the earldom, and he didn't want your father to die."

"He just told us he was leaving," Lily said. "With hardly any warning at all. All he said was that he wanted to expand our interests in India."

"James wanted to prove his worth," Matthew continued. "He told me he wanted to rebuild the family's wealth by reaching beyond England."

"But you don't really believe that," Lily said, resting her hands on her knees. "I think he was running away." Her brother had no reason to pursue wealth, but she'd sensed that he was restless and eager to cast off the chains of the earldom. And he hadn't wanted to face his father's death.

"I agree. And that's part of the reason why I followed him. I suspected if he left England alone, he would never return."

She reached for Matthew's hand, and his fingers closed around hers. "I am grateful you did."

"He was like a younger brother to me," Matthew admitted. "I thought I could watch over him and bring him back to your family."

His expression was pensive, and she wondered if he was ready to talk about what he had endured. "Will you tell me more about what happened when you arrived in India?"

Matthew kept her hand in his, but his gaze fixed upon the

wall. She didn't press him, but simply held his hand and let him say anything at all. He took a breath and finally began. "I knew the East India Company was trading cotton and spices. There were profits in that. But one of the sailors was talking of rubies and sapphires. He convinced James to go out on his own in search of the gemstones, even though I warned him not to trust the man."

He shook his head. "The man was always shadowing us. I should have listened to my instincts. I still believe someone hired him to harm us, though I can't prove it."

Matthew's face turned somber, and his face tightened. "The sailor led us all the way toward the northern border of India. He wanted to separate us from the others."

Lily reached out to take his other hand, for Matthew's voice had grown quiet. "Was that how you were captured?"

He nodded. "I thought at first that the sailor meant to ransom us or use us as leverage against the English soldiers in India. But he sold us to a group of rebels."

Deep inside, she felt the chill of his words. A part of her didn't want to hear any more, but he needed to let go of the memories and share his burden.

"Go on," Lily murmured.

Matthew released her hands and stood, as if he could no longer be still. He drank the entire glass of brandy before he crossed the room and went to stand by the window. The drapes were closed, and his form cast a shadow over them.

"They took James first. I don't know what they did to him or what they said. But all I could think of was finding a way to get us out."

He moved toward the table, poured himself a second glass, and broke off a bit of cheese. "They kept me separated from James, and I had no water for two days. I thought I was going to die in chains. They had dug out part of a sand dune, and we were kept in the darkness. It felt as if we were buried alive.

"When they brought James back, they took me in his place.

We were not allowed to speak to one another. But I don't think he could have spoken if he'd wanted to. I don't know what was done to him, and I never asked."

He ate the cheese and rested his palms upon the table, looking down. "Those weeks were the worst I've ever endured."

Lily drank her own glass of brandy, steeling herself for the worst. She wanted to go to him, to wrap her arms around his waist and hear the truth. But she forced herself to stay back, to let him continue.

"The sailor who led us into captivity brought a woman to talk to me. She was beautiful and soft-spoken, but I could understand her English perfectly. Her name was Nisha Amat, and she seemed to know who I was." He paused. "She knew my title, and she spoke of my family members. When I asked her how she knew them, she said James had told her."

He shrugged. "It's possible he did. But she kept speaking of her husband and child, and she claimed they were taken by the British army. There was such...hatred in her voice. I knew she was lying, for what army would have any use for a child?

"I told her that, but it only enraged her." He lifted his gaze to Lily's. "She had a kind of madness in her that I'd never seen before. It was as if all her anger transformed into the purest evil. They deprived us of food and water, and offered it if we would betray one another. As the days passed into weeks, I started to lose my grasp on what was real and what was not. I tried to think of you and our life in England, but as they broke my bones and burned my skin, I realized I was never going to leave India alive. Nisha had no interest in answers—only torture."

He turned away and said, "She wanted both of us dead, but only after we suffered as much as she had. I don't know who took her husband and child, but she blamed the British."

"It's over now," Lily whispered. "She's gone, and you will never see her again."

He faced her, and his expression had a hard cast to it.

"That's not the worst of it, Lily." He paused a moment and said, "One night, she brought in a child."

Lily felt the tears rise to her eyes before they spilled over. The pain and guilt in his voice was agonizing. She didn't want to hear it, but she knew he needed to release the nightmares that haunted him.

"They blindfolded me, and I heard the little girl crying. Nisha told me they had taken her from a British family. If I would tell her where her own lost child was, she would return this girl to her parents. And if I refused to talk, the child would suffer instead."

His hands clenched into fists. "My mind was so broken, I couldn't even make up lies. I could say nothing at all, and they tortured an innocent child. I still hear her screams when I try to sleep at night." He lowered his head and admitted, "It's my fault she died."

Lily stood from the chair and went to stand by him. Matthew's face was haunted, grim lines of emotional pain carved into his face. She drew her arms around his neck and murmured, "There was nothing you could do."

"She wasn't even English, I learned later. They took a child from one of their enemies and used her to torment me."

She embraced him, resting her cheek against his pounding heart. "It wasn't your fault, Matthew."

"I still blame myself. Though I know Nisha was truly a madwoman, I wish I could have saved that girl."

Lily understood his pain, but there were no words that could change what happened. Instead, she held him close and let him take comfort in her arms. "How did you finally escape her?"

"James got out and brought back help to save me." His mouth twisted in a wry smile. "It's ironic, really. I left England because I wanted to protect him and bring him home to you. But in the end, he had to free me from captivity."

Lily traced the lines of his face, past the scar, framing his cheeks with her hands. "But you are both home now. And I am glad of it." She raised up on tiptoes to kiss him softly. Though she did not know if revealing the past would help him, she could only hope that sharing the burden would do him good. It would take time to overcome the harsh memories of India—but she loved him still.

"How are you feeling?" she asked.

He drew back to look at her. "You were right, Lily. It did help to talk about it. And despite all that has happened, I hope you don't think less of me."

She shook her head slowly. "I understand you better, Matthew. And it doesn't change the way I feel about you. If anything, I admire your courage. You survived at the hands of a murderer."

"I don't think I can ever forget what happened," he murmured. "Those memories will remain with me for the rest of my life."

"But I will be with you," she whispered. "And we will face them down together." The words were a promise she believed in. Her pulse pounded, but she wanted Matthew to know that her heart still belonged to him.

The library was dark, except for the fire in the hearth. His eyes were filled with desire and a hunger only she could sate. "I want that more than anything, Lily." He kissed her wrist and ventured, "If you will have me."

Both of them had changed over the years, but she wanted to believe she could heal the scars of his past. Her pulse thrummed in her veins, and she reached out to touch his face. He caught her hand, closing his eyes as if drinking in her touch.

And she was utterly lost to this man.

"Help me take off this wet riding habit," she whispered.

His expression grew heated, but he moved his hands to the buttons lining her back. One by one, he flicked them open. When he had undone five of them, he turned her to face the other way, lowering his mouth to her bared skin. With each button, he traced a path down her back with his lips. Shivers erupted over her flesh, and she understood what she had begun. There was no turning back now.

When her gown hung open, she faced him. Matthew helped her lift it away, leaving her in her corset, chemise, and petticoats. He lowered his mouth to her throat, kissing a path along her neckline.

"Help me," she whispered, untying her petticoats and turning her back for him to unlace the corset. Her body felt alive with need, and she remembered well what it was to lie beneath him, to take him inside her. It felt like that hurried wedding night, when she had first given herself to him.

No, it had not been a true wedding, but they had spoken vows to one another. And she could not let him leave for India without those promises. In her heart, he had been her husband, and he had sworn to love her.

After she had stepped out of her numerous petticoats, Matthew slid the laces from her corset. She felt herself trembling with anticipation, until at last, she stood in her chemise and pantalettes.

"Your turn," she whispered, sliding the coat from his shoulders. His face was rigid with desire, and when she unbuttoned his waistcoat, he lowered her chemise to her waist, baring her breasts.

She felt herself flush but made no effort to hide herself from his view. Around her throat, she wore the silver chain with the gold signet ring.

Matthew slid his fingers beneath the chain, before he reached to her nape to unfasten the clasp. He removed the ring from the chain and held it for a moment. She was caught up beneath his spell when he held the ring between his fingers and traced the heavy gold over the curve of her breast. Slowly, he circled her nipple with the ring, and her areola tightened with the pressure of the metal. An ache rose between her legs, echoing the sensation.

Matthew removed his shirt, pulling her closer until her breasts touched his bare chest. Softness against hard lines, her cool skin against his warm flesh. Between her legs, she yearned for this man, needing his touch.

"Do you want to know what the black silk was for?" he asked. "Shall I show you?"

She felt a rush of nerves but nodded. Matthew took her by the hand and led her over to the chaise longue. Then he removed the rest of her clothing until she stood naked before him. His gaze lingered over her, as if he were memorizing every curve and line.

"You're even more beautiful than I remembered." He guided her to sit upon the chaise longue and picked up the black length of silk. Then he blindfolded her with it. "When you cannot see, the sensations are stronger."

He was right. Without her vision to guide her, she was only aware of the chaise longue beneath her body and his hands beside her face. Her skin prickled, her breasts straining in the chill of the air. Matthew traced his hands across her shoulders, and without warning, his mouth encircled her nipple.

A sharp spear of pleasure caught her unawares, and she grew wet between her legs. A moan escaped her, and she reached for Matthew, clutching his hair as he feasted upon one nipple, then the other. The scalding sensation of his tongue caressing her, coupled with the gentle suction, made her go breathless with desire.

"I remember this." She shuddered as a sudden arc of pleasure washed over her. "It feels so good."

He continued to suckle at her, and she cried out when his hand moved between her legs. She could see nothing, and the exquisite torment of his fingers touching her was deeply arousing. "You're like silk here," he said, brushing his thumb over a sensitive place. Then he slid one of his fingers into her wetness and sucked hard against her breast. She nearly came off the chaise longue, as a sudden bolt of ecstasy rippled through her. He continued his wicked torment, sliding his fingers in and out as he kissed one breast, then the other.

"Take off your trousers," she pleaded. "I want to feel your body upon mine."

"Soon," he promised. "We were so rushed on our first night together. I want to savor you right now."

Lily felt as if liquid heat were pulsing through her veins, her body arching involuntarily. His hands moved beneath her bottom, and he lifted her hips. For a moment, she could not tell what was happening. His hands remained beneath her, but she did not know what he would do next.

Then she felt the warmth of his breath between her legs. His cheeks abraded her thighs, and her mind went wild at the thought of what he would do.

"Do you want me, Lily?" he murmured. The gentle vibration of his voice was nearly her undoing.

"More than anything. Touch me, Matthew. Kiss me. Anything."

He seemed to guess what she wanted, and he lowered his mouth to kiss her intimately. She gasped, her fingers digging into the chaise longue, and sensations roared through her. She quaked as he worked the nodule above her entrance, his tongue exerting a gentle pressure. Deep inside, her body rose to his call, her body straining for the release she wanted.

"Please don't stop," she begged, when he started to kiss her inner thigh. He didn't listen, but kissed the other thigh, drawing his tongue away from what she wanted. She was trembling hard, seeking the rush that she had known before.

And when he took her again, suckling between her legs, she felt a shimmering pressure building higher and higher, echoing throughout her body as the release took her hard. She was shaking at the force of it, helpless to do anything but ride out the storm.

Matthew kissed her lower stomach, then removed her

blindfold. It took a moment for her eyes to adjust, but she stared into his brown eyes, treasuring this man.

"Take me," she said. "I want your body inside mine."

He removed his trousers and underclothing, moving atop her, though he was careful not to put his full weight on her. He raised her right leg to wrap around him, and poised his shaft at her entrance. "Are you certain, Lily?"

In answer, she moved her hands to his hips and pulled him within her. He slid easily, though it was tight after being without him for so long. There was no pain, only a slight stretching that felt as if he were coming home.

His face held wonder, as he sheathed himself. It was gentle at first, but her body welcomed his slow thrusts. He slid easily, and as he sank into her depths, she felt another pleasure building.

She guided his mouth back to her breasts, and she reveled in the feeling of his tongue caressing her nipple while he sank and withdrew. The chaise longue was narrow, and she closed her legs, crossing her ankles when he was embedded deep.

He hissed, his face taut. "God, Lily, I can feel your tightness. Don't move."

She loved pleasuring him in this way, and as she squeezed his length, his breathing grew harsher. "I need to go faster, Lily."

He gripped her hips, then pulled her to the edge of the chaise longue. He was half kneeling, but he managed to thrust deeply, sending a savage thrill of pleasure deep within her center. She was quivering now, meeting his hips with her own as he penetrated and withdrew.

She hadn't known it was possible to feel such mindless lust, but she gripped him with her legs, as he drove inside her.

Without really knowing why, she touched her own breasts, stroking the nipples, and it elevated her sensations, until she was keening for this man.

Matthew continued to thrust until she broke free of all else and shattered against him. She could hardly think or speak as her body erupted with a rush of tremors and her body milked his hard length.

He ground himself within her until she heard him groan, and his body released, his strokes penetrating in rhythm until he collapsed atop her.

Their skin was slick with sweat, and she could not tell where her body began and his left off. She hardly cared at all, but it felt as if the man she loved had finally returned to her. Emotion welled up so deeply, she struggled not to cry.

But he saw her tears anyway and wiped them with his thumbs. "I'm so sorry, Lily. I lost myself."

He started to pull away, but she refused to let him go. Her voice cracked in a sob, and she admitted, "I'm not crying because you hurt me. I'm crying because I missed you so badly. I love you, Matthew. Don't ever leave me again." She traced the lines of his back, feeling the scars there, and then moved until his body was fully embedded within hers.

"I won't," he swore. For long moments, they lay together, their heartbeats returning to a slower pace. "Am I getting heavy?"

Small aftershocks caused her body to arch against him, but she welcomed the pleasurable sensations. "I love feeling your body upon mine." She kissed him softly and added, "Thank you for telling me about what happened to you."

He framed her face and looked into her eyes. "I am not the same man after what happened in India. It changed me, Lily."

"You survived," she said softly. "And it's the only thing that matters."

"Will you marry me, Lily?" he asked. "I need you by my side." He slid his hands down to her shoulders and then to her waist.

She smiled and kissed him. "I do want to marry you. More than anything else."

Chapter Fifteen

The sky had darkened into evening, and Matthew lay with Lily sleeping atop him. Her skin was rosy, her body utterly pliant against his. He caressed her bare spine, and decided he would buy a new ring for her, a betrothal ring that would suit her.

He kissed her lightly, and her eyelids fluttered. "Must I get up?" She rolled to her side, and he held her close to keep her from falling off the chaise longue.

"I'm afraid so." He moved his hands over her skin, feeling more content than he'd been in a long time.

Lily sat up, and against the firelight, he drank in the sight of her. Her brown hair held a slight hint of red in the golden light, and he marveled at her beauty. She stood up and walked toward the table of food, breaking off a piece of cheese.

He came up behind her, kissing her throat. His body responded to her sensual form, and he drew her close, pressing his hardened shaft to her hips. He could not stop himself from cupping her breasts, his body rigid with need.

But she surprised him when she parted her legs and bent over the table. The invitation was unmistakable, and he stroked her erect nipples. The sight of her exposed opening was too much to bear, and he guided his shaft to her entrance. She gasped, but welcomed him into her body. He slid inside her easily, and the new position allowed him to go deeper. He clasped her hips, rocking inside her as he plunged and withdrew.

She gripped the edge of the table, backing against him in counterpoint.

He felt the pressure building within, the need to claim her as his own. Lily laid her head down and whispered, "I want you, Matthew."

He gave in to his dark desires, intensifying the rhythm. She squeezed him tightly as he thrust, letting the reckless storm take them. Lily convulsed against him, her breathing harsh as she panted against him. Her cries grew higher pitched, and when she seized around him, he erupted within her, spilling his seed. A guttural cry tore from him, and she shuddered with her own pleasure.

He held her close, and Lily rested her cheek against the table, before at last he raised up.

"I should be apologizing for that," he said, withdrawing from her body. "But I cannot be sorry." He caressed her bottom, and then slid his hands up to cup her breasts. She sighed when he stroked her nipples, and he slid his arms around her waist. "And I cannot wait to marry you."

She turned to him and kissed him. His tongue mingled with hers, and she smiled. "I will marry you whenever you wish, Matthew."

He kissed her hard, their bodies skin to skin, until she grew breathless. At last, he broke away, and she tried to calm herself. "As much as I love being here with you, we should probably get dressed. Heaven only knows when Lady Castledon will send someone to let us out."

She returned to the other basket and pulled out the clean blue gown from inside. Beneath it, she saw a corset and chemise, both made from sapphire silk. "I've never seen undergarments like these before," she admitted. "They're from Aphrodite's Unmentionables, don't you suppose?"

"I wouldn't doubt it." Cousin Amelia and her sisters had created the business over thirty years ago. Evangeline's mother, Margaret Sinclair, was now the owner. Their fortunes had been built upon an empire of scandalous corsets and chemises.

"Do you need my help?" Matthew offered. Though he knew little about helping with a corset, he guessed he could figure it out.

Lily pulled the blue silk chemise over her head and drew the corset around her waist, holding it in place. "Will you lace me up?"

He did, though he was afraid to lace it tightly for fear of hurting her. Then she stepped aside to pull on her pantalettes and petticoats. At last, she put on the blue gown. It was a plain muslin fabric, but it fit her beautifully, revealing the dip of her slender waist. Matthew came up behind her and gave her the silver chain with his ring upon it.

"I will get you a ring of your own soon," he promised. "Do you prefer silver or gold?"

She turned to him, fingering the heavy ring. "I would wear a bent horseshoe nail if it meant being with you, Matthew."

Her words warmed him, and he kissed her again. "Perhaps we will marry by Christmastide, if that will suit you."

She smiled. "Perhaps." Then she bent down and picked up her damp riding habit. When she went to peer inside the basket, she frowned. "Matthew, do you know what this is for?" In her hand, she held up a sponge. "It's too small for washing."

He choked back a laugh. "It's for...preventing the conception of a child." Feeling awkward, he explained about the sponge and vinegar.

Lily blushed and remarked, "I suppose it's too late for that, isn't it?"

"So it is." But he hardly cared. The idea of Lily becoming pregnant with their baby was a welcome vision. She would make a beautiful mother, and he wouldn't mind having a daughter with her smile.

Matthew donned his clothing once again, hardly caring about the damp fabric. Then he joined Lily at the table where they feasted upon bread and butter, cold roasted beef, cheese, and a dish of blancmange. The gelatinous creamy dessert wobbled as he spooned up a bite and fed it to Lily.

"I can't eat any more," she protested. "Really, it's enough."

He was about to pour her wine when there came a sharp knock at the door. Lily's face froze, and she stood. Matthew whispered, "Hide behind the drapes until I know who it is."

She moved behind the curtains, but the knocking resounded again.

"What is it?" Matthew called out.

"It's Amelia," his cousin said. "I am so terribly sorry to interrupt, but I've just received word from Lady Arnsbury."

A sudden coldness came over him, and he moved to the door. "Come in."

The key turned in the lock, and then he saw his cousin. Amelia's face had gone pale, and she handed him a note. "You need to return to London immediately, Matthew. Your mother is very ill."

It felt as if her words had cut him off at the knees. Despite the secrets Charlotte had kept, despite his birthright or lack thereof, she was still his mother. He had been in denial of Sarah Carlisle's claims, but he realized none of it mattered. Charlotte was, and always had been, his mother. Matthew would stand by her and their family legacy no matter what happened. He didn't want to face the reality that she might die soon enough. She had been in good health until now, and he hoped it was nothing serious.

Yet if the worst came to pass, he did not want the past to stand between them.

216

A rustling noise sounded from behind him. Lily emerged from her hiding place, and she murmured, "Of course, you must go at once."

He took her hand and squeezed it, thankful for her support. There was no question that she had to remain at Penford with her mother. But once matters were settled in London, he intended to marry Lily and retire to one of the more isolated estates.

"I will return as soon as I can," he promised. He ventured a crooked smile at Amelia. "And you can tell Lady Wolcroft that you won the wager."

After Matthew had gone, Lily returned to Penford, accompanied by her footman. All throughout the ride, she could hardly contain her scattered thoughts. Matthew wanted her to be his countess, and she believed they could now make a good marriage. The thought thrilled her…and yet, she felt a sense of worry for his sake. He had to rush back to London, and she prayed that his mother would be all right. Matthew had lost his father several years ago, and it would wound him deeply to lose Charlotte.

Lily wondered if she ought to follow him to London. Would he want her there? Or would her presence only invite gossip after her mother's outburst, weeks ago? Her thoughts were a muddle right now, even more so, now that she had indulged in a wild liaison in Amelia's library.

Her cheeks flamed at the memory. And no matter how she might try to justify it, the choice had been hers, and she did not regret loving him.

When she arrived home, she dismounted from her horse and gave her gloves and bonnet to the footman. As she walked into the house, she was startled to find her mother sitting in a corner of the hallway on the floor, shivering.

Lily sent a questioning look toward a servant, but he shook his head with regret. "It has been a difficult day for Lady Penford. Lord Penford said it was best if we leave her be."

She ignored him and walked slowly toward the corner so as not to frighten her mother. Iris was seated with her knees curled up beneath her gown. Her stare was glassy, and the sight of her made Lily want to weep. The mother she had loved all her life was trapped within a broken mind. No longer could Iris be the steadfast rock she could turn to. Instead, her mother was like a child again, in need of someone else to take care of her.

Lily lowered herself carefully to the floor, adjusting her skirts until she sat by her mother. For a moment, she said nothing, not wanting to frighten Iris.

When the older matron remained silent, Lily reached out and took her hand. Her mother's skin was thin with soft veins protruding from her hand. Her fingers were cold, and Lily held them, still saying nothing.

After nearly five minutes, Iris squeezed her hand. The gesture of affection was enough to break down her control, and Lily let her tears flow freely over her cheeks. She knew now that her mother would never return to London. Iris could not attend a wedding in a large cathedral while Lily spoke her vows to Matthew.

No, the wedding would have to be here. And perhaps that was right and fitting if they held the ceremony in her mother's garden.

"Would you like to join me for tea?" she whispered to her mother.

Iris didn't answer, but when she put her arm around her waist, her mother stood up from the floor. Lily helped Iris into the sitting room and guided her into a chair. Then she rang for tea and refreshments. The footman agreed to send for them, but before he left, Lily inquired, "Where is my sister?"

"She is in her room resting," he answered. "She was not feeling well today. Lord Ashton is with her."

"Did my mother hear of this?" The news might have sent her mother into a decline if she was worried about her unborn grandchild.

"Unfortunately, Lady Penford did learn of it and was most upset. She feared Lady Rose would lose the baby."

"And?" Lily raised her eyes to the servant who shook his head.

"Your sister will be fine. Lady Rose said it was merely dizziness and exhaustion." He excused himself and went to fetch the tea.

Lily was relieved to hear it. Once the footman was gone, she pulled her chair closer to Iris. "Did you hear what he said, Mother? Rose is going to be fine. She's only resting. The baby is fine, too."

Iris clenched her hands together, squeezing them in her own rhythm. Her eyes remained clouded, as if she saw something off in the distance.

Lily tried another tack. She withdrew the chain and signet ring and held them out. "Matthew asked me to marry him. And I—I've said yes."

She hoped to see a reaction from her mother, but there was still nothing. Even when the tea and refreshments arrived, Iris did not eat or drink.

But then her brother arrived. Lily breathed a sigh of relief and ran to hug James when he entered the room. "I'm so glad you're here. I didn't know what to do."

"There's no change?" he ventured, and she shook her head.

"Nothing I say seems to break through to her. Not even this." She held up the ring and added, "I told her that I've agreed to marry Matthew."

James eyed her with a sidelong look. "He never asked *me* for permission."

"I am old enough to make my own decision." She faced him with confidence, and her brother studied her.

"Matthew has improved, I will agree. But I still do not

think it a wise match, Lily. He could hurt you without even meaning to."

She fingered the heavy ring, ignoring his warning. "I have loved him for years, James. And it is my choice to wed him."

"He loves her," their mother interrupted. They both turned to Iris, startled that she had spoken. Her mother's expression grew dreamy, and she added, "I would like to see them wedded."

Lily exchanged a glance with James and smiled at her mother. "Then you shall have your wish."

⁙

Matthew sat at his mother's bedside, watching over Charlotte. Her face was pale, her eyes lined with shadows as if she hadn't slept well.

"Matthew," she murmured in her sleep.

"I am here." He reached for her hand, bothered by how cold her skin was. It was hard to believe she had grown so ill this quickly.

She rolled to her side, and eventually her blue eyes opened. A smile warmed her face at the sight of him. "You're here. I was so hoping you would come."

"I came as soon as I heard you were ill."

Charlotte sighed and squeezed his hand. "Dr. Fraser said I will get better. It was something to do with my heart. It was working too hard, he said." She studied him for a time and admitted, "Sarah Carlisle came to see me."

A tightness seized his gut, and he tried to hide his anger. "Did she? I told her already that I would not pay her anything further."

"You may want to reconsider." She released his hand and rolled back on her pillow. "She could cause a great deal of embarrassment to us."

"Is she my mother?" he demanded. "Did Father have an affair with her?"

Charlotte's expression dimmed. "No. He was always true to me." She closed her eyes again as if wanting to avoid the subject.

"Do you know who my parents were?" he asked. Right now, he was searching for any answers she would give.

She nodded. "Let the past lie buried, Matthew. There is no need to dredge it up." For whatever reason, she did not want him to know the truth. It was another invisible blow, knowing he was not fathered by the earl. It meant that he had no claim at all to the title, and it bothered him deeply.

"Why do I look like Sarah Carlisle?" he asked again. His mother didn't answer but rolled over and closed her eyes. He prompted, "I know you aren't sleeping."

Then it occurred to him that his true parents might still be living. Was she trying to protect them?

"Why did my father pay Sarah for her silence?" he asked. "I doubt if anyone would listen to her, even if she did spread rumors."

"He didn't want to take the chance of anyone casting a scandal upon our family name. It's a nuisance, easily avoided by a small payment. She has no one to support her, and it was a charity worth offering."

It frustrated him to no end that Charlotte refused to give him any answers. But pressing her would not help her health to improve. For that reason, he let the matter go. He might have better success confronting Sarah Carlisle.

"How is Iris feeling?" Charlotte asked. "Did you see her at all?"

"Lady Penford had more bad days than good ones," he answered honestly. "I do not think she will be able to return to London any time soon."

"That will be difficult for the family."

"Indeed." But he decided to offer her some better news to cheer her up. "But you will be glad to hear that Lily has agreed to marry me."

As he'd hoped, Charlotte turned to him, and her face lit up with joy. "Oh, my dear. I am so pleased for you both."

He nodded, and his mother went on about wedding plans and asking when the ceremony would be. "I have to ask Lily and consult with her on her wishes."

"Right you are." But it did seem that his news had brightened her day, and he was glad of it. His mother patted his hand, and soon enough, he heard a knock at the door.

Matthew went to answer it and saw Dr. Fraser had arrived. The doctor carried a black bag, and his face held a somber expression as he entered the room. "It's glad I am that you've come, lad. I know your visit has done your mother good. She has pined for you for several weeks now."

Matthew lowered his voice. "Will she improve?"

The doctor sobered. "I believe so, yes. But she must rest and not go out for some time. Excitement would do her more harm than good. Her heart troubles came about by a shock of some kind. The servants found her in a faint."

Likely from news of Sarah Carlisle, Matthew thought. "Is Cousin Juliette with you?" he asked.

"Aye, she's downstairs. I asked her to wait until I'd examined Charlotte, and she would come up afterward. I know she would enjoy your company."

"I'll go and speak with her," he offered. To his mother, he said, "I'll let Dr. Fraser examine you and will return shortly."

He walked down the stairs and found his cousin in the library. She was studying the rows of books, and her face lit up when she saw him.

"Why, Matthew! I am so glad you've come home." She embraced him, and he returned the hug. "Tell me all the news."

He did, but after he revealed his engagement, it occurred to him that his cousin might have heard stories about what had happened so long ago with Sarah Carlisle. Juliette was in her midfifties and had likely been a young lady when Charlotte had gone into her confinement.

Juliette continued to gush on about the impending wedding and then broke off with a thoughtful expression. "You haven't heard a word I've said, have you?"

"Forgive me, but no," he admitted. "I've other things on my mind just now."

"Is something the matter? Don't you want to marry Lily?" Juliette bade him to sit down, and her green eyes held worry. His cousin studied him, waiting for him to speak.

"My distraction has nothing to do with the wedding. It's more about my mother." He wondered how to begin with a secret that Charlotte would not want him to share. Perhaps it was better to cast hints and see if his cousin knew anything.

"I'm certain she will heal in time," Juliette reassured him. "Paul will see to it."

"She had a visit from a woman named Sarah Carlisle," he said.

His cousin's expression grew stricken and pale. Her reaction struck him as odd, for how would she even know the woman? Though Juliette tried to gather command of herself, he saw that her hands were shaking.

He didn't know what to think, but he had a feeling she would avoid all questions about Miss Carlisle. Instead, he tried a different tactic. "I think you know why it upset my mother."

Juliette didn't speak at all. Her eyes remained frozen with fear, and tears gleamed within them. Her reaction was so swift, so visceral, it felt as if he lost any ability to breathe. She never voiced a single word, but her silent tears cut him to the bone.

There was no reason for her to be afraid—none at all, unless she was part of the terrible secret.

"I'm sorry," Juliette whispered, reaching for his hand. "So

very sorry. I wanted to tell you for so long. But I had to keep the secret."

Matthew stared at her, noting the shape of her nose that was so similar to his own. Her hair held the same color as his, and he suddenly guessed the truth she had not spoken.

"It was you, wasn't it?" He moved closer and knelt down beside her chair. "*You* are my true mother." He kept his gaze fixed upon hers, now understanding why Charlotte had taken him in—to protect her niece from scandal. All his life, he'd had a special bond with Juliette, never realizing that she was not merely his cousin—she was his true mother.

But there was another piece to this puzzle that was missing. "How do you know Sarah Carlisle?"

Juliette closed her eyes as if pushing back the pain. "Your father's name was Brandon Carlisle, the Earl of Strathland. Sarah is his sister." A darkness slid over her face, and she admitted, "He raped me, and I became pregnant from it."

He squeezed her hand, deeply troubled by her confession. The thought of someone hurting this kindhearted woman brought out a flare of rage. He knew that Strathland was dead—but it didn't diminish the dark fury Matthew felt at knowing he'd been sired by such a monster.

With effort, he tamped down his emotions and kept Juliette's hand in his. "I am sorry for what he did to you."

She nodded. "It was terrible. But I endured, thanks to Charlotte." She steeled herself and admitted, "I confided in her, knowing she would help me. She pretended she was taking me away on a tour and that I would be her companion. But Lord Arnsbury knew the truth. They planned that Charlotte would claim you as her baby. Everyone was told that she stayed in Norway to give birth, being fearful she might lose the child."

Her grip softened on his hand, and she said, "The labor was very difficult, and I nearly died. I was only eighteen when I gave birth to you, and you meant the world to me. I visited

Charlotte often, because I needed to see you. I needed to hold you in my arms and be a part of your life. It's why I was named your godmother."

She reached out to touch his face. "I wish I could have told you the truth sooner, but we decided it was the best way to protect your inheritance. Only a few people know the truth."

"Your husband?" he questioned.

She nodded. "Yes, of course. I told Paul long ago, before we married. And I was fortunate that he did not go off and kill Lord Strathland, as he wanted to. But the earl died when you were only a year old, after he was shot." Her green eyes turned pensive. "I was glad of his death, as terrible as that might sound."

He didn't find it terrible at all. "Perhaps it is a good thing I never knew him. Else I might have shot him myself."

"I am thankful he was not part of your life. And believe me when I say you could have had no better father than Lord Arnsbury. He and Charlotte could not have showered you with more love. It broke my heart to give you to them, but at least it gave me a chance to see you often and to know you were well cared for."

Matthew handed her his handkerchief, and Juliette wiped her eyes. "As for Sarah, she may cause scandal if she speaks of it, but she cannot threaten your place as earl. Your father baptized you as his son. Furthermore, you were formally recognized in the House of Lords, and no one can take your title from you. Be assured of it."

"Why did my father pay her anything at all?"

Juliette stood from her chair and said, "Her life was controlled by her brother, and she was struggling to survive. Lord Arnsbury promised to give her a small yearly sum in return for her silence." She paused a moment and added, "Then, too, before you were born, she was infatuated with Lord Arnsbury. She was caught alone with him at a soiree, and though nothing happened, Lord Arnsbury refused to marry her to save her reputation. She was unable to show her face in society, and she was treated poorly. I think the earl felt sorry for her, and the money was meant to atone for her shame."

He thought of Lily and the seduction. They had been fortunate she had not become pregnant on their first night together, before he'd left for India. Otherwise, she could have been in the same situation as Juliette, alone with a newborn child.

"And would you continue to pay her?" he asked.

"Either that, or try to arrange a marriage for her. Sarah has led a difficult life and has been a spinster all her days."

Matthew could not imagine finding a husband for such a woman, but he finally said, "I will think upon it."

He rose from his chair, studying Juliette. It felt as if his life had been turned upside down and then right side up all over again. But he was glad to finally know the truth.

For that reason, he opened his arms and embraced his mother once again. Though he understood the reasons for their secrecy, he was grateful for the truth.

Juliette cried when he hugged her, and she whispered, "I love you, my son. And I pray that you will find the same happiness in your own marriage that I have known in mine."

Chapter Sixteen

Two weeks later

"Are you feeling any better?" Lily stood at the doorway of her sister's room, hesitant to enter. Rose was lying on her bed, propped up on pillows. For the past fortnight, her sister had remained in this room, struggling to keep down any food. Iain had been reluctant to return to Ireland alone, but she could not have endured the journey.

Rose gave a weak smile. "It's been a grueling morning, I fear." She grimaced and reached for a cup of water.

Lily stepped inside the door and asked, "Can I get you anything?"

"Another stomach?" Rose closed her eyes. "Or perhaps you could transform time so that it's four months from now. They say it will get better, but I have my doubts."

"I'm certain it will." Though what did she know about it? She had never been pregnant before. A blush stole over her face as she thought of what she had done with Matthew in the library. Though her courses had not yet come, she felt no cause to worry. He had written several letters to her and said that his mother was improving, and he would try to return to her soon. They would marry, and all would be well again.

"You're daydreaming," her sister predicted.

"I'm missing Matthew." It felt empty with him gone, and even though she tried to occupy her days helping the neighbors with their dogs and horses, the mantle of loneliness crept over her at night.

A knock sounded at the door, and her grandmother and her brother entered the room. "Good morning, Rose." James held out a small beribboned box. "Your husband bade me give you this. He said it would help with your illness."

He gave the offering to his sister, and when Rose opened it, she exclaimed, "Caramels! Oh, James, thank you." She nibbled at one, and the confection seemed to improve her disposition. Her pallor grew rosier, and when James tried to reach for one, Rose swatted him, laughing. "These are mine. You cannot have any."

He narrowed his eyes at her. "You wouldn't have them at all if it weren't for me."

Lady Wolcroft stepped forward and intervened. "A man should know better than to try and steal food from a pregnant woman. It isn't wise."

But Rose smiled and tossed him a caramel. Turning the subject, she said, "I think it's time that Lily returned to London. She and Matthew need to make their wedding plans." With a nod to Mildred, she asked, "Can you accompany her, Grandmother?"

The older woman sat down in a chair beside the fireplace. "Of course. Amelia has been pestering me about it for the past fortnight. She won her wager and cannot stop gloating about it."

A tension seemed to knot in James's forehead. "Lily, you won't be rushing into marriage. There are some rumors I've heard recently that need to be considered."

She had no idea what he was talking about. "James, I am not rushing into anything. I've known Matthew for years, and I love him."

228

"You may think you know him, but—"

"He told me about India." She did not want to hear anything more about Matthew's past. "I know what happened, and we will put it behind us."

"Walk with me," he said, lifting a hand in farewell to Rose. Lily knew it was because he did not wish to upset their sister. Lady Wolcroft started to follow, but he shook his head and closed the door behind them.

"What is it, James?"

"People are saying that Matthew was not the earl's son. There are stories about him being a bastard, adopted while the countess was traveling with her niece."

She recalled the note she had received from Adrian Monroe. Matthew had dismissed it, saying that his cousin was only trying to gain money, and she had believed him. "That's ridiculous. Matthew was the earl's pride and joy. Lord Arnsbury acknowledged him as his heir." She saw no reason to give rein to idle gossip. "No one can take his title from him."

"True, but they can cause a scandal. It was the cause of his mother's heart trouble. She was deeply upset by the stories."

IAnd it must have upset Matthew as well, she knew. Lily wished she could be there with him now, to reassure him and offer her love. She needed to go to him and do everything she could to help.

She met her brother's gaze. "I don't care what others may say. I am going to marry Matthew."

"Not yet. It would not be wise," James said. "Let the talk die down, else it will overshadow the wedding."

But she had no desire to wait, not anymore. "I want Mother to attend the wedding." Her voice thickened with emotion, but she held back tears. "She's not well, James. I don't know how much longer she will have."

Her brother's expression turned grim. "A few weeks longer, Lily. Don't rush into this."

"We will be married at Penford. That way, Mother can be

here, and there will be no gossip about her madness." She pushed back her feelings, not giving him the chance to argue any further.

Emotions roiled inside her, and she passed by the drawing room where her mother was sitting with a basket of dying flowers in her lap. Iris was tracing the outline of a dried chrysanthemum bud, her face pensive.

More than anything, Lily wished her mother could share in her happiness and join in the wedding plans. But Iris's temperament was fragile, and more often than not, she spoke without any clarity.

Her brother came up behind her. "Leave her be. She is content right now."

"But I am not." Her words came out as a whisper. "I wish she could share in my happiness and help me with the wedding plans."

James rested a hand upon her shoulder. "It may never happen, Lily."

"I don't want to believe that." And when she pulled away from him, she added, "But I am going to London in the morning. I will have my gown made for the wedding, and we will return here to be married as soon as Matthew can get the license."

But her brother did not appear willing. "You don't know what sort of scandal you will face in London. I'm trying to protect you, Lily."

"It doesn't matter." She couldn't believe he was even asking her to delay the wedding because of idle talk. "I intend to wed Matthew by Christmas, no matter what anyone says."

Her brother's hand tightened upon her. "Then I am coming with you, Lily." His tone held a warning, and she didn't doubt that he would remain an overprotective brother.

"And what of Mother?"

"She must remain here. I think Grandmother should stay with her, along with Rose."

Their mother was busy making a chain of dead chrysanthemums, threading the stems through one another. She was singing to herself lightly, and her eyes were vacant.

Lily took a breath. "All right. But when we return, I will marry Matthew."

Her brother said nothing and only squeezed her hand.

Matthew refused to stand aside and allow anyone to threaten his family. He had arranged a meeting with Sarah Carlisle and intended to put an end to the blackmail.

But more than that, he wanted to learn more about the night she had been caught in a compromising position with Lord Arnsbury. She held Matthew's adopted father responsible for ruining her.

He walked up the stairs to the tiny townhouse where she lived. Years ago, it might have been a quiet dwelling of luxury, but it had fallen into disrepair. Ivy covered the brick façade, and the stone steps were cracked.

Matthew knocked upon her door, and Miss Carlisle answered it without a word, opening it wide so he could enter. Her face was tightly drawn, and she led him inside before she finally spoke. "Why have you come?"

He gestured for her to sit down. "We need to come to an understanding. I have the right to know what happened with my parents."

She folded her arms and took a chair. He did the same, sitting across from her. The look in her eyes spoke of a woman who had no intention of cooperating. "And why should I tell you anything?"

"Because you want money. You want to continue living here in your brother's house where it's safe. I want to know what happened to you, to my parents, and anything about my father." He stared hard at her. "And by that, I mean your brother."

Her expression softened slightly. "So you discovered the truth, then."

"I know who my parents are, if that's what you mean. But you should know that, even if you expose our secrets, it won't matter. My father, the rightful earl, formally recognized me as his son. My inheritance and title cannot be stripped away." He wanted to disarm this woman, so she would not try to harm his family.

"Perhaps not. But words can harm a family, nonetheless." She straightened in her chair. "And there are others who want to cause a scandal."

He wondered if she was speaking of Adrian, but she did not elaborate. In her face, he saw the lines of hardship. Her eyes were not those of a cold-blooded vulture. No, she was a woman fighting to survive. His father had pitied her and had given her a small stipend for years. But Matthew suspected that money had not solved her hardships.

"What is it you truly want?" he asked quietly. "A husband? Perhaps a family of your own?"

Her mouth thinned with disdain. "Don't mock me. I know no man would ever have a woman like myself. I am ugly and poor. And my brother—your father—was an arrogant madman who deserved to die."

The vitriol in her voice took him aback. They were the bitter words of a forsaken woman. But he needed to know more about her circumstances. "What did Lord Arnsbury do that caused you to be ruined?"

She let her gaze drift toward the dirty window. For a moment, she paused, her expression turning sad. "I was a different girl then. So filled with dreams. I thought I could win the heart of an earl, and Lord Arnsbury was kind to me."

Matthew waited for her to continue and pressed further. "What did he do?"

Miss Carlisle shrugged. "He saw me among the wallflowers and smiled, that was all. He might have been smiling at someone else, but I wanted to believe that—if I could only talk to him—we might become friends."

Her face turned distant, and she shook her head. "It was my fault that I was enchanted by his handsome face. I followed Lord Arnsbury down a hallway, hoping to speak with him. He was already conversing with the Duke of Worthingstone, and I lost my courage. I hid inside the conservatory to avoid them. But there was...another man already there." Her voice trailed away, and a deep flush suffused her face.

"He was intoxicated and tried to kiss me. H-he tore my gown. I struggled and called for help. Lord Arnsbury heard me. He struck the man and forced him to go." There was a pained note in her voice. "I was caught alone with Lord Arnsbury, and my dress was torn. I hoped that the earl might offer to marry me, because I was found in a compromising position. But he refused."

She took a breath and admitted, "I know it was my fault for following him. He had done nothing wrong and certainly didn't want to wed me. But my brother was...difficult about the situation. I never told him which man attacked me, for I didn't want to be forced into marriage with that blackguard. And certainly Lord Arnsbury wouldn't have me. But after I was ruined, Brandon was insufferable. We were no longer invited to balls or soirees, and he blamed me for our lack of invitations." There was a weariness in her voice, and Matthew suddenly understood his father's sympathy toward her. This woman had endured her older brother's ridicule and had been a spinster all her life.

"Brandon did not know he fathered you until just before he died. Be glad of it," she said. "There was a darkness in him, a terrible anger that he could never control. I pray you have none of his madness within you."

Her words speared him with an uneasy fear. Matthew had told himself that it was the torture in India that had brought out his darker side. And yet…what if there was something of Brandon Carlisle within him? What if there was a madness in him created by the blood of his father?

He didn't want to imagine it. "I am sorry to hear of your misfortune," he said quietly. "And while I understand that my father was willing to pay you a small stipend for your misfortune, you might be happier if you made a new life for yourself. Perhaps with a husband of your own. My family could make the introductions on your behalf."

But Miss Carlisle stood, her face dark with anger. "I know I am too old. No man would have someone like me."

He hadn't considered it in that way at all. "I was only trying to help you. It was never meant as an insult."

"I kept your secrets all these years," she said. "I let you believe you were a legitimate heir."

"Until now," he murmured.

"I had no choice!" she snapped. "I am fighting for every penny I have. If you would not pay me, there were others who would." A sullen expression crossed her face.

Matthew stiffened, for he had not spoken of money. He had come here hoping to end the blackmail relationship and change it into one where Sarah Carlisle could have a better life of her own.

From his pocket, he took out a bank note and handed it to her. "For the sake of my father, I am willing to help you. But the past should lie buried."

She took the money, her wrinkled face holding only pain. "It won't be buried until I am."

Lily stared outside the coach window, thankful to be back in London and eager to see Matthew once again. When the coach came to a stop in front of their family's townhouse, James opened the door and helped her out. But to her surprise, there was a dog waiting upon the doorstep. Lily exclaimed with joy when she saw Sebastian waiting outside. He was sniffing and circling the entrance. The moment the dog spied her, his tail wagged with delight.

"Sebastian!" She opened her arms as she went up the stairs, and the dog crashed into her, sniffing and licking her hands. Foolish tears sprang from her eyes, but she didn't care. "I never thought to see you again. Now what are you doing here?"

For a moment, she wondered if Lord Davonshire had come to pay a call, but why would he? They had only just arrived home from Yorkshire, and he would not even suspect she was here. It was nearly evening, and the sky had already grown dark.

The footman caught up to her and apologized. "I am sorry, Lady Lily. I will remove the dog if you wish it."

"Not at all. Bring him inside. He may be hungry or thirsty." She had no idea how Sebastian had run away from home again, but she intended to enjoy his company for a few hours until she returned him to his owner.

And she could hardly wait to see Matthew. Though it had only been a few weeks, she missed him terribly. She hoped to pay a call upon him at Lady Arnsbury's residence first thing in the morning.

James followed her inside the townhouse, handing his hat to another servant. "Why is that dog here again?"

"I have no idea. But I will keep him for a while, at least. I've missed him so." She guided the Landseer into the drawing room and sat upon the floor, letting the dog flop against her. He rolled onto his back, exposing his stomach, and she rubbed it. His tongue hung out of his mouth, and she could not help but smile at his ridiculous expression.

Her brother shook his head with a sigh and took a seat across from her. "You've a soft heart, Lily."

"So I have." She saw nothing wrong with that and continued cuddling Sebastian. She ran her fingers over the dog, checking to ensure that his wounds were fully healed. He continued to lick her, and her heart warmed to the affection. She supposed she would send a note to Lord Davonshire to let him know the whereabouts of his dog, but in the meantime, she would enjoy the love of this animal.

Her brother rang for refreshments and asked the footman to bring him the collection of notes and invitations from the past few weeks. After the servant returned, he added, "And this one just arrived, my lord." He gave him the stack of papers, and James sat at his writing desk to begin sorting through them.

"I need a secretary," James remarked. "This has gotten out of hand. It will take days to answer all of the notes." He set aside a small stack and then opened the recent letter the footman had just given to him. Frowning, he tore it open. Lily paid it no heed, busy petting the dog, until James abruptly stood. He crumpled the note and shoved it into his coat pocket.

"What's the matter?"

"I'm not certain." His expression tightened, and he turned to face her. "Can you imagine any reason why Evangeline would ever send for me?"

"Heavens, no." Lily knew how deeply her friend despised James. "She never would. Why would you ask that?"

"Because of the note she just sent asking me to pay a call. She says it's urgent."

"That *is* strange." Lily didn't know what to think of it, but she was distracted when the footman returned with sandwiches and tea. She stood and directed him to place the tray upon a low table near the chairs. When she sat, she immediately reached for the food, feeling ravenous.

"I've a mind to go just to satisfy my curiosity," James remarked. "Perhaps she is plotting my murder."

"Be careful," Lily warned with a smile. The last time she'd spoken with her friend, the young woman had decided she was through with James. Everyone thought that was the end of it.

She finished her sandwich and offered a scrap to the dog so her brother would not see the forbidden excitement on her face. Right now, she had no qualms about urging her brother out the door. She yearned to be in Matthew's arms and hoped he could come pay a call on her, despite the late hour.

James took two sandwiches from the tray and lifted his hand in a wave farewell. As soon as he had gone, Lily hurried to the writing desk and scrawled out a note to Matthew, telling him of her arrival. She folded it and gave it to the footman to be delivered immediately.

She could hardly wait to see him again.

Chapter Seventeen

Evangeline Sinclair despised embroidery, but she engaged in the necessary evil to pacify her mother and to give the illusion that she did possess a few womanly skills. Her mother Margaret sat across from her in the drawing room, sewing violet lace to a corset, while Aunt Amelia studied a sketch of a new design.

It was such a paradox to see her impossibly proper mother adorning undergarments more befitting a courtesan than a lady. But then, it was the reason for her family's wealth, so Evangeline could hardly complain. She let out a sigh and glanced over at the hearth where Annabelle slept beside her puppies.

"You have a caller, Miss Sinclair," the footman announced to Evangeline. "Lord Penford is here to see you."

"Now why would he be here?" her mother wondered aloud. "I thought the two of you had parted ways." Margaret stared hard at her daughter, before a faint smile edged her mouth. "Clearly, I was wrong."

"Put your matchmaking thoughts out of your head, Mama," Evangeline warned.

"Matchmaking is such marvelous fun," Aunt Amelia said dreamily. "I've already arranged a wedding for dear Lily Thornton and Cousin Matthew."

Evangeline stabbed the needle through the linen of her embroidery. Without looking at the footman, she remarked, "Tell Lord Penford I am not here."

But Amelia beamed and contradicted her. "Show him into the library, Harrison. I will send Evangeline in shortly."

"I have nothing to say to that man. He is horrid, and I will not be part of your scheming," she informed her aunt. Evangeline would not allow them to make a fool of her.

"If you do not see him in the library, I will send for him here," her mother said. "I know Amelia and I would both like to know why he has come. Perhaps to renew his courtship?"

She was aghast at the idea. Anger roiled up inside her, but Evangeline tossed the needlework aside and stood. "That is the very last reason why he would be here. But if you insist, I will find out and return within one minute." She had no idea why James would dare to set foot here, but it would not take long to be rid of him.

"Evangeline, your hair is falling from the pins," her mother warned. "Take a moment and make yourself presentable."

She ignored her mother and strode out of the room. As soon as she reached the mirror in the hall, she tousled her hair even more, letting a few pins dangle from the strands. Good. Now she looked frightful.

Evangeline took long steps toward the library, but something made her pause before she entered. Her heartbeat was unsteady, her pulse racing. Why did that man always have such an effect on her? She wished James were unattractive or portly. Instead, when she stopped in the doorway, she took a moment to gaze at him. He stood with his back to her, and his light-brown hair held glints of blond. His coat hugged his frame, outlining the lean muscles, and his trousers molded to his legs like a second skin.

She pinched herself roughly before she walked inside. *Gather control of yourself. He's only a man.*

The man she had worshipped for five years, until that fateful day when he had finally noticed her.

She bit her lip and said, "Why are you here, Penford?"

James turned at the sound of her voice. A faint smile creased his mouth when he saw her rumpled appearance. Then his expression softened, as if he were glad to see her. Her traitorous heart leapt at the sight of him, and she tried to tamp down her emotions. From his coat pocket, he withdrew a crumpled piece of paper and held it out.

Evangeline entered the room and took it from him, smoothing the edges. When she read the note, she frowned. "I did not send this."

She examined the handwriting, which was nothing like her own. The letters were large, and one of the words was misspelled. It asked Penford to come at once to meet with her. "Who would have sent this to you? And why?"

"I don't know." He leaned back and sat upon her uncle's desk. "Especially when it was delivered an hour ago, and we've been traveling all day. I thought it best to find out in case something was wrong."

"Why would you care?" she blurted out without thinking. Her cheeks burned when she realized how rude she'd been. "I apologize. That came out before I could stop myself from speaking."

James eyed her a moment. "You're still angry with me."

She was. A rush of humiliation washed over her, and she wished he would simply leave. "You've seen for yourself that we are all fine. Just go back home, and we'll leave it at that." She started to go, but he caught her hand in his.

The warm pressure of his palm unraveled her with confusion. He had such a strong effect upon her that she could not resist. "Regardless of what you believe, Evangeline, I am not your enemy."

She wasn't certain she wanted to hear this. It was easier to hate him, to wallow in the humiliation. She had fallen beneath his spell, believing he cared for her. And every time she saw him, she was reminded of her weakness.

And his wickedness.

She raised her chin and regarded him. "I know that, Lord Penford. You may return home, and there's no need to concern yourself with my welfare."

James studied her for a long moment before he nodded. "Still, I wonder why anyone sent that note."

Her face furrowed, and suddenly, she grew uncertain. "To draw you away from Lily?" She clenched her hands together. "Perhaps someone wanted you to leave her alone."

He stiffened and let out a low curse. "I believe you may be right. I should go back." But before James left the library, he remarked, "I meant what I said. I don't want to be your enemy, Evangeline."

Her face flushed with the memories. If she could go back and blot out those mistakes, she would do so in a single moment. But it was hard to let go of her own embarrassment and grant him a truce.

"I will try," she said quietly.

He ventured a light smile, but when he departed, she felt a sense of terrible sadness. She had clung to animosity, for it protected her wounded heart. It was far easier to despise him than to forgive him.

Because forgiving him meant letting go.

Lily had sent off the note immediately to Matthew, hoping he would be able to see her for a short time. In the meantime, she snuggled with Sebastian, nuzzling his nose and delighting in his slobber.

But then, abruptly, the hair stood on end upon his spine.

He let out a low growl and bolted up from her lap, snarling as he reached the doorway. Lily stood, uncertain of what had bothered him, but she relaxed when she saw Lord Davonshire arriving. Sebastian's hind quarters hit the ground, and his tail wagged as the man reached into his pocket for a treat.

"Now how did you find your way to Lady Lily's again?" he murmured to the dog, giving him the piece of bacon and rubbing the animal's head. "I must apologize for Louis. He hasn't wandered off in a long time. I suppose he must have been missing you."

His tone held a trace of interest, and Lily brushed it aside. "I will admit that I missed your dog as well," she said. "Especially his kisses." She laughed as the dog licked at her fingertips. He sat and stared at Lord Davonshire, politely begging for more bacon.

"How is your mother?" the earl asked. "I presume she has improved, since you have returned to London."

Her smile grew pained. "No, I am afraid she could not come with me." She knew that Rose would take good care of their mother at Penford, and Iain would be there from time to time.

"I am sorry to hear that. But delighted, of course, to see you again." He sent her a warm smile and took a seat, making it clear he intended to visit.

Which was not at all what she'd hoped for. Matthew would come soon enough, and the last thing she wanted was a gentleman caller to interrupt.

Something about Lord Davonshire's visit bothered her. It was too convenient, almost as if he had been waiting for her brother to leave.

Without knowing quite what to say, she sat down. "Would you care for tea?" It was late, but perhaps he would have a cup and then go.

"I should be glad of spending more time in your

company," he answered. She rang the bell and ordered tea, but then decided it was time to inform him of her new circumstances.

"Lord Davonshire, I should tell you that my fiancé is on his way here," Lily began. "Lord Arnsbury and I are now engaged to marry."

At that, the earl's face grew pained. "I know I should offer my congratulations, but I can see that you have not heard the stories circulating around London. Lord Arnsbury is involved in a terrible scandal. You may want to reconsider marrying into his family."

The edge of anger crept into her voice. "I care nothing for idle gossip. I have been in love with Lord Arnsbury since before he left for India."

The earl glanced at the door and then back again. Sebastian left his side when it was clear he would get no more bacon. He settled at Lily's feet, resting his head upon her shoes.

"They say he was not the Earl of Arnsbury's son," Davonshire continued. "Others claim that he was adopted from an unwed acquaintance. And I cannot think that you would want to marry a bastard."

"I could invent the same stories about you," she countered. "I could pretend that you were a man laden with debt, that you needed to wed a wealthy woman. But it would be nothing more than a story, would it not?" She gave him a pointed look, and his gaze turned away. "I will not abandon Lord Arnsbury, regardless of what anyone says."

"Then you are not like other women," he admitted.

The tea arrived, but his demeanor had shifted into concern. "There is something else. I know that Lord Arnsbury suffered a great deal while he was away in India. The stories suggest he fell into madness. Even his servants say he became aggressive. Are you not fearful that Lord Arnsbury could be dangerous?"

Lily distracted herself with pouring the tea. She didn't

know why he was trying to cast aspersions on Matthew, but she simply sipped at her cup and ignored him. "Thank you for your concern, but no."

She rather hoped that Matthew would arrive, but it was growing later, and he still had not come. At last, when Lord Davonshire finished his tea, he stood. "I suppose I should be taking Louis back with me now." He withdrew a length of cord from his pocket and fashioned it into a leash. "I apologize for his unexpected arrival."

The dog let out a low growl when Lord Davonshire attempted to place the loop around his neck. With an exasperated sigh, the earl took a sandwich from the tea tray and offered it to the animal. The dog instantly quieted and waited politely while the earl put the leash around his neck. He whimpered when the man led him away, and Lily longed to snatch him back again.

He's not yours, she reminded herself. But she had been grateful to visit with the dog for a short time, even if he had run away.

"I hope I will see you again, Lady Lily. And please do remember my warning about Lord Arnsbury. I should hate for anything to happen to you."

She stood from her chair and folded her hands. "I will be fine, thank you."

After he had gone, she paced across the drawing room, feeling restless. She longed to see Matthew, but it was possible that he knew nothing of her arrival. From the window, she saw Lord Davonshire departing just as another carriage arrived. Her heartbeat quickened, and she couldn't stop her smile when she saw Matthew disembarking.

Lily longed to run to the door and meet him, but she forced herself to remain in the drawing room. At least she ought to maintain the pretense of being a lady. But when he finally appeared at the doorway, she tossed aside her inhibitions and threw herself into his arms. He dropped a small package on the floor and caught her, holding her in an embrace as he backed against the door to shut it.

She lifted her mouth to his, and the kiss was that of a starving man. There was reckless joy in the embrace, and she could scarcely catch her breath.

"I love you," she whispered.

"And I love you. This fortnight has been the longest of my life," he murmured, his hands moving to her waist and pulling her close. He moved her against the wall, kissing her throat. "Why was Davonshire here? Did he bring the dog to see you?"

Shivers erupted over her skin, and her breasts tightened at the thrill of his mouth upon her. "Sebastian ran away, and Lord Davonshire came to retrieve him."

Matthew's hands moved over her bodice, and she let out a shuddering breath as his thumbs grazed her sensitive nipples. Despite the corset and layers of fabric, she could feel the pressure of his touch, and it drove her toward wildness.

But then he stilled upon her and backed away. "How did he know the dog was here?" There was an edge in his voice, and she could not tell if it was jealousy or worry. "Davonshire lives nowhere near you. The dog would have had to travel for miles across London."

"I thought the same myself. It might be that he intended to pay a call upon me, and the dog got away from him." Even so, she found the entire situation strange. It almost seemed as if Davonshire had placed the dog there for her to find, thereby giving him an excuse to retrieve him.

Matthew's expression was grim, and his suspicions were heightened. "And he waited until your brother was gone." His finger slid beneath the chain she wore, lifting the ring from her bodice.

"It doesn't matter. Regardless, I told him I was going to marry you."

"And how did he respond to that?"

"He...warned me about you." She wondered whether Matthew would be offended by Lord Davonshire's gossip. But it was better for him to know the truth, she decided. "He said there was a great deal of scandal surrounding your name. And that many people believed you were a bastard."

At that, Matthew's expression tightened, and he stepped back from her. His demeanor sobered, and he reached for the fallen package. "I learned of the rumors, too. And we should talk about them."

"I don't care about the gossip," she said. "Let people say what they will. It changes nothing between us."

He handed her the wrapped package. "Open it."

The package was heavier than she'd expected, and she sat down, untying the string. When she pulled away the brown paper, she saw dozens of letters. "What are these, Matthew?"

"Open one and see. The rest are the same."

She chose the top letter and opened it, reading the note in silence. Then she folded it and regarded him. "They no longer want you to attend their ball."

"No. And every last invitation I've received in the past fortnight has been revoked." He reached for the package and pulled the letters free. "All the invitations are from families I believed were my friends. Even the invitations sent to my mother were rescinded."

She was shocked to hear it. "Why would they do this? It's just idle gossip, isn't it?"

He took back the letters and set them aside. "And what if the rumors were true, Lily?"

"What do you mean?" He was behaving as if he knew something, when she'd expected him to deny it. Hadn't he dismissed the stories the last time?

Matthew took a seat near the hearth, resting his wrists upon his knees. "I recently learned that Charlotte was not my mother. She and my father adopted me as a newborn infant and claimed me as their own."

For a moment, she could say nothing, for it didn't sound like it could possibly be real. "If that were true, why would she reveal it now?"

"Because we are being blackmailed."

She came to sit closer to him, listening as he revealed everything...how he had been conceived, that Juliette was his true mother, and how Sarah Carlisle had been demanding money. While he spoke, she reached for his hand, realizing how difficult this was for him. His entire life had been built upon a lie, and he had to grasp a new truth.

But he needed to know that she would stand by him, no matter what. "Matthew, you are the Earl of Arnsbury, and nothing can change that. Your father—Lord Arnsbury—raised you to be his son, and since he swore to it, it must be accepted. He *was* your father in every sense of the word."

He squeezed her hands. "I know it. But all the families in London suddenly don't believe I am the earl. They think I am an imposter, as if I tried to deceive them. They want nothing more to do with me." He reached for the notes and dropped them on the floor of the drawing room. "This would be our life, Lily. Ostracized from polite society. It's not right or fair."

She moved closer to him. "I don't care. I want to be with you as your wife. For better or for worse."

"But this isn't the life I want for you." He stood, stepping over the letters. "You've done nothing wrong, and I don't want you to be isolated because of this."

"It doesn't matter." She didn't truly believe her friends would turn their backs on her. And Matthew was still the man she loved, the man she wanted to spend the rest of her days with.

"It *does* matter," he said dully. "And nothing I say or do will end the talk." He took a step away from her. "It's a war I don't know how to fight."

This revelation had changed him, tearing away the childhood he had known. She didn't ask how he had learned of this. What mattered was letting him see that she loved him still.

She drew her arms around his waist and rested her cheek against his chest. "Then let me fight with you."

Juliette Fraser sat with her three sisters, Amelia, Victoria, and Margaret, and their aunt Charlotte. Despite being around her dearest family, she felt a sense of fear drawing around her like a cloak. During the past hour, she had spilled out her darkest secrets, secrets that Charlotte already knew, but her sisters did not.

She was almost afraid to look at them, worried that they would be ashamed of her. But she could no longer keep them from knowing the truth about Matthew. Not now, when he needed her.

Margaret was the first to speak. Her face drawn with worry, and she spoke softly. "I think I always suspected it. You loved Matthew more than a cousin, and whenever we visited Charlotte, he was always in your arms." Then her tone shifted. "Had I known what Strathland did to you, I would have shot him myself."

Victoria said nothing but reached out and squeezed Juliette's hand.

Amelia appeared stunned into speechlessness. Juliette had never before seen her sister so taken aback. Finally, she spoke. "I cannot believe you kept this from us all these years." Her emotions were bright, her eyes gleaming with tears. "How could you bear this burden alone?"

"Because it meant keeping Matthew's inheritance safe. There was no other choice." Juliette leaned back in her chair, releasing Victoria's hand. "Now the gossip is circulating, and I have to protect my son. For that reason, I have asked Sarah Carlisle to pay a call on us today."

"Why on earth would we want anything to do with that woman?" Margaret interrupted. "After all that her brother did to you—"

"I was not the only victim," Juliette said. "Matthew said she is destitute, and any stories she might have spread were out of desperation. I want to see her for myself and discover how we can force the gossip to die down."

"Are you certain she is the source of it?" Victoria ventured. "Could there be someone else who holds a grudge against Matthew?"

Juliette shrugged. "I cannot say. But for now, we can meet with her and find out what may be done. She should be arriving at any moment."

Amelia's expression held steel. "If she was the source of the gossip, she deserves whatever ruin she lives in. I'll not lift a finger to help her."

In answer, Juliette held out the note she had received from Matthew. "Look at this." Though she understood Amelia's hatred toward the Earl of Strathland and his sister, she did not hold Sarah to blame for the attack. Rather, she pitied the woman for having to live with such a brother.

Amelia took the letter and read it, but her annoyance didn't diminish. "Why would Matthew want to help a woman who tried to ruin him?"

"Because she was the victim of gossip, and Matthew's father was caught with her—though I don't think they did anything wrong. But the scandal ruined her chances of marriage. Matthew believes if we set her up with a good husband, she will let the matter go. Though he did say that she was rather...angry and reluctant."

"I cannot imagine a woman like Sarah Carlisle would let it go," Amelia said, handing back the letter. A footman arrived at that moment, and she shrugged. "But if she's already here, I suppose we can hear what she has to say."

The servant inclined his head in silent admission that their guest had arrived. As he departed to show her in, Juliette turned to Amelia. "Let me speak to her first."

After a moment, Sarah Carlisle appeared in the entrance. She was dressed in gray, and her hair was coiled atop her head. Time had carved ridges of unhappiness on her face. At first, she didn't seem at all eager to join them, but Juliette stood. "Please come in."

The woman eyed them all as if she were entering a pit of vipers. But she took the chair Juliette offered. Silence descended, and for a moment, it seemed that the woman wanted to flee their presence.

Juliette took a moment to calm herself. Sarah had changed over the years, and bitterness had stolen her looks. But the question was whether the woman still possessed a heart.

"Will you have a cup of tea?" she offered.

Sarah hesitated. "That depends on whether you've put poison in it." Her posture remained ramrod straight, and Juliette didn't stop her smile this time.

"We're not that terrible, Miss Carlisle."

At that, the woman shook her head. "I have no idea why I even came here. I know you loathe and despise me."

"Because you're trying to destroy our cousin's inheritance," Amelia snapped.

Juliette pushed back a groan, knowing there was no stopping her sister now. Once Amelia decided someone was an enemy, she would not reverse her course.

But Sarah turned to face the animosity. "Don't you mean your nephew?"

Amelia's glare turned heated. "My sister asked me not to interfere, and for her sake, I will not. But were it up to me, I would have nothing to do with you."

At that, Juliette stood between the women. She guided Amelia to sit back and sent her a warning look. To Sarah, she said, "I have only just told my sisters about Matthew's birth."

Miss Carlisle met her gaze, and she eyed the door. "Shall I go, then? It seems that my presence here is a waste of time."

"No." Juliette said. "Matthew asked me to intervene, and so I shall. I believe you want our help, else you would not have come."

At that, the woman's expression turned tired. "There is nothing you can do to help me. And despite what you might think, I did not spread the stories about him. Someone else did."

"I don't believe y—" Amelia started, but Juliette cut her off.

"Enough." She pulled her chair beside Sarah's. "What we all want is for Matthew to be happy and to put the past behind him. And if you are willing to put it to rest, we may be able to help you find your own happiness. If you wish to try."

"No man would have someone like me," Sarah said quietly. "I'm too old, and I would only make myself into a fool."

It was then that Victoria spoke up. "All of us have seen better days. But I know many widowers who are quite lonely in their years. Some desire only companionship."

She studied them, and Juliette saw a wistful glimpse of hope in the woman's eyes before she shuttered it. "I don't know."

"If you agree to never speak of Matthew's past—and if you help us silence the rumors—we will do everything we can to help you," Juliette said. "Speak up on his behalf, and insist that Matthew is legitimate. Do this for him and for us. And in return, you'll have another chance at your own happiness."

"Next Friday," Victoria said. "I want you to attend my Christmas ball. There will be hundreds of people there, and you will be treated like an honored guest."

"I don't belong in a duchess's house," Sarah insisted, her face coloring. "I wouldn't know what to say or how to act. It's been far too long."

At that, Margaret released a sigh. "I cannot say as I trust you, either, but I know what it is to be stared at by society. When Cain and I took over Aphrodite's Unmentionables as our family business, many households refused to receive us. But we learned how to overcome it." She assessed Sarah and said, "I even know a few of the widowers Toria spoke of. Some would marry a stick of wood if it smiled at them."

A horrified choking sound came from Sarah, and Juliette realized it was a laugh. The woman covered her mouth and gathered her composure. "Well, then. I suppose if they would marry a stick of wood, then there's hope for me."

Chapter Eighteen

"They are behaving as if we don't exist."

Matthew didn't miss the discomfort in Lily's tone as she took his arm. And she was right. Although the Christmas ball was hosted by the Duchess of Worthingstone, most of the guests had turned a cold shoulder to them.

"Does it bother you?" he asked quietly. "We could leave." On her cheeks, he could see the flush of embarrassment. Though Lily had insisted that she wanted to face them down, it angered him that people were ignoring her. There was no cause for it whatsoever.

"I would not give them the satisfaction," she said, raising her chin and entering the ballroom. There were garlands of greenery hung throughout the rooms, and the scent of mulled wine filled the air. A few oranges were set about for color, along with holly. And near the far end of the room, a bundle of mistletoe hung above a discreet corner.

Matthew guided her inside, but several of the older women leaned toward one another, whispering. Lily tried to brave a smile, but it didn't meet her eyes.

She walked toward one of the matrons and nodded in greeting. "It is so good to see you, Mrs. Everett. And how is your daughter? I understand Viscount Burkham is courting her."

The matron's eyes glazed over as if she didn't see Lily, and she turned to her friend. "Lady Compton, I must say, I am surprised at the duchess's guest list for this ball. One would think she would allow the rabble off the streets to come and mingle with us."

Matthew was not going to let the spiteful cats have the last word. "Quite right," he said. "Lady Lily, you would not wish to lower yourself to converse with"—he narrowed his gaze at the women—"*rabble*."

He didn't give the older women the chance to reply but took Lily's hand and led her further into the ballroom. Her face was bright with color, as if their words had been a physical slap. "I never expected them to be so terrible to our faces," she confessed. "I knew there were whispers of gossip, but this went beyond my expectations."

He studied her closely, wondering if he could give her the life she deserved. This woman had stood by him through the worst moments he'd ever endured, and it meant everything to him.

"We will go and speak with my cousins," he said. "They will not spurn us." A waltz had begun, and he took Lily toward the dancing. Matthew rested his hand upon the small of her back, but she had grown pale. He didn't know why she was putting herself through this, but for the moment he said, "Look at me, Lily." She raised her gaze to his, and in her hazel eyes, he saw fear. "We don't need them."

"We have to make our peace with the scandal," she corrected. "You will have to live in London for part of the year."

He knew his Parliamentary responsibilities, but there were other possibilities. "You need not come with me. We could build a house nearer to Penford so you could see your mother whenever you wanted."

Her face softened. "I would like to live near her for part of the year. But we cannot run away from this scandal. We must confront it and face it down." Her hand squeezed his, and in that moment, he loved her courage.

"There is nothing that will part us again, Lily. I promise you that."

She managed a smile, and the warmth of it slid over him like a caress. After the dance, she tucked her hand in the crook of his arm as he led her toward the Duchess of Worthingstone. He was confident that the matrons would shield Lily from the gossip. And in the meantime, he wanted to find out exactly whom he could number among his true friends.

Just then, he saw an older woman join the duchess and her sisters. She wore a demure gown of light blue, but there were traces of silver thread within the fabric that made it gleam in the candlelight. The woman appeared nervous, twisting her hands as she glanced around.

The Duchess of Worthingstone smiled at him as he approached, and Matthew understood what the women had done. Instead of casting out Sarah Carlisle, they were attempting to make her an ally, doing just as he'd offered.

And it did appear to be working. He was uncertain what to think of it.

He greeted the duchess, bowing to her. "Your Grace. Thank you for the invitation this evening."

"We are delighted to have you with us, Lord Arnsbury." She held out her hand for him to kiss, and then Matthew received warm greetings from her sisters, Amelia, Margaret, and Juliette, who held his hand the longest.

He had always been close to his godmother, and now he understood why. There was another blood bond between them, one that would never be broken. And instead of being encircled by cousins, they were his aunts.

Sarah Carlisle had tried to slip away, but Amelia caught her arm. "Oh, no, you don't. You're not running away this time. Not after all the trouble we went to."

Miss Carlisle let out a sigh. "I feel like a fool," she admitted. Her gray hair had been swept into a newer style. "I wanted to wear a black gown."

"It would make you look old," Amelia countered. "And that is not our intention this evening."

"I *am* old," Miss Carlisle insisted. "Why should I pretend to be someone I am not? I cannot believe I let you talk me into a gown like this."

"It will get you noticed," Margaret said. "And we have chosen three gentlemen to introduce to you. You know what you must do in return."

"I've never felt so ridiculous in all my life." She fanned herself, but Matthew saw that they had indeed made her look better. Instead of wearing a bitter frown, she appeared to be a nervous debutante.

"Would you like me to walk with you?" Lily offered.

Sarah appeared taken aback. "I'm...not certain."

He exchanged a look with her, and Lily said, "Don't be afraid. Mrs. Sinclair and I can accompany you." She offered a mischievous smile to Amelia. "I realize that Lady Castledon would terrify all of your suitors."

"Why would you want to help someone like me?" the old woman asked bluntly. "After all that I've done."

Because Lily has a heart greater than nearly every woman in this ballroom, Matthew thought. She was generous and kind, seeing the good that lay beneath the surface.

"You made your choices out of necessity, I think." Lowering her voice, she added, "And besides, there are better ways of supporting yourself than blackmail."

Sarah shot her an indignant look, but Lily only laughed. "Come along."

After they departed, Juliette turned to him. "How badly are the guests treating you?"

Matthew shrugged. "Apparently I do not exist, according to them." He had passed by many so-called friends whose gazes had turned distant when he and Lily walked by.

"I hope Miss Carlisle will keep her promise and begin spreading her own story that the rumors are not true."

"I would not rely on it," Matthew said. "But if she found a husband, the blackmail would stop, and that would be a relief." He hadn't been certain Sarah Carlisle would even entertain the idea, but she had agreed to let the women dress her, and she *was* here.

Still, he didn't want Lily to feel the shame of his past. She had done nothing wrong and did not deserve their scorn.

Juliette rested her hand upon his arm. "There is something else we could do. Toria could announce your engagement, which would force the others to acknowledge you."

He understood that no one would risk offending the Duchess of Worthingstone. But he shook his head. "Not yet. It would create a strained atmosphere. Perhaps later, when the talk has died down."

He studied the crowded ballroom, and for a sudden moment, he thought he spied Adrian. To Juliette, he asked, "Was my cousin invited this evening?"

She shook her head. "No, of course not. His presence would only undermine what we are trying to accomplish."

And yet, he could have sworn he caught a glimpse of the man. He murmured his excuses, and departed Juliette's side, wanting to ensure it was not Adrian.

An unsettled suspicion took root within him that sooner or later, he and his cousin would have a confrontation that would not end well.

"Psst—"

James turned and saw Evangeline lurking against the far wall. He couldn't quite understand why she was hissing at him, so he drew closer. She slipped through the doorway and beckoned for him to follow.

It wasn't at all a good idea to be alone with her, but he suspected this had something to do with Lily. If nothing else, he was confident that Evangeline would not attempt to trap him into marriage.

When he reached the hallway, she picked up her skirts, tiptoeing toward another room. James stopped where he was and waited. What on earth was she wanting? She beckoned again, but this time, he rested his hands on his hips and stared at her. Until he knew what this was about, he intended to stay precisely where he was.

Evangeline rolled her eyes and tiptoed back to him. "You need to hear this. It affects Lily."

"Are we eavesdropping, Miss Sinclair?"

"Yes. Now are you coming, or are you intending to abandon your sister in her hour of need?"

He smiled at her melodramatics. "Do you even know where you are going?"

"They are inside the library. I thought we could go in the adjoining room."

"They?" He followed her this time, and she silenced him with a finger to his lips. She led him into the music room, closing the door behind them.

Warnings flared within his mind, for despite his tentative truce with Evangeline, he knew how improper this was. But he followed her to the far end of the room. There was a door that was not properly set upon its hinges. It did indeed connect to the library, but from the crevices along the edge of the door, he could clearly hear the conversation of two men. He recognized Adrian Monroe's voice, but not the other gentleman's. It sounded familiar, but he couldn't quite place it.

When he leaned in closer to catch what they were saying, he grew acutely aware of Evangeline's presence. Her skin held the light aroma of gardenia, as if she had bathed with scented soap. James gritted his teeth and pushed the idle thoughts away.

"I thought you said Miss Carlisle would help us," the other gentleman was saying.

"And so she has. She has sown the seeds of doubt, which was precisely what I wanted," Adrian answered. "The stories I have spread will make her claims seem genuine. It matters not if she tries to deny what she said before. *My* evidence is far more damning."

James exchanged a glance with Evangeline, who had gone pale. She looked as if she were about to say something but stopped herself.

"I have a surprise for my cousin this night," Adrian said. "One that will drive him past the brink of sanity into madness. It has taken a great deal of time and effort, but I have no doubt it will work. Everyone will be shocked at his behavior, and it will lend credence to my claim that he is incapable of handling the estates due to his mental state. I will be permitted to govern Arnsbury on his behalf."

"Good," the other man answered, his voice sounding more relaxed. "We can then repay our debtors."

"*I* can repay my debts," Adrian corrected. He paused as if admiring his own efforts. "I have been waiting a long time to gain the property that should have been mine."

James had no idea what the pair intended, but it sounded as if Matthew ought to leave the ball immediately. Whatever Adrian planned sounded like a true threat.

There came a slight cough from the other gentleman. "And what of *my* debts? I thought we were working together."

"You may pick up the pieces of Lady Lily's broken heart," Adrian said drily. "She has a good dowry, if you can win her hand. Let her pay your debts, for I don't care what happens to her now."

James's lips tightened into a line, his anger rising at the mention of his sister. He wanted to shove his way through the door, but Evangeline put herself in front of the entrance, shaking her head.

There was no further conversation coming from the room, and James heard the faint click of the library door closing. He started to turn, but Evangeline caught his hand. "Wait a moment."

She paused, and then without warning, she drew his head down and crushed his mouth to hers. The kiss caught him completely unawares, and he was stunned enough not to protest. Evangeline's warm mouth held a hint of citrus, like the lemonade she had drunk earlier. But the heat of her embrace left him reeling.

"Forgive me," he heard a male voice say, before the door closed again.

Only then did Evangeline jerk away. "I'm sorry," she whispered. "But...I was afraid they would suspect we were eavesdropping. It was the only thing I could think to do that would explain why we were here alone."

He didn't move, but when she tried to take a step back, he held her waist with one arm. "It has been a long time, Evangeline."

"I know it. And I shouldn't have done that at all."

In all honesty, her quick thinking had likely deterred the intruder. But from the deep flush upon her cheeks, she looked as if she wanted to die. And he didn't want to humiliate her.

James took her hand and led her from the room, carefully looking around before he escorted her out. He needed to speak with Matthew to warn him about whatever Adrian was planning. There was no sign of the men, and he discreetly led her back to the ballroom.

"I—I saw the other man," Evangeline whispered. "It was Lord Davonshire."

Now it made sense what Adrian had proposed, about Davonshire picking up the pieces of Lily's broken heart. But James didn't intend to let either man near his sister. "I will protect Lily from them."

"Will you speak with Lord Arnsbury?"

He nodded. "And I want you to come with me, Evangeline. You can warn Lily in case she won't listen to me." He was less concerned about his sister, since it did not seem that the men were threatening her overtly. Matthew was their true target.

There was a waltz playing, and James led Evangeline into the steps, pressing his hand against her spine. Her face was still bright with color, and he couldn't think of what he could say to ease her embarrassment.

"The kiss wasn't that bad, was it?" he teased.

"No." She closed her eyes for a moment and admitted, "It was that good."

Her confession took him by surprise, though he knew she was right. Her lips had been softly yielding, reminding him of the last stolen moment between them.

She had a good reason to despise him, for he had not wanted to marry her. It wasn't Evangeline—it was any woman. He had felt the trappings of his father's dictates closing around him like a cage. At the time, he had been only twenty-three years old, and yet, his father had treated him as if he were already the earl. Every day, he'd been forced to read ledgers and surround himself with duties he was unprepared to face.

Now, he understood that his father's desperation was born from a man who had known he was dying. There had been so little time, but James had cast off responsibility and sought adventure in India. He had wanted to escape the title he didn't want.

But time and hardship had filled him with regret. Evangeline hadn't deserved to be cast off.

"Why didn't you marry someone else while I was away?" he asked. He guided her closer toward Matthew and Lily. The waltz would end soon, and he wanted to speak to both of them.

"Not many men would have me," she answered. "Because of my family's...business. And others were only interested in my money."

Her parents had built their fortunes upon an empire of scandalous ladies' undergarments, but it had never bothered James. "You are a beautiful woman with a good dowry," he reminded her. "It's what every gentleman wants."

Her expression cooled. "Not even you wanted me, Lord Penford." The dance ended, but Matthew and Lily were still on the far side of the room. He was about to approach them when he caught sight of another woman. His blood turned to ice, and he let out a low curse. God above, what was *she* doing here?

Evangeline frowned. "What is it?"

"Go back to your parents," he ordered. "I know exactly what Adrian is intending. And if Matthew sees that woman..."

He didn't bother finishing the sentence. Adrian wanted command of Arnsbury, above all else—and his ruthlessness would send Matthew over the edge.

"What can I do to help?" Evangeline asked.

God above, he didn't even know. All he could do was try to get Matthew out of this ballroom before he saw the woman who had clearly not been invited by the duchess.

"I have to stop him." He glanced around and added, "Tell a footman to summon Lord Arnsbury's carriage. I need to get Matthew out of here before he sees her."

"Before he sees who?"

There was no time to explain. "Please go and summon the carriage. I will tell you everything later."

Evangeline squeezed his hand before she hurried toward her parents. And in the meantime, he crossed through the room of people, hoping to warn Matthew.

Before he caught sight of the woman who had tortured him in India.

Chapter Nineteen

Lily left Matthew's side after the waltz, feeling slightly out of breath. Matthew had promised to fetch her a glass of lemonade while she went to see about Sarah Carlisle. The older woman had chosen a chair on the far end of the room, and another gentleman with gray hair was standing near her, leaning on his cane. Sarah's face was flushed, and Lily hid her smile, wondering if she had indeed found a suitor.

Just as she was about to approach, she overheard two men arguing. "I don't think it's true," the gentleman said. "We've known Arnsbury all his life. And Adrian Monroe is stirring up trouble for his own benefit."

Lily paused, her heartbeat quickening. She wanted to believe that Sarah Carlisle had done what she could to dispel the gossip—but no one could know for certain.

She was about to approach the older woman, when she heard a female voice calling out to her. "Lady Lily?"

Lily turned and saw a beautiful woman with dark hair and skin the color of rich caramel. Her features held an exotic cast, as if she had been born in India, and she wore a dove-colored ball gown with two flounces. A warm smile curved over the woman's face.

"I do not believe we have met," Lily said. She felt a sudden uneasiness, though she masked her feelings.

"No, I have not had the pleasure. I am Priya Shavanastu." With a nod in the other direction, she added, "I am the guest of Mr. Monroe."

I am certain you are, Lily thought. She had no notion of what Adrian's intentions were, but if he had brought this woman from India, it could not be good. Whether this woman had any connection to Matthew hardly mattered at all— Adrian was attempting to dredge up terrible memories. And Lily intended to shield the man she loved from his cousin's animosity.

"Forgive me for interrupting you," Miss Shavanastu continued, "but I have been wanting to speak with Lord Arnsbury. Mr. Monroe thought he would not be far from your side."

"He may return shortly," Lily answered. Although she gave the appearance of serenity, inside, her stomach was churning. If Matthew saw this woman, it might bring back all the torment of India. And she would never allow that.

She took the woman's arm with the pretense of walking with her. "Forgive me, but how do you know the earl? Did you meet him during his travels in India?" She kept her tone light, as if she were discussing the weather. But she wanted to read the woman's response to determine her intentions.

Miss Shavanastu gave a soft laugh. "We did, yes. In fact, he is the reason I traveled this far to London. I owe him a great deal and wanted to thank him in person."

Every hair upon Lily's skin seemed to stand on end, but she forced herself to smile at the woman. "Then let me take you to him," she lied. Her instincts warned that this woman was up to no good, so she guided her in the opposite direction. "He was speaking with a friend outside. Let us go and join him."

The woman had clearly not seen Matthew, for she followed Lily readily. "I should be glad to. My daughter would not be alive were it not for Lord Arnsbury's assistance."

Lily did not believe any of her words but murmured, "You have traveled a great distance. It could not have been an easy journey." She guided the woman toward the doors, letting the woman speak of her voyage onboard the ship.

All the while, Lily was conscious of the deceit. She did not doubt for a moment that this foreigner had been brought to disturb Matthew. There was danger in her very presence, and Lily was determined to take her away from the duchess's ball. A footman could help to discreetly escort Miss Shavanastu away, claiming she was an uninvited guest.

When they reached the garden, the woman turned to study the men and women milling about, but as Lily had intended, there was no sign of Matthew. "We must have missed him," she said apologetically. "But if you wish to wait here, Miss Shavanastu, I can fetch a footman to bring him to us."

The woman's expression shifted almost imperceptibly, revealing a trace of annoyance. "Let us return to the ballroom, and I am certain we will find him there."

"Perhaps in a moment." Lily walked across the stone terrace, pretending as if nothing were amiss. "Do let me show you the gardens."

The woman stared at her. "There are no flowers blooming in December, Lady Lily."

"No, but it will give us a chance to speak without anyone eavesdropping." She intended to give this woman a warning of her own. As she'd hoped, Miss Shavanastu followed.

During his revelation, Matthew had admitted that he believed someone had paid a sailor to kidnap him and James, bringing them at the mercy of their captors. But James had not been tormented in the same way, and when he'd escaped, no one had followed. Likely because he was of no consequence to the men.

Adrian had known that Matthew was leaving for India with James. Would he not arrange for his cousin's death, particularly since he was the immediate heir to the earldom? It was easy enough to hire an assassin, but for whatever reason, Matthew had been tortured instead.

"Your English is flawless," she said to Miss Shavanastu. "How did you learn to speak it so well?"

The woman smiled. "We were servants in an English household. I learned to speak it as easily as my own language." In spite of her friendly tone, Lily detected a hardness in her eyes, a flash of hatred toward those she had served.

Now that they were alone, away from the other guests, Lily wanted to provoke a reaction from the woman to see if her premonition had any merit. She had her own theory of the woman's true identity and decided to voice it.

"I seem to recall that Lord Arnsbury *did* mention you to me." Before the woman could speak, Lily added, "But I believe your true name is Nisha Amat, is it not?" She kept a smile fixed upon her face, but the woman's expression faltered in a moment of shock.

Miss Shavanastu shook her head. "No. You must be thinking of someone else."

How stupid do you believe I am? she wanted to retort. Had it truly been an error, the woman would not have reacted at all. And for that reason, Lily made no effort to conceal her hatred. "I don't know why you've traveled all this way, nor do I care whether you were paid by Mr. Monroe or anyone else. Return to India, and leave Lord Arnsbury alone."

The woman finally dropped the façade of friendliness. "As you said before, it was a long journey from India. I was paid well for what I did there. But I will not be paid the rest until I have finished my task. Mr. Monroe was quite furious that Arnsbury survived and returned home."

A surge of fury rose up within her that this woman had

ordered Matthew's torture. Lily's hands curled into fists, and she barely kept herself in control. "What you did to him was not human. I want you to leave immediately."

"I liked torturing him," Nisha said smoothly. "I held power over him, the way your people held power over me. I enjoyed breaking his mind as well as his body. And I had to return, to finish what I'd started. I knew where he would go, and I followed him here."

The woman's madness was a part of her, ensnared so deeply, it terrified Lily. Words would not convince her to stop, and she had no doubt Nisha meant to kill Matthew. The thought drew out her own protective instincts, lending her courage.

"You will not lay a single finger upon him," she warned. "Go now, or I will have you thrown out."

Nisha's face curved in a dark smile. "I don't think you will." She reached out and caught Lily's wrist, tightening her grip.

And in her other hand, Lily saw the glint of a knife.

Matthew searched for Lily, but she was not standing where he had left her. He held a glass of lemonade, feeling foolish while he stared at the ballroom guests.

"There you are," James called out. He hurried toward him, and Evangeline trailed behind. Both appeared out of breath, and he wondered what had happened.

"Have you seen Lily?" he asked.

James exchanged a glance with Evangeline. "No, but I overheard a conversation between your cousin and Lord Davonshire. It seems that both men are attempting to cause more trouble."

Likely the rumors were spreading rapidly, and he guessed, "Because of Miss Carlisle?"

James shook his head. "There's something far worse. If you will come with me now, I'll explain, in private."

He couldn't imagine what was worse, but his greater concern was his fiancée. "Let me find Lily first. I told her I would bring her a glass of lemonade, and she may want to hear this, too."

But James caught his sleeve and lowered his voice. "There isn't time for that, Arnsbury. It seems that Adrian brought a...guest with him this evening. He's trying to push you into madness, the way you were when we returned from India."

"Nothing he could say or do would accomplish that," he answered. Over the past few months, he had managed to shut away the past, locking it out of his consciousness. And regardless of his cousin's machinations, Matthew intended to remain strong for Lily's sake.

James started to argue, but then Evangeline paled. "Lord Penford, I think we should go to your sister. I saw Lily on the terrace, and she—"

"Yes, I agree." Matthew turned around, intending to go after Lily.

James joined him, but before Matthew could take another step, his cousin Adrian blocked their path. Beside him was Thomas Kingston, Viscount Burkham.

"I've been wanting to speak with you," Adrian began. "I was just telling Lord Burkham of your trials in India." His voice was silky, as if he delighted in Matthew's ordeal. "You were imprisoned there for such a long time. Any man would go mad after such torture."

Matthew ignored the man, knowing that his cousin was only trying to bait him. "Excuse me, Adrian."

But the man refused to move. "In fact, I spoke with other members of Parliament over the past few weeks. They know what you suffered and how you've struggled since you returned to England."

At that, Matthew stopped. "Spreading lies and rumors does

not become you, Cousin. Anyone with half a brain"—he eyed Viscount Burkham—"would see that you are trying to claim Arnsbury as yours. But you are not the earl, nor can you take command of my property."

"Not while you are here, no," Adrian admitted.

"Is that a threat?" he demanded. "Because everyone here knows of your debts. You hope to gain Arnsbury so you can strip its wealth away for your own gain."

"I have no need to threaten you," Adrian answered. "You may put on the airs of a man who has recovered, but your true nature will reveal itself."

Matthew shook his head in exasperation and pushed his way past his cousin. But before he could take another step, Adrian added, "In fact, once you see Lady Lily, I believe all of your madness will come roaring back. Everyone will see exactly the man you are—one unfit to care for the estate."

He didn't know what Adrian was talking about, but it was clear that he was trying to provoke him. And right now, he needed to find Lily to ensure she was all right. He eyed James, and his best friend nodded in silent agreement.

Matthew pushed his way past Adrian, walking across the ballroom to the doors leading to the terrace. James trailed behind him, his expression grim.

Outside, it was freezing cold, and the stone terrace was slick with frost. Matthew hurried toward the far end of the garden where two women stood.

Fury roared through him when he recognized Nisha Amat. This woman had caused the torment and vicious nightmares. She had broken his spirit and mind, until he'd thought he would never have a normal life. The very sight of her made him want to close his hands over her throat until she breathed her last.

He didn't have to wonder how or why Nisha was here. Adrian had arranged her transportation—and Matthew now knew exactly what his cousin had plotted and why. God above,

Adrian had planned all of this. He had hired Nisha to abduct and kill him in India, for if Matthew was dead, Adrian would inherit the earldom to pay off his debts.

Now, his cousin hoped to provoke him past the edge of sanity by forcing him to face his torturer. Matthew's gut hardened, as the pieces slid into place. If he were locked away in an asylum, Adrian would have full command of the earldom and its fortunes.

Lily cried out, struggling against Nisha, and all Matthew could think of was protecting her. He ran hard toward the women, his mind seething with rage. Nisha was gripping Lily's wrist, and in her other palm, he saw a curved blade.

Dimly, he heard James warning him to be careful, but he ignored the words. He cared nothing about himself—only shielding Lily. Never would he allow Nisha to hurt the woman he loved. With one stroke of the knife, his torturer could end the happiness and peace he had found. And God help him, he would snap Nisha's neck first.

Time ground to a stop, and the world blurred. Matthew pushed back all rational thoughts, surrendering to actions. He threw himself toward the woman and felt the blade sink into his flesh. He didn't feel any pain, but he reached for Nisha's throat, closing his hands around it. Abruptly, she stumbled, twisting, as he pressed her toward the ground.

He heard none of the voices calling out to him, nor was he aware of what was happening. All he knew was that he would give up his own life for Lily.

Strong arms dragged him backward, and the blade clattered to the stone terrace. His blood pumped wildly through his veins, and he saw the fallen body of Nisha. Lily was doubled over, blood all over her gown.

"No!" The hoarse cry tore from his throat when he saw her sobbing.

Two men pulled him away, and he saw James kneeling beside his sister. There was a pounding echo in Matthew's ears, and he fought to free himself from the men grasping his shoulders.

"My lord, you must leave now," a servant was saying. "Go with your men back to your carriage. The duchess has demanded it."

"Lily—" He needed to know if she was all right, but dizziness washed over him, and he dropped to his knees. The two men hauled him upright, and he grew aware of a searing pain in his side.

"We must go." The footmen should not have been able to overpower him, but Matthew realized that Nisha had indeed wounded him with her blade. His hands were covered in blood, and it seemed he'd been stabbed in the ribs.

He tried to break free of the men, but dizziness made him stumble. "I need to see if Lily is hurt."

"Her brother is looking after her," the footman insisted. "But my lord, you are bleeding. You should go home and order your servants to summon a doctor."

The servant's words made little sense. He could have sworn Dr. Fraser was among the guests, but the men were pulling him back inside the house.

"Send the doctor to…Lady Lily," he gasped. He fought to remain conscious, but the loss of blood made it impossible. His vision wavered, and his last image was of Lily cradled in her brother's arms beside the fallen body of his torturer.

⁂

"I must go to him," Lily told James. "I-I need to see if he is all right." Her hands were trembling, and she hardly knew what had happened. When Nisha had pulled the blade on her, Lily had not been afraid for herself—she had known the threat was meant to drive Matthew over the brink.

And so it had. Everyone had witnessed him diving at the woman, his hands closing over her throat.

Everything had happened so fast, yet for Lily, time had seemed to slow down. All she remembered was being pushed away while Nisha staggered forward with the blade in her hand. The woman had slashed Matthew deeply, but he didn't seem to feel the pain at all. Instead, he gripped Nisha by the shoulders to keep her away from Lily. Then he tried to force her to the ground.

Lily didn't know what she could do to help, but she kicked Nisha's leg hard. The woman lost her balance, and when she stumbled forward, she fell upon her own blade. Within a few moments, she was dead.

God help her, Lily had only been trying to save Matthew. Others were already saying he had killed Nisha for her sake, but that wasn't true at all. The blood and the guilt lay upon Lily's shoulders. And the very thought made her sick.

Her brother had guided her into their carriage, and she hoped they were following Matthew. But within minutes, she realized he had taken them home. "James, I need to see him. Take me to his townhouse."

"Give it a little time, Lily. They are investigating the cause of death, and I don't want you there."

She knew full well what the cause of death was. "I will not stay at home. I need to know that Matthew is all right. He was injured by the blade."

Because of me.

She now understood the terrible guilt he had suffered when she had dislocated her arm. He had never meant to harm her, just as she would gladly have sliced her own skin before wounding Matthew.

"Lily, there was an uproar after he left. It's not a good idea to go and see him so soon." Her brother reached for her hand and squeezed it before he opened the carriage door.

"I will go with or without your approval." In this, she would not be swayed.

His mouth tightened as if he didn't want to, but at last he

nodded. "Then I will take you there myself. Unless you...want to change first?"

She realized that her ball gown was covered in blood. James was right—she could not visit Matthew looking like this. It looked as if she had been wounded herself, and that might cause him even more distress. "All right, but quickly."

She followed her brother into the house and rang for Hattie to help her change into a demure gray gown. Her hands trembled as she donned her gloves once more, and James waited to escort her.

"You don't have to come with me," she argued. "I can take a footman."

But in this, he was adamant. "After all that has happened, I am not leaving your side." He guided her outside to the waiting carriage, and she admitted to herself that she was grateful for his protection.

Lily needed to see how badly Matthew had been wounded. Although his cousin had tried to provoke him, she knew within her heart that he had not fallen into madness. He had reacted out of rage and the desire to protect her. Afterward, she'd heard him calling out to her. It made her believe that he'd known what was happening and had done everything he could to keep her safe.

Lily felt a dark sense of satisfaction that the woman was gone. Though she had never wanted to cause anyone's death, she was grateful that Nisha could not harm either of them again. She only prayed that they would not be blamed for her death. Surely enough witnesses had seen the attack and would know the truth.

James helped her climb into the carriage, and she sat across from him, her worry multiplying with every minute. But then he interrupted her thoughts, asking, "Why did Nisha Amat travel this far from India?"

"She came of her own accord, because she was hired to kill Matthew. Adrian only paid her a portion of what was promised. And because she... wanted to finish the task and kill him." Lily closed her eyes and clenched her fingers together. Another thought took hold, and she regarded her brother. "Did Nisha torture you in the same way?"

James shook his head. "They questioned me but only to get information about Matthew, I see now. I tried not to tell them anything, but..." He grimaced. "It was difficult to hold my silence. And they didn't really care when I escaped."

She didn't ask him what had happened. Instead, she reached out to hold his hand. "I am glad you came back, James. Thank you for bringing Matthew to me." It was then that she noticed her gloves were stained with Matthew's blood. She should have changed them when she'd chosen another gown, but now it was too late.

The journey to Matthew's townhouse was short, and James helped her disembark from the carriage. Her brother rang the bell, and when the footman answered, James said, "We came to see if Arnsbury is all right. Did you send for Dr. Fraser?"

The footman frowned. "Lord Arnsbury is not here. He was attending the Duchess of Worthingstone's ball and has not yet returned. Has something happened?"

Lily froze, exchanging a glance with James. Her brother prompted, "Then his carriage is not here?"

The footman shook his head. "No, my lord. Is there...anything we should do?" The servant appeared uneasy about the turn of conversation. "Was Lord Arnsbury hurt?"

James shook his head. "We will go and find him." He didn't bother explaining himself to the footman. Instead, he led Lily back to the carriage once again.

She waited until they were both inside before speaking. "What's happened to Matthew?"

James's expression turned sober. "I fear Adrian or his servants may have taken him somewhere. But I cannot say where."

She was not going to give up so easily. If it meant confronting the man herself, she would find Matthew and bring him back.

"We should return to the duchess's ball," she informed her brother.

"He won't be there."

"No, but we can ask questions of the servants. Someone might know where Matthew was taken." Emotions swelled up within her, fear that he was still wounded and in danger. Though she didn't think his cousin would go so far as to take Matthew's life, he might let him bleed to death.

Her brother thought for a long moment, his expression furrowed. Then he looked back at her. "Evangeline and I overheard a conversation at the ball that we weren't meant to know about. Adrian Monroe was conspiring with Davonshire. They wanted to take command of Arnsbury's estates and wealth to pay off their own debts."

A coldness gripped Lily's senses, though she tried to hold back the fear. "Do you think they've taken him?"

"I don't know," James answered. "But I think Monroe was trying to prove that Matthew was incapable of managing the earldom. He wanted everyone to believe that Arnsbury went mad after what happened in India. Then Adrian would be in charge of the estates."

"But what does Davonshire have to do with it?" Lily shook her head, not understanding.

"He and my cousin are close friends. Both are heavily in debt," her brother said. "Perhaps Davonshire intended to renew his courtship of you, hoping to get his hands on your dowry."

"He did come to pay a call on me when you were gone," she said. "He was trying to discredit Matthew, telling me he was illegitimate and should never have been named earl." The more she thought of it, the more she wondered what else Davonshire had done.

She sat back in silence, trying to keep her hopes up. If those footmen had not led Matthew home again, where could they have taken him? And then, the answer came to her.

"We should go to Adrian Monroe's residence. He must know something."

Her brother called out to the coachman and gave the orders. "It's possible."

Lily was afraid to get her hopes up, but she held faith that they would find Matthew before it was too late. "We will find him," she insisted. "No matter how long it takes."

⟞⟝⟐⟞⟝

Matthew's head was pounding, and it felt as if his brain had been encased in cotton. Every muscle in his body was frozen, and he could hardly move. He was dimly aware of blood seeping from a wound near his ribs. The pain had been constant, a dull ache that gripped him and would not let go.

He hadn't recognized the two footmen who had taken him from the duchess's ball, but he'd been furious at the sight of Nisha threatening Lily. It had been a living nightmare, one he hadn't wanted to believe.

One of the footmen had forced a tonic down him, and the opiate effects of the drug had not yet worn off. His lips were dry, and he could not rid himself of the bitter aftertaste. His vision blurred, and he heard voices talking as they approached. He closed his eyes, hoping he would learn what Adrian wanted.

"What do you want to do?" came the voice of Lord Davonshire. "Blame him for the murder of the woman? If he is imprisoned, he cannot oversee the estates."

"There were too many witnesses who saw Nisha pull the knife on Lady Lily." Adrian let out a disgruntled sigh. "Already they are saying the earl was only defending her. That the death was accidental." He let out a foul curse and muttered, "There has to be another way. He was supposed to lose all sense of reason and show that he was unfit to be the earl."

"And so he did," Davonshire agreed. "All you have to do now is prove his madness."

"No one will believe it." But he thought a moment and said, "But they might believe a doctor. If we take him to an asylum, they can fill him with enough opium that he won't even know his name." Adrian's tone brightened, and he added, "We can bribe someone to testify that he isn't fit to manage the estates."

"He's still bleeding," Davonshire reminded him. "Should we have a doctor heal his wounds?"

"It's better if he dies," Adrian answered. "He was *supposed* to die in India, so that I would become the earl."

"Why did you hire a woman to kill him?" Davonshire asked.

"I didn't," Adrian snapped. "But her brother was aboard the ship with them, and he turned Arnsbury over into her hands."

Matthew kept his eyes closed, feigning an unconscious state. But inwardly, he felt cold inside. His cousin's greed was boundless, it seemed—enough to want him dead.

"We should bring him to Bethlem Hospital," Adrian suggested. "No one will think to look for him there."

Matthew gritted his teeth. He would rather bleed to death than be committed to an asylum.

The sound of their footsteps retreated, and their voices grew quieter as they departed. When there was only silence, Matthew forced himself to open his eyes and discern his surroundings.

His cousin had brought him inside the house, but it appeared that they were within the servants' quarters. The narrow bed he lay upon had hardly anything more than threadbare sheets and a wool coverlet. If he was on the lowermost level, he could follow the corridor to another set of stairs that would lead outside. But he didn't know if he possessed the strength to make his own escape.

There was a strong chance that he wouldn't be able to get out of bed, much less find a way out of the house. But he steeled himself with the image of Lily's face. He remembered the soft curve of her cheek, the rose lips that had kissed him...and the golden brown strands of hair framing her beautiful face.

She would be worried about him, and if she dared to track him here, it would endanger her. He had to get himself home again, one step at a time. Though his body did not want to cooperate, his mind remained strong. He had to get out of here.

One by one, he swung his feet over the side of the bed and managed to sit up. Dizziness rushed to his head, but he took slow breaths to steady himself. He touched his ribcage, and his fingers came away sticky with blood. The wound throbbed, but he could do nothing except hold his hand against it, keeping pressure upon the ache.

He kept Lily's face fixed in his mind as he made his way to the open door and paused to look for Adrian or Davonshire. He heard the distant sounds of arguing, but it did not seem that either man was within view. He had a few precious moments to get out, and Matthew forced himself to stagger down the hallway toward the stairs leading outside.

The pain in his ribs was vicious, tearing through him with every step. It was likely they hadn't bothered to secure the door, knowing he could barely move.

But when he reached the stairs at the end of the hall, he didn't know if he had the strength to climb them. Droplets of blood had leaked upon the floor, and if the men decided to search, it would be an easy matter to find him.

He had to continue fighting for his life, for Lily's sake. She had brought him back from the edge once before, and he would use her love to do it again.

Matthew nearly stumbled at the first step, but he bit his lips hard and forced himself onward. His wound felt like fire, burning his ribs. Each step was agony, but he refused to give up. His vision blurred, and he continued onward.

In his mind, he focused on what he would do once he reached the outside. He would hail a hackney and go home. There were drivers out, even this late at night. Surely, he could find someone.

When he managed to push open the door, the night air was frigid and malodorous. And yet, it held the scent of freedom. Step by step, he ventured beyond the property lines, keeping his gaze fixed in the distance. He thought he heard voices, but when he turned, there was no one there.

Twisted memories invaded, causing him to hallucinate. He heard Nisha's laughter in his mind, and he continued to hobble forward, trying to push away the visions that were not real. He closed his eyes, telling himself that he only had to make it a little further until he reached the London streets. He heard the soft nicker of horses, and it gave him hope. He trudged onward, trying to lift his hand to signal for a hackney, but his arm would not move. Every muscle in his body ached. The slick flow of blood, mingled with the effects of the opium, made it impossible to lift his hand.

He surveyed his surroundings and saw none of the London streets. There were horses, yes, but he had come out by the mews instead. God help him. He didn't think he possessed the strength to prepare a horse, much less ride away from Adrian's townhouse. Every last bit of strength was draining away from him.

He managed to enter the stable, but he could not take more than a few steps before his knees buckled. He tried to pull himself back up, but the tide of dizziness swept over him until he collapsed to the ground.

Behind him, he heard voices. "Should we bring him back?"

"No. Leave him there. He'll be dead by morning."

And with that, the heavy wooden door closed, leaving him in complete darkness.

Chapter Twenty

Outside Adrian's house, Lily stood beside her brother, her heartbeat pounding. *Please let him be here,* she thought. *Let him be alive.* "Do you think Matthew is here?" she asked her brother.

"Even if he is, Adrian will lie about it." James pounded on the door once again, waiting for a servant to answer.

"It's long past midnight," she said. "I doubt they will let us in."

Her brother stiffened. "Oh, they will. If I have to break a window, we'll find him."

In that moment, her heart swelled with love for her brother. Although she and James had not always gotten along, in this moment, she knew she could depend on him. "Thank you."

At last, a footman answered the door, a disgruntled expression on his face. "Mr. Monroe is not receiving guests at this late hour."

Before the man could slam the door in their faces, James shoved his way inside and held the door for Lily. "Mr. Monroe has a great deal to answer for. And we will not wait until the morning."

"Mr. Monroe is sleeping," the footman said. "I will not disturb him."

"No matter," James replied cheerfully. "I have no qualms about disturbing him."

But a moment later, there came a low growl from one of the rooms, followed by exuberant barking. Lily turned toward the sound and nearly stumbled when a large dog jumped up on her, licking her with joy.

"Sebastian!" she called out. She knelt down, ruffling his ears. Joy filled her at the sight of him, but she also realized why he was here—because of Lord Davonshire.

Sebastian sat back and scratched his ear with his hind legs before he stood and wagged his tail. And she fully intended to use the dog to help her. Lily stripped off one of her stained gloves and knelt down. "Find Matthew, sweet dog. And I will give you as much bacon as your heart desires."

The word bacon caught the animal's attention, and he licked his chops, his tail wagging with delight. The dog sniffed at the carpet, but instead of following a trail inside the house, he returned to the front door.

Lily pulled him further inside, but the dog held little interest in finding Matthew's trail. Instead, he rolled onto his back, exposing his belly to be rubbed. She tried again, but he only licked her fingers and wagged his tail.

She wanted to groan with frustration. It had been foolish to pin her hopes upon Sebastian when he was not her dog and was not trained. She had relied too much on the impossible.

So be it. If he could not find Matthew, then they would get the truth out of Adrian.

But a moment later, the dog jerked to his feet and began snarling. The hair stood up on his back, and then he bolted toward the drawing room. Lily followed him, trailed by James. Although the room was dark, she heard a man yelp, "What the devil?"

James took the lamp from the footman and entered the

room, revealing the presence of Lord Davonshire. The moment he saw them, he blinked. "Lord Penford and Lady Lily. Isn't it a bit late for you to come calling?"

"I might say the same for you," Lily answered. She went to stand by Sebastian, her suspicions alert. "And for a man who claims to have owned Sebastian for years, he doesn't seem to like you very much just now."

The earl stiffened and took a step backward. "He's not very intelligent."

"I disagree." And the more she thought of it, the more her suspicions heightened. "I think he only obeyed your commands because you had bacon in your pockets."

Davonshire's expression turned annoyed. It infuriated her to think that he had stooped to something so low.

"He's never been your dog, has he?" Lily prompted.

"Easy now—" His words were cut off when Sebastian snarled at him once more. "All right, no, he wasn't. But it gave me a reason to see you again. Is that so wrong that I used him to get close to you?"

His confession infuriated her, for she now knew that Lord Davonshire was only interested in getting close to her dowry. "Yes, it *is* wrong that you would take my dog away, pretending he was yours. Why would I ever want to see a man like you again?" She had wept over the loss of this furry creature, and she would never allow anyone to take him from her. Her hands curled over Sebastian's fur, and she vowed, "I am keeping him. You cannot have him back."

Lord Davonshire shrugged. "He was a nuisance, and you are welcome to him."

Lily rather wished the dog would relieve himself upon Davonshire's leg. But she squared her shoulders and demanded, "So why are *you* here at this late hour, Lord Davonshire?"

He appeared dumbfounded by the question. "Well, I. That is…"

"Because he was helping me bring back my cousin," came a voice from behind them. Lily and James turned to see Adrian who was still wearing his dark tailcoat from the ball. "You were there, and you saw the madness that came over him. Matthew was not himself."

"Because that woman tried to stab me," Lily insisted. "The woman you hired from India." Rage was seething within her, and James tried to hold her back. "I never thought you would take matters that far. How could you do such a thing?"

Adrian's expression was smug, and she wanted to strike out at him.

But James intervened, still keeping a firm grip on her waist. "Where is Matthew now?"

"Where he belongs," Adrian said. "I rode with his footmen, and we delivered him to Bethlem Hospital."

Lily was aghast at the idea. "Why on earth would you do such a thing?" Her mind was spinning with horror. How could it even be possible?

But then, in a moment of clarity, she understood. If Matthew were locked away in an asylum, the property would fall into Adrian's hands. He would have complete command of Arnsbury and its wealth.

"You are despicable. And what's more, you—"

Before she could say another word, her brother took her by the hand. "Thank you, gentlemen. We bid you a good night."

She wanted to protest, but James sent her a sharp look to be silent. For that reason, Lily allowed him to lead her from the drawing room. Her brother was up to something, and she didn't know what it was. She had to trust that he knew how to help Matthew.

Sebastian happily trailed them, sniffing the carpet along the way. James continued to lead her outside, but Lily could not believe any of Adrian's claims. When they were outside and alone, she asked her brother, "Do you think he actually took Matthew to Bethlem Hospital?" She had heard terrible rumors about what had been done to the criminally insane patients.

"No," James answered. "For one, they would never accept a new patient at this hour, unless the police were involved. Adrian is trying to throw us off."

"Then where—" Her words broke off when Sebastian began sniffing the ground. His nose locked upon the scent, and he trotted toward the rear of the house by the mews.

She started to hurry, afraid the dog had caught a wrong trail. But she held hope that he was close to finding Matthew.

Sebastian sniffed a path toward the stables and then whined at the doorway. Lily unlatched it, and the dog bolted forward...only for him to stop suddenly and gobble up what appeared to be a fallen piece of food.

She let out a sigh of dismay. "I can't believe it. For a moment, I wanted to believe that he had tracked Matthew this far." Frustrated, she reached for Sebastian and guided him back outside. There was only the soft nicker of horses in the stable, and certainly nothing else was visible in the darkness.

"Let's go home, Lily," her brother urged. "It's late, and Matthew isn't here. I'll reach out to our friends, and we will see what can be done. And if he is in Bethlem Hospital, by some chance, I will get him out."

With reluctance, she closed the door behind them and followed her brother back to the carriage.

They had left.

Matthew groaned in the darkness, struggling to call out to her. "Lily," he rasped. But his voice was hardly above a whisper. She would never hear him.

He didn't know how much blood he'd lost, but it felt as if his heartbeat were slowing down. Weariness overtook him, and he tried to call out twice more. The earthen floor was damp and cold beneath his face. It struck him as ironic that he had escaped torture in India at Nisha's hands, only to be killed by her in the end.

His skin had turned to ice, and he was trembling hard. Matthew thought he was hallucinating now, for the world kept flickering in and out of his consciousness. There was a whining sound, and he thought he heard voices again. Or perhaps he was dying from loss of blood.

A tongue rasped against his face, and he blinked, only to see Sebastian beside him. He couldn't quite grasp how it had happened, but the dog continued to lick him.

"Matthew!" Lily's voice called out. "Dear God, James, we have to get him out of here."

It was her voice that jolted him back. In the darkness, he tried to glimpse her face, but he could only see shadows. He moved his lips, trying to speak Lily's name, but no words would come out.

It was already too late, he knew. He was shaking badly, his voice locked in silence. He couldn't tell her how glad he was to see her, even if it was for the last time. How beautiful she was or how much he adored her.

She was openly weeping for him, but it would do no good now.

It was the middle of the night when James carried an unconscious Matthew to the house of Dr. Fraser and his wife, Lady Falsham. Lily pounded on the door, her worries heightening with every moment. So much blood. She hadn't known he'd been that badly wounded, but she had bound the wound tightly, trying to stop the bleeding. Her heart froze with the fear that he might not survive this ordeal.

She kept pounding and calling out for the footman. When one eventually opened the door, he suppressed a yawn. But once he realized what had happened, the servant sprang into action. "Oh dear. Lord Penford, Lady Lily, do bring him inside. I will awaken the doctor."

The footman led them over to a smaller room off the parlor that had been set up for patients. "Put Lord Arnsbury there upon the bed." He rang for other servants, and when they arrived, he gave orders for hot water, bandages, and supplies the doctor would need.

Within a few minutes, Dr. Fraser strode into the room. The moment he spied Matthew's bloody shirt, his demeanor transformed. "Now what's happened to you, lad?" he murmured, pulling back the shirt to examine Matthew. Without looking up, he said to James, "I need more light. Hold the lamp so I can have a look at his wound. Lady Lily, fetch me that basin of water and bring some linen so I can clean it."

Her hands were shaking so badly, she nearly spilled the water, but she hurried to obey. Inwardly, she voiced a thousand prayers, hoping Matthew would live. The doctor's face remained grave as he cut away her makeshift bandage to examine the jagged wound.

"It hasn't struck a vital organ," Dr. Fraser said, "but the amount of blood he's lost is disturbing. His heart is struggling to beat."

A cry sounded from the doorway, and Juliette entered the room. She was wearing a nightgown and wrapper, and she moved to kneel beside Matthew. "How did this happen?"

James explained hurriedly, but his voice held a quiet tone of fear. "He's been bleeding for three hours."

Dr. Fraser examined the wound closely. "It looks as if he tried to bind his ribs before you did, Lily. Or perhaps he lay upon his side, and that put pressure upon it. But I wouldna be lying if I did no' say 'tis a miracle he's still breathing."

"Save him, Paul," Juliette pleaded. "He cannot die." Tears slid down her cheeks, and Lily reached out to take her hand, sharing in her grief. But she had fallen into such numbness, she could scarcely breathe.

Dr. Fraser cleaned the wound and began treating it. It tormented Lily to see Matthew lying so motionless, and it appeared he was already dead. Her heart refused to accept the thought. She murmured a litany of prayers all throughout the doctor's ministrations, until Matthew's wounds were bandaged.

"I dare not give him laudanum," he admitted. "It would stop his heart." Eyeing the women, he added, "The most you can do now is pray."

"I will stay with him," Lily promised. "And if anything happens, I will send for you."

"I will join you," Juliette said to Lily, but the doctor guided her back.

"Give them a moment alone first," he said.

A terror lanced Lily's heart when she understood why. He believed she needed a chance to say goodbye to Matthew before he died. *Dear God, no.*

One by one, they left her alone with him. Matthew's pallor was so gray, she feared the worst. He had battled death in India once before, but she didn't know if he could overcome this.

"I am here, Matthew," she said gently. She slid her fingertips over his face, but he did not react. She wished for any response at all, even if he spoke to her the way he first had when he'd returned from India.

"I suppose I should have brought Beast with me," she offered. "Or even Sebastian. He did help us find you, you know. We had given up, but he kept pulling me back and whining until we opened the doors and searched again." A tear rolled down her cheek, but she didn't bother to brush it away. "I told Lord Davonshire that I'm keeping Sebastian."

Lily kept talking, telling him stories about the dog. She poured out her heart, never ceasing as she begged him to fight for each breath. And when she could hardly talk about anything else, she laid her cheek against his chest and held his hand. It shattered her that she could do nothing to ease his suffering.

She had loved this man for so long, and they had battled the demons of his past together. He had survived those moments of darkness, only to come out stronger. And somehow, he knew her more deeply than anyone else.

"I need you to get well," she whispered. "So I can marry you." His hand was terribly cold, so cold, she didn't know if he had heard anything she'd said. Tears slid down her cheeks, and she squeezed his palm. "I love you, Matthew." She brought his hand to her mouth and repeated, "I love you."

She needed him by her side, for they belonged together. The thought of losing him was a dagger in her own heart.

Lily leaned down and brushed her mouth against his. Though he didn't kiss her back, she could only hope that he had heard her words.

It was then that she felt the slight pressure of his palm squeezing hers. And it gave her a faint trace of hope.

Chapter Twenty-One

Six months later

Matthew stood while his valet adjusted his cravat, brushing away any visible lint from his tailcoat. His best friend, James, stood on the far end of the room, a slight smirk on his face. "Monroe should enjoy his new home, I should imagine. I personally think you should have shot him. Accidentally, of course. Or perhaps sent him to India to endure what you did."

"I hold more power over him this way," Matthew answered. "I bought up his promissory notes, his mortgaged estate, and I command his entire fortune. And I think America will be a better home for him."

"An ocean between you is a good start."

"And he has nothing to return to. If he dares to set foot back in England, he will face criminal charges."

"I still say you were too forgiving." James picked up his top hat and opened the door. "But then, it *is* rather torturous for a man of Adrian's upbringing to live on the frontier. He may not survive. And Davonshire's new wife has him well under her thumb. He'd be in debtor's prison if it weren't for her dowry."

"Both of them will have to make the best of their new lives." Matthew followed James out of the bedroom and toward the stairs. A sense of anticipation thrummed within him of the moment when he would see his bride walking toward him in her mother's walled garden. He had fought his way back from death's embrace for her sake, and Lily had come to see him every day over the past few months, until he was fully healed.

There were no longer any nightmares to torture him. Nisha's death had been ruled an accident, and he had found his own peace knowing that justice had been given by Fate. The rumors his cousin had tried to spread about Matthew's birthright had died down thanks to the efforts of his friends and Sarah Carlisle. The scandal of Adrian's crimes had cast a greater shadow over all that he had said, and no one believed his stories now.

Matthew felt as if his life had been returned to him, only now, there was a very different kind of torment—waiting to marry the woman he loved. Lily had wanted to wait until their wedding night to make love again, and every kiss sharpened the yearning. He longed to wake up beside her, to see her hazel eyes shining with joy before he took her in his arms.

And this day, he hoped to give Lily the wedding of her dreams.

Outside, the sun was shining, and he and James made their way outside Penford toward the walled garden. The door leading to the garden was open, and he entered the space where the wedding guests awaited them.

Dark-pink roses climbed along the brick wall, while a stately willow hung beside a clear pool of water. In the shade, blue hydrangea bushes were in bloom, the deep color vivid against the green leaves. Dozens of chairs were set up in rows, and the guests smiled as he walked past them. James returned to the door to await his sister.

Matthew took his place near the minister, waiting for his bride. He was eager to see Lily, feeling so grateful that this day had come at last.

When she appeared in the doorway of the garden, it stole his very breath to see her. Her ivory gown rested at her shoulders, covered in seed pearls that beaded across the neckline and over the cap sleeves. The gown clung to her slender waist, and yards of white fabric cascaded behind her. A lace veil covered her face and draped down her back. She walked with her hand upon her brother's arm, and her beauty transfixed him.

Behind her trotted Sebastian. The black dog was wearing a knotted cravat around his throat, and Matthew smiled at the sight. Even more startling was seeing his young cat, Beast, trailing behind the dog. The cat evoked a laugh from several guests, before he scampered up the willow tree in search of a bird.

The dog took his place behind Lily, lying down in the grass while James lifted back his sister's veil. Matthew tucked Lily's gloved palm into his arm and saw that her eyes were gleaming with unshed tears. In a low voice, he murmured, "I hope those are tears of joy, Lily."

She lifted shining eyes to his. "They are, indeed."

The wedding was beautiful, and Lily did shed a few tears of happiness when Matthew kissed her at the end of the ceremony. The wedding guests applauded and stood. Her mother beamed at the sight of them, and in her arms, she held her first granddaughter. Baby Lavender had been born only a week ago and was asleep in Iris's arms. Rose and Iain stood with her, and as soon as Lily drew near, Rose stood from her chair to embrace her sister.

"It was a perfect wedding, Lily."

"It was. And I could not be happier."

She hugged her sister tightly, and Rose glanced back at her infant daughter. "Oh, I don't know. There may come a time when you find someone who brings even more happiness to your life." Her husband leaned in to kiss her cheek, and at the sight of their baby, Lily felt the tug of envy. *One day*, she thought.

Sebastian got up from the ground and trotted beside her while they accepted congratulations from the guests. Within the garden, they celebrated among family and friends, enjoying a wide variety of food and confections. At the far end of the garden, Lily spied an older man and woman seated together. She leaned in closer to Matthew and whispered, "Is that who I think it is?"

He brushed a kiss against her temple. "It is. Sarah Carlisle has a suitor. Lord Eversleigh has been widowed for three years now, and most of his children are grown. Except for his nine-year-old son, that is. There is a rumor that he may ask her to marry him." The white-bearded gentleman had a distinguished air about him, and he offered Miss Carlisle a glass of lemonade. The older woman smiled and blushed, but there was no doubt she was flattered by the attention.

"I am glad for her," Lily said. She had to give the woman credit—Miss Carlisle had dispelled so many rumors around London, claiming she had no doubt Matthew was Charlotte's legitimate son. Now that Adrian was gone, the talk had died down, and their lives had returned to normal.

From behind them, Lily heard a woman call out, "Matthew." They turned, and Juliette Fraser embraced him, a warm smile on her face. "I am overjoyed for both of you."

Matthew kissed her cheek, and Lily saw the similarity in their features. Lady Falsham had made a difficult decision to give up her son, but it was one that had brought him a better life and future. "Thank you, Juliette." He winked at her, and then they circled around to speak with each of their guests.

As their wedding celebration continued on through the afternoon and evening, Lily grew aware of her husband's eagerness to leave. At last, he drew her knuckles to his lips. "I am taking you away now. I don't care what the customs are." His eyes grew hungry and heated. "I've waited long enough."

"Shall I send Hattie to prepare our room?"

He shook his head. "If you think I'm going to spend our wedding night in your brother's house, you are quite mistaken."

She didn't understand what he meant by that. "Then where will we go?"

"You'll see." He took her around to bid farewell to each of the guests, and Lily's curiosity was intrigued. He had spoken nothing of this before. The dog trotted behind her, and she wondered whether to leave him. But then, Matthew bent near one of the trees and scooped up Beast, making it clear that both animals would come along.

After they departed the garden, she saw a black coach waiting for them. Matthew helped her inside, using both hands to tuck her voluminous gown inside. He placed Beast on the opposite seat.

"What about Sebastian?" she asked.

"He is coming with us, don't worry." He signaled for the dog to jump up, and Sebastian rested his head against her knee. After Matthew closed the door, she laughed at how much space was taken up by the wedding dress and the dog.

"I'm nearly drowning in silk," she laughed. "But I do love this gown."

"It suits you," he said. "And I could not have asked for a more beautiful bride." He knocked on the ceiling of the coach, ordering the coachman to drive on, and then he leaned in to kiss her, nudging Sebastian aside. The dog claimed the opposite seat, lying across the entire width of the coach. The cat hissed at him and then claimed his own space.

Lily clung to Matthew, welcoming the embrace of the man she loved. He rested both hands on either side of her, and she ran her hands through his dark hair, bringing him as close as she could.

Abruptly, he switched their positions, taking her seat and pulling her onto his lap. The gown was twisted beneath her, and she struggled to free herself. Matthew helped, until she straddled him. Beneath her thighs, she felt the heated length of him, and he continued to kiss her until she grew molten with need.

"Thank God, we've only a short drive," he said. "Else I might take you right here in this coach." He gripped her waist, and she shuddered at the shocking sensation of his erection pressed against her core. The image of riding him was a scalding vision that tempted her.

"Another day," she murmured. With a wicked smile, she added, "Promise me."

He kissed her hard and agreed, "Any day you wish, Lily."

He was right that the drive was indeed short, only a few miles away. When the coach pulled to a stop, she asked, "Where are we?"

"It's my wedding gift to you," he said. He opened the door and led her outside. The dog hopped down and trailed them, followed by the cat.

Lily walked along the gravel pathway, and ahead lay a small brick house. Candles were lit in the windows, and they were a welcome sight.

"It's too small for now," Matthew apologized, "but we will add the rooms we need. I bought up the surrounding land, so we can make the house as large as you wish."

"This is ours?" she breathed. Emotion bundled up in her so tightly, she could hardly breathe.

"I knew you wanted a home near your mother, since she has been so ill. This is close enough that you can see her as often as you like." He drew her palm to his lips. "You could even build a house for her behind this one if you want to bring her to live here."

Lily threw herself into Matthew's arms, feeling as if he'd just handed her the moon. She had been so worried about Iris, but now this gave her a means of taking care of her. "I love you, Matthew. Thank you for this."

He kissed her again and then lifted her into his arms. She yelped, laughing as he handed her yards and yards of silk. "You'll have to hold this while I carry you over the threshold. That *is* the tradition, isn't it?"

"So it is." Thankfully, a servant opened the door for them, smiling as Matthew carried her inside. An older woman greeted them, introducing herself as Mrs. Ferns, the housekeeper.

"Your rooms are all prepared, my lord."

"Thank you, Mrs. Ferns. And we've a few other guests we've brought with us." He nodded toward the dog and cat.

"The cat can stay but not the dog," the housekeeper groaned. "He should stay outside. I'll have no muddy paws here."

"Sebastian stays with my wife," Matthew answered. And with reluctance, the housekeeper let the dog inside, muttering to herself about wiping his paws.

He continued walking toward the stairs, and Lily gripped him harder. "Don't drop me," she warned. "Perhaps I should walk."

"Do you think I would ever let you go?" he murmured against her lips. Then he continued up the stairs and into the narrow hallway. "This house isn't nearly big enough. But it was all I could find near Penford."

"As you said, we can change it as much as we like."

At last, he lowered her to stand in front of their bedchamber. Matthew opened the door, and inside, she saw a four poster bed with the coverlet drawn back. Beast followed them inside and hopped onto the bed, curling up into a ball. A warm fire burned in the hearth, and within another moment, the dog trotted inside and flopped down in front of the fireplace.

Matthew picked up Beast and set him down by the dog.

The young cat sniffed at the dog's nose and then sprawled out next to him. Then Matthew turned back to Lily. "Will they bother you?"

"Not at all." She smiled at him. "Now help me out of this gown."

He took his time unbuttoning her, pressing his mouth against her back as he revealed each inch. Shivers erupted over her skin, and at last, the gown lay pooled upon the carpet. He helped her remove her corset and petticoats, revealing layer by layer, until she turned and stood naked before him.

The fire warmed her skin, but her breasts grew taut at the cool air in the bedroom. Matthew leaned in to take a nipple into his mouth, and the heat of his tongue made her gasp. She hurried, trying to undress him while he tormented her. And when he wore only his breeches, he picked her up and laid her down on edge of the bed. She started to move back, but he shocked her when he knelt before her, lifting her legs on his shoulders.

"I want to taste you." His warm breath warmed the intimate flesh between her legs, and she felt the spiral of anticipation arousing her senses. When he bent and licked between her folds, she let out a cry and gripped the sheets, arching against him. His tongue teased her, finding the nodule of her pleasure until she grew wet. A burgeoning sensation of need heightened, balling up inside her until she was breathing in a harsh rhythm. He replaced his mouth with his fingers, stroking her closer to a release she desperately wanted.

Dimly, she grew aware of Matthew removing the rest of his clothing. She closed her eyes, moaning when he slid two fingers inside her. He caressed her, coated with the essence of her desire, and she felt herself rising higher, aching for her husband.

"Are you ready for me?" he asked.

"Yes," she said, trembling as he increased the rhythmic

stroking of his fingers. A shattering white-hot sensation caught her, and then she came apart when his hard length invaded her. Pleasure arced through her, and she sobbed with the devastating release that rolled over her. Matthew continued to plunge and withdraw, and she squeezed his length, surrendering to the pleasure of lovemaking.

"Look at me," he demanded. She obeyed and saw the fierce desire in his brown eyes. His hands imprisoned her wrists, and she wrapped her legs around his waist. "I love you, Lily. And I always will."

She wrapped her arms around him, "I love you, too." He kissed her as he continued to thrust within her. She gloried in the pressure of his body moving within hers, clasping his head as he hastened the tempo.

And when at last he found his own pleasure, his body shuddered against hers, and he collapsed atop her. For a moment, their bodies lay joined, and he placed soft kisses against her face. "I'm glad you waited for me, Lily."

She lifted her mouth to his, kissing him in return. "I would have waited the rest of my life to love you again."

He lifted her back to the bed, their warm bodies mingled together, facing each other. And as they lay in the firelight, with their animals asleep on the hearth, Lily touched the gold signet ring on Matthew's finger. It had rested against her heart for the two years she had waited for this man.

"It was you who brought me back," he whispered. "On the night you found me in the stable, I nearly died. But your voice kept me alive, along with your love."

"Probably because I wouldn't stop talking," she teased. "But I needed you to know that I was there."

"I knew," he said. "And you will continue to be here at my side."

There was no doubt of that. They belonged together, and this man filled her with such happiness, she could scarcely breathe.

Lily reached out to trace the handsome line of his face. "Every day, for the rest of our lives."

And in front of the hearth, there came a low snore, followed by the thumping of a tail.

THE END

With special thanks to Dr. Brittany Ashworth for her veterinary advice regarding the care of wounded dogs. Any mistakes in the written manuscript are my own.

Did you miss the first book in this series, *Good Earls Don't Lie?* Enjoy an excerpt from book one in the *Earls Next Door* series about Lady Rose and Iain Donovan.

Chapter One

Yorkshire

May 1846

His head was killing him. It felt as if a hundred horses had trampled his skull, and right now he tasted blood and dirt in his mouth. After a moment, Iain Donovan gathered his senses, clearing his head.

The last thing he remembered was riding toward the Penford estate. He dimly recalled having passed a grove of trees when, abruptly, he'd been knocked off his horse. A shattering pain had crashed over him, and he vaguely remembered voices arguing and shouting.

But no one was here now.

Iain tried to sit up, and blood rushed to his head, threatening a loss of consciousness once again. He reached out to touch his brother's signet ring, only to find it gone. A sense of fear rose up in him, and he uttered a foul curse.

No one knew him here. He'd never left Ireland before now, and this country was completely foreign to him. While his mother had taken his older brother Michael to London every Season, teaching him all the skills necessary to become the Earl of Ashton, Iain had been left at home. She had done everything in her power to ensure that he was the invisible spare, the hidden son of no importance.

None of that mattered now. He was the only heir left, and he intended to prove that he was a man of worth. He would rebuild Ashton and help his people—even if that meant traveling across the Irish Sea to meet with strangers.

The wind sent gooseflesh rising over his skin, and when he realized he was no longer wearing a shirt, he let out another curse. Who would do such a thing? The bloody bastards had seized the shirt off his back, devil take them all and eat them sideways.

The thieves had stolen not only the ring and the few coins he possessed, but his horse, his coat, waistcoat, and shirt—even the shoes he'd worn. A fine welcome to England this was. After leaving the nightmare of Ireland behind him, he'd thought that here, everything would be better.

Apparently not.

Iain rose to his feet and studied the land around him. It was a fair day with the sun shining over rolling hills and meadows. He supposed he could walk the remaining distance to the Penford estate, for it was only a few miles farther. Though he didn't particularly like the idea of walking in his trousers and stocking feet, he had no other choice.

He grimaced as he followed the road leading toward Penford. All the baggage he'd brought from Ashton was gone now. He'd have to borrow clothes and shoes, and no one would possibly believe he was the Earl of Ashton. Without a coach, servants, clothing, or a signet ring, they'd think him a beggar at best.

His head was pounding from the mild wound, but more than the physical pain was a rising sense of panic.

Calm down, he ordered himself. He would tell the truth

about his ill luck, and surely someone would believe him. Lady Wolcroft had visited Ashton a few years ago. Surely she would remember him. After all, she was the one who had invited him to visit when she'd learned of the troubles they had suffered with the famine. His mother, Moira, and Lady Wolcroft's daughter, Iris, had been good friends at boarding school. Moira had spent all her school holidays with Iris's family and was like another daughter to them.

But friendship aside, he couldn't suppress the rise of uneasiness. Aside from Lady Wolcroft and his tenants, very few outsiders even knew there *was* a spare, in addition to the heir. His gut twisted at his mother's disregard, but he pushed the anger back.

Despite the circumstances, his younger sisters were depending on him to save their estate. For Colleen and Sybil, he would not fail. *Could* not fail. The task before him was greater than any he'd ever imagined, but he was determined to prove his mother wrong and restore Ashton to its former wealth.

And so it was that Iain had decided to travel across the sea, to leave his familiar homeland and dwell among strangers. And most of all, to offer himself up in marriage, in the hopes of wooing a wealthy bride.

Most men would never dream of such a thing, but his pride had crumbled as surely as the estate of Ashton. His brother was dead, and his sisters needed him. He'd be damned if he'd turn his back on them, forcing them to wed strangers. No. There was a way out of this mess, even if it meant offering himself up as the sacrificial lamb.

With each step, Iain gathered command of himself until he was confident that he *would* be welcomed at Penford, despite his bedraggled appearance.

As he continued along the dry road leading toward the hills, he saw sprouts of barley and rye emerging from the soil. The sight was a sobering contrast to the rotting fields he'd left behind at Ashton. The blight had destroyed their potato crops, until there was naught left, save a crumbling castle and enough debts to bury the family alive.

His mother and sisters had gone to stay with their aunt in New York, while he managed the affairs at Ashton. He had no intention of abandoning the estate or the people who had called it home for all their lives.

For they were starving. Too many of them had watched their crops rot in the earth, and they had nothing left. No livestock, no money—nothing to trade for food. Hundreds had left in the hopes of finding work elsewhere, but no one wanted Irish refugees.

Iain knew that if he wed an heiress, his bride's dowry could help the tenants survive until the crops improved. And though he had little to offer, save his Irish charm and a decrepit castle, he had to try.

The road curved over a hill, and when he crossed the apex, he saw Penford within the valley. On the west side of the estate, he spied a lake, gleaming silver and gold in the morning sunlight. For a moment, he paused to enjoy the sight. The estate was near a village, though it lay in an isolated part of Yorkshire—not exactly the best place to find a wife.

But Lady Wolcroft had her own motives for bringing him here ... and he would do anything necessary to form an alliance with the matron. She could bring him into her circles in London, introducing Iain to potential brides—and he was well aware that she had her own unmarried granddaughters. He would certainly consider the young ladies as marriage prospects before he left for London.

He continued the painful walk down the road, and when he turned the corner, he spied two adolescent boys on horseback. On *his* horse, Darcy.

Damn them all and may the crows feast upon their bones.

Iain didn't call out to them, for they could easily outpace him. Instead, he began running lightly, hoping he could overtake them before they noticed his arrival. The rocks dug into the soles of his feet as he ran hard, and he bit back the pain. Almost there . . .

"The horse is mine," one of the boys insisted. "I found him first."

"No, he's mine," the other boy glared. "I'm going to tell Father that he followed me home."

They couldn't have been more than thirteen, he guessed. Their thievery was likely adolescent mischief, and he fully intended to get every last one of his possessions back. He quickened his pace, but within seconds, Darcy grew skittish and neighed, alerting the boys to his presence.

At that, Iain shouted out, "Stop, both of you! That's my horse!"

"I told you we shouldn't have done it!" one cried out, urging Darcy faster. "Go!"

His idiot horse obeyed the command and galloped hard until there was no hope of catching up to them. Iain ran as fast as he could, hoping to glimpse where they were going, but the boys disappeared into the trees.

He cursed beneath his breath, furious at the way this day had begun. It was bad enough to be robbed, much less by boys. But it wouldn't take long to identify them to the authorities.

His feet were bleeding through his stockings, and his body was perspiring from the hard run. A sight he would be, arriving at Penford like this. He'd have to improve his appearance before arriving, or else they'd toss him back into the road like yesterday's breakfast.

Iain walked the remaining distance to the manor house, keeping off the gravel road. Several of the tenants eyed him as he passed, but he kept walking, his shoulders held back as if it were the most normal thing in the world to arrive at an estate wearing only trousers.

Tall hedges stood beside the house, and a small arbor led into a garden. He hurried toward it, feeling sheepish about his lack of attire. It might be that he could find a footman or a gardener who could help him with clothing. But as he approached the garden, he realized that he had entered a maze of hedges. Curiosity got the better of him, and he began wandering through the boxwood aisles.

At one end, he saw a stone fountain with rosebushes planted beside it. Deeper within the maze, he found a bed of irises, their purple blossoms illuminated by the sun. And when he reached the farthest end, he saw lilies of the valley.

He stood for a moment at the edge of the maze, where it opened onto a green lawn. A lovely woman was seated upon a stone bench, a book lying beside her. Her hair was reddish brown, tucked into a neat updo beneath her bonnet. She closed her eyes for a moment, lifting her face toward the sun like a blossom.

The sight of her stole the words from his brain, and Iain decided that his missing horse could wait, for the time being.

Who was this woman? One of Lady Wolcroft's granddaughters? It was possible, given her white morning gown trimmed with blue embroidery. Every inch of her appeared to be a lady. Iain took a few steps closer, fascinated by her.

The young woman dug her fingers into the stone bench, and her face tightened. Slowly, she eased herself to the edge of the seat, and she hunched her back. She gripped the bench hard, as if every movement was a struggle. Iain tensed, trying to understand her difficulty. It was only a moment later when he realized what she was doing.

She was trying to stand up.

The woman leaned heavily against the bench as she tried to force her legs to bear weight. When her knees buckled, she sat down again, her spirits dismayed.

Iain let out the breath he'd been holding. The pieces were beginning to fall into place. It might be that Lady Wolcroft had asked him here to help her granddaughters. If this young woman couldn't walk, there was no chance of her finding a husband.

And yet, she had a courage that he admired. There was a quiet determination in her eyes, of a woman who would not give up. He understood her.

Softly, he emerged from the hedgerow, wanting to know who she was.

There was a strange man standing in her garden.

Lady Rose Thornton blinked a moment, wondering if her imagination had conjured him. Because he was also half-naked and smiling at her, as if nothing were the matter.

"You'll have to forgive me for being half-clothed, *a chara*," he apologized, "but I was robbed on my journey here by a group of damned thieving boys."

Now what did he mean by that? Rose shut her eyes tightly and opened them again. No, he was still there. She filled her lungs with air, prepared to scream for all that was holy.

"I won't be harming you," he said, lifting his hands in surrender, "but I would be most grateful for some clothes. Not yours, of course." He sent her a roguish grin.

She gaped at him, still uncertain of who he was. But she had to admit that he *was* indeed an attractive man, in a pirate sort of way. His brown hair was cut short, and his cheeks were bristled, as if he'd forgotten to shave. She tried not to stare at his bare chest, but he cocked his head and rested his hands at his waist. His chest muscles were well defined, his skin tawny from the sun. Ridges at his abdomen caught her eye, and it was clear enough that he was a working man. Perhaps a groom or a footman. Gentlemen did not possess muscles like these, especially if they lived a life of leisure. His green eyes were staring at her with amusement, and Rose found herself spellbound by his presence.

"Do you not speak," he asked, "or have I cast you into silence with my nakedness?"

"Y-you're not naked," she blurted out. Her anxiety twisted up inside her, and she began babbling. "That is, you're mostly covered," she corrected, her face flaming. "The important bits, anyway."

Not naked? What sort of remark was that? She was sitting in the garden with a stranger wearing only trousers, and she hadn't yet called out for help. What was the matter with her? He could be an intruder bent upon attacking her.

But he laughed at her remark. It was a rich, deep tone that reminded her of wickedness.

Rose couldn't help but wonder why on earth a footman was naked in her garden. "Stay back," she warned, "or I'll scream."

He lifted his hands. "You needn't do that. As I've said, I have no intention of harming you. I fear you've caught me in a kettle of pottage. Could you be helping me, if it's not too much trouble?" With a slight lift of an eyebrow, he added, "I am here at Lady Wolcroft's invitation."

That nudged her curiosity. Why would her grandmother summon a stranger to Penford? Mildred loved nothing better than to meddle, but she wasn't even here at the moment. She had gone to Bath only a few weeks ago.

Then again, it was entirely possible that this man was lying. Probable, even.

"Who are you?" she managed to ask. "And why are you here?"

"I am Iain Donovan, the Earl of Ashton," he answered. "At your service." He bowed, and in his grin, she detected a teasing air. An Irishman, she was certain, given his speech patterns. But an earl? Exactly how empty-headed did he think she was?

Rose folded her hands in her lap. "There is no need to lie, sir," she told him. "I know full well that you are not an earl."

He blinked at that, his face furrowed. But honestly, had he really thought he could pull off such a deception? She was no country miss, easily fooled. "An earl would travel in a coach with dozens of servants. Never alone."

Before he could argue with her, she continued. "You may go to the servants' entrance, and our housekeeper, Mrs. Marlock, might have some old clothes to lend you. Perhaps a bit of food, and you can be on your way." Though she kept her tone reasonable, she had no way of knowing whether this man was dangerous. Perhaps she should have screamed after all. There was still time to do so.

The man crossed his arms over his chest and regarded her. In an even tone, he said, "I've not spoken any lies, miss."

"It's Lady Rose, Mr. Donovan," she corrected. As far as she was concerned, this man was a commoner with no claim to any title. "I should like for you to leave. Now." Her nerves tightened, for if this man dared to threaten her, she could do nothing to stop him. Especially since she couldn't run.

Even if she did call out to her footman, Calvert, he might not arrive quickly enough. Her gaze seized upon a rake nearby, and she wondered if she could reach it, if the need arose.

"I've no reason to speak untruths," he said. "As I told you before, I was robbed on my way here." He paused a moment, adding, "The axle broke on our coach, and my servants stayed behind to fix it. I thought it best to continue on horseback, since Lady Wolcroft invited me to stay as her guest."

"An unlikely story," Rose countered. "If you really *were* the earl, you'd have brought several footmen with you."

He raised an eyebrow. "And how many footmen was I expected to have?"

"Enough to bring several of them with you. A gentleman never travels alone."

The man's expression turned thunderous. "He does, when there's no other choice." It looked like he was about to argue further, but instead, he tightened his mouth and said, "Lady Wolcroft's eldest daughter and my mother were friends. She wants to marry me off to an Englishwoman, and that is why I am here."

She didn't believe him one whit. No, he had to be a vagrant of some sort, a man down on his luck who was attempting to take advantage by lying. "Well, sir, you do spin an entertaining tale. I've heard that the Irish are excellent storytellers, but you can take your story back to our housekeeper."

"It's not a story, Lady Rose. I *am* here to find a bride." The intensity in his voice was rather strong and made no secret of his annoyance.

She leaned as far over as she dared and managed to reach the rake handle. It made her feel better having a makeshift weapon.

"What are you planning to do with that rake, *a chara*?" he inquired, taking another step closer. Rose gripped the handle with both hands and drew it closer, using the tool to keep him at a distance.

"Nothing, if you go away." Truthfully, she didn't know exactly what she would do with the rake. It wasn't exactly suitable for stabbing someone. She could poke him with it, but not much else.

This time, she did call out to her footman. "Calvert! I have need of your assistance!" She hoped he would guard her against any threat. Right now, she wanted the strange man gone from her presence.

Even if he was quite handsome. And a charming liar.

The Irishman's mouth twisted, and he bowed. "As you like, then, Lady Rose. I'll be seeing you later, when I've better clothes to wear than these."

She wasn't certain what to think of that, but she gripped the rake tightly. "Be on your way." *Or I'll have my footman remove you.*

But as the stranger disappeared into the maze, she was

aware that her heart was beating swiftly, out of more than fear. Although she had seen her brother without a shirt before, never had she seen a man like Iain Donovan. His dark hair had a hint of curl to it, and those green eyes fascinated her. His cheekbones were sharp, his face lean and chiseled. He looked like a man who had walked through hell itself and come out stronger.

There was nothing at all refined about him. She'd wager that he'd never worn gloves in his life.

No. He could not possibly be an earl.

And yet . . . she'd been intrigued by his physical strength, wondering if his muscles were as firm as they appeared. His form could have been carved out of marble, like a statue.

When Calvert arrived upon the path to take her back to the house, she stole a look back at the maze. As soon as she was safely inside, she intended for her footman to follow Mr. Donovan and find out the real reason why he was here.

***

"Well, now, I don't know as I'm believing ye, lad." Mrs. Marlock planted her hands upon her broad waist. "Lady Wolcroft said naught about a houseguest arriving from Ireland. But if'n I'm wrong, I'd be a fair sight embarrassed to turn ye out again. I suppose ye mun have some clothes, aye?"

"Aye, that is true enough." Iain was well aware of his impoverished appearance, but there was naught to be done about it. "If I could speak with Lady Wolcroft, I'm certain she will sort it all out."

Mrs. Marlock tilted her head to the side as if assessing his story. Her gray hair was bound and pinned up beneath a cap. She reminded him of a soldier, though she had a ring of house keys instead of a sword at her plump waist. "Lady Wolcroft isn't here, and I can't be certain when she'll return from Bath."

Bath? Why had she gone there after she'd invited him to come visit? Well, now this was a fine kettle of fish. He had no clothes, no money, no signet ring, and no one to welcome him to Penford.

The housekeeper continued, "Have ye any other proof of who ye are?"

No, he had nothing at all. He'd been stripped of everything, may the thieves be eaten in tiny pieces, bite by bite. Iain's frustration rose up, but he forced himself to tamp it down. The last thing he needed was to frighten the housekeeper.

He searched for a believable lie. "My servants will be arriving today with my belongings, once my coach is repaired," he said smoothly. "That should be all the proof you need." He spoke calmly, keeping his tone even so as not to intimidate Mrs. Marlock. If he gave her any reason to doubt him, she would throw him out.

He was on borrowed time, and he had no means of proving his identity. If Lady Wolcroft were here, there was some chance she might recognize him. But no one else would.

The housekeeper didn't appear convinced. "Ye say ye've come from Ireland, is that so?"

"I come from Ashton," he answered. "In County Mayo." For a moment, he waited to see if she had other questions. When she said nothing, he added, "I imagine Lady Wolcroft may have spoken of my mother, Moira, has she not? Or my brother, Michael, God rest him?"

Mrs. Marlock folded her arms and frowned. "Nay, she hasn't." She eyed him as if trying to make a decision. At last, she said, "Well, there could be some truth in what ye say, but until Lady Wolcroft returns, I can't be letting a stranger into the house. Ye can return in a few days, and see if she's back home again."

Her refusal didn't surprise him at all. But he didn't want to be turned out in the middle of Yorkshire with no shelter, no money, and no food. Thinking quickly, he decided upon an alternative. "I'll swear to you that I *am* the Earl of Ashton. Allow me to stay this night, and once my servants arrive at Penford, I should be glad to compensate you handsomely for the trouble." He wasn't quite certain how he'd manage it, but he would find a way.

The housekeeper only smiled. "And when the Queen arrives, she'll offer me proof that I'm her long-lost daughter." With a shake of her head, she added, "Nay, sir, ye'd best go now. I'm certain ye can find someone in the village who'll be giving ye a place to bide for a wee bit."

Iain highly doubted it, given his state of undress. No, it was far better to talk Mrs. Marlock into letting him remain at Penford. "And what if I offered to . . . that is—" He hesitated, wondering if it would hurt his cause to lower himself further.

What choice do you have? he thought to himself. *No one knows who you are.*

He bit back his pride and asked, "What if I gave you my assistance on the estate? At least until my servants can prove who I am." It was the best compromise he could give. He'd done his share of menial labor on Ashton, after most of the tenants had left or died. It had been unavoidable, and he would set aside his pride if it meant gaining shelter for the night.

Mrs. Marlock frowned, crossing her arms as she stared at him. "I already asked ye to leave, sir. Ye've no references, and despite yer manner of speech, ye're a stranger among us. There's no place for ye here."

Iain straightened and regarded her with all seriousness. "Mrs. Marlock, what will Lady Wolcroft say to you when she learns that you turned away her guest?"

The old woman hesitated, and her uncertainty made him press further. "All I ask is to remain here for a single day. I need not stay in the main house, if it makes you uncomfortable."

She narrowed her gaze. "I don't know ye, sir. And it's our

butler, Mr. Fulton, ye'll have to speak with. I cannot give ye a place to stay within this household. It's nae possible."

"A few hours, then," he bargained. "Just until my servants arrive."

Though he had no desire to sleep outside, if he couldn't convince Mrs. Marlock or Mr. Fulton that he was the earl, he'd have no choice. And while he might be a slightly adventurous sort, sleeping on the moors would be colder than the devil's conscience.

He sent her a warm smile and added, "You do seem to be a charitable woman, Mrs. Marlock. I know you'd not ask a guest to sleep out in the freezing rain when there's shelter to be had."

"There's no rain today, lad," she said. "And ye'll find a place in the village, as I said before. If ye *are* the earl, they'll be glad to help ye." Her tone suggested that she didn't at all believe him. But as proof of her charity, she handed him a large hunk of bread. Iain tore off a piece, devouring the food, since he hadn't eaten in hours.

He wasn't going to give up on gaining a place to sleep. Not when he was convinced that he could prove himself by evening at the latest. All he needed to find was the signet ring that had been stolen.

When he'd finished the bread, he asked, "What of clothing, Mrs. Marlock?" He lowered his arms to his side, giving her a full view of his bare skin. "I can't be going around with naught to wear."

A faint blush rose over her cheeks, and she sighed at last. "I suppose ye're right, at that. I'll see what rags we have before ye gang to the village."

"I am grateful indeed. And thank you for the food." He inclined his head, and she eyed him as if not knowing what to do. In the end, she bobbed her own curtsy.

"Hattie!" she called out. One of the maids hurried inside the kitchen, a *cailín* of about sixteen. The girl sent him a curious look, and her gaze slid over his bare torso in open admiration. Though he rather felt like a roasted goose on display, Iain said nothing, in case the maid turned out to be an unexpected ally.

Mrs. Marlock said, "Stop yer gawpin, Hattie, and fetch the man some clothes."

The maid blushed and gave an embarrassed smile before hurrying away. Though Iain kept his expression masked, Mrs. Marlock moved in front of him and glared. "Once yer dressed, ye'll be leaving Penford. If ye *are* her ladyship's guest, ye'll get a full apology from me at that time." The look on her face said she doubted he would return.

"You'll see," he told her. "I will be dining at your table tonight." Once he had located his stolen belongings, he was confident that they would accept him.

Mrs. Marlock offered nothing more than an indignant "humph."

A few minutes later, Hattie brought him a ragged shirt and an equally tattered coat, along with a pair of shoes. Given the young girl's age and her attire that was slightly better than a kitchen maid's, he surmised she was a maid-of-all-work. And although he doubted if anything would fit, it was better than remaining half-naked and unshod. Iain thanked her for the clothes.

Unfortunately, it seemed he would be spending the next few hours out of doors, wearing servant's rags. A fine day this was turning out to be.

You never expected it to be easy, he reminded himself. *Why should they believe you're an earl? Without any proof, how could they?*

He put on the ill-fitting shirt, coat, and shoes, taking the time he needed to make plans. Although he had hoped his men would join him here, it was beginning to seem that they had abandoned him. And with no servants to vouch for him, his circumstances had become dire indeed.

But he would never give up. Too many people were dependent on him.

After he was dressed, he followed Hattie down the servants' hallway. She turned to him and with a hopeful smile said, "I do wish you well, sir." Pointing to the door at the end, she added, "You can go out that way."

He eyed the door and then regarded the maid for a moment. "Do you believe that I am the Earl of Ashton, though I'm looking as if I'd been dragged through the midden heap?"

Hattie appeared uncomfortable and lowered her gaze. "It—it's not for me to be sayin', sir." With that, she continued leading him toward the back door.

He didn't argue with her, for she was only obeying orders. His mind was already conjuring up where he would stay this night. Possibly in the stables or somewhere sheltered. He hadn't a single coin to call his own, so no one in the village would give him a place.

Iain had only walked a few steps when he heard a woman screaming. The piercing noise made it sound as if she were being attacked. He didn't stop to ask questions but hurried up the stairs leading to the hall. He found a middle-aged woman running toward the front door, her hair tangled and hanging down her back. She wore a long-sleeved blue serge gown, and her eyes were wild. Far too young to be Lady Wolcroft, he guessed, but it could be the woman's daughter.

"Lady Penford!" Hattie exclaimed, rushing forward to her aid. "Please . . . let me help you."

Iain looked around to see what the woman was fleeing from, but there was nothing at all.

The woman's face was deathly white, and her hands shook badly. When Hattie put her hand out, Lady Penford gripped it hard. "Please, you have to help me! The—the wolves. I heard them howling. They're coming for me."

The maid sent a look toward Iain and shook her head in

warning. Though Iain wasn't certain what was happening, it was clear that Lady Penford was suffering from visions that weren't real.

The woman started to bolt again, and Hattie tried to stop her, holding her by the waist. "My lady, no. You mustn't leave the house."

Whatever illness had captured her mind, Lady Penford might injure herself if she was allowed to flee. And though it wasn't his business, Iain stepped toward the doorway to keep her from escaping.

"Let me go," Lady Penford insisted, wrenching her way free of the maid. But when she moved toward the front door, Iain remained in place to block her. He sensed that this woman was trapped in a world of her own imaginings, one where reality made little sense.

"Where are the wolves?" he asked calmly. He kept his voice quiet, as though soothing a wounded animal.

His question seemed to break through Lady Penford's hysteria, and she faltered. "They—they were chasing me." Her face held confusion, and she appeared unaware that he was a stranger.

"Would you feel safer in your room?" he asked. "Perhaps Hattie could take you there."

"No." Her breathing grew unsteady. "I can't go back there. The wolves will find me." She gripped her hands together and took another step toward the door. "Summon my coach."

He met Hattie's gaze, and she moved closer to Lady Penford. Iain took another step backward to prevent her from reaching the door.

A slight noise caught his attention at the top of the stairs, and he saw Lady Rose being carried by a footman. "Mother, please wait a moment." Her face paled at the sight of the matron, and she ordered, "Calvert, take me downstairs."

It sobered him to realize how difficult Lady Rose's life must be, having to rely on others to carry her where she wanted to go. The simple act of helping her mother would be quite beyond her abilities.

When she saw Iain standing by the door, her face tightened in dismay. Color flooded her cheeks as if she was embarrassed that he had witnessed her mother's outburst. Hattie brought a chair close to Lady Penford, and the footman set Lady Rose upon it, retreating to a discreet distance.

"Are you all right?" the young woman asked. In her voice, there was the gentle tone of compassion, no censure for the madness. She held out her hand, but Lady Penford ignored it.

At this close proximity, Iain noticed that Lady Rose's eyes were the color of warm sherry. A few tendrils of reddish-brown hair framed her lovely face, and he found himself wanting to ease her worry.

"Did you hear me, Mother?"

Lady Penford gave no answer, but she stared down at her trembling hands.

"I was just talking with Lady Penford about the wolves," Iain said, as if there were nothing at all wrong. He fixed his gaze upon the young woman, hoping she would play along, since the older woman seemed to be caught up in confusion.

But Lady Rose paid him no mind. "Everything is all right now, Mother. I am here." She reached out a hand, but the woman ignored it.

"I'm afraid," her mother admitted. Her eyes welled up with tears, and she twisted her hands together. "So afraid."

He glanced over at Lady Rose and saw her flushed cheeks. The maid and footman eyed one another before casting their gazes downward. Clearly the woman's madness was not a new occurrence.

"Is there anything I can do to help?" Iain asked.

The older woman turned back to him, and her mood suddenly shifted. "I've not seen you before. Do you know my son James? Is that why you are here? Has he returned from

India?" Her voice was edged with emotion, and he suspected that grief and worry had led her into this agitated state.

Iain risked a glance toward Rose, who shook her head. It wasn't clear whether her brother was dead or gone, but he decided not to upset the woman any more than necessary. It was simple enough to continue with the ruse. "I might have seen him. Will you remind me of what he looks like?"

A sudden moment of clarity passed over the woman's face, and her expression filled up with sorrow. "James has been gone for a long time. I pray he will return, but he hasn't answered my letters. He must come back, you see. He is the new Earl of Penford." Her voice lowered to a soft whisper. "Now that my husband is . . . gone, there is so much to do. So many decisions to be made, and I can't—I simply can't—" Lady Penford covered her mouth with her hands, panic rising in her expression.

"You needn't worry," Rose reassured her. "Lily and I will manage. Right now, I think you should go into the drawing room and have a cup of tea. Mrs. Marlock might have scones with clotted cream. Would you like that?"

The mention of food successfully diverted the matron's attention. "I—yes, that would be lovely."

"Hattie will take you to the drawing room, and we will join you there." Rose signaled for the maid to come forward, and Hattie guided Lady Penford down the hallway.

When her mother was gone, Rose turned back to Iain, and her expression held sadness. "Thank you for stopping her from leaving. She's been grieving ever since my father died."

He nodded. "She seemed very upset." *And not in her right mind,* he thought, but didn't say so. "Will she be all right?"

Rose sighed and straightened in the chair. "No one knows the answer to that question. There are good days and bad days."

He glanced back at the footman. "Do you need assistance? That is, if you wish to join her, I could—" But he stopped short, realizing how inappropriate it would be for him to carry her.

Lady Rose didn't appear to take offense but simply answered, "Calvert will bring me there." Then she glanced at Iain's bedraggled clothing with a questioning look. "Do you still claim to be an Irish earl, sir?" Her words held a dry humor, and the look in her eyes said she didn't believe him at all.

Iain's mouth twisted in a smile. "My name is Lord Ashton, *a chara*. And you'll have to wait and see, won't you?"

Did you enjoy the sample?
To learn more and to purchase this book
at a retailer of your choice, visit:
www.michellewillingham.com/book/good-earls-dont-lie.

Don't forget to claim your free e-book by
signing up for Michelle's newsletter here:
http://www.michellewillingham.com/contact

About the Author

Kindle bestselling author and Rita® Award finalist **Michelle Willingham** has published more than thirty-five romance novels and novellas. Currently, she lives in southeastern Virginia with her husband and children, and is working on more historical romance books in a variety of settings, such as medieval and Viking-era Ireland, medieval Scotland, and Victorian and Regency England. When she's not writing, Michelle enjoys baking, playing the piano, and avoiding exercise at all costs. Her books have been translated into languages around the world and are also available in audio editions. Visit her website at www.michellewillingham.com to find foreign translations.

Made in the USA
Lexington, KY
27 October 2017